# The Long Ears

## The Dragon Flyers

*Dear Rhiannon, Sian, & Rhys,*
*Enjoy the journey!*
*Love,*
*Debbie*
*xxx*

### Debbie Daley

Published in 2014 by FeedARead.com Publishing – Arts Council funded

This book is dedicated to my two beautiful and talented children. They are my inspiration and my life. Go live your dreams, strive to be different and never have a moment's regret. Love you always.

Book cover by Sarah Aumeer

Other illustrations by Natalie Ifill

www.debbieddaley.co.uk

## *Acknowledgements*

I'd like to extend my love and thanks to all those people who have believed in me and given me every encouragement to pursue my dream to see this second book in print. There are too many of you to mention but special thanks must go Sheila Sykes, Linda Chidgey and Elenya Daley my eagle-eyed Elvenites for their proof reading and suggested edits for the book. To the amazingly talented Sarah Aumeer, for once again designing and creating a fabulous cover and capturing the essence of Lizzie and her dragon so beautifully. To a very talented young lady, Natalie Ifill, who translated my ideas for the map and pterotorial illustrations into two wonderful pieces of art. To all my family and friends, who spur me on and keep my spirits up in times of doubt. And last, but by no means least, to you my readers, who are following Lizzie's story and who have encouraged me to tell you what happens next. I can never thank you all enough.

N.b. For those of you with the first print of The Harp of Elvyth, please note that the character of Melificent has been renamed Melisha in this and all future books.

# CHAPTER 1

## Too Hot to Trot!

It was an unbearably hot Saturday morning and the sun beat down remorselessly on Lizzie Longton's white blond head. Lizzie's usually pale complexion had turned a bright shade of pink in the intense heat which, in turn, had made her hair look faintly pink too.

Lizzie sat by the pond near the old willow tree in the gardens of her home, Longton Hall. Her chin resting on her knees, she watched as the water-bugs paddled their way across the pond's murky surface. The fish in the pond were nowhere to be seen, as they had dived into its depths to escape the burning heat. Dragonflies flitted around, their multi-coloured wings beating so fast that they were just a blur. The giant insects' startlingly beautiful coloured bodies drew Lizzie's gaze hypnotically toward them, and she smiled as they made their way on their jerky flight-paths. Only the soothing sound of the bees buzzing about their business and the chirruping of the song birds disturbed the silence of what was a perfect summer's day.

Summer had come early and, although it was only the second week of July, a drought order had been in place for several weeks. This had meant that anyone using a hose-pipe to water their gardens or wash their cars was in for a hefty fine. Longton Hall's gardens, however, were a green oasis in the midst of a dry and parched landscape. Over his many years of tending the Hall's gardens, amongst all the other jobs he did around the place, Bob Crowther had learnt a thing or two about conserving water during dry periods.

As Lizzie's mind flitted from one thought to another, much like the pale blue butterfly that had briefly landed beside her, her mind drifted to a programme she'd watched on the TV the previous evening. It had been about saving the planet and, in particular, the causes and effects of global warming. Lizzie had felt immensely sad as she watched footage of a magnificent polar bear drifting on a chunk of ice that had broken away from the polar ice-cap in the vast Arctic Ocean. The programme's presenter had informed the viewers that these wonderful creatures were in danger of extinction, as many were drowning because they were unable to swim the increasingly huge distances between the ice floes and the nearest land mass. Lizzie, curled up next to her grandmother on the sofa, had watched with growing anger at what was unfolding on the screen and listened with interest to the views and opinions of the scientists and environmentalists who had been interviewed. The general consensus was that much of the damage being done to the Earth's atmosphere was down to man's quest for wealth and so called progress, but there had also been surprise expressed at how, over the past few months, global warming seemed to be gaining pace.

Like many people, Lizzie knew that the pollution caused by humans had done terrible damage, but she also knew that there was another contributing factor, unknown to most humans, that was speeding up that damage and she was determined that she would somehow help to combat that hidden factor. It was linked to a rather unpleasant and dangerous individual wreaking havoc a world away from the one she was currently living in.

Earlier that year, around her eleventh birthday, Lizzie had made an amazing discovery. She had always believed that the only family she had was her grandmother and an absent father, following the death of her mother Ria on the night she was born. Lizzie had always understood that her mother had been an orphan and so had been stunned to discover that this wasn't the case at all. In fact Ria's father and sister were alive and well and living in a place that Lizzie had no idea even existed. Lizzie's newly discovered grandfather and aunt were actually elves and, not just any old elves, but the King and Princess of Elvedom. This, of course, meant that Lizzie's mother had also been an elf which, in turn, made Lizzie a half-elf. As if all this wasn't enough for Lizzie to contend with, she also had the shock of finding out that her mother had been the eldest child of King Elfred, which meant that Lizzie was now the heir to the Elvedom throne. So, after years of feeling alienated from most people around her, by way of her unusual looks and abilities, she was finally beginning to understand the reason why.

Lizzie wasn't able to tell anyone about any of this, of course, as they would never have believed her but, more importantly, they would think her even more peculiar than they already did; especially the gruesome twosome, Regina and Veronica Bray. Lizzie didn't want to think about what those two would do if she let slip her secret.

Regina and Veronica, together with their little gang of followers, were the reason Lizzie lived such a lonely existence in her home village of Chislewick. They made her life a misery with their bullying ways but Lizzie knew that one day she would have the last laugh on that pair. She just had to bide her time.

Since discovering her true heritage, Lizzie had gained in confidence enormously. Although it still hurt to have no real friends of her own age in the human world, she would take secret pleasure in knowing that she was loved and valued by her family and friends in her "other" world. After her confrontation with the horrid Bray twins, when she told them they no longer scared her, they had backed off for a time. However, it wasn't long before they and their gang had started their nasty bullying once more. The difference now was that when they were being mean, she would just think about the wonderful time she had spent in Elvedom and look forward to when she would next be with her new family and friends. The thoughts would often make her smile to herself, which unfortunately made the Brays think Lizzie was even odder than ever. What amused Lizzie even more was that they believed they were insulting her by using the nick-name Long Ears, when they were actually complimenting her. "And to think I used to hate that name," Lizzie had thought.

Lizzie could speak with her grandfather and aunt any time she wished by means of a magical locket, bequeathed to her by her mother. The locket had sat in the bottom of her trinket box in her bedroom since she was born and it was the only treasure that her mother had left her. She had never worn it as it was far too precious and she was afraid she would lose it. Whilst she was in Elvedom she had discovered just how valuable it was, as it allowed her to contact her family in Elvedom. Her aunt Elenya had an identical locket and had shown Lizzie how it worked. So, when she wanted to speak to either Elenya or her grandfather, all she needed to do was to rub the surface with her thumb three times, flick open the catch and kiss the portrait of the person she wished to speak to. She would know when Elenya or her grandfather wanted to speak to her as the locket would glow warm and vibrate. Then all she had to do was open it for them to do so. The locket now never left her. At school she kept it in a special pocket that her grandmother had sewn into her school skirt or sports shorts. When the other kids were being especially horrid, she would place a hand on the locket in her pocket to gain some comfort in the knowledge that she was truly "special".

Because of the locket, Lizzie had been kept up to date with events in Elvedom by her grandfather, but more usually by her aunt Elenya. Most of the elves that Lizzie had met during her time in Elvedom were small and slight, but not Elenya. She was tall and willowy and, with her long golden hair, was strikingly beautiful. Lizzie hoped one day to be just like her but her grandfather said she was more likely to take after her own mother who had been just like him, rather on the short side. Lizzie had smiled when he said this as it was all too evident to see that height wasn't exactly King Elfred's strong point.

Lizzie flopped onto her back and closed her eyes against the blazing sun above her. She felt a trickle of sweat dribble down behind her infamous ears and soak the hair at the nape of her neck; it wasn't a particularly pleasant sensation. Once again, her thoughts returned to events unfolding in Elvedom.

Lizzie had spoken with her aunt Elenya via the locket just a few days previously. Elenya had told her that the spy Ella, who had infiltrated Eldorth's inner most circle, had reported that his fury at the loss of the Harp of Elvyth had been terrible to witness. It had increased significantly when he had found out about Lizzie's involvement and her subsequent escape from Maladorth.

Duke Eldorth made Lizzie's troubles with the Bray twins seem like a like a minor irritation. It was due to the curse that Eldorth had placed on Lizzie's mother, following her rejection of him, that had caused her death. Eldorth was now hell bent on destroying the Elvedom royal family and, having discovered that Lizzie had survived the curse after believing that she had died with her mother, he was now determined to terminate her. Elenya had told Lizzie that Eldorth was wreaking havoc on the northern territories of Elvedom that bordered Eldorth's own lands of Maladorth. Vast swathes of land were being poisoned by the dark magic of Eldorth and his side-kick, the evil witch Melisha. Rivers and streams were drying up and any richness was being leeched from the soil. The devastation was spreading south from Eldorth's lair and the land was dying.

Lizzie had witnessed first-hand the effects of Eldorth's poison on his own lands when she, her grandmother and her Elvedom friends – Elrus, Max and Eloise – had fallen through a Threshold (a magical doorway that allowed a person to move between different places) and deposited them in Maladorth. It was a dry, arid land where no animals thrived and no birds sang. Only the one small wood that had given them shelter had shown any trace of green to be seen in that terrible terrain. King Elfred and his advisors were convinced that the destruction Eldorth was causing was so damaging that its effects were seeping through the layers of the Earth and affecting the other worlds surrounding it. Something had to be done to stop Eldorth, and the little voice in Lizzie's head told her that she had to be involved in bringing him down.

"Lemonade, ma'am?" said a high pitched voice from somewhere above her.

The sudden interruption to the peace of the garden, and to Lizzie's train of thought, made her jump. She jerked her head up to see Elwood Doogoody – her friend, guardian and mentor appointed by her grandfather – standing over her. He was holding a tray containing a jug of Mary Crowther's home-made iced lemonade and two glasses. Lizzie sniggered when she saw that Elwood had a lurid pink baseball cap perched on top of his head. His long pointed elven ears squashed outwards from his head at comical right-angles.

"Suits you, Elwood," she smirked, her eyes flicking up to the cap.

"Thank you, ma'am, but actually your grandmother asked me to bring it out for you to wear," he grinned; Elwood just never seemed to get sarcasm. He placed the tray on the ground beside Lizzie. "I think it may suit you a little better than it does me," he said as he removed the cap with a flourish and passed it to Lizzie, who put it on carefully to make sure that it didn't have the same effect on her ears as it had on Elwood's. Elwood plonked himself down onto the ground next to her and poured them both a tall glass of the lemonade.

"Thanks," Lizzie said, taking the glass and swallowing a long draught of the cold sweet liquid.

"It surely is a very warm day," puffed Elwood, removing a handkerchief from his shorts pocket and dabbing his brow. "Your grandmother says that your weather forecasters are predicting that this heat is going to continue for some time yet."

Lizzie placed the cold glass to her forehead and looked at Elwood from beneath it. "And we know why, don't we Elwood?" she said knowingly. "When am I going to be able to go back to Elvedom? I want to help in some way."

The elf looked at Lizzie and raised an eyebrow. "And how, may I ask, do you propose to do that, ma'am?" he queried. "Your grandfather has said that you are to remain here until your school lessons finish in a week's time. It is important that you are kept here safely for the time being. In the meantime, we can continue with our lessons and then you will be ready to return."

Lizzie placed the glass back on the tray and put her chin petulantly on her knees, hugging them tightly. She was fed up with being here in this world. It was months since she had spent those brief few days in Elvedom but she felt it was where she truly belonged. She loved her grandmother and the Crowthers, and of course her dogs, Basil and Rathbone; but there was nothing else here for her. No friends who would miss her like her friends in Elvedom did. She had received several letters from Elrus and Eloise, and a couple from the busy Max, although she wasn't quite sure how they had got there, just that Elwood had presented them to her. She had replied but there was so little to tell them, apart from that she couldn't wait to see them again, whereas theirs were full of the stuff they were doing.

Elrus had been concentrating on his favourite lessons of history and calculations, which Lizzie assumed was something akin to maths. In addition, he was helping his father in his role as village chieftain. He had happily recounted the various festivals and festivities that had been held in her absence, the main one being Midsummer Solstice. She had laughed at his account of how he had danced till he dropped, imagining him whirling around the dance floor like some mad red-haired spinning top.

Elwood had told Lizzie and her grandmother how the Solstice was an important festival in the Elvedom calendar and so they had had their own little ceremony in the gardens of Longton Hall. They had released Chinese lanterns into the reddening skies as the sun had set. It was a wonderful moment and one which would have raised some eyebrows in the village had anyone witnessed the event. It must have been quite a sight seeing the three of them prancing around the garden barefoot with flowers in their hair and Elwood playing a merry tune on a wooden flute.

The letters from Eloise were even more enviable as Lizzie read about the life she led in Elcarib, playing on the white sandy beaches, swimming in crystal clear seas in the company of dolphins and turtles. Eloise's life seemed a world away from the worries of Eldorth and his vicious assault on the lands close to Elrus and her grandfather. Elwood sat silently beside Lizzie, watching her face as her thoughts played across her pointed features.

"Are you alright, ma'am?" he asked gently.

Lizzie looked at him and nodded slowly. "I'm fine, Elwood," she grinned half-heartedly. "I'm just frustrated at having to stay here. I thought that I might have been able to go back during half term holidays but the King said it wasn't safe. I kind of feel cheated at having been there and then kept away. Still, it's only a week before I finish school and then there are six weeks holiday before I start at Markham High. I was kind of hoping that I might be able to go to school in Elvedom." She added longingly.

Elwood looked surprised. "I think that is most unlikely, ma'am," he stated. Lizzie gave him a lop-sided grin.

"It was just a wish, that's all, Elwood. Anyway, Gran's already organised my uniform for Markham so I couldn't let that go to waste, could I?" she smiled resignedly.

Elwood stood up and picked up the tray. As he did so, Lizzie felt a vibrating sensation at the top of her leg and she reached into the pocket of her shorts and took out the cause of it. Glinting in her hand was her mother's locket. She looked up quickly at Elwood.

"I think someone wants to speak to me," she said excitedly. Elwood promptly sat back down and looked at the locket expectantly.

Lizzie rubbed her thumb over the surface of the locket three times and flicked open the catch. There, smiling up at her was the image of her grandfather.

"Grandfather!" Lizzie cried, her face beaming with pleasure. "Hello!"

"Good afternoon, Elizabeth," said her grandfather, his face crinkling in a broad grin. "I hope I find you well this fine day."

"Oh yes, I'm good thanks. Although it is pretty hot here," she added, sticking out her bottom lip and blowing up towards her nose as if to emphasise the point.

Her grandfather nodded. "We too are experiencing something of a heat-wave, although Marvin is working on something to counteract the effects. However, Elizabeth, I have not contacted you in order to discuss the weather." The King's face became a little more serious. "I understand that you have been disappointed that it is taking so long for you to be able to return to Elvedom."

Lizzie cast down her eyes and then peered up at her grandfather's face in the locket.

"Well...," she started. She flicked her eyes in the direction of Elwood who must have been the source of this information. The little elf looked away nonchalantly.

"I am sorry but the reasons for this have been explained to you," he added. "However, I have some good news that I hope will help you see out the next week before you travel here once more." Lizzie's eyes lit up in anticipation. What could her grandfather have planned?

The King smiled broadly. "I have arranged with Elmer and Elmara for their son, Elrus, to visit you in your home at Longton Hall. He will return here when it is time for you and your grandmother to come to Elvedom once more."

Lizzie's mouth dropped open. Then, whooping excitedly, she pulled Elwood up and began to dance him around in a circle with the locket dangling from her hand. "Yes, yes, yes!" she chanted.

"Elizabeth? Elizabeth!" A little voice calling her suddenly made her stop and, raising the locket in her hand, she looked at her grandfather's face. "Elizabeth, you are making me feel quite dizzy," her grandfather laughed.

"Sorry, grandfather," said a contrite Lizzie. "I got a bit caught up in the moment. Oh, but thank you so much for arranging for Elrus to come here. It'll be great to see him."

"Well," continued the King, "His father and I both feel it is important for the future when he is an advisor to you, that he understands your life in the human world. This, I hope, will be the first of a number of journeys he will undertake to your world."

"When can we expect him, Your Majesty? So that arrangements can be made to accommodate Master Elrus," asked Elwood, peering over Lizzie's shoulder to speak to the King.

"Marvin is arranging a temporary Threshold for the purpose as we speak," said King Elfred. "You may expect Master Elrus tomorrow morning."

"Tomorrow?!" Lizzie squealed in delight.

Having said goodbye to her grandfather, she put the locket away. Turning to Elwood, who was the picture of calmness, she asked, "Did you know anything about this, Elwood?" The little elf looked at her sheepishly.

"Well, ma'am, I did know that Master Elrus would be coming but not the exact date. Your grandmother and I didn't want to say anything to you in case there was a change of plans at the last moment. We wanted to avoid any possible disappointment. Your grandmother has spoken to your school to say that he may be coming before you finish for the holidays and asked if he can attend with you. They have been most accommodating."

Lizzie gave him a stern look. "So gran knew too?" Elwood looked down at his feet and nodded.

"Well, yes. She had to make sure that it was alright for him to attend school with you," he explained.

Lizzie's face showed her surprise that even her school had known before she had.

"Well never mind now I suppose," she said, her face breaking out in a wide grin. "We'd better get ready for our visitor. There's shopping and stuff to do." Then, jumping to her feet, and with Elwood trotting along behind, she ran into the Hall to start the preparations for her friend's stay.

# CHAPTER 2

## The Visitor

Preparations for Elrus's arrival didn't take long that Saturday afternoon. Lizzie and Elwood took the bus – something Elwood found a real treat – into Markham Town to buy some supplies for the visitor.

When they returned to the Hall, they started arranging Elrus's room. The windows were thrown open to expel any musty air from the bedroom that he was to occupy for the duration of his visit. Fresh bedding was eventually put on the bed once Lizzie and her grandmother had laughingly wrestled the duvet into its cover, although given how hot the nights were it was unlikely to be used much. Elwood watched them in amusement as he whizzed around the bedroom flicking the old wooden furniture with a large fluffy duster. Their labours finally over, the three workers stood, red faced and weary, and surveyed their efforts. Mrs Longton nodded sagely.

"Well, it may not quite be up to Elvedom Castle standards, but it'll do for Master Elrus. Don't you agree, Elwood?" she added, turning to the little elf standing between herself and her granddaughter.

Elwood smiled with satisfaction. "Indeed, Madame. Indeed."

An excited Lizzie found it difficult to sleep that night as she churned over in her mind all the things she wanted to show and share with her friend. At King Elfred's request, Mrs Longton had spoken to Lizzie's school to arrange for Elrus to attend there for the last week of term as a visitor. The Head Teacher had said that it was an unusual request, but Mrs Longton had argued that Elrus was Lizzie's cousin who was coming on a surprise visit from Greenland and that it would be good for international relations. Lizzie tried to imagine the faces of the other children when they saw that she finally had a friend and ally. The Brays were going to flip. The thought made Lizzie chuckle; she could hardly wait. It was going to make the last few days at school before they broke up for the summer holidays very interesting indeed.

Lizzie must have eventually dropped off to sleep because she woke with a start the following morning when a big wet nose was unceremoniously thrust into her face followed by a slurping lick. Basil and Rathbone were sitting beside her bed and one of them, being tired of waiting for his young mistress, had decided it was time she was up and about.

"Ewww, you two," she groaned, pulling the sheet over her head and rubbing the slobber off her cheek. She peeked out from under the cover and looked at the two dogs, their tongues lolling and tails wagging in greeting. "Okay, okay, I'm getting up." Lizzie threw back the sheet and swung her legs out of bed. The dogs, taking this as a good sign, barked excitedly at her and ran from the room, their claws skidding on the wooden floor of the landing outside Lizzie's bedroom as they made their way back downstairs.

As Lizzie entered the kitchen, having quickly showered and dressed for the day, she was greeted by the sight of Elwood tucking into a large bowl of his favourite cereal, Choco Krispie Rice Pops. As always, when Elwood saw Lizzie for the first time each day, he jumped to attention and bowed low and bade her good morning.

The smell of frying sausages and bacon filled the kitchen. Mrs Longton was standing at the range, making breakfast and humming happily to a song playing on the radio.

"Good morning, darling," she called. "Full English as usual? *Oh, I do love Sunday morning fry ups.*" She sang to the tune of the old Beatles song that was playing.

Lizzie sat down at the table and tore off a chunk of bread that Mary Crowther had baked the previous day. It was warm from having been resting on top of the stove, and as she spread some butter over its surface, the golden spread

19

melted into it. As she bit into the soft centre, Lizzie felt it was like biting into a little piece of heaven.

"What time is Elrus arriving?" she mumbled through a mouthful of bread.

"Elizabeth! What have I told you about speaking with your mouth full?" admonished her grandmother, placing a plateful of bacon, sausage, egg and beans in front of her.

Elwood looked up from his cereal and, ensuring that his mouth was not full, said grandly, "I believe that he should be arriving at 10:30 hours Greenwich Mean Time, ma'am."

It never failed to amuse Lizzie that Elwood was always so precise. She looked up at the kitchen clock, it read a quarter to ten. Just enough time to eat breakfast, help gran clear up and he'll be here, she thought, slicing off a piece of sausage and popping it into her mouth. She was about to take a forkful of beans when the dogs suddenly ran out of the kitchen, barking madly. A voice coming from somewhere in the Hall's depths could be heard.

"Good boys, get down. Down now, that's a good boy."

The kitchen's occupants looked at each other. "Elrus!" they shouted in unison.

Dropping her fork, Lizzie ran to the kitchen door and there, walking down the hall towards her, was her good friend Elrus. A kitbag slung over his shoulder, his red hair flopping into his eyes and a broad grin across his face.

Lizzie leaned against the kitchen door frame and crossed her arms. "And what time do you call this?" she said with mock severity. "You're early!"

Elrus hesitated a moment and then, dumping his bag on the floor, said, "Good to see you too, Princess. Mmm... Is that sizzling meat of some sort I smell?"

Mrs Longton gave Elrus a big hug and then, with an arm around his shoulder, led him into the kitchen. "It's so lovely to see you, Elrus. Did you have a good journey?" Elrus looked up at her.

"Pretty straight forward actually," he said, matter of factly. "I just stepped over the Threshold and turned up in one of your old sheds. I was a bit confused at first as to where I was but I just followed my nose." Elwood picked up Elrus's bag and, hoisting it over his shoulder, said he would deposit it in Master Elrus's room.

Entering the kitchen, Lizzie and Elrus sat down at the table and Lizzie continued to tuck into her breakfast as Mrs Longton threw together a "full English" for Elrus. The young elf watched Lizzie with interest.

"So, Princess, how's things?" he asked, as a steaming plate of food was placed in front of him and he began devouring its contents.

Lizzie stopped chewing on her bacon for a moment and said that everything was much the same as she had said in her last letter to him; and it was. Lizzie was still on her own most of the time. None of the other kids ever went to her defence or wanted to be associated with her in case the Brays' attention turned to them, but she did get the occasional admiring glance from some of the younger ones for having stood up to the twins. The only saving grace for Lizzie was the knowledge that any day now she would be returning to Elvedom and the company of her mother's family and her new friends. Now Elrus was here she couldn't wait to see how things went over the next few days. What would he make of the Brays and, more to the point, what would the Brays make of him?

When Lizzie had first met Elrus, she had been slightly taken aback by his forthright manner. She remembered with pleasure the first sight of his cheeky face grinning out from under his long red fringe and how he'd winked at her. He showed no embarrassment or shyness and threw himself into things with abandon. Even in elvish terms, Lizzie thought he must be considered a little wacky, as most of the other elves she'd met had been quite serious. Lizzie trusted Elrus implicitly, as she knew that he had been raised to be one of her protectors, but more than that, he had proved to be a

21

good friend. She looked at him fondly now as he sat opposite her, attacking his breakfast with gusto.

Finally having munched their way through their large cooked breakfasts, which Elrus announced to be the best he'd ever had, the two of them left the table. Followed by the dogs, they made their way out into the garden. As they walked out of the coolness of the house, the heat of the day hit them as if someone had opened a raging oven door.

"Are you having such hot weather in Elvedom?" Lizzie asked Elrus, taking a sharp intake of breath, her face turning pink and beads of sweat breaking out on her forehead and above her top lip.

"Yeah, it's a nightmare. It's been like it pretty much since you left," Elrus nodded, his face beginning to resemble the colour of his hair. They walked quickly over to the shade of the big willow, close to the garden pond, and sat down on the grass beneath the tree's drooping branches.

"So, I've told you my news, or lack of it," Lizzie began. "So what have I been missing in your neck of the woods?" Elrus looked at her nonplussed.

"Neck of the woods?" he quizzed.

"It's an expression, it means, where you come from," she explained impatiently, eager to hear his news.

"Oh," nodded Elrus. He must remember that one, he thought. "Well, our spies have been gathering more information. I was with my father, the King and his head of security..."

"Elnest," Lizzie interjected.

"Yes, Elnest. Well, they were discussing how Eldorth is gathering more forces to his cause. He went ballistic when we got away with Elvyth's Harp and it's made him more determined than ever to keep the other sacred relics hidden and to wreak his revenge. There've also been more sightings of the pterotorials."

Pterotorials were large flying dinosaur type creatures, similar to the extinct pterodactyls, and were being used as spies in the skies by Eldorth. Their large wing spans and great speed meant that they could cover huge areas, in order to see what was happening on the land below.

"We also now know how the information that the pterotorials are picking up is actually being fed back to Eldorth – something that had confused the Great Council."

"Can Eldorth speak to them?" Lizzie asked in awe.

"Well they thought he could but apparently he can't. He's using wraiths." Elrus whispered conspiratorially, looking left and right as if to check that there was no-one eavesdropping.

"Wraiths? What are wraiths?" Lizzie asked, looking around too.

"Wraiths are the spirits of dead people or creatures," Elrus began.

"You mean ghosts," Lizzie suggested.

Elrus raised his eyes to the branches above his head. "Look, Princess, are you going to hear me out or are you going to keep interrupting me?" Lizzie looked sheepish and apologised. Elrus continued.

"Ghosts are the spiritual remains of someone who's unable to rest. Wraiths are the spirits of evil people or creatures that have been raised from the dead by dark magic. They're bad news as they can only be destroyed one way – by dragon fire!" Elrus concluded dramatically.

Lizzie stared at Elrus open mouthed. Then, blinking as if just realising she was gawping, she said sarcastically, "Well that's going to be easy – not!" After all, she thought, everyone knew there were no such things as dragons; or were there? She'd thought that elves and fairies weren't real and look how that turned out.

Elrus nodded knowingly. "The King and his advisors are working on that. The problem is that while they're working on it, Eldorth is gathering an army of wraiths to add to his armies of other nasties. It's going to be a hell of a battle when the time comes."

"Do the Council think it will come to that?" Lizzie asked, horrified by the thought.

Elrus shrugged. "It's possible I guess."

Lizzie looked down into the murky depths of the pond at their feet. The thought of war was terrifying. Hopefully, it would never come to that but then who knew what the future held. Whatever happened though, Lizzie knew in her bones that she had a part to play in it and it wasn't going to be an easy ride.

Most of the rest of the day was spent mooching about the house and garden, as it was too hot to do much else, and discussing their plans for the coming week. Later, when the heat of the day had cooled a little, Mrs Longton suggested that they take the dogs for a walk. She said it would be good for Lizzie to show Elrus around the village before dinner. As they walked through the village streets there were very few people about. Most of the villagers seemed to want to stay home in the cool of their houses with electric fans or air conditioning units blasting their faces.

Lizzie pointed out the local highlights, such as the park with its swings, slide, roundabout and climbing frame – all of which Elrus found huge fun. He spun the roundabout so fast that Lizzie thought she'd be sick. They then passed the library and the village green with its war memorial to the young, and not so young, men who had sacrificed their lives in the two World Wars. Elrus found the memorial fascinating and read through each of the names, several of whom were past relations of Lizzie. He turned to her sadly.

"We don't have anything like this in Elvedom," he said solemnly. "Of course we do celebrate the lives of fallen heroes in songs and poems, but we don't carve their names on stone. I think I'll tell my father about this so we can do something similar in our village."

"Let's hope that won't be necessary," Lizzie said gently and smiled at him sadly, knowing in her heart that if war with Eldorth did take place, then in all likelihood there would be sacrifices.

They walked across the green where they saw Lizzie's school. She explained that this was where they would spend the next few days and that Elrus would have the very dubious pleasure of meeting the Bray twins. As he looked at her, a cheeky grin spread across his face and he said he couldn't wait.

"Well, that's enough sightseeing for now. I'm starving!" he announced. "And after dinner I want to look at that telly thing you told me about." Then, laughing, he grabbed her by the hand and, with Basil and Rathbone racing along beside them, they ran for home.

# CHAPTER 3

## Elrus's Education

The following morning, Lizzie and Elrus were up early and, after a hearty breakfast, made their way to school. Elrus was wearing some of the clothes that Lizzie and Elwood had bought on their shopping trip. Lizzie had needed to keep a close eye on Elwood's purchases as he tended to be very fond of bright colours which no human kid would be seen dead in. Elrus was wearing some baggy blue shorts, a bright green tee-shirt – that Lizzie thought clashed a bit with his orange hair but had been unable to persuade Elwood out of this – and a grey baseball cap. The cap was there to keep the intense heat of the sun off his pointed features, but more importantly to keep his elvish ears under cover. It had also been agreed that his elvish name, Elrus, was likely to raise questions too and so they would just explain that it was a common name in Greenland.

As they walked along the lane towards the village, Elrus babbled on excitedly about how much he was looking forward to the experience. Education in his world was usually undertaken by village elders in small groups and within a young elf's own home until they were thirteen, and so school for Elrus was a new and exciting experience. Lizzie grinned at his beaming, animated face and thought that he might be just a little disappointed as, in her opinion, school was to be endured rather than enjoyed. She would much prefer to be educated the elvish way.

As they came into sight of the school, and could see the other kids making their way through the gates, Lizzie suddenly stopped. She felt a building sense of dread at what the day held in store. What would the Brays reaction be to her supposed cousin's arrival? Would they be mean? Or sickeningly sweet to entice him away into their gang, which was another of their strategies to lure unsuspecting kids into their lair. Elrus, initially unaware of his companion's abrupt halt, was several steps ahead of Lizzie before he realised that she was missing. Turning around and seeing the doubt etched on her face, he smiled his cheeky lopsided grin at her reassuringly.

"Come on, Princess. Don't worry, I won't embarrass you, promise," he said, drawing a cross with his long fingers over his heart.

Lizzie smiled back at him and, walking towards him, said sternly, "It's not you I'm worried about and don't call me Princess – it's Lizzie from now on, remember?"

"Absolutely, Lizziekins," he laughed, as Lizzie shot him a withering glance.

Walking through the school gates, Lizzie's heart skipped a beat as she spotted Regina and Veronica Bray with a little group of their followers standing close to the entrance to the school building. She saw that Veronica had seen them and watched as she nudged her sister whose back was towards them. Regina turned around and stared, planted her hands on her ample hips and took the defiant stance of an overweight Peter Pan. Elrus was oblivious of the Brays as he looked around the playground at the other children running around, skipping, jostling each other, or just talking in excited groups and pairs as they told each other about their weekend exploits.

"Come on then Prin..., Lizzie," he said happily, almost forgetting to call her by name, but as he turned towards her he could see the frozen look on her face. Following her gaze, Elrus knew immediately the focus of her attention. "Ah....," he sighed knowingly, the smile falling from his face.

Lizzie had described the twins to perfection and he would have recognised them without having to witness his companion's discomfort at being in their presence. Elrus touched Lizzie's arm; "It's going to be okay," he grinned at her. "You know, this could even be fun." Lizzie saw the glint of mischief twinkle in the young elf's eyes and couldn't help but smile.

Lizzie had been told that she should take Elrus to the office of Mr Meacham, the Head Teacher, first thing that morning and so the pair marched towards the school building under the intense glare of the Bray twins and their gang. As they approached the doors, Regina stepped forward and blocked their progress; a sneer spread across her podgy face. As she opened her mouth to speak, Elrus stopped right in front of her. His green eyes from under his shock of red hair bore into Regina's black beady ones and she blinked rapidly against the intensity of his glare. A flicker of something akin to fear flashed momentarily across her face before it was quickly replaced by her usual arrogant, defiant countenance. Veronica stood at her sister's shoulder as always, hovering just in the background, silently urging her twin on. Regina tore her eyes away from Elrus and turned them onto Lizzie.

"Morning, Long Ears," she sneered. "So who's ya boyfriend?" Her posse, gathered behind her, giggled.

Lizzie was sure that the pounding of her heart could be heard all around the playground but, taking a deep breath and buoyed up by the company of Elrus, she swallowed down her feeling of fear and sidestepped the Brays. Then, without a word of acknowledgment, she and Elrus strode into the building. The sensation of the Brays' hateful eyes burned into the back of Lizzie's head. As she and Elrus entered the foyer, he grabbed her by the arm and she swung round to face him. The action took her by surprise.

"So that's the Brays?" he sounded incredulous. He shook his head slowly from side to side. "I don't think your description did them justice." Lizzie looked at him puzzled and then watched as a wry grin spread across his lips as he added, "My... they is *ugly*."

Lizzie burst out laughing and, as she did so, the bubble of impending doom burst too. It was going to be okay because she trusted her friend to make sure that it would be. Feeling a hundred times lighter in mood, and daring to think that her last week at the village school might actually be fun, she led Elrus to Mr Meacham's office.

As they approached the office door, the Head Teacher's secretary, Mrs Watts, greeted them.

"Good morning, Elizabeth," she smiled. "And this, I take it, must be your cousin. Elrus isn't it?"

Lizzie nodded as Elrus put out his hand to shake that of Mrs Watts.

"Good morning, madam," Elrus said brightly. The secretary smiled down at his hand and shook it warmly, thinking what a polite young man he was. She took in his unusual pointed features and could see the similarities between him and Lizzie, concluding that he must indeed be a relation.

"I'll let Mr Meacham know you're here," Mrs Watts said, going into the office behind her.

Lizzie turned to Elrus and quickly whispered that it was usual to call the women in school Miss or Mrs whatever their surname was, not madam, and that it was okay to call the men Sir. Elrus nodded in understanding as Mr Meacham, accompanied by Lizzie's teacher Miss Finley, came out of his office to greet them.

"Good morning, children," smiled Mr Meacham, his round face beaming a friendly smile. Lizzie liked her Head Teacher as he was kind but firm when necessary. He did, however, have one fault in Lizzie's opinion and that was his blindness to the activities of the Bray twins. Elrus stuck his hand out once more in greeting; Mr Meacham shook it heartily. "Welcome young man, welcome."

A smiling Miss Finley was introduced and then she and the two children made their way to 6F's classroom. As they entered the room, Elrus's face lit up. He let out a whoop of delight as he took in the sight of the walls covered in pictures and maps and paintings and drawings that had been done by the children. A bookcase stretched the length of the room, on top of which sat pieces of pottery and craftwork also created by the children. He ran over to the bookcase and took out a large illustrated storybook and flicked through its pages.

"Wow," he breathed. He lifted his face and grinned at Lizzie. "This is great!" Miss Finley watched his reactions with fascination.

"Surely your school has similar books?" she asked. Elrus shook his head emphatically.

"Not like this," he said. "The pictures are so bright. Our books are so...," he paused in thought. Finally adding, "... old."

Miss Finley laughed. "Well, maybe we'll see if we can let you take a couple of books back with you as a gift to your school," she said. As Elrus thanked the teacher for her kindness, there was a loud ringing sound that came from outside in the playground. Elrus shot Lizzie a quizzical glance.

"That's the bell to start school," Lizzie explained. The pair watched out of the window as the rest of the children fell into neat lines, at the front of which stood a teacher or an assistant. Then, as another bell rang, the lines marched one by one into the building.

Lizzie sat on her usual chair by the window and, as the seat next to her was never occupied, Elrus plonked himself down in it just as the rest of the children filed in, led by the loathsome Regina Bray. As Regina and her twin sat down, they shot the newcomer a disdainful glance. Elrus paid them back with a big cheesy grin and then turned to face Miss Finley as the rest of the class settled into their seats.

"Good morning, children," said Miss Finley.

"Good morning, Miss," the children chanted in reply.

"This morning we are joined in class by a visitor," Miss Finley began and then, indicating Elrus to her right, said, "This is Elrus and he has come to Chislewick to stay with his cousin Lizzie. Elrus has come all the way from a country called Greenland, so I hope you will make him feel very welcome." She stared intently at the Brays as she finished her sentence.

The Brays, sitting in their usual place just behind Lizzie, smiled sickly sweet grins as they looked at their teacher. As Miss Finley turned away to pick up the class register, one of the twins gave Lizzie a sharp poke in her back with a pencil. As she turned she saw their sneering faces. It was look that Lizzie recognised all too well and she knew that the pair was no doubt already planning something unpleasant.

As she turned to face the front once more she heard Veronica say, "Elrus? What kind of stupid name is that?"

Quick as a flash Elrus turned around and stared at her. "Actually it's very common in Greenland," he said proudly. Causing the twins to look at each other and snigger.

Miss Finley turned to the class once more to take the register, she noticed that Elrus still had his baseball cap on.

"Please remove your cap, Elrus," Miss Finley told the young elf.

"Yeah, you're not allowed caps in school," piped up Regina.

"Thank you, Regina!" Miss Finley admonished sharply.

As Elrus slowly removed his headgear, a flurry of whispers rumbled around the room.

"Look at his ears." "Oh my god! Look, he's got ears like her!" Then, Lizzie and Elrus with their sharp hearing heard Veronica murmur to her sister, "Another freak! What a loser."

Miss Finley glared at the children that were making comments. Her usual gentle face flushed pink with anger.

"That is quite enough," she said, through barely concealed gritted teeth. "Elrus is our guest here and you will show him courtesy." The children fell silent and most looked down at the table in front of them, except the Brays whose smug faces looked defiantly at their prey sitting near the

31

window. Miss Finley returned to her register and began the roll call of names.

The first lesson of the day was literacy, which went relatively smoothly as the children took it in turns to read pages from a story book about witches. Elrus was mesmerised by the story and listened in rapt attention as Lizzie took her turn in telling how an evil witch turned a young boy into a rat. The only slight hiccup was when Elrus clapped enthusiastically as Lizzie sat down after her reading. She shot him a warning glance and hissed that he should stop and that he'd promised not to embarrass her. As she looked around, she spotted the Brays and some of the other kids giggling at Elrus. Miss Finley, however, thought it was charming that he should enjoy the story so much and smiled at him as she asked another pupil to take their turn at reading.

At the end of the literacy lesson, the school bell sounded once again – this time to signal it was time for break. The children got up quickly, pushed their chairs haphazardly under their tables and made a dash for the classroom door with Miss Finley calling after them to stop running. Lizzie and Elrus hung back to allow the other kids out before they made their way to the playground for morning break. Elrus replaced his baseball cap over his red hair and tucked the tips of his ears inside. Lizzie looked at him and grinned.

"Too late, mate," she laughed. "No point in trying to hide them now. You wait till we get outside and see what I've had to put up with." Elrus grinned back at her.

"The future holds no fear for me," he said dramatically, and the pair were still laughing as they walked out into the bright, sun-drenched playground.

The playground was buzzing with activity and Elrus stood fascinated as he watched kids running around, throwing things to each other or playing various games. Clusters of girls stood gossiping and giggling and groups of lads messed about, pushing and shoving each other and laughing boisterously. Over to one side of the playground was a collection of wooden tables and benches, and perched on one of the tables sat the Brays holding court over a gaggle of their followers. Lizzie looked at Elrus's beaming face and suddenly felt sad. She knew he would love to join in with some of the antics taking place but also knew that was not going to happen whilst he was in her company. She looked over at the Brays and their followers and hatred suddenly welled up inside her.

Over the years, she had learnt to stifle the feeling of loneliness and isolation that she had endured because of them, but now she had a friend who, even for a brief time, would also suffer at their hands. She glared across at the pair and saw Veronica look over in her and Elrus's direction and promptly nudge her sister. Regina's piggy face turned its malicious expression their way too. Elrus was too busy watching kids having fun to notice as the Brays clambered off their perch and began to walk in Lizzie's and his direction, their gang trailing in their wake.

Lizzie's stomach did a quick flip and her hand instinctively rested on the locket contained in the secret pocket of her school skirt. The locket had often been a source of comfort to her during the few months since she had learnt its true purpose, as it represented her other life amongst family and friends who cared for her. As she had moved her hand, her arm had accidently brushed against Elrus and he turned a questioning glance at her. Upon seeing the pinched look on her face, and her resolute stare towards the approaching mob, he turned to watch as the Brays sauntered up to face them.

"So, this is your cousin is it, Long Ears?" Regina began, taking her usual role as chief spokesman of the pair. A sneer spread across her porcine features.

Elrus drew himself up to his full height, which was a fraction taller than the girl in front of him but slightly less than her lanky, vulturous sister. His green eyes glared into the squinting piggy eyes of Regina's own.

"Her name is Lizzie," he said slowly and precisely. The group now surrounding him and Lizzie laughed mockingly and some oo'd and ah'd in ridicule.

"Her name's Lizzie," mimicked Veronica, looking around at her audience for support and gaining it through more laughter. Some of the gang members nudged and jostled each other in mirth.

Lizzie stood rooted to the spot watching the group, her face set and showing little sign of emotion. Elrus's face, however, began to show signs of feigned disbelief and suspicion. He nodded deliberately, a wry grin playing across his lips.

"Lizzie's told me all about you two," he smiled, looking almost evil as a mischievous glint twinkled in his eyes.

"Oh yeah?" Regina asked defiantly.

"Oh, yeah," he nodded, the grin widening. "By the way, are you always so rude and obnoxious?"

The Brays faces showed surprise at the insult and then seemed to heighten in colour as anger rose up in them. Regina, hands on hips, leaned forward threateningly. "Who the hell do you think you're talking to?" she snarled.

Elrus looked about him innocently. Then, leaning forward so that his nose almost touched that of his adversary, he said quietly and to maximum effect, "That would be you."

Lizzie, standing beside him, felt as if her heart would burst with happiness that her friend was standing up for her. No kid had ever done that before. She saw the look of uncertainty cross Regina's usually self-assured face and waited to see who would pull out of the confrontation first. Then she heard the shrill tone of Mrs Crabb, who was supervising the playground.

"Now, now children. What's going on here?" asked the teacher, a large overweight lady with a fierce countenance. She had spotted something amiss from across the playground and had made her way over to stop it from escalating.

Regina pulled back, looked up at the looming Mrs Crabb and a smarmy insincere grin spread across her podgy face. "Nothing, Miss," she said sweetly. "Just saying hello to the new boy."

The teacher took in the scene and, before going about her business, said, "Well, play nicely now."

If looks could kill, Elrus would have been residing with his ancestors in the Spirit world from that moment on. Regina and Veronica's glares were of pure, unadulterated hatred. Elrus had not only stood up to them but had embarrassed them in front of their gang and they would neither forgive nor forget that moment. They turned on their heels and, with their followers muttering and glancing back at the young elf standing confidently watching their retreat, took up their position on the wooden table they had vacated shortly before the encounter.

Lizzie looked at Elrus and had an overwhelming urge to hug him, but knew that if she did it would probably cause them both acute embarrassment. Instead, she slapped him sharply on the back.

"That was brilliant," she beamed. Then, looking more serious, said, "You do know you've made two enemies there?"

Elrus stared across at the twins. "I certainly hope so; I'd hate to think they were my friends," he said and then, turning to look at her, asked that she give him a tour of the school.

After break, the class of 6F returned to their room for a maths lesson at which Elrus demonstrated his skill. Miss Finley began the lesson with a short test to check that the children had done their homework over the weekend. Elrus found the questions very easy and in his keenness kept shouting out the answers. Miss Finley explained that he shouldn't shout out but should raise his hand to give the other children a chance. In his eagerness to be chosen, Elrus's arms waved about like a demented scarecrow in a high wind for the remainder of the question and answer session. Lizzie gave up telling him to put his arms down when it seemed to make no difference in dampening his enthusiasm. The question and answer session over, Miss Finley thought it would be interesting to learn from Elrus how maths was taught where he came from.

"The teaching of numbers and calculations is very practical where I come from," Elrus began. "I live in a mainly farming community so my father and his council must work out how to maximize the use of the land without exploiting its resources."

Miss Finley raised her eyebrows. She didn't know much about Greenland but from what she did know, she had understood it to be a country dominated by the cold and snow and so the fact that it was agricultural took her by surprise. Also, the news that his father led some kind of council implied that he must hold an important position within his community. She let the boy continue.

"My father lets me sit with him in council meetings and I have learnt how to make those calculations," Elrus explained. Lizzie shifted in her seat. She was beginning to feel uneasy that he was getting carried away and might end up saying too much. "I can show you if you like," he beamed. Lizzie groaned.

Before Miss Finley had a chance to decide whether or not she wanted Elrus to show her how the calculations were made, he was up out of his seat and at the whiteboard, pen in hand. He proceeded to talk about lengths and distance and ratio of grain weight to grains per square acre and so on. He scrawled formulas of numbers and letters on the board and spoke so quickly that the rest of the children, including Lizzie and Miss Finley, could only observe with mouths hanging open. Elrus finished the demonstration with a flourish and bowed to his audience. He was greeted with stunned silence. Elrus's eyes flicked around the room, waiting for some kind of response, and then settled on Lizzie, his head tilting to one side as if to say, "Well?"

Lizzie felt that she should show him her support in the way he had shown her his and began clapping. Miss Finley slowly began to follow suit and looked to the children to follow her example, some of whom did. Elrus's face lit up in pleasure and, replacing the marker pen on Miss Finley's desk, he sat back down next to Lizzie.

Miss Finley thanked Elrus for his interesting demonstration and then asked the children to take out their exercise books. As she turned to the whiteboard, she felt reluctant to remove the elegant squiggles and swirls of the boy's writing and felt strangely inadequate in what she was about to ask the class to do. Still, she had to stick to the curriculum and so the maths lesson proceeded.

With the lesson over, it was time for lunch. Those children who had packed lunches went to collect their lunch-boxes stored at the side of the classrooms, whilst the others made their way to the school hall. Many of the tables and chairs were already occupied by the time Lizzie and Elrus arrived and they made their way to the back of the queue to collect their food. Over on the far side of the hall, they could see the Brays and some of their gang already seated and tucking into their food. Elrus sniffed the air.

"Smells good. What do you think we're having?" he asked Lizzie.

"Well, it smells like burgers to me," she said, turning up her nose.

"What are burgers? Don't you like them?" Elrus asked. "They're bits of flattened minced beef that are usually over-cooked and served with chips and peas. And no, I don't much like them. After what you're used to eating Elrus, don't expect too much of school dinners," Lizzie said disdainfully.

After collecting their burgers and chips, which this time came with salad instead of peas, and a pudding of raspberry yoghurt, they found a quiet table as far away from the Brays as possible. Elrus began tucking into his burger. As he chewed a mouthful of the meat, he raised his eyes to Lizzie. Swallowing hard, he said, "Umm… I see what you mean."

The remainder of the lunch break was spent avoiding contact with the Brays and, in order to do this, Lizzie and Elrus went and sat in the book corner of the school. Lizzie often hid herself away there, as it was somewhere the Brays never went unless forced to by Miss Finley. Elrus loved looking through the books and was especially interested in those that contained pictures and facts about the countries of the world. As Lizzie and Elrus pored over a world atlas, the pair discussed what the equivalent countries in his world were called.

The afternoon went quickly and was spent doing arts and crafts. By the end of the day, Elrus was proudly holding a clay pot that he had created. It was actually very good and Lizzie could see the venom emanating from Veronica Bray who usually took the praise for her pottery. Miss Finley said that the pots would be put in the kiln overnight and should be ready to decorate the next morning. As the class concluded for the day, Miss Finley reminded the children to bring in their sports kits for Sports Day the following afternoon.

"And please make sure that you bring in your sun hats and plenty of sun lotion. We don't want anyone suffering from sunstroke in this weather," she called out, as the children made their hasty exit out of the room.

Lizzie and Elrus hung back until the others had gone and then made their way slowly out of the building. Lizzie wanted to give the Brays plenty of time to be well away before leaving the school grounds. The twins' silence towards her and Elrus made her uneasy. She knew only too well their spiteful ways and that there was no way they would allow Elrus's comments at break that morning to pass without some form of retribution. As they walked through the school gates, Lizzie looked both ways down the street. She could see lots of kids making their way from school but there was no sign of her adversaries. She let out a sigh of relief. Elrus watched as Lizzie's face relaxed and gently touched her arm.

"You okay, Princess?" he asked, feeling that it was alright to now use the form of address he was most comfortable with.

"I'm fine, thanks," she smiled. "Let's go home."

A mischievous look crossed Elrus's face. "Race ya!" he said and began running, hotly pursued by Lizzie.

As Lizzie and Elrus reached the end of the road and turned the bend, they got a nasty shock. Hanging around on the corner of the next street, the one they needed to turn down to take them home, was Regina and Veronica Bray and their gang.

# CHAPTER 4

## Granny Fimble Found Out

Lizzie grabbed Elrus's arm and dragged him back behind the hedge that bordered the house alongside them. "I'm not going to go past that lot!" she hissed vehemently.

Elrus peered around the hedge and looked at the gang.

"You know, you and I could run past them *so* fast they wouldn't know where the draught had come from," he said, accompanying the words with a whooshing noise as if to emphasis the point. "I could even give that Regina a poke in the eye as we passed, if I could get through the folds of fat that is."

Lizzie couldn't help but laugh at the thought but shook her head. Like all elves, Elrus had the amazing ability to run exceptionally fast and Lizzie, through her mother's bloodline, had inherited the gift.

"No, I don't think so," she said. "I think we should just wait here a bit until they get bored and leave."

"Quite right, dear," an elderly woman's voice said from the other side of the hedge. Lizzie and Elrus peeked over the foliage to see the wrinkled face of the rumoured village witch, Granny Fimble. The old woman smiled at them, revealing a row of brown, chipped teeth, several of which were missing.

Lizzie had always avoided Granny Fimble because of the rumours. Even though she'd been told whilst growing up that there were no such things as witches, her recent adventures in Elvedom had proven the contrary. Lizzie's grandmother had said that there was no reason to avoid Granny Fimble, and that she was just a simple old lady who loved the company of her several cats. Mrs Longton had grown up in the village, as had Granny Fimble, and so knew the old lady reasonably well. As the years had passed,

Granny had become more and more reclusive, spending her days pottering around her garden apart from making the occasional trip to the village shop for her meagre supplies. Mrs Longton said that Ada Fimble, whom she referred to as "Daft Ada", was always a bit of a loner, even when she was younger.

Elrus suddenly shoved a hand in the old woman's direction and said, "Good day, madam." Granny Fimble looked at his hand for a moment as if confused by the action and then up into the boy's eyes.

"Good afternoon, young man," she replied. Elrus dropped his hand to his side but continued to smile brightly at her.

Granny then turned her rheumy gaze in Lizzie's direction. It was the first time that Lizzie had been close enough to a get really good look at Granny and what she saw surprised her. The woman's face was in no way scary or hostile but soft and gentle. There wasn't a hint of "witchiness" about her, apart from perhaps the black cat that lay in her arms. Granny was running her hand along its sleek coat in slow, deliberate strokes. The cat's green eyes shone like tiny light bulbs in its elegant head and Lizzie found its stare unnerving as it turned to look at her.

Lizzie's expression must have changed because Granny said, "Don't mind Liquorice; he likes to weigh people up before he lets them make friends with him. Very sensible, don't ya think?"

"Yes, very," Lizzie agreed, eyeing the cat warily. She had always been more of a dog person herself.

"Most wise," Elrus contributed. "Is Liquorice your only cat?"

"He's not *my* cat," said the old lady. "Cats don't belong to anyone. No, no. Cats are their own souls. Liquorice just choses to live here with me and I'm glad he does. We are good friends, aren't we, Liquorice?" She looked down at the cat and it looked back at her before slowly closing his eyes, as if enjoying the massage she was giving him. Granny Fimble turned back to the children.

"I have seven cats that live with me," Granny continued.

"Seven?!" exclaimed Elrus. "That's a very good number. Some would even consider it lucky." Lizzie looked at her companion. If she didn't know better, she would have thought he was mocking the old lady but that wasn't Elrus's way. He, like all elves, was very respectful of his elders.

"Seven is a lucky number," Granny Fimble agreed, as if giving them a lesson in the laws of suspicious beliefs. Elrus nodded.

"I know," he nodded.

Whilst the young elf and the old lady discussed lucky numbers, Lizzie grabbed the opportunity to have a peek around the corner of the hedge to see if the twins had gone. To her dismay, they had not. In fact, the Brays and their gang seemed to have settled down on the grass verge and were mucking around as if they were going to be there for quite a while. Lizzie turned back towards Elrus and Granny.

"Those Bray brats giving you trouble, girl?" Granny asked.

"Well…" Lizzie began.

"You don't have to say anything. I know they're chips off the old block. Their dad was a bully in his day; still is by all accounts," said Granny. Lizzie was stunned at the change in the demeanour of the old lady. Her voice had become stronger and the rheumy eyes seemed to clear as a flint-like glint appeared in them. They then seemed to soften once again as she said, "While your waiting for that lot to disappear, would you two young'uns like to come in for a nice cold glass of my home-made rosehip cordial? It's great if you're feeling under the weather but I like it any time."

Elrus and Lizzie looked at each other. Lizzie's face showed her uncertainty but before she could say anything, Elrus said, "Thank you so much. We'd love to."

Granny suggested that the pair go around to her back gate to avoid the Brays. As they walked through the wooden gate, they found themselves in a neatly tended garden. To one side of it, there were some old fruit trees, unripe apples, pears and plums hung amongst the leaves, promising a good crop by autumn time. In one corner was a small vegetable patch and flowerbeds bordered a well mown lawn. Standing by the back door of the cottage was Granny Fimble, still holding Liquorice in her arms. She smiled at her visitors and invited them to sit at a little metal table and chairs set under the shade of a heavily laden cherry tree. Lizzie's mouth watered at the thought of the cherries juicy sweet flesh.

Granny noticed the look on Lizzie face and, as she put Liquorice gently on the ground, told her and Elrus to help themselves. Elrus needed no second bidding before he was standing on one of the chairs and reaching up into the lowest branches.

As he passed handfuls of the round red berries down to Lizzie, who in turn piled them onto the table, she whispered, "This is weird. I've spent my whole life avoiding Granny Fimble and you're here five minutes and I find myself in her garden picking her fruit."

"Why are you whispering?" Elrus whispered back. "She's inside so she's not going to hear you," he continued, raising his voice to a more normal level. "Anyway, why have you always avoided her? She seems perfectly nice to me."

Lizzie glanced over at the cottage door to make sure that there was no sign of Granny's reappearance before saying, again in hushed tones, "People say she's a witch."

"So?" Elrus asked.

"Well," Lizzie began, starting to feel slightly foolish. "Because witches are supposed to practice magic, it was always believed that they were wicked. Years ago, women were burnt at the stake for any suspicion that they might be one. Nowadays they just tend to be avoided. And anyway, people in this world are a bit wary of anyone who's seen as different. Look at how the other kids treat me."

"Is she a bad witch?" Elrus asked, now looking a little worried.

"I don't think so," said Lizzie, thoughtfully. "If truth be told, my gran has always said that it's nonsense for people to think Granny's a witch. She thinks that she's just a bit odd."

As the old lady came out of her back door, carrying a tray laden with glasses and a bottle containing a red coloured liquid, Elrus hastily said that he thought they should give Granny the benefit of the doubt.

Lizzie pushed the cherries to one side of the table so that Granny could place the tray in front of the children. As well as the cordial, they saw that it also contained a plate of delicious looking biscuits. Granny sat down on one of the other remaining chairs and proceeded to pour some of the liquid into each of the glasses and pass them to Lizzie and Elrus.

"Oh, this is a treat," sighed Granny, as she leant back in her chair, clasping her glass to her chest. "I don't get many visitors." She then added, "Actually, I can't remember the last time." The look on Granny's face appeared sad and Lizzie suddenly felt sorry for her.

"So, I know that this young lady is Amy Longton's granddaughter, Elizabeth, but who else do I have the pleasure of entertaining this fine afternoon?" Granny asked.

Elrus jumped up and bowed and almost introduced himself as Elrus of Elvenholme, before remembering how he should introduce himself in this world.

"I am Lizzie's cousin, Elrus," he pronounced grandly. Granny gave Elrus a shrewd look and then smiled, giving Lizzie the distinct impression that she didn't quite believe him.

"Well, Lizzie's cousin Elrus, you are most welcome to my little cottage," Granny said.

He sat back down and took a sip of his drink, and Lizzie almost giggled when she saw the look of unpleasant surprise on his face.

Granny smiled at him. "Delicious, aye boy?" she said, taking a sip from her own glass and eyeing Elrus steadily over its rim.

"Mmm..." replied Elrus weakly, swallowing reluctantly and trying to turn the grimace forming on his lips into a smile. Lizzie sniffed her drink suspiciously and wondered how she might escape taking a sip herself. Looking at the biscuits, she thought that these might be her saviour. As she began to think about asking for one, it suddenly occurred to her that she didn't know how to address the old lady. Granny Fimble was a village nick-name for her that sounded slightly disrespectful, and she certainly couldn't call her Daft Ada. She decided to plump for a formal approach.

"Those biscuits look delicious, Miss Fimble, may I have one?" Lizzie asked.

"Of course, my dear," the old lady said, pleasure brimming over in her face. "I baked them fresh this morning. Oats and honey," she added, as she offered the plate to Lizzie. "Home-grown honey it is too. See my little hive over there," she added, indicating a bee-hive hidden in another corner of the garden. Lizzie hesitated slightly as she put the biscuit to her mouth but when she bit into its crisp surface, she discovered that it tasted even better than it looked. She smiled over at Elrus.

"You should try one," she encouraged him. "It'll go well with the cordial." She winked conspiratorially and Elrus quickly took one of the biscuits and stuffed it into his mouth. As he swallowed the honey flavoured crumbs, he sighed in relief as took away the sickly, cloying taste of the rosehips.

Granny Fimble looked across the table at her two young visitors and, smiling gently, asked, "So, young man, how are you enjoying your visit to our part of the world?"

Lizzie and Elrus were astounded. How did the old lady know he was a visitor when she rarely appeared to venture out of her home? Who had told her? As if reading their minds, Granny leant back, laughed and said, "There's not much that goes on in this village without me knowing about it."

"I'm enjoying it very much, thank you," Elrus said. Then, unable to contain his curiosity, he asked, "May I ask how you know I'm just visiting?"

Granny leant forward, as if about to share a great secret, "Let's just say a little birdie told me."

"You can talk to birds?" he asked, wide-eyed in wonder that a human could hold such a skill.

"It's just a saying, when you don't want to tell someone who it was that told you something," laughed Lizzie.

"That too," acknowledged Granny, to Lizzie's amazement. What was the old lady implying; that she really could talk to birds?

"Also your name gave the game away a bit. Elrus, it's a very unusual name," Granny added thoughtfully.

"Oh, it's very common in Greenland, which is where I come from," Elrus assured her, feeling that he wasn't exactly very convincing. He and Lizzie looked at each other and the look that passed between them was one that said, "hope we've got away with that explanation".

Elrus decided a change of subject was a good idea and, looking around the garden, complimented Granny on how beautiful it was. Granny gazed around her little domain with pride and said that her garden was her favourite thing, next to her cats that was. Lizzie had spied a number of the animals lying in strategically shaded places around the little plot and asked Granny about them.

"Well, that's Zeus," she said, pointing to a ginger giant spread out under a rosemary bush. "Like his name-sake, he's the boss. He puts the others in their place if there's any squabbling." As if knowing he was being talked about, the cat opened a lazy eye and peered at the children disinterestedly before closing it again and continuing with his slumber. Granny then indicated a pretty little tortoise-shell stretching languidly from her place between the plant pots on Granny's patio.

"That there is Isadora. She's a proper little actress if she doesn't get enough attention." A further three cats, Bandit, Jester and Shadow, were introduced and Granny explained that the only cat that was missing tended to stay mainly in the cottage. "Dodger is shy and happiest indoors. Would you like to meet him?"

Curious to see the inside of Granny's cottage, Lizzie said she would love to meet the missing cat and, if it meant avoiding drinking any more of the repulsive rosehip cordial, Elrus agreed with her.

As they walked into the cool of the cottage, the first thing that struck the pair was a strong smell of something aromatic burning. It reminded Lizzie of a time she had been to church and the vicar had been swinging a thurible full of incense. It wasn't an unpleasant smell but Lizzie did find it a little over-powering.

From a short back hall, they followed Granny into her kitchen and were confronted by what could have passed for an old apothecary shop. Herbs and plants hung, drying from a wooden rack suspended from the ceiling, and a huge dresser dominating one wall was full of jars that appeared to contain a mixture of powders, pastes and potions. Bowls of varying sizes occupied an old wooden table in the middle of the room. Curled up on a chair in the corner, lay a black and white cat. The markings on the cat's face gave him the look of a pirate, as he had a black patch covering one eye. Disturbed by the entrance of strangers to his home, he sat up and stared intently at them.

"This is Dodger," Granny said by way of introduction. "Say hello, Dodger," she cooed. The cat did not move but continued to watch the intruders warily.

"Hello, Dodger; nice to meet you," said Elrus, keeping his distance as the cat made a hissing noise.

"Don't mind him," excused the old lady. "Like I told you, he's shy. He'll be fine once he gets used to you. Just like Liquorice and most cats, he doesn't trust people straight away. Not like dogs – silly creatures. Much too trusting – that's why they get taken advantage of so easily."

Lizzie thought that the old lady had a point, but she still felt that the unconditional love that dogs gave their owners was preferable to the often aloof nature of cats. The devotion that Basil and Rathbone gave her was something she treasured, as it had seen her through some of her loneliest moments.

Elrus walked over to the dresser and peered at some of the labels on the jars lining its shelves. He recognised some of the names on the labels and, taking down one of the jars, he turned and looked intently at Granny.

"Some of these are medicines," he said slowly. As if he had come to some realisation, he asked, "Are you a healer?"

The old lady smiled her gentle smile. "That I am," Granny admitted proudly.

Before her mouth had engaged with her brain, Lizzie blurted, "So you're not a witch!" She then clamped a hand over her mouth in horror at having been so rude. Her grandmother would have killed her if she had been present.

The old lady threw back her head and chuckled loudly. Lizzie sighed in relief as it seemed that Granny hadn't taken offence. Regaining her composure, the old lady looked Lizzie straight in the eye and said, "I didn't say that."

Lizzie felt a flutter of fear in the pit of her stomach. She and Elrus had been stupid to come into a relative stranger's home and eat and drink with someone she had always avoided. They could have been poisoned by that disgusting rosehip cordial. Fairy stories of children being fattened up by witches and then eaten flew into her imagination.

Granny sat down at the kitchen table.

"Don't be frightened, Elizabeth; I've waited a long time for this chance to speak to you. Please sit down. There's something I want to explain." The way Granny spoke stirred memories in Lizzie from when she had first met her grandfather in Elvedom, and so she did as she was asked. Elrus followed her lead and sat down close to her, his role as her protector foremost in his mind. They watched the old lady expectantly.

The expression on Granny Fimble's face was one of someone thinking about how best to start and, after a few seconds, which felt like minutes, she began.

"Like you, Elizabeth, I am different and because of that I have led a lonely life, apart of course from the company of the cats that have lived with me over the years," she said. "I had a sister but she was very different to me in many ways. Lively and outgoing, she wanted to experience a wider world so she moved away years ago." Lizzie was surprised by this as she had never heard that Granny had a sister. Granny continued, "Then my parents died, leaving me all alone. People in small communities can help and support each other but sometimes it makes them close-minded and suspicious, especially if you don't fit their idea of 'normal'.

Because people shunned me, I, like you, had a difficult time at school and hated my time there. I was happiest at home where I could be with the cats and my beloved mum and dad. My sister was usually out with her friends. My mum understood me because she too was different; she was also a healer."

Amazed at how much Granny seemed to know about her, Lizzie now felt a sudden empathy for the old lady. If anyone should have understood how lonely Granny was, it should have been her. She was beginning to realise that she had been terribly wrong to have avoided the old lady for all those years. As if reading her mind, Granny continued.

"Over the years, I've watched you from a distance Elizabeth, and have been sad that you have had to suffer much the same fate as me. When I saw you yesterday, with this young man here, I was delighted that you had got yourself a friend at last. Cherish him, for true friendship is a rare and precious thing. Take that from someone who's been denied it."

Lizzie got up from her chair and walked around the table and squatted down beside the old lady. She took one of the woman's wrinkled hands in her own and looked up into her face. The action seemed to take Granny Fimble by surprise, but she didn't flinch from the contact. Instead, she looked down at Lizzie with red-rimmed eyes that looked ready to overspill with tears.

"I'm so sorry, Miss Fimble, that I haven't been to visit you before. I should have understood how lonely you must get and I'm so glad that you invited us in today. I hope that you will let me come and see you often," Lizzie said with true emotion.

"Oh, that would be lovely, Elizabeth," Granny beamed. "And if you're interested, perhaps I could show you some of my spel..., recipes for my ointments and potions," she added. Lizzie felt sure that the old woman was about to say another word before deciding upon recipes. Surely she wasn't about to say spells, was she? Lizzie wondered but she decided not to press the point.

"I would really like that," said Lizzie, smiling brightly. It looked like she had another new friend. "But can I ask you a favour?"

"Of course, my dear," Granny agreed.

"Please call me Lizzie; my gran calls me Elizabeth when she's cross with me," she grinned.

Granny threw back her head and chuckled, her broken and chipped teeth clearly on display.

Elrus stood up from his chair where he'd been watching the exchange and made a sound as if clearing his throat.

"Excuse me Prin.., Lizzie, but I think we should check if the coast is clear. We need to make our way home or your grandmother might start to worry," he said.

"Quite right, young man," Granny agreed, getting up from her chair. Then, still holding Lizzie's hand, she helped the girl to her feet. The three of them walked through the cottage towards Granny's front door where the old lady opened it and peered out. She turned back to face the children.

"Well, it looks as though it's safe to proceed," Granny smiled. "Now, you get yourselves off home."

As Lizzie and Elrus said their goodbyes and headed for the Hall, Elrus turned to Lizzie.

"Well, she seemed a really nice old lady to me," he said. Lizzie nodded in agreement. "Just one thing though," he added.

"What's that?" Lizzie quizzed.

"She really needs some urgent dental work!" he grimaced and, laughing, they began jogging for home.

Back at the cottage, Granny stood watching and waving until they were out of sight. Finally, she turned and walked back inside, stopping to pick up Liquorice who'd been watching the departure with interest. She stroked the cat lovingly.

"Well, wasn't it nice to have visitors, Liquorice?" said Granny happily. The cat purred contentedly at her caress. Then, turning once again to make sure the children could no longer be seen, she added, "I know, boy, she's so like her mum."

# CHAPTER 5

## Sports Spectacular

When Lizzie and Elrus finally arrived home, they found Mrs Longton pacing up and down the kitchen in an agitated state. As the children plonked themselves down at the kitchen table, she began berating them for their lateness and told them how worried she had been.

"Where have you been? Elwood's been dashing round the village like an elf possessed trying to find you," she stormed. Elwood bobbed up and down beside her, nodding his head frantically in agreement.

As Lizzie and Elrus made their apologies, and began explaining that the reason behind their lateness was due to their visit to Granny Fimble, Mrs Longton's anger quickly faded. It turned first to surprise and then delight that they had shown such kindness to the old lady. She wasn't going to let them off too easily however.

"Well, that was nice of you to spend some time with Daft Ada but couldn't you have asked if she had a phone so that you could have called me?" Mrs Longton frowned.

"Oh, please don't call her that anymore, gran," pleaded Lizzie. "She isn't daft at all. In fact, she seems pretty clever to me. We didn't really think to call as we were having such an interesting time."

"Lizzie's right, Mrs Longton," agreed a serious Elrus. "To be a healer you have to be very clever. Don't you, Elwood?" Elwood looked surprised.

"A healer, you say?" he asked, not really requiring an answer. "Well, well, well."

"What do you mean a healer?" Mrs Longton asked, looking from one to the other.

"Well, her kitchen is full of herbs and jars of stuff. Elrus recognised some of the things she's made as medicines." Lizzie explained. Mrs Longton looked surprised. As the children told them what had happened whilst they had been at Granny's cottage, Mrs Longton and Elwood listened in fascinated silence.

"I think she can speak to birds too," Elrus finally added.

"Really? How interesting," said Elwood, looking most impressed.

"I told you that it's just an old saying," Lizzie said. Although she wasn't totally sure that she was right about that, given Granny's passing comment at the time.

Enthralled by the news that Granny was a healer, Elwood then began to explain about healers in Elvedom. He told them how they had special powers to aid them in their roles within their communities.

"Many are considered to be closely akin to witches, as they use chants and rituals when creating their medicines and ointments," he concluded.

"Would healers in this world be the same as those in Elvedom?" asked a fascinated Lizzie.

"I believe many would," Elwood said. "Sadly, in this world healers have had a very difficult time. For hundreds of years they practised their craft in secret because of the distrust and suspicion that humans had for witches and witchcraft. Things are much better these days, with more people turning to the old ways and realising the benefits of nature's remedies. Granny has lived through less tolerant times though and so has no doubt been shunned and even ridiculed for her ways."

Mrs Longton looked a little shamefaced. "The Fimbles were always a bit apart from most of the folks around here. They tended to keep themselves to themselves."

"Did you know that Granny had a sister, gran?" Lizzie asked.

Mrs Longton thought for a moment before saying, "Oh yes. Gosh! I'd forgotten that. She moved away years ago, she went abroad I believe. She had a bit more spark about her I seem to recall; quite different to Ada. I remember that when I was young, I'd often see Ada wandering around the village and the surrounding fields on her own, collecting plants and other stuff. If truth be told, I think she had a bit of a hard time from some of the other children; not unlike you my darling," she said, looking at Lizzie tenderly. "I remember Ted Bray, the twin's grandfather, being particularly unkind to her on more than one occasion," she added sadly.

It was agreed that the Brays were really not a nice family. It seemed that, for several generations now, they had bred bullies to plague the village children.

After dinner, the evening was spent playing board games and, Elwood's favourite game, charades. Lizzie always found Elwood's enthusiastic performances hilarious, especially when he got frustrated with her and Mrs Longton's inability to interpret his charade accurately. Their laughter at his antics only served to increase his levels of agitation and irritation.

To avoid Elwood getting too excited, Mrs Longton suggested they watch some TV before bed. Elrus asked if he could choose the programme, but after his incessant flicking through the various channels – watching a series of brief clips of mind-numbing reality shows, American police dramas and occasional bits of comedy – Mrs Longton decided that Elrus couldn't be trusted with the remote control and said it was time for the children to go to bed.

As they climbed the stairs to their bedrooms, and out of earshot of Mrs Longton and Elwood, Elrus asked Lizzie what she thought about their visit to Granny Fimble.

"I think that I feel sad more than anything," Lizzie replied. "To think, I've been scared of her for years just because of some silly rumour about her being a witch."

Elrus looked at her earnestly. "You know, she still could be."

Lizzie pulled him a "don't be silly" face but said, "Okay she might be. But even if she is, she's not going to hurt me; in fact, probably quite the opposite. She just seems to want to help people. It's a shame that because they won't go near her, she hasn't been able to. I really will go and visit her from now on and maybe one day I'll be able to help her put her knowledge to good use."

Elrus grinned. "And how do you hope to do that when here in Chislewick you've as many friends as she has?" he asked sceptically.

Lizzie shrugged. "I don't know yet but I can dream can't I?" The pair laughed and, having said good night, went off to their respective rooms.

The next morning as they passed Granny's cottage on their way to school, they spotted her picking up the milk bottles from her doorstep. She looked up and saw them and waved cheerily. They returned the wave enthusiastically and happily went on their way. Lizzie had thought long into the night about Granny and had felt strangely comforted in the knowledge that someone close by knew exactly how she felt. A kindred spirit, she thought.

When Lizzie and Elrus entered the school yard, they could see the other children carrying little bags containing their sports gear for the afternoon ahead. Mrs Longton had packed them both off that morning with appropriate sports attire. Elrus only had one pair of human footwear and they were the trainers he had on his feet at that moment.

"They will have to do," Mrs Longton had said, as she popped an old pair of Lizzie's navy blue shorts in the bag. Elrus had looked slightly comical when he'd tried them on the previous evening – his white skinny legs sticking out the bottoms of the slightly too short shorts. She had also put some sun lotion and a bottle of water each in their kit bags. Elrus was intrigued by the sun lotion, as it wasn't something he'd come across before. Although, when he was helping his father in the fields back home, his mother sometimes made him put some special ointment on his face to stop his nose from burning. Maybe that could be called sun lotion, he supposed.

Lizzie spotted the twins in their customary place by the wooden table area of the playground, surrounded by their usual crowd. They really are creatures of habit, she thought. As the bell rang for the children to line up for class, the Brays pushed their way to the front of the queue as they always did. Lizzie and Elrus brought up the rear, keeping as far away from them as possible.

After yesterday's lessons, where Elrus had shown off his mathematical prowess, and embarrassed Lizzie by applauding her reading, Lizzie had given him a few pointers on how he should behave in class.

"Try to tone down your enthusiasm a bit," she'd warned him. Elrus had looked downhearted at her comments; it was going to be hard to contain his naturally ebullient personality but he said he'd try. In Elvedom, elves were encouraged to be true to themselves at all times, he'd explained. Humans were so constrained, he'd said petulantly.

After their first lesson, where they painted their clay pots created the day before, Lizzie and Elrus followed the other children to the playground for mid-morning break. As they walked out into the sunshine, their way was suddenly blocked by the Brays.

"We missed you after school yesterday," said Veronica sarcastically.

"Yeah, where'd you and your freaky friend disappear to, Long Ears?" added Regina nastily.

"I think that's Lizzie's and my business and nothing to do with you," Elrus said, stepping forward so that his body slightly shielded Lizzie from the Brays.

"I wasn't talking to you, weirdo," Regina spat, leaning towards him threateningly. Elrus suddenly burst out laughing. He laughed so much that tears started running down his face and he held his sides as if they would split. His sudden outburst was so unexpected that Regina almost fell backwards in surprise, crashing into her sister in the process. The rest of the gang just looked at him in confusion. Some of them backed off, putting some distance between themselves and Elrus, in case he was slightly mad.

The gang weren't the only ones who'd been surprised by Elrus. Lizzie watched him, unsure of what he was playing at.

As suddenly as his outburst started, he stopped laughing and, with a serious face, stared intently at the twins.

"You know," he paused for effect and rubbed his chin as if thinking about something really important. Then glaring at the twins said, "You two really are a sad act, aren't you? Do you really think that Lizzie and I are frightened by you? These silly kids here," he said, pointing to the gang behind the pair, "will grow up one day and realise that you are just a horrid fat kid with an ugly sister."

If Elrus was about to add anything else, it was dramatically cut short as "the fat kid" pounced on him, knocking him to the floor as she began trying to hit him. Shouts of, "Fight! Fight! Fight!" rang around the playground, as kids came running and surrounding the fracas. As quick as a flash, Elrus was up and, before Regina knew what was happening, he was sitting on top of her, holding down her arms and wriggling, squirming body in a vice-like grip. Her face was almost purple with rage as she hurled a torrent of abuse at him. Veronica loomed over the pair urging her sister to flatten the freak, but wasn't brave enough to get physically involved, whilst Lizzie stood watching the pair on the floor wide-eyed and ashen-faced in shock.

Suddenly there were teachers hauling the combatants apart. One grabbed Elrus whilst another dragged the prone Regina to her feet and held onto her as she tried to attack Elrus once again. To Lizzie's horror, Elrus and Regina were then frog marched into the building with threats that they were being taken immediately to Mr Meacham's office. As she watched her friend disappear into the building, Lizzie received an unexpected shove in the back and turned to find Veronica Bray's face inches from her own.

"Your mate's dead meat," Veronica spat at her and, turning, strode away with the remains of her gang in her wake.

In the Head Teacher's office, Elrus and Regina stood facing Mr Meacham whilst, standing between them and still holding tight to Regina's arm, Mrs Crabbe relayed details of the events that had just occurred outside.

"So, what do you two have to say for yourselves?" demanded Mr Meacham, his usual friendly face taking on a fierce expression.

"He started it!" yelled a puce-coloured Regina.

"I did not," replied an indignant Elrus. "I simply defended myself from her verbal and physical attack."

"You called me fat!" stormed Regina.

"I was merely stating a fact," Elrus said, holding his head high. Mr Meacham suppressed the laughter that almost escaped him, as he watched the girl's face almost burst in outrage. What a strange young man, he thought.

"Anyway, this girl began by threatening my lady," Elrus explained, addressing Lizzie as he would in Elvedom. He had forgotten in the heat of the moment. Quickly correcting himself, he said. "I mean my cousin Lizzie."

His face flushed in annoyance with himself and looked down at the floor awkwardly, hoping that no-one had noticed the slip up. As he peeked up through his fringe at the man standing in front of him, he saw a look of suspicion cross Mr Meacham's face. He and Mrs Crabbe exchanged a look of surprise at Elrus's term of address for Lizzie. Regina was so mad that she was too preoccupied with blustering about the insults to notice.

"Well, Elrus, we do not resort to violence in this country. We resolve our differences by discussion," Mr Meacham said seriously, choosing to ignore the question he wanted to ask about why Elrus would call Lizzie "my lady". Perhaps it was a Greenlander term for a family member, he thought.

"As do we in mine, Sir," Elrus announced proudly. "But when physically attacked, it is only natural that we defend ourselves and this girl attacked me. I just sat on her to make her stop." At which point a snigger emanated from Mrs Crabbe. Mr Meacham shot her a warning glance, although he too thought the boy's manner amusing. He then turned to Regina.

"Is this true, Regina? You attacked Elrus?" he asked.

"But he called me fat," Regina blustered.

"And she called me a weirdo first," retorted Elrus, matter of factly.

Mr Meacham shook his head. "I am disappointed in you both but I am more disappointed in your behaviour Regina. Elrus here is a guest in our school and should have been treated accordingly. I really should send you both home but, as it is the last week of school, I shall not. However, I will ask Miss Finley to keep a very close eye on the pair of you and I too shall be watching for any further signs of poor behaviour. Now, go to class and I don't want to see either of you in my office again."

As the two children left Mr Meacham's office, with Mrs Crabbe following closely behind, Regina hissed out of the corner of her mouth, so that only Elrus could catch it, that her dad was going to hear about this. Elrus ignored the comment and, looking straight ahead, walked into the classroom.

During lunchtime, Lizzie and Elrus sat at their solitary table in the lunch hall, enjoying plates of spaghetti bolognese. Elrus was having great fun, sucking the long strings of pasta through his teeth and making a noisy slurping sound. Several kids smiled at them as they passed on their way to their own seats. One even gave Elrus a "thumbs up" sign.

"I think you've got the beginnings of a fan club," Lizzie grinned at her friend. "I'm sure there are loads of kids here that would love to flatten Regina Bray."

That afternoon, as the sun beat down on the field behind the school, the children of Chislehurst Primary made their way outside to take part in their annual Sports Day. Running tracks and field event areas were clearly marked out on the short grass. In another part of the playing field there was a five-a-side football pitch and in others a rounders pitch and a netball court. The children gathered excitedly in class groups, as teachers organised individual competitors and teams. Miss Finley and the other year six class teacher, Mrs Dorey, were organising their classes into teams of both boys and girls to take part in the games of football, netball or rounders.

Elrus looked on excitedly then, turning to Lizzie, said, "Where are the archery targets? And I don't see the wrestling ring."

Lizzie giggled. "They may be the types of sports that are held in Elvedom but we don't do archery here; it's much too dangerous for school kids. My god, could you imagine letting the Brays loose with bows and arrows?" Elrus nodded in amused agreement at the thought.

"But what about the wrestling?" he asked. "I'd love to take on Regina."

"We don't do that either. Teachers don't encourage fighting, as you found out today. Although, I'd love to see you up against Regina again," Lizzie smirked. As the two giggled at the idea of Elrus pinning Regina on the floor once more, they heard their names being called by Miss Finley.

"Lizzie, I'd like you to join the girls over there in the rounders team and Elrus, you can join in the 5-a-side football," Elrus looked at Lizzie in alarm.

"What's football?" he queried, with a worried expression across his face.

"Exactly what it says, you kick a ball around a pitch and try to score goals. Just follow the others on your team and remember that you mustn't touch the ball with your hands. Oh, unless you're in goal when you have to use them to stop the ball going in," Lizzie said hurriedly.

Lizzie walked towards the rounders pitch, full of dread at what lay ahead but her heart lightened when she saw that the Brays weren't there. Looking around the field, she saw them over by the netball court and watched Regina bossing the other girls around, telling them where to stand and what to do.

The rounders teams were made up of children from each of the school year groups, and the following few minutes or so were some of the most fun that Lizzie had experienced at the school. She was just getting into the swing of things, and was holding the bat in readiness for the ball to be bowled, when she noticed that much of the activity on the field had come to a halt for some reason.

As she looked around, all eyes seemed to be trained on the football pitch over on the far side of the field. Lizzie held her breath; she had a very good idea who was likely to be causing such interest. People were pointing and beginning to walk towards the pitch and so Lizzie decided she ought to follow suit.

As she got closer, she could see that her suspicions were right. There, running around the pitch like a whirlwind, was Elrus. The ball seemed to be glued to his feet as the other boys on the pitch stood, watching him in bemusement. Mr Meacham, who was acting as referee, was blowing his whistle frantically and calling for Elrus to stop but the young elf was too caught up in the moment. He shot the ball at goal and the power behind it sent the goalie diving for cover. Elrus whooped with joy and then, scooping up the ball, began running with it in the opposite direction and scored a similar goal at the other end of the pitch. Lizzie groaned. Mr

Meacham, whose face was bright red with exertion from blowing his whistle, made several attempts to catch Elrus but Elrus was too quick for him. Kids were now laughing and enjoying the spectacle and Lizzie too though that it was very funny but she also knew that drastic action was needed and so, without thinking twice, shouted:

"ELRUS, STOP!"

The sound of Lizzie's voice boomed out across the field. She even shocked herself at the volume that had just come out of her small body. Elrus came to an abrupt halt and stared at her. Mr Meacham's whistle fell from his lips whilst everyone else turned and gaped at Lizzie. Her face reddened in embarrassment and her ears burned as if little glow plugs had suddenly ignited in them.

Then, meekly, she said, "I mean, Elrus, please stop."

Elrus looked around at the other boys surrounding him, as if seeing them for the first time. One of them picked up the ball and hugged it as if it had been assaulted in some way. Mr Meacham walked over and placed a hand on Elrus's shoulder. The poor man looked exhausted.

"My dear boy, have you ever played football before?" he asked breathlessly.

Elrus looked up at him and shook his head. "No," he said brightly, his face lighting up in a happy grin. "But I'm going to take a ball home with me and show others how to play."

Mr Meacham nodded wearily. "Well, perhaps we need to go through a few of the rudiments of the game before we carry on," he smiled. He pulled a handkerchief out from his shorts pocket and mopped his profusely sweating brow.

As the teachers called the children back to their respective sports activities, most eyes were now focussed on Lizzie. She kept her own cast down to avoid contacting any others but her sharp ears picked up some of the excited and incredulous whispers being shared around her.

"How loud was that?" "Scary." "I didn't know she could even talk!" Then, above the rest, she heard Veronica Bray, "Oh my god! She's an even bigger freak than we thought; her and her weirdo cousin."

After the team games were over, there were field sports and, much to the disgust and anger of the Brays, Lizzie and Elrus swept away the prizes at the various running events, throwing the bean bag – the school wasn't allowed javelins or shot-puts for fear the children would harm themselves – the high jump and the long jump. Both Lizzie and Elrus knew that they could have run faster, thrown further and jumped longer and higher but they had to content themselves with just doing enough to beat the other children without raising suspicion.

At the end of the afternoon, there was a presentation ceremony where winners received their medals and certificates. Elrus clapped and whooped as children came to collect their second and third prizes but he was particularly effusive as Lizzie picked up her awards. Lizzie's face ached from smiling so much and she looked down happily at Elrus as the Brays sat stony faced, arms crossed sullenly. Then it was Elrus's turn and Lizzie enthusiastically returned the applause. Finally, Mr Meacham, who was handing out the prizes, said that they had one more thing to award and, as he waved over to his secretary, he asked Elrus to come forward. Mrs Watts came onto the podium and handed the Head Teacher a brand new black and white football which he then passed to Elrus.

"I should like to present you with this small gift from the school for you to take back to Greenland, Elrus. I'd also like to thank you for an entertaining, if somewhat unusual, game of football this afternoon. May this give you and your friends much enjoyment." Elrus thanked everyone for their kindness and, sticking out his hand, vigorously shook that of the older man.

"Thank you, Sir. I will enjoy it very much."

The afternoon of sport concluded, the children began making their way back to the school buildings to collect their belongings before leaving for home. As Elrus and Lizzie chatted excitedly about their successes, the football was almost knocked from Elrus's grasp as he was shoulder barged by the hefty bulk of Regina Bray. As she and her sister strode past without looking at the pair, she snarled threateningly, "You two think you're so clever. Well, just you wait."

As Lizzie and Elrus entered the school yard, Lizzie spotted Elwood hovering around by the school gates. He was wringing his hands and looked a little agitated. His strange ears were, as usual when out in public, hidden under a large green beanie hat. Lizzie ran over to him, closely followed by Elrus.

"Elwood! How lovely, you've come to meet us," Lizzie exclaimed.

"Thank you, ma'am," he replied. Looking at her and Elrus's necks festooned with medals, he said, "It would appear that you've both had a successful afternoon."

Lizzie looked down at her medals proudly and nodded. A smile beamed happily across her face.

Elwood continued in hushed tones, "I should let you know that I am not here alone, ma'am. Your grandmother is currently awaiting your Headmaster. There has been an urgent communication from your grandfather and it would seem that we shall be leaving for Elvedom earlier than anticipated."

Lizzie looked at him excitedly and then, turning to Elrus with her smile shining even more brightly, she punched the air.

"Yes!" she cried.

# CHAPTER 6

## Spy in the Camp

A world away, and far to the North of the Kingdom of Elvedom, Duke Eldorth sat in his castle. His dark, handsome features were spoilt by the cold, contemptuous sneer spread across them. The fingers of his hands, resting upon the ornate arms of the large throne-like seat, tapped impatiently – the only indication of the inner turmoil coursing through his body. No one but no one would ever see any sign of vulnerability on his part.

His eyes bore down onto the kneeling body of a young she-elf in front of him. Her thin, white arms reached out towards him and her forehead, resting on the floor, was encircled by a halo of white blond hair. She almost appeared to be praying to the figure seated before her.

"I ask again, girl, what were you doing when you were caught outside the castle's confines?" Eldorth's voice was so icy it could have frozen the blood of those bearing witness to the encounter.

Ella raised her head from the floor and sat back on her heels. She looked up at her interrogator. One of her clear blue eyes was almost closed and a deep purple bruise was blossoming around it. She stared directly into the eyes of Eldorth.

"Sire, I have explained that I had gone foraging for some herbs and plants to make a remedy for my maiden's malady," her voice rang clear and confidently around the cavernous hall. Eldorth winced at the words. The thought of female bodily functions were disgusting to him. He leant forward and peered down into the girl's one good eye.

"You lie," he said, slowly and deliberately. "You know full well that no plants or herbs grow here about. The lands are too dry and arid for any to survive. You were seen releasing a bird. Where were you sending it?"

Ella sighed, as if tired of going over old ground; she had answered his questions several times now. "I stumbled across the bird floundering on the ground. I picked it up as it was gasping for water. I gave it a little from my water pouch and sent it on its way. I was making my way to a wood nearby that I thought may contain the plants I needed."

"How do you know that there is a wood nearby? Have you been outside the castle before?" Eldorth asked suspiciously. Servants and other castle personnel were brought into his service in the utmost secrecy. They travelled there in carts, blindfolded and under a muffle charm, to prevent them hearing any sounds which might indicate their location.

"No Sire, I have not been outside before but I remembered spotting the image of a wood on a map that you were studying when I was serving you once."

"You spied upon me? How dare you!" Eldorth's voice increased in volume as he rose from his seat and towered over the girl.

Ella bowed her head. "I was not meaning to spy, my Lord. I could not help but notice it and took my chance at finding the wood. I realise now that it was wrong of me and I am sorry."

Eldorth slowly walked down the steps from his dais and circled the girl, moving like a panther on the prowl. The robe he was wearing swished softly about him. He bent down and grabbed a handful of the girl's silken strands of hair. Its softness stirred something in him but the feeling was fleeting as he wrenched her head backwards. Ella's face showed no fear even though her heart was pounding and her nerves jangled.

"Your story does not stack up, girl. The castle is well guarded and yet you managed to slip out unnoticed. How was this possible? Who knows what you may have got up to if my reconnaissance party hadn't been returning at the time? If you needed a remedy as you say, you could have gone to Mistress Melisha for help. There is more to this than you admit to and I *will* get to the bottom of it."

Eldorth released the hair entangled in his fingers, thrusting Ella's head forward so that she fell to the floor once more. Then, turning to two hill trolls standing to the side of the hall, he shouted for them to remove her.

"Get her out of my sight and tell Mistress Melisha to come to me," he said through gritted teeth.

The trolls lumbered over to Ella, each of them grabbing one of her arms with their clumsy rough hands and pulled her to her feet. Eldorth returned to his seat on the dais as Ella's face, now hidden from him, showed the flicker of a smile of satisfaction. Her tiny body was then dragged from the hall and down to the castle's dungeons. Her message to her sovereign must surely have reached him by now, she thought, as the trolls' huge mitts bit into her frail flesh. If she were to die in this gods' forsaken place, she would do so in the knowledge that she had done her duty.

*

In another part of the castle, a squat, unkempt woman was pouring over an ancient leather-bound book. Her straggly strands of mouse brown hair drooped across her sweaty brow, as her finger with its dirty broken nail trailed across the page following each symbol written upon it. Her blubbery lips mouthed the words silently as she read the page's contents, seeking enlightenment on how a child had survived a curse that should have destroyed it. The implications of the curse's failure pricked her conscience.

Melisha had read her way through numerous books and scrolls since Elethria's child had been brought to Elvedom months earlier, but she had not yet been successful in finding the information she was seeking. Although extensive, Eldorth's library did not hold the types of tomes she needed. To find those, Melisha knew that she must travel to the great library of Eldinburgh in the realm of Elcaledonia. She had to think of a way of persuading Eldorth to let her travel there alone, as she was less likely to draw the interest of Elfred's spies than if she travelled with a group of others. She knew, however, that this would be almost impossible due to Eldorth's increasing paranoia and insistence that she be at his beck and call.

Eldorth was proving difficult. She had thought to manage him better when she had taken him as her apprentice, but he had become more powerful over the years following his banishment from Elfred's court. Then having the Harp of Elvyth snatched from his grasp, he had become even more embittered and determined to seek revenge upon King Elfred and his kin.

There was also another problem to overcome, should Eldorth agree to her travelling to Eldinburgh. There was the little matter of her being banned from ever entering the library's hallowed halls again, having been caught attempting to steal one of their precious manuscripts many years previously. Searching through her old books and scrolls had proven very useful in that respect however, when she'd discovered that the Wild Woods held a secret that would solve the problem. It would also help with avoiding Elfred's spies.

Knowing that there was nothing to be gained from her continued perusal of the documents in front of her, she shoved them away in frustration.

"What the bliddy 'ell am I bovvering with this for? I know what I want ain't here," she stormed. Waddling to an over-stuffed and grubby floral armchair in the corner of the room, she plonked herself down heavily into it. The mangy cat that had been curled up on the chair escaped just before the witch's large bottom squished it flat. It stalked away with its tail held high and quivering in annoyance, his one good eye glancing back at her disdainfully.

Melisha laid her head back on the chair and closed her eyes. Stretching her short stubby legs out in front of her, she kicked off her battered boots and wriggled the toes that were protruding from the holes in her wrinkled stockings.

"Oo… that's better, me feet are killin' me," she sighed.

Just at that moment, the door crashed open and one of the hill trolls that had escorted Ella to the dungeons appeared, stooping and squeezing himself through the aperture. Melisha's eyes sprang open and she almost fell out of the chair in fright.

"What the…" she spluttered. "Can't you blinkin' knock?"

The troll looked confused and then proceeded to bang with his huge fist on the open door. Melisha sighed scornfully.

"Too late now, you blivverin' idiot," she yelled. "You're meant to do that before you come in." The troll took this to mean that he should go out again and knock to come in and so began squeezing himself back out of the room.

"What are ya doin'? There's no point now you're in 'ere. Oh, for gawd's sake!" Melisha grumbled. She couldn't understand why Eldorth kept these cretinous creatures so close to him. They were all brawn and very little brain and so dealing with them was extremely irritating in her opinion.

"Well, what d'ya want?" she asked the troll impatiently.

"DUKE ELDORTH," bellowed the Troll. Melisha clamped her hands over her ears and screwed up her face.

"Quieter!" she screeched. Trolls voices, like those of ogres, were very loud and they always forgot to turn down the volume when speaking to species other than their own. The troll looked sheepish and did his best to speak less loudly.

"Duke Eldorth," he began again.

Melisha removed her hands from her ears and said, "That's betta."

The troll attempted a smile; not easy when you had such hard-skin as it tended to crack at the corners of the mouth. Its small brain registered something akin to pleasure at having pleased the witch. It continued, "Wants to see you now." Trolls worked best when they didn't have to use overly long sentences.

"Is he in the Great 'All?" Melisha asked. The troll nodded his huge head. "All right then, I'm on me way."

As Melisha reached down to retrieve her boots and pull them over her smelly feet, the troll eased out of the room, slamming the door behind him.

"Those blinkin' trolls will be the death o' me," she grumbled, struggling to her feet.

When Melisha entered the Great Hall several minutes later, Eldorth was pacing up and down the dais once again. He swung round and faced her as she shuffled up the Hall towards him.

"Where have you been, woman?" he fumed. "When I summon you, I expect you to come immediately."

Melisha took a deep breath to calm the anger welling up in her. At one time, Eldorth had treated her with respect. That was when, as a young elf, he had wanted to learn from her. Now he treated her with the contempt he showed to most of the others in his service. She had loved the child as a son and had taught and nurtured him into adulthood, only for him to treat her this way now. It was only the love she still felt deep down for him that kept her at his side and prevented her cursing him to kingdom come. She hoped that when they succeeded in their quest to overthrow Elfred, Eldorth would change his attitude towards her and she would be there to assist his rule.

"What is it you needed me for, Lawd?" Melisha asked, bowing low. She had to keep him sweet.

"I believe we have a spy in our midst," Eldorth announced. "A servant!"

Melisha looked at Eldorth and shrugged. "Why are you worried? The castle's protected by enchantments. No messages or missives can get through to anyone on the outside. I made sure o' that."

"She was outside the castle walls when one of our reconnaissance teams found her. She claims that she was looking for herbs for some remedy or other she says she wanted to make." He couldn't bring himself to mention the words "maiden's malady".

Melisha looked bemused. "How the 'ell did she get out? Didn't anyone try to stop 'er?"

"Well of course no one tried to stop her, you stupid woman!" Eldorth boomed.

"Well, why not?" the witch asked, biting her tongue to stop the retort that hovered on it. How dare he call her stupid!

"Because, no one saw her leave!" Eldorth exclaimed, as though talking to an imbecile. "She managed to get out through the enchantments and I believe that she sent a message to someone, using a bird that she was seen releasing. She claims she was trying to find a wood close to the castle that she had spotted on a map that we were reading when she was serving us. If she was quick-witted enough to see that, should she be telling the truth, what else has she seen or picked up on? I don't believe her story that she was foraging for herbs and just came across an injured bird. There's more to this than she is telling."

"But it's impossible to get out of the castle wivout the pass spell," Melisha blustered. How could a serving girl thwart her enchantments? "This is all very suspicious, Lawd," she mused.

"Quite!" snapped Eldorth. "That is why I want you to go and have a little chat with the girl. Find out exactly what she was up to. I can't use the trolls as I don't trust that they wouldn't crush her skull before they elicited anything useful. Whereas you, my dear, are sure to have other – more persuasive – means at your disposal." Eldorth's voice had turned silky and he smiled a cold smile in the witch's direction. His earlier high-handed manner momentarily forgotten, Melisha almost preened at the compliment.

Then, cracking first the knuckles of one hand and then those of the other, she said, "It'll be a pleasure, me Lawd.

# CHAPTER 7

## Return of the Heir

At Longton Hall, the arrangements for leaving for Elvedom were in full swing.

The Crowthers said that they would be happy to stay at the Hall and look after Basil and Rathbone. Mrs Longton had told them that urgent family business had arisen and that Lizzie, and she, together with Elwood must return their guest, Elrus, to his folks in Greenland. They would also take the opportunity of visiting the rest of Lizzie's mother's family.

The Crowthers had, like Mrs Longton, always believed that Ria had no family. Then around Lizzie's birthday, Ria's father and sister had suddenly come out of the woodwork. It appeared that, by some miraculous coincidence, they had been staying with Elwood at the same hotel to which, Lizzie had won a holiday. If the Crowthers had any suspicions that there was something amiss with this story, they didn't admit to it. They had known Mrs Longton a very long time, and Lizzie her whole life, so if weren't being given the whole story, then it must be for a really good reason. Everything Mrs Longton did, when it came to Lizzie, was in her grandchild's best interest.

"Isn't it exciting?" burbled Mary, as she watched Bob help to load bags and suitcases into the boot of Mrs Longton's old Jaguar car. For the story to appear authentic, Mrs Longton had decided that they would seemingly travel to Heathrow Airport, in order to take a plane to Greenland. In truth, the plan was to drive the car to a remote farm out in the country, park it safely, and then Lizzie would contact her grandfather via her locket so that Marvin could arrange for a Threshold to open that would transport them to Elvedom castle. Bob had said that he would drive them to the airport to save money on parking but Mrs Longton had said that she knew someone who lived nearby and so would leave the car with them. Bob thought it strange, as he didn't recall her ever having mentioned such friends before, but he didn't pursue the matter. In fact, he had thought that since their trip away for Lizzie's birthday there had been a definite air of something iffy going on. What with the appearance of the strange little Elwood and now this long lost relative Elrus. Still, he was just pleased to see young Lizzie happy and blossoming with newly found confidence. As far as Bob was concerned, they could fill the Hall with as many unusual long lost relatives as they saw fit.

"Have you got your passports, Mrs L?" asked Bob.

"I have, Bob," Mrs Longton answered, waving the documents as proof. She tucked them safely into her handbag. "I don't think I've forgotten anything. I'm not sure how long we'll be away. It may be just a few days or possibly a few weeks. We have an open plane tickets so we can decide when we, or our hosts, have had enough."

"Now don't you worry about a thing," Mary reassured her. "You just do what you have to do. What's the problem over in Greenland, did you say?"

"Oh, Lizzie's grandfather wants Lizzie to meet some of her other relatives who are in Greenland for just a short time this summer. He doesn't want her to miss meeting them." Mrs Longton hated lying to the Crowthers, who were like family to her and Lizzie. She looked forward to the day when she could tell them the truth about Lizzie's heritage.

"Won't that be great, chick?" Mary said to Lizzie, who was kneeling down beside her making a huge fuss of Basil and Rathbone. Lizzie looked up into the beaming, cherry-cheeked face of the lovely Mary.

"It will, Mary. I'm really looking forward to seeing my grandfather and aunt again," Lizzie agreed, continuing to scratch her dogs behind their ears, much to their pleasure. Lizzie nuzzled her face into the soft fur of each of her dogs in turn and told them how much she would miss them. Apart from the few days earlier that year when she had travelled to Elvedom, Basil and Rathbone had been her constant companions. They would wake her in the mornings and, since her return from Elvedom, would lie by her bed when she went to sleep at night – their company a reassuring presence. She wished they could go with her but she knew that it was impossible as who knew what adventures lay ahead. It also wouldn't have fitted in with the story that they were going to fly to Greenland, she thought.

Their goodbyes said, and hugs from Lizzie for Mary and Bob shared, the little party climbed into the car and Mrs Longton pulled slowly away down the drive. Elrus was particularly excited as it was the first time he had been in a motor car and he pumped Elwood for answers about Jaguar cars and how they worked. Elwood was in his element explaining the history of the motor vehicle and revealing his extensive knowledge of engineering. Lizzie never failed to be impressed by the things Elwood knew, he was like a walking encyclopaedia.

As the car drove through the country lanes, away from the village of Chislewick, Lizzie gazed out at the countryside she knew so well. In many ways it was not dissimilar to that of Elvedom once you were away from the towns and villages. The only difference she recalled was that the colours in Elvedom had seemed clearer and more vivid.

After a few miles Mrs Longton began slowing down at some dilapidated old farm buildings. As she drove the car through an old five bar gate hanging from its hinges, Lizzie and Elrus could see that they were in what appeared to be a deserted farmyard. Ancient rusted pieces of farm machinery were scattered about the yard with weeds growing up and around them as if choking them to death. A large stone barn, parts of which were crumbling with age, dominated one end of the yard; its big wooden doors secured with a huge iron padlock. Mrs Longton stopped the car.

"Well, this is it kids. Elwood and Elrus can you go and open up the doors to the barn?" she asked, taking an old metal key from the car's dashboard compartment and handing it to Elwood. The little elf jumped out of the car with Elrus close behind and the pair made their way over to the barn. Lizzie watched as Elwood struggled with padlock hanging from the door's latch. Finally, having succeeded in his quest, he, together with Elrus, swung wide the huge doors to reveal a large open space inside. Shafts of sunlight streamed in through the gaps in the roof where tiles had slipped.

"Grandma, what is this place?" Lizzie asked. She'd never been there before and certainly had no idea why her grandmother would have possession of a key to its barn.

"This is Hogs Trough Farm, darling. It's belonged to the Longton's for years and was run for generations by tenant farmers called Baker. Sadly, after the last tenant died about twenty years ago, it fell to rack and ruin. It's the ideal place to keep the Jag whilst we're away. I just hope she starts again when we get back but she's not let me down yet, have you girl?" Mrs Longton said, patting the car's steering wheel affectionately before driving forwards.

The car purred its sleek way into the barn. Elwood and Elrus closed the barn doors and secured it from the inside, hiding the car from any potential prying eyes. The group retrieved their bags from the boot and Mrs Longton locked the car securely, putting the keys in her handbag. She then turned to Lizzie.

"Are you ready to contact your grandfather, my love?" she asked. Lizzie nodded and took the locket in her hands from around her neck where it now hung. She rubbed her thumb over its intricate silverwork three times, so that it felt warm to her touch, and then flicked open the clasp. Her grandfather's image and that of her aunt, Elenya, gazed up at her. It made Lizzie smile every time she looked at them. She then kissed the image of her grandfather and the picture misted over to be replaced by the animated face of King Elfred smiling out at her.

"Good day, Elizabeth," the King said.

"Hello, Grandfather," Lizzie grinned down at his loving face.

"Is your grandmother there?" he asked. Lizzie said that she was and passed the locket to Mrs Longton.

"Good morning, Your Majesty," said Mrs Longton brightly. "I trust we find you well?"

"Very well, thank you," smiled the King. "I take it that you are all ready to enter through the Threshold that has been arranged? We don't like to keep it open for too long in case it is breached by others for whom it's not intended."

As soon as Mrs Longton said that they were all set to go, there appeared in the shadows at the far end of the barn what seemed to be the glowing outline of a door frame. Bright rays of light shone and spread out from its edges. The members of the little group grinned at each other and, grabbing up their things, and with Elrus holding on tight to his treasured football, Elwood led them through the Threshold.

King Elfred's smiling face was the first to greet them as they found themselves in the entrance hall of Elvedom Castle. Standing at his right shoulder was the tall and imposing figure of the Court Sorcerer, Marvin; his long, purple robes glittered from the light still emanating from the Threshold. Suddenly, a loud yell of delight was accompanied by a figure rushing towards them and Lizzie found herself caught up in the tight embrace of her beautiful aunt, Elenya.

"You're here at last and about time too," Elenya beamed, holding Lizzie at arms' length and taking a good look at her. "I think you may have grown a little since I saw you last," she said, eyeing Lizzie appraisingly. Lizzie laughed shyly and looked down at her sandaled feet as if checking that they were indeed a bit further away from her face.

Then, letting go of the girl, Elenya turned her attention to Mrs Longton and, sticking out her hand, shook the other woman's warmly. "It's so good to see you again, Mrs Longton," Elenya smiled.

"You too, Your Highness," said Mrs Longton, dipping her head in a brief bow.

Elenya waved her hand as if in dismissal, "Oh call me Elenya, please," she implored. "After all, we're family."

Lizzie felt a surge of love and warmth flow through her at Elenya's words. It amazed her to think that these two very different women, one human and one elf, were her family. They were the two halves of Lizzie's heritage that made her whole and once again she felt like she had come home.

King Elfred, who had let his daughter dominate the visitors arrival now stepped forward and held out his arms to Lizzie. As she stepped into his enfolding embrace, she let out a sigh of contented relief and, looking up into his face said, "Hello again, grandfather."

The King smiled gently down at her and, placing his chin on her white silken head, said softly, "Welcome home again, my darling."

The special moment between them was quickly interrupted by Elrus who professed loudly to be starving. As all eyes turned towards the young elf, they laughed and Elbert, the ancient butler who had met Lizzie and her grandmother when they had first arrived at the castle earlier in the year, came forward to say that refreshments were ready when they were. The group made their way towards one of the rooms that led off the entrance hall and, as they entered it, Lizzie could see that large glass doors opened out into a beautiful garden at the centre of which a large fountain played. A table to one side of the room was laid with a selection of snacks and drinks and Elrus, still holding on tightly to his football, made his way hungrily towards it. Lizzie remembered from her last visit the copious amounts of food and drink that always seemed to be available in Elvedom.

"May I ask what that thing is that Elrus seems so attached to?" the King asked, drawing Lizzie's attention away from the laden table, which Elrus was now delving into. She laughed and explained the ball's purpose and how Elrus had come by it.

"I don't think he's put it down since it was given to him yesterday," she laughed. "I think he may have even slept with it." The King laughed with her and said he looked forward to seeing it in action.

King Elfred looked across the room to where he could see his daughter in deep discussion with Mrs Longton and, excusing himself from his granddaughter, went to join them.

Lizzie took the opportunity to join her friend at the table where Elrus was tucking into what appeared to be a large chunk of meat pie. Taking the look of pleasure on the boy's face as good recommendation of the pie's merits, Lizzie took a chunk herself and bit into the light, crisp pastry and succulent centre. "Mmm….," she sighed in satisfaction.

"Good, eh?" came the muffled reply from Elrus; his mouth still full of the delicious pie. Lizzie nodded in agreement.

Over on one of the sofas, with a cup of tea in hand, Mrs Longton was asking King Elfred about what had been happening in Elvedom since her and Lizzie's last visit.

"Our allies are still keeping Eldorth and his forces contained within the boundaries of Maladorth. There are, however, rumours that some of his supporters may have crossed the border of Elcaledonia which is to the north of his lands," the King explained.

"The Elcaledonians have been our allies for centuries but there has always been an uneasy truce between us," Marvin told Mrs Longton. "The capital of their land is the ancient seat of Eldinburgh. It is there that the great Elven library is sited. The library holds many ancient tomes that contain a wealth of knowledge and secrets that, if they fell into the wrong hands, could cause untold damage to this world and yours."

"That is why it is well protected by representatives of all our allies, so that no one race of people can take control of the library and it's contents," continued the King.

"The problem we face is that it is not known at this time how many of Eldorth's supporters have breached the border," Elenya said. "But we do know why."

Mrs Longton saw a troubled look pass between the King and his daughter as he said, "We need to send troops up to ensure the library to reinforce the security of the library but this is difficult as we don't want to raise Eldorth's interest in our movements. It is better to have an element of surprise," he explained.

"Can't you just open up a Threshold to take them to Elcaledonia?" she asked, as if the solution was obvious.

Marvin smiled wanly. "I'm afraid it isn't that easy," he said. "Thresholds are, in the main, used for small parties or individuals to transport them from one place to another. To open up a Threshold that would allow the numbers needed to enter Elcaledonia would mean a huge risk of potential undesirables slipping through as well. So, in answer to your question, no you cannot just open up a Threshold."

The King taking up the story once again said, "We have been looking at other possible ways of getting into Elcaledonia. Securing the library is fundamental, of course, but we also understand that there is another equally important reason for travelling there. We have received intelligence that another of the sacred relics has been hidden within Elcaledonia's lands and this is why its borders have been breached."

"Do you know which relic it is?" Mrs Longton queried.

"We believe it to be the Chalice of Elaria; a magical chalice that has the power to heal anyone who drinks from it.

Legend has it that it can even bring those who have just died back from the brink," the King explained.

The King's eyes turned towards his young granddaughter, now eating from a large bowl of what appeared to be chocolate mousse, and a sad smile crossed his lips. Mrs Longton, watching the expression on his face, felt a sudden sinking feeling spread through her insides. Her eyes flicked from the King to Lizzie and back again.

"Why was it so urgent that Lizzie and I travel here before she finished school?" she asked curiously.

The King turned his head towards her. His eyes betrayed the doubt and turmoil that lurked behind them. "There is a meeting tonight of select members from the Great Council. We will discuss the arrangements for a small party of individuals to journey to Elcaledonia to retrieve the Chalice. We believe that Elizabeth must be an integral member of that party."

Mrs Longton looked across at Lizzie tucking into a large piece of cake. As she laughed at something Elrus was saying, Lizzie looked as though she hadn't a care in the world. The King's words formed like a rock in the pit of Mrs Longton's stomach and the sinking feeling that had spread through her, sunk even lower.

# CHAPTER 8

## The Best Laid Plans

After the delicious lunch, Lizzie and Elrus went in search of their friend Max, Marvin's apprentice. They found him in Marvin's laboratory, grinding away at some powder in a massive mortar and pestle. As they entered the room, the young apprentice's face lit up in a huge grin of delight. He let go of the pestle and bowed low to Lizzie.

"Max! It's so great to see you," Lizzie smiled happily, thrilled at being back in her friend's company.

"Your Highness," Max said as he raised his head to look at his princess; his floppy blond hair falling into his bright blue eyes. He brushed his fringe away from his sweating brow.

Lizzie giggled. "It's Lizzie, remember?" she said, smiling brightly at the boy. Max nodded shyly.

"Lizzie," he repeated, almost in a whisper.

"So how's things, mate?" asked Elrus cheerily.

"All the better for seeing you, Master Elrus," Max said, giving his friend a wry grin. "So, what scrapes do you both plan to get us into this time?"

Lizzie and Elrus laughed. "Well, we'll have to wait and see, won't we?" Elrus said impishly.

The three friends fell easily into each other's company as Lizzie and Elrus told Max all about Elrus's visit to Lizzie's home in Chislewick. The young apprentice listened with genuine interest, a wistful look on his face. Lizzie suddenly felt a little guilty.

"Perhaps grandfather can arrange for you to come too next time," she said to the boy. Max's eyes widened.

"Do you think he would allow that?" he asked doubtfully.

"Of course," Lizzie said confidently, she would make sure she asked her grandfather at the next opportunity. The thought of spending time at Longton Hall with her two friends was something to really look forward to. Max's eyes travelled to the ball that Elrus was holding in his hands. Elrus noticed the boy's interest and explained that it was called a football.

"Hey, why don't we go and play with it. I can show you how," Elrus said excitedly.

Max shook his head sadly. "I can't, I'm afraid. I've got chores to finish and I've already spent too long talking now." He stood up and went back to his work bench and picked up the pestle, ready to start pounding away at the powder once more. Elrus and Lizzie stood up and were about to say their goodbyes, and that they would see him later, when the door to the laboratory opened and Marvin walked in. He looked at the three friends and watched as Max began to grind the pestle into the mortar with gusto.

"Have you not finished the preparation of that powder yet, Max?" Marvin asked, his voice was stern but his face showed that he was only teasing his apprentice.

Max looked sheepish as he admitted that he had not. His face turned a brilliant shade of red, not only from the embarrassment of being caught slacking by his master but also from the exertion he was putting into pummelling the powder.

"For goodness sake lad, give the arrowroot a rest and get yourself outside in the fresh air before you burst a blood vessel. The powder can wait but I can see that your friends cannot." Max looked uncertainly from his master to his friends and back to his master once again when Marvin boomed, "Go boy, before I change my mind!"

As the three friends made a hasty retreat out of the door, they could hear Marvin's deep rumbling chuckle filling the room behind them.

The rest of the afternoon was one of the most enjoyable that Lizzie could remember ever having spent, as she and her companions enjoyed playing out in the summer sunshine. Although the sun blazed down, it was as if Elvedom Castle and its grounds were protected in some cocoon that prevented the harmful heat rays from penetrating it.

After eventually falling down exhausted from playing football – which Max said was the best game ever – they went for a dip in the lake. As the cooling water eased their aching limbs, they splashed about, raced each other and challenged one another to see who could hold their breath under the surface for the longest. As Elrus and Max then took it in turns climbing on to each other's shoulders and diving into the water's depths, Lizzie clambered out and flopped down at the lake's edge to watch them. Laughing happily at the antics of her two friends, she wished, not for the first time, that she could stay here in this world forever. Her thoughts were interrupted when a shadow fell across the ground in front of her and she looked up into the familiar face of Elwood.

"Hi, Elwood," she greeted her guardian happily. "Do you fancy a swim?" The little elf shook his head emphatically.

"Oh dear no, ma'am!" he exclaimed. "I'm far too busy making preparations."

Lizzie looked confused. "Preparations? Preparations for what?" she asked.

Elwood looked flustered. He must remember to be more careful what he let slip; he was always speaking out of turn and it wasn't for him to tell Lizzie what was being prepared for her. So, he said more sharply than he intended, "You'll find out in due course." Then, softening his tone, he added, "I'm afraid I must ask you and your friends to come along in now and get ready for dinner. There is to be a special meal held this evening for your dep… arrival!" He had just stopped himself saying departure, oh dear, oh dear, he nearly did it again he thought. Lizzie was too happy and preoccupied laughing at her friends to notice and so, getting to her feet, she called to Elrus and Max that it was time to go in.

That evening, after having bathed in her beautiful bathroom, in the same rooms that she and her grandmother had occupied the last time they had come to Elvedom, Lizzie and Mrs Longton made their way down to dinner. They were escorted to the Great Council Chamber by Eldora Cherrytree, who appeared to have been given the role of personal servant to them both.

As they entered the Chamber, they were greeted by King Elfred. Looking around, they saw that this time the large oval table was laid out for what appeared to be a State banquet. As the rest of guests around the table stood, Lizzie was surprised to see that those gathered were not all elves and was delighted to recognise the familiar faces of Prince Finnion of the Fairies, Flaxon the faun, Digby the Dwarf and the warty features of Gorin the Goblin.

Everyone present appeared to be dressed in their best clothes and so Lizzie was glad that the dress she had found lying on her bed was suitable for the occasion. The fine material, in a subtle shade of the prettiest green, fell to her knees in soft folds and she had clipped her hair back from her face with pearl encrusted combs that had also been left for her use. She felt pretty; not something she ever experienced back home in Chislewick.

As Lizzie and her grandparents made their way to their seats, the guests around the table dipped their heads in respect. Lizzie took a chair between her grandfather and aunt Elenya, whilst Mrs Longton sat to Elenya's left. As those present proceeded to sit down, Lizzie glanced around the table and saw, to her relief, Elrus sitting with his father across the table to her right. He gave her a cheeky grin and she felt the tension that had formed in the pit of her stomach melt a little. A whispered compliment came from her left.

"You look lovely, Lizzie." Lizzie turned to thank her aunt and caught her breath; Elenya was possibly the most beautiful creature she could have ever imagined. The princess's golden hair was piled up in soft curls, and peppered with crystal beads above her perfect features, and her flawless skin glowed in the flickering light of the myriad burning candles that lit the room. She was wearing a dress of the shimmering blue of a summer sky and it completed the picture of a perfect elven princess.

"Thank you. You look lovely too," Lizzie replied shyly, although the compliment seemed grossly inadequate to her. Elenya briefly touched Lizzie's arm lovingly and then turned her eyes to her father who had just clapped his hands together. Upon this signal, what appeared to be an army of servants suddenly entered and began serving food from great silver platters.

Despite the formality of the occasion, the meal was an enjoyable experience as the guests chatted animatedly amongst themselves. Following several delicious courses of perfectly cooked and presented dishes, Lizzie lay back in her chair feeling as though she would burst if she ate another morsel. "Thank goodness this dress seems to be made of something stretchy," she thought, wriggling to make herself more comfortable.

As plates were speedily cleared away and more drinks served, King Elfred stood up. "My brethren, now with our appetites sated, let business commence." The general hubbub of conversation died and all eyes turned to the King as he continued.

"As you are aware, the return of The Harp of Elvyth to its rightful place was a huge blow to our arch enemy, Duke Eldorth. It has been a set back to his plans to gather an even greater following amongst those most vile or vulnerable in our world and so he has withdrawn into his own lands. This does not, however, mean that he will remain there or has given up his plans as he still has three other sacred relics in his possession.

We now have information that Eldorth has sent his agents into the realm of Elcaledonia. Our spy has discovered that the purpose of those agents was to move one of the relics into those lands. It is clear that Duke Eldorth will use the ploy of relocating the relics in an attempt to keep us from discovering their whereabouts. Some of you here present are the chosen few who will travel on a secret mission to retrieve that relic. To achieve this, you will join forces with our special allies in the Principality of Elcambria."

A flurry of murmurs spread around those sitting at the table and Lizzie watched as Prince Finnion stood up, his wings fluttering gently.

"Before we go any further, Your Majesty," he began. "Surely these children should be allowed to leave as they cannot be part of the chosen few?" he continued, indicating Lizzie and Elrus.

"I am afraid you are wrong, Prince Finnion, these two children are indeed part of the chosen few," the King declared. Lizzie and Elrus stared at each other and then looked up at the King as the murmurs increased in volume. Lizzie felt elated. She was going on another adventure; brilliant! Elrus grinned at the look of delight on his friend's face. "And," the King raised his voice above the cacophony echoing around the table. "They won't be the only ones. They will be joined by two others." Several of the guests at the table jumped to their feet, calling out their dissent at such a notion.

"We're not baby sitters," growled the dwarf, Digby.

"Why should we be responsible for having to watch over these children when we need our wits about us just keeping ourselves out of harm," grumbled Gorin, his high squeaky tones cutting through the noise around him.

King Elfred watched the group silently for a few moments and then patiently, as if taking control of a group of unruly school children, held his hands up in front of him. His voice echoed around the chamber as he called the meeting to order. His disgruntled guests sat down reluctantly, their voices fading to silence as King Elfred's icy stare bore into them.

"There are reasons why there will four young people travelling with you but these will not be divulged at this time. Suffice it to say that it is imperative they go on this journey with you and are protected by you."

Lizzie's mind went into overdrive. Two other children were going with them; one must surely be Max but the other? Could it be possible that Eloise would join them? The thought filled Lizzie with joy. They would be the fabulous four, the four musketeers; Lizzie smiled to herself and looked across at Elrus who gave her a resounding thumbs-up. Her excitement fell away sharply though as she then glimpsed the expression on her grandmother's face. The pained look of fear and sadness as Mrs Longton stared off into the middle distance made Lizzie want to run to her and hug her tight, but the formality of the occasion prevented her from doing so. She willed her grandmother to look her way, but Mrs Longton was lost in her own thoughts.

The King continued. "As I was saying, you will join special forces in Elcambria who will aid you in your quest. More will become clear when you reach their hideaway. The journey will mean crossing Eldorth's lands and it would be too perilous for you to travel them alone."

"When Duke Eldorth stole four of the sacred relics he did not only steal the symbols of the Throne of Elvedom. Each relic contains ancient magical properties, which when used together for the purpose of good, are very powerful. These powers keep these lands and their people prosperous and healthy and allow peace to reign. However, the powers of the relics can also be used for evil and it is to that purpose that Eldorth plans to put them. Eldorth used the Harp of Elvyth's magic to call undesirables to his service and had we not retrieved it, I have no doubt that in time he would have used the Harp's power to influence the good souls of our world to follow him also. The retrieval of the Harp has prevented that from happening. Now we must endeavour to seek out the remaining three relics in his possession so that we can stop his poisoning of the land and its people from spreading further.

Since the retrieval of the Harp from Eldorth's castle, his anger has been vented on the lands and people surrounding his own. Great swathes of the Northern territories are now barren and he is controlling the provision of food and vital supplies needed by those living in those lands. His propaganda machine is sending out the message that their hardships are caused by me and my followers and so he is beginning to gain more support. The sacred relics must be returned their rightful place in our keeping."

There were sounds of general agreement from those seated around the table. The discussion then turned to the practicalities of preparing to leave Elvedom Castle the following day. As the King sat down another elf with a large grey grizzled moustache stood up.

"By keeping your party small, we hope to ensure that your journey will not be discovered by Eldorth's 'spies in the skies' the wraiths riding upon pterotorials," announced Elnest, King Elfred's Head of Secret Surveillance. "You will travel overland and make your way to the Mountains of Snow in Elcambria. Horses and mules are to be your mode of transport and safe havens have been arranged for you to take your rest, although there may be occasion that you will have to make camp en route when needs arise."

Marvin then took up the narrative, "Your party will be led by her Highness, Princess Elenya, who is the only one of you who will be privy to the full details of your mission. Heed her well."

Those gathered nodded resignedly as Prince Finnion stood once more.

"We place our faith in the Princess as always," he said, bowing his head in respect in Elenya's direction. "I am sure I speak on behalf of my comrades here when I say that we have our reservations about taking these young people with us. However, we trust you when you say that it is imperative that we do. We will lay down our lives in their protection, if the cause demands it."

At this point, Elenya stood up and spoke to the group for the first time.

"Thank you, Prince Finnion," she said, bowing her head firstly to the fairy prince and then to each of the remaining guests in turn. "You are all our most valued allies and friends. We have faced adversity together in the past and come through victorious. I feel confident that in our unity we can once again thwart our enemy. I look forward to the challenge."

The delegation all stood up and raised their goblets in salute. The action stirred Mrs Longton from her reverie and she looked around at the gathering with an expression of resignation on her face. Slowly, she got to her feet and raised her drink to toast the success of the mission.

Lizzie's heart went out to her grandmother. She felt such a mixture of emotions; excitement, fear and sorrow at the pain that this journey into the unknown was causing her beloved gran. As the guests sat down once more, and began talking amongst themselves, Lizzie took the chance to go to Mrs Longton. She knelt down beside her and placed her hand on her grandmother's; it was trembling uncontrollably.

Mrs Longton looked down into her granddaughter's face and could see the love and concern etched upon it. She pulled Lizzie into her arms and hugged her as if she would never let her go.

"It's going to be okay, gran. I'm sure of it," Lizzie said reassuringly.

"It feels different this time," Mrs Longton said, releasing Lizzie a little and looking into the girl's eyes. "Last time I didn't have this sense of utter dread that I feel now."

"That's because we didn't have time to think the last time we came here. Everything was so new and exciting and when we fell into Maladorth it was by accident and we just had to get on with it," Lizzie said wisely. "This time there's a plan and I just know that Elenya will look after us."

"Oh, I know," Mrs Longton stressed. "And you're probably right about there being a proper plan this time but it doesn't stop me from worrying about the danger you're going to be facing."

As Mrs Longton spoke, she looked up to see Elenya beside them. The princess was smiling.

"Mrs Longton, I will do everything in my power to protect Lizzie; of that you can be sure," Elenya said gently. "But then you will bear witness to that as a member of our party."

Mrs Longton's jaw dropped open in shock.

"Yay," crowed Lizzie, squeezing her grandmother tight. "You're coming too!"

# CHAPTER 9

## Another Journey Begins

The next morning after breakfast, the group of travellers met in the cobbled courtyard of Elvedom Castle. Dressed in garments made of light, comfortable material, in shades that would shield them from prying eyes, they greeted each other warmly.

The yard was a bustling hive of activity with elves and other creatures going about their business. While grooms checked that saddles and harnesses were secure on several horses and a couple of mules, elven servants finished packing the mules' panniers with food, clothing and the equipment needed for the travellers to use on their journey.

Mrs Longton, standing alongside King Elfred and Lizzie, was eyeing the horses warily.

"Oh dear, it's been a long time since I've ridden," she said dubiously. King Elfred laughed.

"Don't worry, Mrs Longton; these horses are very well trained. The horse you will be riding will just follow along behind its leaders," he said reassuringly.

"It's not *that* I'm worried about; it's the state of my poor bottom by the time we arrive at our destination I'm concerned about," she said. Lizzie and her grandfather laughed heartily.

"Oh gran, I'll rub it for you when we get there, shall I?" Lizzie giggled.

"Now, now young lady; don't be so cheeky," Mrs Longton admonished, chucking her granddaughter under the chin and joining in the laughter. The seriousness of the journey ahead of them was momentarily forgotten.

Just then, there was a commotion on the other side of the courtyard as a group of elves, dressed in brightly coloured outfits, came striding into the frenzy of activity taking place. Leading the way was a huge dark-skinned elf and, if he hadn't been smiling brightly, his size and presence would ordinarily have appeared threatening.

"Elroy, my dear friend," said the King, offering his hand in welcome. Elroy took the King's hand and shook it warmly.

"Your Majesty, I bid you good day," Elroy's deep voice rumbled through the noisy preparations taking place around them. "I am sorry for the lateness of our arrival but we were delayed due to rough seas."

"You are here now and that is what matters," the King said.

Elroy turned to Lizzie and her grandmother and dipped his head in a brief bow.

"Your Highness. Mrs Longton. I trust I find you both well," he greeted them. They said that they were indeed well and that they were glad to see him again.

"I believe you remember my daughter, Eloise," Elroy said and, turning to the group of elves standing in his wake, called to his young daughter. Eloise stepped out from behind a tall elf wearing a multi-coloured shirt and shorts, the sun's rays bouncing off her black curls. Lizzie was thrilled to see her. It was great to have Elrus and Max coming along but it was even better to know that she would have a girl to share in the adventure too.

"Eloise! Hi! It's so great to see you," Lizzie said excitedly and, running forward, took the girl's hands in her own.

"Hello, Princess," Eloise said, dipping her knees in a curtsey.

Lizzie leant forward and whispered in the girl's ear. "It's Lizzie, remember?" Then, linking Eloise's arm over her own, she said, "Come and meet the boys again. They're just finishing packing their stuff. Oh Eloise, isn't it exciting to be going on another adventure?"

Eloise looked at Lizzie with less conviction than her words portrayed. "Yes Lizzie, it's exciting," she said, the slight tremor in her voice betraying her nervousness about what lay ahead.

Max and Elrus were standing next to two of the horses and Elrus was having, what seemed to be, an animated discussion with Elwood who was directing some of the servants. Max watched the proceedings with a slight air of amusement.

"But why can't I take it with me?" Elrus was asking Elwood.

"It has been explained to you several times now, Master Elrus, that you can only take the essentials needed for the journey. A football does not constitute an essential item," Elwood explained, as if coming to the end of his patience.

"But it's essential to me!" exclaimed Elrus.

"Can you eat it? Will it keep you warm at night? Will it save your life if you are in danger?" asked the exasperated Elwood.

"Well, okay I can't eat it," Elrus acknowledged. "But I have been taking it to bed with me so I could use it as a pillow and I could always throw it at the enemy if attacked; it hurts quite a bit if it hits you," he argued.

Lizzie, who was now standing next to Max watching the altercation, whispered in the boy's ear, "I told you he was sleeping with it." Max sniggered.

Elwood seemed to have finally come to the end of his tether. "Oh, for goodness sake; all right! Take it with you but I'm warning you, Master Elrus, the first time it gets in the way or becomes a liability you must dispose of it. Think on that. You may be wise to leave it here where it will be kept safely for your return."

Elrus looked a little unsure of himself for a moment but then, not wishing to be defeated, said that he would still take it with him. As Elwood walked away huffily, Max went over to his friend and, from his pocket, took out what appeared to be a piece of netting. As he opened it out, the other children could see that it was a bag of some sort.

"Here, take this." Max offered the bag to Elrus. "You can put your ball in that and hang it from your saddle. Just make sure that it doesn't bounce about too much or you might spook your horse." Elrus thanked his friend and, placing the ball in the bag, tied it securely to the horn of his saddle.

Preparations completed, the travellers began their goodbyes. Elroy lifted his daughter in a bearlike hug.

"Now, Eloise, you do exactly as you're told," Elroy began. "The King has assured me that you will be kept safe. You have a role to play, what that is I'm not privileged to know but I am sure that the King would not have requested your presence were it not vital to this mission. I love you, my darling. Stay safe. May the gods go with you."

Eloise threw her arms around her father's neck and held him tight. "I love you too, daddy, and don't worry; I'll be back before you know it."

Elrus's parents, Elmer and Elmara, stood proudly by their son. Elmara bent and kissed Elrus's red head. "Stay safe, honey, and behave yourself. Do as you're told and no harm should come to you," she said gently but firmly.

"Your mother's right, son," agreed Elmer. "Take care and remember there is safety in numbers. I know you can be daring but sometimes the safe option is the best option."

Max was receiving his final instructions from his master, Marvin. The look on the sorcerer's face was serious but, as he looked down at his young apprentice, his eyes showed the care and affection he felt for the boy. After reassuring Max that this would be a great lesson in life, he briefly ruffled the boy's blond hair before turning and standing next to his sovereign.

The King spoke to Lizzie who was now standing with her aunt and grandmother. "Elizabeth, in the past you have been a little…" he hesitated, as if trying to find the right words, before saying, "reckless on occasion. On this journey you must listen and take your lead from your aunt. She and those travelling with you are experienced in covert operations and they know best how to keep you from danger. Your and your friends' roles in this mission will become clear in time but, until that time comes, keep safe and enjoy this experience. It is a good opportunity to see more of the realm you will one day rule." Turning to Mrs Longton, he wished her safe passage and, taking her hand in both of his own; he shook her hand firmly as a parting gesture.

The King then faced his daughter and his love for her was almost palpable. He took Elenya's hands in his and squeezed them tightly. All those present in the courtyard watched and listened as the King spoke.

"Elenya, my child, you know what you have to do," the King announced. "The success of this mission rests on your shoulders. I have every faith that you will do whatever's necessary to ensure that success. Just keep safe and return to me as soon as you may."

With the King's hands still grasped tightly in her own, Elenya curtseyed low to her father. "I will do everything within my power to keep those entrusted to my care safe, and return them to you as they have left you; whole in body and soul. With the aid of our great friends and allies who accompany me on this mission, I know that we can bring it to a successful conclusion." Elenya then stood and she and the King embraced each other. As the pair parted, Lizzie ran to her grandfather and threw her arms around his waist, burying her head into his chest. The action seemed to take the King by surprise but he quickly regained his composure and placed his arms around his granddaughter's slender shoulders. He bent his head and kissed Lizzie's soft white hair.

"Take care, my love," he murmured into the silken threads and, with that, released her gently.

The travellers then went to their respective horses and proceeded to mount them. Lizzie was surprised to see that Prince Finnion too would be riding. She bent and said as much to Elwood, who was assisting her by making sure that her feet were safely in their stirrups.

"Flying such a distance would be both tiring for the Prince and difficult for him to maintain the same pace as the rest of you on horseback. Fairies tend to fly very quickly," Elwood explained.

Lizzie looked around at the other riders and could see that Digby the D    warf and Gorin the Goblin both seemed to be a little out of their comfort zones. Digby was grumbling about much preferring to be marching on his own two feet, whilst the groom helping Gorin into his saddle was having to shorten the straps on the goblin's stirrups so that his short legs could reach them properly. Lizzie wanted to giggle but thought it might appear rude if Gorin were to see her.

She looked across at her grandmother who was settled comfortably on a beautiful chestnut coloured mare. Mrs Longton had ridden a lot in her youth and had several cups and rosettes back at Longton Hall as evidence of her success at various gymkhanas. She looked most impressive in her large floppy straw hat that was to give her some protection from the sun beating down upon them. Lizzie could see the rest of the party on their various mounts; Elwood was seated upon a small black and white piebald close to her grandmother; Max, Elrus and Eloise were on horses similar in size to Lizzie's own; Willo the Wood Sprite, dressed in a green outfit that complemented his green hued complexion, sat upon a shaggy-haired pony and Lizzie noticed that there were two more fairies who, she was sure, had been in the raiding party in Maladorth, and two elves she didn't recognise but who carried longbows and quivers strapped across their backs.

The only member of the party not seated upon some steed or other was Flaxon. Lizzie supposed it would have been difficult for the faun to manage riding on the back of another animal. Flaxon saw her looking at him and smiled; he made his way over to her, his goat's feet clip clopping across the cobblestones.

"I am guessing you have realised that I shall not be joining you on horse back, Your Highness," he said in his softly spoken voice. Lizzie nodded. "Horses get a little skittish at a part-goat sitting upon them," he explained.

"Couldn't you just play them a tune on your pan-pipes to calm them down?" Lizzie asked. Flaxon grinned.

"You have a good point, Highness, but I have to admit that I would rather travel on foot as I am just as able to keep up with you all. Anyway, I could do with the exercise," he concluded with a wink.

A loud blast on a horn suddenly sounded and Lizzie and Flaxon turned sharply to see where the noise had come from. Sitting on a small grey horse, Elwind – Elwood's twin – removed a hunting horn from his lips and passed it to one of the fairies that would be riding with them. Next to Elwind sat Elenya mounted on a huge white stallion; its coat shimmering in the bright early morning sun. The animal pawed the ground with its front hoof as if impatient to be off. Elenya raised her arm in salute to the King, and those remaining with him, and the small entourage led by the Princess, with the two archer elves bringing up the rear, trotted out of the protection of the safe haven that was Elvedom Castle.

# CHAPTER 10

## Mind Games

"Well, that Ella's a tough nut to crack." Melisha was seated at one end of a large wooden table in the private chambers of Duke Eldorth. The table's only other occupant was Eldorth himself who was picking at a plate of fruit; the sharp knife in his hand was peeling back the skin of a ripe, juicy peach as if he was pulling back the skin of one of his most hated enemies, slowly and deliberately.

"But you will break her," he said; his voice was cold and his eyes even colder as they looked up from the peach and into those of his accomplice. He shuddered at the sight of her; the woman was repulsive to him but he knew he must keep her reasonably sweet until she was of no further use to him.

"It's possible that she is a Secret Keeper which is why her mind's impenetrable to anyone seekin' to read it," Melisha continued.

Secret Keepers were a special tribe of elves who had the power to learn and keep secrets that they would only divulge to their chosen recipients. They had very high pain thresholds so no amount of persuasion, be it verbal or physical, would make them submit to pressure. They were also skilled at going about their business barely noticed or remembered by those that they came into contact with. All of these attributes made them excellent spies.

Eldorth looked doubtful. "If she's a Secret Keeper, how was she so easily spotted and caught outside the castle walls?"

"I don't know. Maybe she got sloppy," Melisha suggested. The girl had certainly got the better of the witch so far and Melisha was determined that she would get to the bottom of what the young elf knew and had passed onto her contacts.

"The girl getting sloppy is not what's important here, Melisha; what concerns me more is your sloppiness. If she is a Secret Keeper and you are unable to break her secret, that says more about your inadequacies than hers," he said smoothly, laying down the knife and popping a piece of the sweet peach flesh into his mouth.

Melisha's lips pursed in annoyance at the rebuke. She swallowed her pride and decided that getting into a row at this time would not benefit her plan to make the pilgrimage to the Great Library of Eldinburgh.

"As you say, Lawd," she simpered, bowing her head so that Eldorth couldn't see the anger flare in her eyes. "I shall be makin' the girl another visit later."

Eldorth placed his elbows on the table and, with his hands held as if in prayer, tapped his fingers together; the action helped to calm him. "So, how do you propose to break her?" he asked; his eyes boring into the top of Melisha's bowed head. The witch raised her eyes slowly to his.

"The problem we 'ave is our limited resources 'ere, Lawd. I've exhausted me own library of spell books and, even though I do have a wealf of knowledge in me own brain, like everyone else I still 'ave fings to learn," Melisha explained, with fake humility.

Eldorth eyed the witch suspiciously; she was after something. "So how do you suggest remedying this lack of knowledge?" he asked critically.

Melisha took a deep breath to quell the anger that was seething in her chest. Once upon a time, she'd have slapped the young pup down but their roles at this time were reversed. She knew that something within the walls of this castle was draining away her powers and she needed to get to Eldinburgh to seek out the spells and enchantments to replenish them. By doing so, she could not only bring about the defeat of the Elvedom King but also pull Eldorth back into line. She would play the subservient until the time came to redress the balance.

"Well, Lawd," she purred. "I fink it would be wise to allow me to travel to the Great Library of Eldinburgh to seek out the books of ancient knowledge that may provide the answers to our problems. I should travel alone and will, of course, be incognito."

Eldorth didn't like the plan at all. He wanted Melisha within his control and the thought of her out in the wider world, gathering greater knowledge, made him nervous. He didn't want to allow her to gain powers that she could use against him. As things were, he had drained much of her knowledge and power to his own benefit in ways that the witch was unaware of. She had been too trusting of him. He knew that she had looked upon him with affection and it would prove to be her downfall; love was a weakness that he would never succumb to.

Then again, Eldorth thought, if she should gain greater knowledge and power by this journey to the Great Library then it would be advantageous to him also. He must ensure that, if he were to allow her to go, she returned to Maladorth once she had achieved her purpose. He would, unbeknown to her, arrange for her to be followed and, if necessary, brought back to him.

Melisha sat watching the thoughts play across the implacable face of the elf sitting at the opposite end of the table. She relished the mind games they played against each other. Eldorth's vanity and ambition were so obvious to her and they were his weakness. She knew only too well that he didn't fully trust her and that she had been foolish in her fondness for him in the past, but he now thought himself too clever for her and this would play to her advantage. She would let him think that her affection for him would bind her to him but she would not be taken for a fool again.

"You know that I already have agents in the realm of Elcaledonia. They are seeking to make alliance with representatives residing in the environs of Eldinburgh, who are weary of their leaders' links to the monarchy of Elvedom," Eldorth said almost unnecessarily, as Melisha had been privy to the plans from the outset. The witch nodded vigorously, her thin hair wafting around her head like rats' tails.

"Those agents will no doubt prove useful once you arrive in the area," Eldorth continued.

Melisha smiled a sickly grin of satisfaction.

"Fank you, Lawd; you know it makes sense. I shall make immediate preparations for my departure," she smirked. Then, standing and making a swift dip in an attempt at a cursory curtsey, she scuttled from the room.

Eldorth released a sigh of relief that she had gone. At least she had been at the end of the table closest to the door, thereby eliminating the need for her to pass by him and saving him from having to hold his breath. The woman's odour was not to be endured.

Out in the passageway leading from Eldorth's chambers, Melisha punched the air in triumph. "Yes!" she crowed. Then, with a glance at the door to her rear, she said under her breath, "You just wait, my Lawd."

*

Down in the dungeons of Eldorth's castle, Ella crouched on the thin mattress that lay on the floor of her cell. The little light that shone through the barred window, high in the wall above her, cast its rays on her blond head. As she raised her pale blue eyes to the warmth of the rays', the discolouration around them was clear to see. She put a tentative hand to her ribs, she felt that two at least had been broken. As she laid her hand upon them, she muttered a few silent words of a mantra and the dull pain in her chest eased a little. She would come through this, she was a survivor. As she sighed to herself at the thought, a small white pigeon landed on the sill of the window.

Ella got slowly to her feet and walked over to the door of her cell and peered through the small opening that afforded her prison warders a view of their captive. She could see one of them – a dim witted hill troll slumped in a huge seat and snoring loudly. She cast her eyes around but could see no one else.

Returning to the window, she reached up as high as she could without hurting herself more than was necessary. The pigeon cooed softly and dropped a small white scroll of paper into Ella's hand. Then, before Ella could say her thanks, the bird had flown. She quickly read the missive and placed the paper in a cup of water standing on a small wooden stool next to her mattress. As the paper disintegrated, Ella smiled a secret smile; her message had got through and she knew what was now expected of her.

# CHAPTER 11

## The Companions

The group of travellers had been journeying for some hours and had passed the time en route by singing songs, telling stories and generally keeping each other entertained. They were travelling along the side of a wide river and as they approached the shelter of some trees, where Elenya said they would rest. Mrs Longton let out a huge sigh of relief, as she announced that she was glad as she needed to rest her aching back for a while and the children all complained that they were starving.

The saddles were removed from the horses, and the panniers from the mules, so that the beasts could recover from the journey so far, take water and graze a little. Elwood took out a rug from one of the panniers and began laying out food for the travellers to eat.

"I think we should give ourselves a name," suggested Eloise, as she chewed on a chunk of crusty bread and a piece of ripe cheese.

"A great idea," agreed Elenya. "Anyone got any ideas?"

"How about the Band of Brothers?" piped up Elrus.

"No! That wouldn't be right," said Lizzie indignantly. "We're not all boys or men. We might just as well call ourselves the Band of Sisters as there are girls amongst us too, in case you hadn't noticed." Elrus made a wry expression; she had a point he supposed.

"Well, I like the idea of Band of something," Max added.

"What about the Bandits then?" Elrus said enthusiastically; he was on a bit of a roll.

"Oh dear no," chirped Elwood, who was filling Mrs Longton's cup with a fruit cordial. "Bandits are bad people who go around stealing things; not a very good image at all."

"Well, we're going to be stealing back the relics aren't we?" Elrus said in hushed tones to his three young friends. Lizzie, Eloise and Max nodded in agreement.

Max then came up with the idea that they could perhaps include the word 'aid' in their name. "After all, we're aiding the greater cause," he said.

The little group thought for a while as they tucked into their delicious picnic. "I know," Elrus suddenly shouted. Elwind almost dropped his drink in surprise. "What about the Band Aids?"

Mrs Longton burst out laughing, almost spraying her mouthful of water all over Digby who was sitting near her. Elrus looked at her nonplussed. "What's wrong with that?" he quizzed.

"Well," she began, gathering her wits about her. "In the human world, we have something called band aids. They're sticking plasters."

"What are sticking plasters?" asked Elenya, who had just joined them. She had been discussing the route ahead with Prince Finnion, Flaxon, the two fairies and archer elves, who were called Fidora, Filip, Elbie and Elgin respectively.

"Sticking plasters are small strips of material that you place over grazes or cuts to the skin to protect them from infection," chipped in Elwood, always ready to show off his vast encyclopaedic knowledge.

"You mean, like a poultice?" asked Elbie.

"Mm… sort of," Mrs Longton said.

"That's not quite the image we're after," laughed Elenya.

The little group went quiet once more as they continued devouring their food and drink, the whirring of their brains almost audible as they thought about a suitable name for the little party. Finally, Mrs Longton spoke.

"Well, I think we should call ourselves what we are and that's companions," she said. Several of the party nodded their agreement. Elenya, who had been sitting on the grass

105

next to Lizzie, rose gracefully to her feet and, raising the cup clasped in her hand, said, "To the Companions." Everyone clambered to their feet and, raising their cups in salute, echoed Elenya's words and drained the contents of their vessels.

When everyone had finished their last mouthful of food, and had rested the parts of them that ached from the morning's ride, they prepared to set forth once again. Lizzie was helped to re-saddle her horse by Fidora. Lizzie found the fairy's wings mesmerising as they shimmered with a multitude of colours in the sun's rays. Fidora, who was pulling tight the saddle straps, noticed the girl's interest and smiled at Lizzie. Lizzie's face reddened in embarrassment at having been found staring; her grandmother had always taught her it was rude to stare.

"Your wings are so beautiful," she said shyly.

"Thank you, Princess," Fidora said. Apart from the beautiful wings, Fidora was nothing like the fairies Lizzie had grown up seeing in story books and in other ways that humans liked to portray them. She had several ornaments of fairies on a shelf in her bedroom at Longton Hall that presented them as pretty, delicate little people surrounded by flowers and tiny creatures. Fidora, on the other hand, could not be classed as delicate. She was every inch the warrior fairy in her camouflaged clothing and the short broad sword that she was attached to her belt. If Lizzie hadn't known better, she'd have sworn the fairy was a boy with her strong features and short brown hair.

Once mounted, the Companions set out again. As they began to move off, one of the mules decided that it wasn't ready to leave and refused to budge. The animal was being led along by a strap secured to Elwood's horse, which was brought to an abrupt halt by the dead weight of the reluctant mule. Elwood clicked his tongue and chivvied the mule along, but still it dug in its hooves and refused to move. Increasingly irritated, Elwood resorted to stern words that were getting louder in his frustration.

"Oh come along, you silly animal; you're holding everyone up," Elwood admonished. As he berated the poor beast Flaxon, who had been walking ahead, turned and walked back towards the stubborn mule. As he passed Elwood, he said, "You need to show patience and kindness to him, Elwood. Mules are very sensitive creatures. He is no doubt aware that the way ahead could be fraught with danger and it is his way of warning you."

Flaxon went to the mule and ran a soothing hand along the soft, brown coat of the animal's neck. He then whispered some calming words in the mule's ear, which those nearby couldn't hear, and the mule took a tentative step forward. Then, with Flaxon walking alongside the nervous animal, the party continued on its way.

As the little group traversed the river bank, Fidora and Filip rode on ahead. The two fairies would scout the terrain to ensure that the route they were treading was safe from potential hazards. Lizzie spurred on her little horse – named Whisper – and caught up with Elenya. She looked up at her aunt sitting regally on her magnificent horse and Elenya smiled down at her.

"How far will we travel today?" Lizzie asked.

"We should reach our destination, where we'll spend the night, at dusk. We must travel through the Forest of Neuwe and it is there that we'll set up camp," Elenya explained.

"Will it take long to get there?" asked Elrus, who, not wishing to miss out on anything important, had caught up with the pair.

"We should be there within another two or three hours," Elenya said. There was a groan from just behind them and Lizzie turned around to see her grandmother almost slump in her saddle.

"Another two or three hours?" Mrs Longton grumbled. "Oh dear; I'm not sure my derriere can stand it." The elves and others travelling with them looked at Mrs Longton in puzzlement.

"Derriere?" quizzed Digby.

"French my dear, for…" began Mrs Longton and, standing up in her stirrups, reached around and patted her bottom before sitting back down gingerly in her saddle. The group of travellers laughed and Digby agreed that his "derriere" had a pain in it too.

"French?" chipped in Gorin.

Mrs Longton laughed. "A human language," she explained. Gorin's face showed that he was none the wiser for her explanation.

Just then, there was the sound of galloping hooves and Fidora on her mottled brown mount came into view. The Companions halted in their progress at her approach. Fidora stopped in front of Prince Finnion and Elenya and, bowing her head briefly, said that she and Filip had found a ford some way ahead, which would allow them to cross the river safely. With Fidora guiding their way, the Companions rode on. After a short while, they could see Filip waiting for them, his horse standing impatiently on a small shingle beach by the river's bank. As they reached him, Elwood and Elwind, who had been leading the pack of mules, quickly dismounted and raised the panniers on the animals' backs to prevent them from getting wet, before getting back onto their respective horses. The group watched briefly whilst Filip's horse picked its way slowly across the fast flowing waters and then followed suit.

As they reached the middle of the river, the water came up to the belly of the smallest horse in their party, whose rider happened to be Gorin. The goblin was making a terrible fuss about hating water and not being able to swim, when suddenly the river to his left began to bubble and churn. The terrified goblin squealed in alarm as his horse began to shy away from the disturbance. Flaxon, who was half-walking and half-swimming just ahead of the goblin, turned quickly and grabbed the halter of the frightened horse. He spoke gently to calm the animal. The other riders ahead of Gorin and Flaxon turned to see what the commotion was about;

just in time to see the beautiful head, arms and torso of a water sprite raise itself out of the churning waters. The creature's long silvery hair fell in rivulets down its grey and blue tinged skin, which appeared smooth and fluid. The water sprite then spoke with a voice that sounded like a stream trickling over a gravelled gully.

"Brother Wood Sprite," she called, looking around at the travellers. "Brother Wood Sprite!"

Willo had almost reached the other side of the river but he swung his horse about and came back to discover the reason for the water sprite's appearance. "I am here," he called in reply. "Who seeks me?"

"It is I, Webba, the guardian of these waters. I have a message for you and your company," she gurgled. "Our sprite sisters and brothers of the forest are keeping watch for you and have relayed a message granting you safe passage through their domain. They will keep watch while you rest in their shelter this night. However, there have been sightings of the dreaded pterotorials beyond their borders and they advise you to keep vigilant."

"Thank you for this information, Sister Webba. We will heed their advice," Willo responded, and bowed his head in a sign of respect to the water sprite.

"Safe passage," Webba called, as she spun around like a whirlpool and disappeared back down into the waters below.

"Well that was scary," squeaked Gorin, who had gathered his composure once more. Flaxon continued to hold onto Gorin's horse and guided it to the safety of the river bank beyond.

As the Companions gathered on the shores of the river, Willo recounted the message given to him by the water sprite.

"We need to make haste so that we can reach the shelter of the Forest of Neuwe as soon as possible," Elenya told the group. "We must pick up the pace." She then instructed Fidora and Filip to once again go ahead to scout for possible danger and seek out the safest route for them. The fairies bowed their acceptance of their role and sped off, leaving a trail of dust in their wake. The rest of the Companions took off at a canter in the direction of the fast disappearing fairies.

Keeping their eyes peeled for any sign of the huge prehistoric type creatures in the skies above them, the Companions made good progress towards their destination for the night. The main party finally caught up with their scouts on a rocky knoll which overlooked the great swathe of trees that signalled the beginning of the Forest of Neuwe. As they looked across the distance from their position on the knoll to the trees bordering the forest, Mrs Longton asked how long it would take to reach them.

"We will be there within the half hour," Prince Finnion assured her.

"Thank goodness for that," Mrs Longton sighed.

"But once we are within the safety of the forest, we have a while to travel before reaching our resting place for the night," Elenya explained. Mrs Longton, Digby and Gorin groaned at the announcement.

"There's no point moaning about it," Lizzie said, matter of factly. "We've still got a long way yet to travel, so we might as well just get used to the idea." The other children nodded their agreement as Elenya looked on and smiled with pride at her young niece.

"Lizzie is right," Elenya agreed. "The Mountains of Snow are still another two days ride away from here."

Mrs Longton's eyes widened in shock and she gasped at the thought of another three days of riding. She was beginning to think that she was too old for all this adventure stuff. Her "derriere" was decidedly sore and she really wanted to have a nice soak in a bath and put her feet up. Three more days of this mode of travel was going to seem like an eternity.

"Well, sitting up here looking at those trees is not going to make them come any nearer, so let's get a move on," grumbled Digby.

The riders began picking their way between the boulders that littered the way down from the knoll. Some of the horses' hooves slipped slightly on the loose stones and gravel of the path beneath their feet. Flaxon, however, made light work of the way down, as his goat-like legs and feet seemed to be specifically designed for this type of terrain.

At the bottom, the ground levelled out and the riders took off at a canter once again. As the Companions began pounding across a wide heathland that sprawled out before them, Lizzie called out to her three friends.

"Come on. Race ya!" she cried and set off at a gallop.

Elrus didn't need asking twice and chased after Lizzie on his little mount and Eloise was quick to follow suit. Max, looking less than sure about the situation, decided that he couldn't appear to chicken out and so set off in hot pursuit, his knuckles white from gripping tight to the reins of his horse and his eyes almost closed in terror.

Elenya and Mrs Longton laughed at the sight of the four friends enjoying the excitement of the race, when a terrible screech from above them pierced the air. Seemingly out of no-where, a huge black shadow passed over their heads and they looked up to see a pterotorial heading straight for the four young riders.

# CHAPTER 12

## Healing Hands

As another terrifying screech rent the air, the four young people turned their heads towards the huge black form of the pterotorial bearing down on them. Max screamed in terror, as he was closest to the creature, and urged his little horse on to greater speed. His three friends ahead of him were yelling encouragement to him as they too pressed their own mounts to go faster.

The massive creature began to swoop in towards the young apprentice. Suddenly there was a series of whooshing sounds and thuds as, from behind the panicking children, the two archer elves, Elgin and Elbie, galloping at full speed, let off a volley of arrows. The pterotorial screamed, the sound reverberating through the riders below, as several arrows hit the creature and it wheeled away from its prey to try and avoid further injury.

Lizzie, Elrus, Eloise and Max raced for the safety of the forest, now almost within touching distance, hotly pursued by the remaining riders and Flaxon, whose goat-like legs were amazingly quick. Lizzie, who was leading the pack, turned to see what was happening behind her, just in time to watch the pterotorial plummet to the ground several hundred feet away; its body flipping over and over as it crashed onto the heath, throwing up dust and debris as it tumbled. She reined her horse to a stop and Elrus and Eloise, who were tearing past her, did likewise. Max, still in a state of complete panic, continued to head towards the trees. The Companions had now reached the children and Mrs Longton, ashen faced and shaking, pulled her horse up close to Lizzie's own and reached across and grabbed her granddaughter's arm in relief.

"My darling, are you all right?" she panted. Lizzie nodded mutely and looked past her grandmother at the stricken pterotorial lying in the distance. It was flapping a great wing as if struggling to get back into the air; as it did so, Lizzie watched something rise wisp-like from the creature and seemingly evaporate into nothingness.

Prince Finnion spoke to Elenya, who was checking that the other children were okay, whilst Filip had ridden on to catch up with Max. "Princess, we cannot stop here. There may be other pterotorials in the vicinity. We should make for the safety of the forest."

Elenya nodded, "You're right, Finnion." Then, turning to the group, told them to gather themselves together and make for the trees as quickly as possible.

Lizzie couldn't tear her eyes away from the injured creature that was trying to drag itself to its feet and her eyes filled with tears. She looked at Elenya.

"We can't leave it like that," she said and, before she could be stopped, she turned Whisper in the direction of the creature and began riding towards it.

"Nooo!" screamed Mrs Longton. "Elizabeth, get back here this instant!" she shouted. Then, turning to Elenya, demanded that the princess bring Lizzie back. Elenya looked at Mrs Longton and a gentle smile crossed her lips.

"I will go with her, Mrs Longton. Don't worry; I don't feel that she will come to any harm, but just in case." She turned to Elbie and told him to come also. "You know what to do should things turn to the worst." The elf nodded. Elenya told the rest of the group to stay where they were unless there was any sign of further danger; then they were to make haste to the forest. Elenya and Elbie then rode off after Lizzie.

As Lizzie drew closer to the pterotorial, it seemed to get more agitated and began using its wings to drag itself away from her approach. This need to escape became more urgent as Elenya and Elbie caught up with Lizzie. Elenya looked down at her niece riding beside her and saw the look of compassion and determination etched upon the girl's face.

113

She reminded the princess so much of her beloved sister that it was almost too painful to see. Elethria would take any creature that was suffering into her care and nurture it back to health, but if she was not able to save it, she would ensure that it suffered no longer.

Elenya broke the silence between the three riders. "What do you plan to do, Lizzie? This creature is not some tiny bird with a broken wing." Lizzie looked up at her aunt with a serious face.

"I know but it's hurt and probably frightened and it would be wrong to leave it to die in pain. I have to help it," Lizzie said, as she turned once again to see the creature flap its damaged wing. Lizzie stopped her horse. "I think the horses are scaring it," she said, and clambered down from Whisper's back. Elenya and Elbie followed her lead and the three of them crept forward towards the pterotorial, leaving the horses behind them to graze. As they drew closer, Elenya placed a restraining hand upon Lizzie's arm.

"Wait," the princess hissed. She then reached inside her tunic and pulled out a small silver pipe and a leather pouch, from which she pulled a tiny feathered dart.

"You're not going to poison it are you?" Lizzie exclaimed, her eyes wide in disbelief.

"No, silly. The dart contains a sleeping draft. It may calm the creature sufficiently for you to approach it more safely." Elenya explained.

"I don't think that will work, Princess. The dart is too small. Save it for another time."

The voice came from the rear of Lizzie and her accomplices, and they spun round in surprise to see Flaxon with Elrus riding piggy-back just behind them. As Elrus climbed down from the faun's back, he gave Lizzie one of his cheeky lopsided grins.

"Well, you didn't think I'd miss out on this bit of the adventure, did you?" he quipped.

Lizzie smiled and looked past the newcomers to see the rest of the group watching her progress, including Max who'd been returned to his Companions, and Eloise sitting astride her horse next to Lizzie's grandmother.

"Do you have your pan-pipes, Flaxon?" Lizzie whispered, turning to the faun.

"I never go anywhere without them, Princess," he assured her, removing the instrument from a leather strap that straddled his chest.

The little group crept stealthily forward towards the pterotorial. Once again, it struggled to get away and let out one of its blood-curdling screeches. The sound was deafening this close up and the little party of rescuers clamped their hands to their ears to protect them. Taking a hand from one of her ears, Lizzie held it up as a signal for the group to stop.

"I think there are too many of us. We're scaring the poor thing," she said.

"Poor thing? Poor thing?! It terrified the daylights out of us. It probably would have eaten us if Elbie and Elgin hadn't shot it first," Elrus exclaimed.

"Well it's hurt and the thing that was that was riding it has disappeared so we're the only ones that can help it now," Lizzie continued. "So, Flaxon, you come with me and you can play your pipes to calm it while I try to help it."

"I'm not sure..." began Elenya, shaking her head doubtfully, but Lizzie interrupted her.

"I am, Elenya. I know I can help. Don't ask me how I know, I just do," Lizzie stated, as Elenya opened her mouth as if to protest.

Elenya nodded. She was intuitive enough to know that Lizzie was speaking the truth. She had no doubt that the child had inherited some of her mother's gift for healing. Elbie then spoke. It was the first time that either Lizzie or Elrus had heard the elf's voice, as he and his side-kick,

Elgin, usually went quietly about their business. Lizzie was surprised that he seemed to have a soft Irish burr to his voice.

"If you can calm the creature, Princess, and keep it occupied, I can then help by removing the arrows in its damaged wing. I have a balm here in my pouch that will aid the wing's healing. We archers always carry the remedy as well as the cause," he explained.

"Thank you, Elbie," Lizzie replied. "Wait here until I give you the signal to join us. Come on Flaxon; let's do this." Then, inhaling deeply, she and Flaxon crept forward once more.

"Just don't get too close to that beak," Elrus hissed as his friend moved away.

As they drew closer to the creature, its size almost took Lizzie's breath away. If it had looked huge when it was in the sky, it was massive close up. The pterotorial's long pointed head with its enormous sharp beak snapped around to look in their direction as they approached. Its black beady eyes peered at them, warning them to come no nearer. Flaxon took this as a signal to begin playing his pipes. The soft melodic notes of the tune he began playing drifted across the distance between the stricken creature and the pair determined to aid it. The creature leant its head to one side as if confused by what was happening and its eyes began to flicker and close. Flaxon continued to play and, as he did so, Lizzie began to talk to the creature in gentle soothing words.

"It's all right. We're here to help you," she cooed, tenderly. "You don't need to struggle anymore."

Flaxon shot her a look but continued to play his pipes. Lizzie smiled at him encouragingly.

"There, there, we'll fix everything up for you," Lizzie continued. The pterotorial opened a sleepy eye and peered at her; the music was making it feel so peaceful. What was this strange little person doing coming so close to it?

Finally, Lizzie and Flaxon were close enough to touch the creature. Lizzie's heart was pounding in her chest with a mixture of fear and elation at having come so close to such a magnificent but terrifying beast.

As Lizzie reached her hands tentatively towards the head of the pterotorial, its eyes flickered open once again and stared into those of its little helper. Lizzie froze in mid motion. A feeling almost like an electric shock passed through Lizzie's body, as she felt a connection of understanding form a bond between her and the creature lying before her. The pterotorial closed its eyes again and its huge body seemed to relax and stop struggling. Lizzie continued reaching forward and gently placed her hands on the huge beast's head. Warmth spread through Lizzie's whole body and, from somewhere deep inside, a song bubbled up to trickle out from her. It was as if some ancient knowledge had been released by the action she had just performed and it surprised her but felt so natural. The pterotorial, now in some kind of trance, lay deathly still and Lizzie, still singing the words of the strange song, glanced towards Elbie and, with a brief nod of the head, signalled him to come and treat the animal's wing.

The Companions, gathered hundreds of feet away, could barely breathe at the sight they were witnessing. Mrs Longton's hand was clasped to her throat in complete and utter horror at what her granddaughter was doing. She could barely look but was too frightened to turn away. Max and Eloise just stared open-mouthed in awe.

Elbie had made his way to the creature and was gently lifting its enormous wing. It was proving difficult for him to get to the arrowheads embedded in the creature's flesh, so he turned towards Elenya and Elrus and silently mouthed that he needed their help. The princess and Elrus lifted the wing aloft with great effort, as it was extremely heavy. Meanwhile, Elbie slid underneath the wing on his back and began to remove the arrows. Dark red blood dripped onto the elf's face and arms as he worked, but he moved quickly and

117

expertly. Having dug out the final arrowhead, he spread some of the balm over the wounds and scampered out from under the leathery shelter of the massive wing. Elenya and Elrus placed the wing down as gently as possible and, together with Elbie, they backed away from it.

Lizzie, now with her own eyes closed, continued to sing. The warmth that had emanated through her to the pterotorial had become a tingling sensation, as if something magical or mystical was passing from her and into the injured creature. As the sensation began to fade, Lizzie opened her eyes. Flaxon was still playing his pipes. Lizzie removed her hands from the animal's great head and motioned to Flaxon that that they should now leave, as she could do no more.

The pair slowly stood and retreated from the pterotorial's side. When they were several yards away, Flaxon removed the pipes from his lips and the last notes drifted into silence. The huge creature still did not move.

"I think the wing should heal well. There didn't seem to be any major damage to any of the bones in it," Elbie said. "The animal is lucky that the arrows weren't a little further to the left or we'd have pierced its rib-cage. I just hope that Elgin and I haven't lost our touch," the elf grinned. Elenya chuckled.

"Well you're fired if you have," she said with mock severity.

"You know us, Princess; we try to avoid killing unless there's no other option. We just needed to scare the thing off on this occasion," Elbie replied. "Maybe we scared it a little too much."

The group remounted their horses and with Elrus now sitting behind Elbie, they turned and began riding back towards the other Companions. As they reached them, Mrs Longton seemed to be almost on the verge of collapse.

"Oh my giddy aunt, to quote one Mary Crowther, what were you thinking, Elizabeth Longton?" she wagged an admonishing finger at her granddaughter.

Lizzie shrugged her shoulders. "Just doing what I had to do, gran," she said.

"Weren't you scared?" asked a wide eyed Eloise.

Lizzie shook her head, nodded, and then said, "Well, kind of scared and excited and, well..." She paused; she couldn't really put into words her exact feelings. "I just knew what I must do. I can't really explain." What she did know, however, was that she now felt very, very tired.

Flaxon, who seemed to sense her need for rest, spoke to Elenya. "I think we need to get to our haven for the night, Highness. Princess Elizabeth needs to rest. I think we could all do with a little less excitement."

"Hear, hear!" agreed Mrs Longton.

As the Companions began to move towards the line of trees that was the start of the forest, they heard the sound of enormous wing beats once again. The first reaction of most of them was to scan the skies for signs of any more pterotorials but Lizzie knew better. She looked across at the creature she and her friends had just helped and watched as it stretched and flapped its great wings. Lizzie felt a huge surge of relief as the animal rose into the sky. It seemed to hover there for a moment as if testing the strength of its damaged wing and then soared into the blue sky, back towards the knoll from whence it had come.

Prince Finnion urged the party to hurry and get to the shelter of the trees and, as they heeded his advice, the sound of wing beats could be heard once more. Elgin and Elbie armed their bows ready, should their arrows be needed once more. Then, from over the knoll and flapping its way towards them, came the pterotorial.

"It won't hurt us," yelled Lizzie above the noise of the beating wings of the creature that was now circling high above them. The pterotorial then let out a call that echoed across the heath, but this time it was not threatening; it was as if the creature was calling its thanks. Then, without further ado, it flew off across the roof of the forest.

119

"Phew," Max sighed loudly. "Can we now get under those bloomin' trees?"

The Companions let out huge sighs as the sense of relief swept over them.

"I'm with you, Max," Elenya laughed. Then, lifting her arm in an exaggerated gesture towards the forest, cried, "Let's get under those bloomin' trees!"

# CHAPTER 13

## Witch Away

It was early morning and the sun was rising in the East; its blood red rays spread across the sky as if warning that there was trouble ahead. Melisha, cloaked and booted, and with a light pack slung across her back, strode purposefully across the parched and barren landscape that was Maladorth. The shuffle in her step that she affected in front of Eldorth was no longer evident. She was on a mission and she would be successful or die in the process, of that she was determined.

As the sun rose in the sky, its heat beat down upon Melisha's head. Sweat broke out on her broad forehead and she licked away the salty taste of it from her upper lip. As her thinning hair began to plaster itself to her pate, she rummaged in her pack and pulled out a scrap of material. Shaking it a few times, the fabric formed itself into a pointed, floppy brimmed hat. She plonked it on her head. She then removed her cloak and stuffed it in the bag. Her shabby, brown cloth dress clung to her chunky body, revealing the rolls of fat beneath.

She was heading for the border of Maladorth and into the Wild Woods of Elumbria to the Pool of Elesbat in the centre of the woods. She had to reach the pool by the night of the full moon in three days' time for its magical waters to achieve their full effect. Melisha knew that Eldorth must not know that she intended to go to visit the pool first, before travelling on to Eldinburgh.

Melisha had considered finding an alternative mode of transport to reduce the time she spent walking. If truth be told, she hated the drudgery of putting one foot in front of the other. Eldorth had refused her a horse and so she must keep a look out to see if she could find some other beast of burden to carry her on her way. She had not had any luck in finding such an animal as yet.

As the day wore on, Melisha began to tire. She was hot and uncomfortable as sweat ran down her back and between her sagging breasts. There was little in the way of shade in Maladorth, as the dry parched earth had sucked the life out of the trees that had once grown there so that, apart from the occasional copse or small wood, there were only stunted bushes and small leafless trees to be found.

She had skirted around the small villages that she had passed en route so far, avoiding contact with any of the inhabitants. The elves and other creatures living in these villages were eking out their meagre existences with little or no hope of growing their own provisions, as other communities outside Maladorth did. She had spotted a few small-holdings where some skinny chickens and the occasional under-nourished goat and pig picked at what scraps of grass or grain they could discover in amongst the stones and dust. She had not come across any that kept an animal large enough to carry her bulky frame.

After some hours, the witch decided that she needed to rest her weary legs and take some sustenance. She was trudging along a winding dusty trail with a rocky cliff face to one side. As the sun had moved further to the west, the cliff cast a shadow over part of the road and Melisha headed for the coolness of its shade. Taking out her cloak from her bag, she threw it on the ground and flopped down upon it. She pulled off her boots and wriggled her toes; her dirty feet seemed to emit a vapour as the fresh air hit them. She then extracted a piece of lumpy parchment, a wrinkled skinned onion and a flask of ale from the bag. As she opened the parchment, the stench of some strong over ripe cheese permeated the air around her. She sniffed the cheese and a look of pleasure spread across her coarse features. The combined smell of the cheese and Melisha's feet would have floored an army should one have been nearby.

"Ahh, Rottenfort cheese; my favourite," she sighed. She tucked hungrily into the food. Peeling back the skin of the onion, she bit into it like an apple. Then, before swallowing the onion's flesh, she bit into the cheese. Popping open the flask of ale, she swigged at its contents before swishing the whole concoction around her mouth and gulping it all down.

"Huuuh…," she sighed, as she leant back against the rock behind her; her short, stubby legs stuck out straight in front. She closed her eyes and rested a while.

Melisha's peace was broken several minutes later when she heard a voice singing merrily and the clip clop of hooves on the stony road away to her right. She opened a single eye and swivelled it in the direction of the noise. From around the bend came a young elf sitting on the back of a donkey. Melisha smirked evilly; here was her chance. She grabbed one of her boots and quickly pulled it on. Having done that, she grasped her other foot and howled as if in terrible pain.

"Owww…" she hollered.

The young elf stopped in his tracks. Eyeing him again, Melisha wailed once more as if the agony was too awful to bear.

"Aww, owww…" she screeched, clasping her fake injury. The little elf looked about him, as if he expected that some other assistance might suddenly appear then dismounting, he took a few tentative steps forward. From what he felt was a safe distance, he peered at the woman now writhing in pain on the ground.

"Are you alright?" he called, reluctant to come any nearer and glancing around to see if anyone was about to pounce on him.

"Do I look alright?" Melisha responded irritably. She wailed pitifully once again.

The young elf was suspicious of finding the old woman alone by the road side but he couldn't just abandon her when she was obviously in some distress. He inched a little nearer, pulling his donkey along with him.

Melisha needed the elf to come closer so that she could achieve her evil purpose. "Aww dear, me poor old foot," she moaned. "I twisted it on that stone over there." She pointed to a small pebble lying in the middle of the track. The elf looked at the pebble, surprised that such a little object had caused the woman such a painful injury. "I can't put me foot to the ground. I don't suppose you have a bandage upon ya person, do ya?" Melisha continued.

The elf shook his head rapidly in an emphatic no. Melisha looked more closely at the young elf and could see that there was something a little odd about him. As she peered into the elf's face, it suddenly dawned on her what it was; she realised that he wasn't a very bright soul. Oh, goody, she thought, the situation just got better and better. She had only intended to steal his donkey but it would be so much better to have a little slave attend her every whim. She smiled a sickly smile at the elf.

"Do ya think you could help me get to me feet, young'un? I need to be on me way and once I'm up I'm sure I'll be fine," she asked, grinning deviously.

The elf still hung back; he sensed that there was something not quite right but he was a good elf and he felt really should help her if he could.

"She's just an old woman. What harm can she do?" he thought. He let go of the donkey's lead and walked towards Melisha. As he approached, she asked his name.

"Elpme," said the elf.

"Well fank you, Elpme," Melisha said sweetly. Elpme smiled; perhaps his instincts were wrong and there was no danger after all. As he bent and offered a hand to help Melisha to her feet, she suddenly yanked on his arm and pulled him down on his knees in front of her. Before the young elf knew what was happening, Melisha had placed a rough hand onto his forehead and, gripping it tight, muttered some words he didn't understand. Elpme slumped to the ground and lay there dazed.

Quick as a flash and belying her bulk, Melisha was on her feet. She grabbed up her boot and slipped it on her bare foot. Then, from a hidden pocket in her dowdy dress, she pulled out a long twisted piece of wood. Waving it over the prone elf, she cast a spell, binding him in servitude to her for as long as she needed him. As she replaced the wand in her pocket, Elpme stirred. He blinked his eyes against the sun that shone across his blank features and, pulling himself up into a sitting position, gazed up vacantly at the witch standing in front of him.

"Get up!" Melisha commanded gruffly. Elpme clambered to his feet, swaying slightly as he did so. "Now pick up me stuff and put it in that bag there. Then you can help me up onto that donkey of yours. Well, mine now," Melisha smirked.

"Yes, mistress," Elpme replied, quickly doing as he was bid.

"That's right, I'm your mistress now and don't you forget it," Melisha threatened.

"No, mistress," Elpme said, his voice flat and emotionless.

Melisha then told the young elf that they were off to the Wild Woods of Elumbria. "So get this ass movin'," she ordered. Then, without a word, Elpme began to lead the donkey along the dusty track.

*

By night fall, the witch and her captive had almost reached the border of Maladorth. They had made good progress with Melisha riding on the poor donkey's back and Elpme running ahead, dragging the poor creature behind him. Melisha wasn't happy as she bumped and joggled along; every bit of her body ached from the roughness of the ride.

Finally, she had had enough and called to Elpme to stop. The elf halted instantly. Melisha looked around her for somewhere suitable for them to rest for the night and spotted some stunted trees a short distance away that would afford some shelter from prying eyes. She decided that they would rest there. She ordered Elpme to take her over to the trees and, once there, the young elf set about making camp. He fixed a little fire and Melisha, having pulled a small pot out from her bag, and a cabbage and onion too, proceeded to make a thin soup for the pair to eat. She knew that if Elpme was to be of any use to her, she had to keep him fed and watered.

Supper over, Melisha drew out her wand and, aiming it at the unsuspecting Elpme, cast a sleeping spell on the young elf. He fell backwards, with arms and legs spread-eagled, and began snoring loudly. Melisha looked at him disdainfully.

"I'm never goin' to get any sleep with that racket going on," she moaned, and, with another wave of her wand, silenced the elf mid snore. Melisha sighed in relief and, pulling her cloak out of her pack, wrapped it around her and settled down to sleep.

As the witch began to drift off, and her deep breaths turned to loud rattling snores, two small pairs of eyes watched from behind a gorse bush a little way back along the track that Melisha and Elpme had just travelled. The eyes blinked at each other in silent understanding, as their owners agreed to take it in turns to keep lookout through the night.

# CHAPTER 14

## Neuwe Camp

Dusk was falling as the Companions rode into the coolness of the forest. The shade from the canopy of branches above their heads was a welcome relief from the oppressive heat that they had travelled under so far. The density of the trees meant that for much of the time, the riders now rode in single file, with Filip leading the way and Elgin bringing up the rear.

A light breeze rustled through the leaves and the sound of a myriad of birds and small animals, calling to one another as they prepared for the night ahead, filled the air. The soothing effects of the forest created a calmness in them that was in stark contrast to the anxiety and fear they had experienced during the events earlier that evening.

As the Companions trotted along, picking their way through the roots and fallen branches that littered their path, Elwind began to sing and was soon joined by his brother, Elwood. The twins' voices joined in perfect harmony as they sang a catchy little ditty:

> The might of the wind
> The power of the sea
> The strength of the wood
> The magic of three.

> Alone they will stand
> As two they are strong
> But all three together
> Is how they belong.

Wind, sea and wood
The mother earth made
And brought forth this union
So fate may be played.

Alone they will stand
As two they are strong
But all three together
Is how they belong.

As nature had planned
They went their own way
Until they are needed
To rescue the day.

Alone they will stand
As two they are strong
But all three together
Is where they belong.

But all three together
Is where they belong.


Elwood and Elwind sang the last line of the song with gusto, trying to outdo each other as to how long they could hold the final note. The song lifted the group's spirits and when it finished, there were calls from Elrus and Digby to sing it again and this time, all the Companions joined in.

"We dwarfs love a good song," Digby called happily, his gruff manner no longer evident in his eagerness to sing the song once more. The song's words and melody drifted through the forest and the evening bird song seemed to complement it beautifully.

Lizzie laughed at the enthusiasm with which the singers sang. She loved the feeling of camaraderie that had grown between them throughout the day. Her sense of belonging in this world grew with every passing moment.

They sang it several more times before Digby announced that he had a song they could all sing. He then began singing one about digging and tunnels and great canyons beneath the ground. He had a rich deep baritone voice and he conducted the other singers in the group by waving his hand around as though conducting an orchestra

From her place, riding just behind Filip, Fidora, Finnion and Elenya, she looked back at the others behind her. Elwood and Elwind, still leading the weary mules along, were singing their hearts out; their heads were thrown back as they warbled the lyrics of the song. Elrus and Eloise were laughing together as they sang the chorus heartily. Max, just behind them, was nodding his head in time with the melody while Flaxon, skipping alongside him, sang along too. Digby's deep voice resonated through the trees forming a great bass line in contrast to Mrs Longton's high soprano tones. The only member of the Companions who seemed not to be joining in with the fun was Gorin, who winced each time Mrs Longton hit a particularly high note. Willo and the two elven archers at the back of the group were busy keeping look out.

As Lizzie turned back to face the direction in which they were travelling, she was sure that she saw one of the trees move. She faced forward for a moment, thinking she must have been imagining things and that it was probably a breeze blowing through the tree's branches. To make sure she'd been mistaken, she glanced back at the particular tree in question and, this time, she was certain that the whole trunk had moved several inches towards them. She then looked around at some of the other trees and noticed several seeming to shuffle towards the path that the group was navigating. The sense of safety and security Lizzie had been feeling evaporated.

"Elenya," she called nervously to her aunt. Elenya turned around.

"Elenya, the trees," Lizzie pointed at the trees unnecessarily. "They… they seem to be moving?"

Elenya laughed. "The trees aren't moving, Lizzie. Trees can't move."

"Yes they are," Lizzie replied determinedly. "I've seen them. I may be tired but I'm not dreaming."

"It isn't the trees you've seen moving; what you have seen are the wood sprites. They are forming a barrier for our protection until we reach camp for the night," Elenya smiled reassuringly.

Lizzie breathed a sigh of relief. How stupid of her not to think that those who were leading the quest would not have noticed a bunch of trees moving towards them. She relaxed once more and the Companions continued on their way. Elvedom would never cease to surprise and delight her.

A little while later the travellers came to a glade in the forest. A small stream flowed through it and the crystal waters trickling over the stones in the stream bed added to the peaceful ambience of the place. Tall straight trees circled the glade and gave it a cathedral-like effect. As the riders dismounted and began preparing camp, Lizzie looked up and could see that there was a gap in the tree canopy, through which she could see stars beginning to emerge in the darkening sky. The effect was magical.

Having removed the saddle and harness from Whisper, Lizzie sent him off to a corner of the glade with the other horses and mules to rest. She took out her sleeping rug from the pack that had formed a cushion behind her on the ride and lowered herself onto it, to watch as the others in the group went about their business. She felt she should be helping but she had been so tired since aiding the pterotorial that she knew she should rest in order to recharge her drained resources. Whatever had passed between her and the beast had sapped some of Lizzie's normally boundless energy.

Lizzie smiled as she watched her grandmother unpack for the night, and straighten and stretch her obviously aching back, then laughed as she saw Mrs Longton gently rub her sore "derriere". Mrs Longton noticed Lizzie watching her and gave her granddaughter an exaggerated wink and broad grin.

Lizzie turned and saw Eloise walking towards her. Her friend put down her own sleeping rug next to Lizzie's and sat down too.

"Are you okay, Lizzie?" Eloise asked. "You look so tired."

Lizzie explained that she had felt exhausted since her encounter with the pterotorial and that she badly needed a good night's rest.

"I'm not surprised," Eloise exclaimed. "What you did was incredible. We were all amazed as we watched you; it was terrifying. I thought Max might faint."

The girls giggled.

"Why did you do it? I mean, that thing looked like it was going to kill us; why would you want to save it? Weren't you scared it might attack you when you got near it?" Eloise continued incredulously.

Lizzie looked at her friend and shook her head.

"I was nervous but not scared, if that makes any sense," she began. "As I said before, it was something I had to do. I knew that if I could get it to relax enough so that I could get close to it, then I'd be able to help heal it. It really helped to have Flaxon with me to use his pipes to calm it and then the others did their bit too."

131

Eloise stared awe-struck at Lizzie. She was so lucky to have such an amazing friend, she thought.

"What did it feel like?" she asked.

Lizzie looked at her friend questioningly. "Do you mean what did the pterotorial feel like or what did I feel like when helping it?"

"Both," breathed Eloise.

"Well," Lizzie thought for a bit. "The pterotorial felt warm and hard but the skin was like soft padded leather. It's kind of hard to describe. And me, well I can't really explain that either, just that it was like some electric current passing through me."

"Electric?" Eloise looked confused.

"Like lightening," explained Lizzie.

"Oh wow," Eloise sighed. Just at that moment, Fidora called to Eloise and asked if she could come and help find some wood to keep the campfire burning.

"Sure," Eloise called and, turning to Lizzie, told her she'd be back later.

The smell of something delicious began wafting through the glade, and Lizzie suddenly realised that she was famished. Eloise, Elrus and Max returned to the fireside with arms full of kindling, and Elwind, who seemed to be in charge of keeping the fire stoked, added some to it. Lizzie felt guilty just sitting there observing the activity whilst everyone else seemed so busy.

She watched Elwood, happy in his role as chief cook, chopping and preparing ingredients and running back and forth to the pot over the fire that was emitting the appetising aromas. Mrs Longton, wiped her brow as the steam from the pot wafted up as she stirred its contents. Gorin was honing what seemed to be a collection of sharp implements including knives, swords and arrowheads on a stone placed between his short legs. The two fairies were rubbing down the horses, whilst Elgin and Elbie were stripping straight pieces of wood and forming them into more arrows to replace those that had been used against the pterotorial. Elenya, Prince Finnion, Digby and Flaxon were in deep conversation and pouring over what appeared to be a map or some other old document. The only member that was missing, as far as Lizzie could see, was Willo.

The children, having completed their wood collecting chores, were now passing the football between them. They still seemed to still have loads of energy, despite having had a pretty arduous day. Mrs Longton, who had been relieved of her stirring duties by Elwood, wandered over to them.

"I can teach you a new game to play with the football," she declared. The three children turned to her excitedly.

"Please do, Mrs Longton," Elrus said politely, picking up the ball and passing it to her.

"What's the game called?" asked Max.

"It's called keepy-uppy," Mrs Longton announced and, with that, began bouncing the ball on her foot. She wasn't terribly good at it and the ball bounced off in all different directions, with Mrs Longton running after it and attempting the feat again. The children laughed uproariously at her antics, none more so than Lizzie who was watching from her place on her rug.

"Well, it's not that easy," puffed Mrs Longton, red faced from the exertion of the activity. Then, passing the ball back to Elrus, she said, "You get the idea. You can compete with each other to see who can kick the ball up in the air the most."

The three children did just as she suggested and their laughter rang around the forest glade in their attempts to stop the ball from hitting the ground.

Mrs Longton went over to her granddaughter and joined her on the rug. She placed loving arms around Lizzie's shoulders and drew her into a warm embrace, placing a kiss on Lizzie's head as she did so.

"Well, that was quite an exciting day," Mrs Longton sighed, "what with water sprites rising out of rivers and big ugly brutes swooping out of the sky trying to attack you. It's not exactly Chislewick is it?" Lizzie giggled at the thought of pterotorials flying around over her village.

"That was incredibly kind and brave of you to help that creature, darling," Mrs Longton continued, looking down into Lizzie's face.

"I keep telling people, I didn't have a choice. I had to help it," Lizzie said, a touch of impatience in her voice. Mrs Longton ran a soothing hand across Lizzie's hair as she brushed the fringe away from her face.

"I know, I know," Mrs Longton said gently. Lizzie leant against her grandmother and drew strength from the love that passed between them. They watched in silence, smiling as Max seemed to get the hang of keepy-uppy and was counting loudly as his number of kicks increased.

Finally, supper was ready and the Companions lined up to have their food bowls filled with steaming hot, thick, comforting stew. It smelt delicious and as they sat around the camp fire and tucked into it, accompanied by some kind of chewy bread. The group ate in silence as they devoured the contents of their bowls and several went back for second helpings. As they ate, they were re-joined by Willo. The wood sprite ate food that he pulled from his own pack, which seemed to comprise mainly of nuts and berries. His absence was quickly explained as he told the group that he had been into the forest to speak with his brother and sister wood sprites.

"They have forged a way through the forest for us to hasten our journey onwards," Willo explained, in his soft, rustling voice. Members of the group nodded in understanding.

"Please thank your kin for their assistance to us," Elenya said gratefully.

"I have taken the liberty of doing so already, Princess," Willo replied, bowing his head slightly in acknowledgement of the thanks.

When supper was finished and the things were being cleared away, Lizzie decided she really should help out as it seemed wrong to not take her turn with the chores. As she went to walk over to Elwood and offer to wash dishes, she felt a gentle hand on her arm. She looked down at the hand and then up into the face of Flaxon standing beside her.

"You should rest, Princess," he said softly. "You did a great thing this afternoon and it will have taken much out of you."

Lizzie nodded. "It has, Flaxon. I've felt so tired since then," she said wearily. Still holding lightly onto Lizzie's arm, the faun led her to her sleeping rug. As she sat down, he sat beside her.

"You have a great gift, Princess," he began. "In fact, you have more than one it would seem." Lizzie smiled politely at the compliment and thanked him but was unsure of what he meant by more than one gift. The faun seemed to read her mind.

"I do not flatter you, I tell you the truth. Did you know that you could speak Dragonian?" he asked. Lizzie looked at him uncertainly.

"What do you mean?" she asked.

"You speak the ancient language of dragons," Flaxon stated. Lizzie's mouth dropped open and she blinked rapidly in shock.

"Wh…, what?" she exclaimed. "How?"

"You obviously did not know," Flaxon said matter of factly.

"Well no, I didn't know. I mean, we don't have much call for it in Chislewick where I live," she said, almost as if speaking to herself. "But how do you know I can speak; what's it called again?" she asked.

"Dragonian," Flaxon replied. "You spoke to the pterotorial in that language. Pterotorials are distantly related to their majestic cousins, the dragons. I should imagine that the creature you helped earlier could understand something of what you were saying, for your song seemed to have such a therapeutic effect on it. If you didn't know that you spoke it, then you must have inherited the ability from one of your ancestors."

Lizzie shook her head slowly from side to side. "I can't believe this," she murmured.

Flaxon smiled at her and, getting to his feet, looked down and said, "Believe it, Princess. You have a very special gift that may come in useful one day."

As Flaxon walked away, Lizzie lay down on her rug and pulled a light cover over her. As she stared up through the gap in the trees, at the multitude of stars twinkling down on the Companions, her mind whirred. It was full of the memories and emotions that the day's events had evoked. The final thought that passed through Lizzie's brain as she fell into a deep, exhausted sleep was, "I can talk to dragons!"

# CHAPTER 15

## Neuwe and Old Friends

The Companions rose early the next morning and, suitably refreshed, and fed on a good hearty breakfast of porridge and fruit buns, they set off for the Elcambrian Mountains of Snow once more.

The way through the forest had, as promised by the wood sprites, been made easier for them so that, instead of picking their way over roots and fallen debris, they could canter along at a steady pace. The forest seemed to go on for miles and whilst within its boundaries, they felt safe from Eldorth's spies. As they approached the forest's edge, Elenya called the group to a halt.

The riders reined in their horses as Elenya turned her own about and faced the forest trees, signalling for the Companions to do like-wise. She then called out, her voice bouncing off the trees and reverberating through the forest flora.

"Good spirits and sprites of the Forest of Neuwe, we thank you for your hospitality and for keeping us safe within your domain. We now take our leave of you and bid you well until we meet again," she pronounced.

Elrus, who was riding next to Lizzie, leant across and whispered to her, "But we didn't meet any."

As if his words had been overheard, there suddenly appeared, from behind and out of the trees and bushes, numerous woodland faces. Beautiful wood nymphs danced forwards and curtsied to the travellers; the colours of their flowing hair and dresses rendered them almost invisible as they blended in with their surroundings. Wood sprites – their tree-like forms swaying and bowing – bade their goodbyes to the visitors. One particularly strong featured wood sprite

137

stepped forward and stood in front of the rest. The creature's voice was deep and resonant when he spoke.

"On behalf of my brethren and our sisters, the wood nymphs, I, Oakley of Neuwe, wish you safe passage. Until you come this way again, we wish you good speed."

Elenya thanked him and raised her hand in an open palmed salute. The rest of her party followed her lead, then turned and continued on their journey.

As the trees thinned, the Companions could see a deep valley spread out beyond the forest borders. With Filip and Fidora scouting ahead, the group picked their way carefully down a steep incline towards the valley floor. A river wound its way off into the distance through the green clad delta, and the sun, now high in the sky, glinted off the water's surface. They spotted a small village several miles away and Elenya said that they would stop there and replenish their provisions for the next stage of their journey.

Lizzie had dropped back a little and was now riding next to Elwood. She realised that they hadn't spoken much since their arrival in Elvedom and so she took the opportunity to catch up with how her friend and mentor was faring.

"I am good thank you, ma'am," Elwood responded. "It's been an eventful venture so far, don't you think?"

Lizzie smiled and nodded. "Yes it has," she agreed. They rode a little in silence, comfortable in each other's company. Lizzie then remembered the song that Elwood and his brother had sung whilst travelling through the forest the previous day.

"I enjoyed the song that you and Elwind sang yesterday. I know that most songs in Elvedom seem to tell a story, what did that one mean?" she asked.

Elwood puffed up his chest and smiled broadly at Lizzie.

"It is a song that my mother used to sing to Elwind, my sister and me when we were children," he said happily. "It is about the three of us."

Lizzie was surprised and her face showed it. "I didn't know you had a sister," she exclaimed and then, thinking about it, said, "But then I didn't know you had a brother till I met him in Maladorth."

"Elwind, my sister Elsea and I are triplets. Elsea lives by the East Coast and so I don't get to see her as much as I would wish, as my duties prevent my visiting her." His face looked sad and it was Lizzie was unused to seeing. She suddenly felt guilty to think that it was probably her fault that he and his little family were apart.

"I'm sorry that looking after me keeps you away from your family, Elwood," she apologised. Elwood looked at her puzzled.

"Why are you sorry, ma'am? It is not your fault that I must serve you. We all have our purpose in life. You have yours, I have mine and Elsea has hers," he said matter-of-factly.

Lizzie nodded; there was truth in that. Elwood seemed quite clear in what his purpose was and she was still finding out hers. She asked what Elsea was doing by the East Coast.

Elwood told Lizzie, "When we were children, my mother and father travelled to the East Coast with us. It was a wonderful time," he said wistfully. "Whilst we were there, we played on the beach and one day we came across a merboy called Walter who was hurt. He was lying in the surf and had a terrible wound to his tail. My mother helped to mend his wound and my sister kept him company whilst he healed. They formed a strong friendship. When he was well enough to return to the sea, his people came to claim him. We returned home but Elsea could not forget Walter. When she was old enough to leave home, she went back to the coast and has stayed there ever since."

Lizzie listened in rapt attention as Elwood told his story. It was like something out of a children's book.

"How romantic," she sighed as he finished. A look of doubt crossed the little elf's face.

"Possibly, but a relationship between a merman and an elf is unheard of," he explained. "It can lead to nothing but heartache." The silence fell between them once more as Lizzie thought about the fact that there were merpeople out there in the sea. After a while, she asked Elwood about the creatures.

"There are lots of communities of merpeople and not just in the sea. Some live in the deepest lakes and lochs. They are very private people and have little to do with land dwelling creatures, believing themselves to be of a higher order – quite incorrectly in most people's opinion. They consequently are most unfriendly and can be quite dangerous to the unwary. Walter is an exception because of his brief time with my family."

The Companions had now reached the banks of the river and they stopped briefly to allow the horses and mules to drink, and the riders to stretch their legs. Elrus was about to reach up and take his football from the horn of his saddle but Elenya said that there was no time for that, as they needed to reach the village.

A grumpy faced Elrus climbed back onto his horse as the other riders remounted. Max looked at the expression on Elrus's face and laughed.

"Don't worry, Elrus. Maybe we'll get time to have a game when we get to camp tonight. Hey, perhaps we could get some of the others to join in," he said brightly. Elrus's face lit up and, as he looked around at the little group, his mind put each of the Companions in a position on the pitch. He decided that none of the fairies should go in goal or otherwise no-one would be able to score, what with the speed the fairies would be able to fly around the goal mouths.

The Companions reached the little village by lunch time and the villagers stopped whatever activity they were performing to watch as the riders approached. Looks of fear and suspicion were etched on the villagers' faces, but these soon turned to ones of shock and then joy as they recognised the beautiful blond rider amongst the newcomers. Elenya's regal bearing shone out from those around her as she sat astride her majestic stallion.

Word obviously spread quickly, as elves and their children came running out of huts and houses and lined the track that passed through the village. The male elves amongst them, who were wearing hats, doffed them and the women curtseyed as the visitors passed by. The Companions waved and children, laughing and calling, ran alongside the riders, until finally the group came to the largest house in the village. As they stopped in front of it, an elderly elf came out; he had a long silver beard and hair and he walked with a stick. As the riders dismounted, he bowed his head towards Elenya.

The princess came forward and took the elf warmly by the hand.

"Eldan, how wonderful to see you," she said, beaming a dazzling smile at him. Then, looking around her, she continued, "So this is where you disappeared to."

The elderly elf laughed softly. "It is indeed, Your Highness, it is indeed. I welcome you and your company to Elvalle; to the home of my people," he said, formally. Elenya then turned to the group travelling with her and called Lizzie to her side.

"Eldan, may I introduce my niece, Princess Elizabeth," she announced, putting a hand gently on Lizzie's shoulder. The elderly elf peered intently into Lizzie's face and she was surprised to see that his eyes seemed to brim with tears as he looked at her. She put out her hand in greeting and, as Eldan took it in his own, Lizzie shook it firmly.

"It is an honour to meet you, Princess," he said.

Elenya then explained to Lizzie that Eldan was one of King Elfred's oldest and valued advisors and that he had retired from court after many years of loyal service. "He is a true friend to the King and he is much missed at court," she said, smiling affectionately at him.

"I knew your mother well, young Princess. She was always the good one, this one here was just a bit naughty," Eldan whispered to Lizzie.

Elenya laughed heartily. "But you loved me really, Eldan," she grinned.

"I loved you both, more than life itself," the old elf said, his face showing the depth of his feelings.

Elenya then introduced the rest of her party to Eldan and he greeted them all with a warm but reserved smile. He then invited them into his house, to take some refreshments and shelter from the increasing heat of the day. As the group entered the coolness of his home, Eldan called to some of the villagers to make sure that the horses and mules were attended to.

In the central hall of the house, there was a large table with several chairs surrounding it. Elves scurried about, laying out food and drink for the visitors as the Companions joined Eldan at the table.

"So, Princess, to what do I owe this honour?" Eldan said, as a serving elf poured wine into their goblets.

"We're passing through on royal business," Elenya began, taking some ham and cheese from a platter that was being offered. "I'm sorry but the exact nature of the business, I am not at liberty to share," she explained. Eldan didn't press her for more, as he knew only too well that if Elenya said she could not elucidate further, then she had good reason.

Eldan asked how their journey had faired until now and Prince Finnion relayed the events so far, including their close call with a pterotorial. Eldan nodded but did not seem surprised.

"We have heard that Eldorth is using the creatures for his malicious purposes. That boy was always going to be bad. We fortunately have been spared those creatures presence in our valley so far, as there is nothing here to warrant their interest. I hope that does not change now," Eldan said warily.

Elenya agreed that she hoped so too. She said that she was sorry that they had disturbed the peace of the village but that they needed to restock their supplies before moving on. They would leave as soon as possible to avoid further detection by any likely pterotorials that might be nearby, she told him.

Eldan then turned to Lizzie.

"So, you aided the fallen creature, Princess?" Lizzie nodded mutely, as a mouthful of strawberry prevented any speech. Eldan smiled. "Just like your mother. She couldn't let an injured animal suffer." Then, raising his eyebrows and looking impressed, he added, "She never took on something the size of one of those things though."

The party laughed and enjoyed the rest of the lunch, talking about news from the court and what intelligence was known about Eldorth's latest antics.

The meal complete, the visitors rose to prepare to leave. Eldan spoke with Elenya and Prince Finnion. "I have a strong feeling that I may know of the direction in which you travel for the remainder of this day." Elenya went to speak but was silenced by Eldan raising his hand. "If I am right, may I suggest that you keep to the west of the river; you can cross at a small bridge about a mile north of here. Keep close to the side of the valley where there is an overhanging cliff that will keep you from prying eyes for as long as possible. About ten miles from where you cross the river, you will find a secret passage through the hills that will save you several hours journey time." Elenya thanked the elderly elf for his advice.

As each of the Companions left the safety of Eldan's home, they took him by the hand and thanked him for his hospitality. Elenya and Lizzie were the last to say their farewells to him.

"Look after this one, Princess Elenya. I think she is truly special," he said tenderly, looking down into Lizzie's little pointed face.

Taking one of Lizzie's hands in her own, Elenya promised that she would do everything in her power to keep her niece safe. Then, releasing her hand, she went to Eldan and hugged him tightly.

"Come and see us at court soon, Eldan. I miss your wisdom and your kindness," she said, her words soft in Eldan's ear.

"I may just do that some time, Princess," he replied and held her tight before releasing her and telling her to be on her way. Elenya quickly mounted her horse and the Companions set off once again. The mules' panniers were filled to their brims with everything the travellers needed for the remainder of their journey that day.

The Companions followed Eldan's advice to the letter and, just as he said, once they had crossed the river they found the overhanging cliff and kept to its recesses. As they trotted along in its shade, Lizzie, riding beside Elenya, asked her aunt about Eldan.

"As I told you when I introduced you both, he was an old and trusted advisor to my father. When Eldorth had been orphaned and came to live at court, Eldan had been his tutor. It was he who persuaded my father of Eldorth's dark ways and banishment from court. It is rumoured that Eldorth has never forgiven the old elf and will one day have his revenge upon him also," Elenya explained. "Eldan's whereabouts, when he finally retired from court, have been kept secret for many years."

Lizzie hoped that now they had discovered Eldan's secret hideaway, it didn't put him at risk. She was sure that none of their party would betray the old elf.

After several miles, they discovered the bridge that Eldon had mentioned and crossed it without incident. Shortly afterwards, they came upon the passage that cut through the hills as he had told them. It was hewn through two high precipices which formed a gorge; the trees and bushes that grew on either side afforded the Companions concealment from anything above. When they finally emerged from the passage some hours later, a wide flat plain spread out ahead of them. In the distance, on top of a rocky tor, sat what appeared to be a huge castle, its spires and turrets stretching up into the sky.

The sun was lowering on the horizon and it cast its orange rays upon the castle walls, so that the building appeared to burn gold in the sun's evening glow. It was a beautiful sight to behold.

As the riders stopped and took in the view, Mrs Longton sighed. "Wow, that's spectacular," she breathed.

Elenya turned and smiled at Mrs Longton. "Well, folks, that's our residence for the night, so we had better get a move on."

"What is it?" asked Eloise, taking in the vista.

But before Elenya could reply, Max said in awe, "That's Elavalon!"

# CHAPTER 16

## The Pool of Elsabet

A heat haze formed a heavy blanket of condensation over the sleeping forms of Melisha, Elpme and their beast of burden, the poor donkey. Melisha stirred and stretched her bulky body as she awoke from her slumbers. She felt hot and uncomfortable and her bones ached from sleeping on the hard, rough ground. She peered across at the young elf sleeping soundly a few feet away and sneered as she took in the peaceful look on his face.

"I can soon shatter that look of contentment on his stupid face," she thought spitefully. Then, loudly, she shouted, "Oi! Oi you! Wake up!"

Elpme jumped, blinking rapidly as the brightness of the day hit his eyes, and clambered onto his knees. He looked around him blankly, as if confused as to where he was. Melisha cackled at the comical look on the young elf's features. Elpme then spotted Melisha sitting close by and stared at the witch expressionlessly.

"Get up and make me somefink to eat," Melisha ordered. "And there's some water in that pouch there. You'd better give some to the ass; I don't want it keeling over while I'm on its back."

Elpme scrambled to his feet and did as he was told. He looked around for something with which to feed his mistress, but saw nothing but a barren landscape that showed no signs of anything edible nearby. Melisha realised the source of the elf's confusion and irritably told him there was some food in her bag and that he should get a move on.

As Elpme went about his chore, Melisha stood and looked around her. She was beginning to think that her and Eldorth's plan to cast dark magic on his lands, so as to make folks living there totally dependent upon him for all their provisions, had its drawbacks. She had only brought enough supplies with her to feed herself on her journey; she hadn't taken into account that she would have another mouth to feed, two if you counted the donkey. She needed to get out of Maladorth and into the more fertile lands of Elumbria, where she could get Elpme to forage for stuff that they could eat. Elves were good at that sort of thing, she thought.

After a meagre breakfast of some watery gruel, the three set off on their journey once more. Unseen by them, just behind were two small figures, darting between the boulders and bushes that littered the way, as they followed the witch and her captives.

As they trudged along under the burning sun, Melisha could hear a humming noise. She looked around her quickly, thinking that some insect or other was buzzing close by. She swatted her hand around at the invisible assailant, not wanting to be stung or bitten, but the humming noise persisted. She then gathered that it was coming from in front of her and realised that the noise was emanating from Elpme. She listened harder and managed to determine that he was humming some tuneless song. It seemed that, despite his befuddled brain and her spell upon him, from deep somewhere inside, he had called upon a memory of a song. She was about to tell him to shut up but then decided that the flat monotony of the tune was actually quite pleasant to her, in a weird sort of way, so she let the elf continue.

A few hours had passed when the travellers came to the border of Maladorth and its neighbour, Elumbria. The stark difference between the two lands was vast; it was as if a physical line had been drawn in the earth. One side of the border, the Maladorth side, was dry, parched and barren whilst the other, Elumbrian side, was completely green and fertile. Melisha could see the trees of the Wild Woods in the distance and an evil smile spread across her face. They could reach the Pool of Elsabet by nightfall if they continued to travel at this rate. What a stroke of luck it had been, finding this elf and his donkey. She had managed to knock a whole day's travel off her journey to the pool.

In addition to the new sights that assaulted the travellers' senses, crossing the border also brought new sounds and smells. Melisha winced, as if in pain, at the sounds of the musical tweeting of birdsong. The smell of vegetation growing by the side of the track would, to most mortals, be pleasant and comforting but to Melisha, whose inherent badness seeped through to every fibre of her being, it was noxious and made her gag. Now she remembered another reason why she had agreed to the decimation of the lands in Maladorth; she couldn't abide anything green and pleasant.Doing her best not to inhale through her nose, Melisha chivvied Elpme and the donkey along.

When, some time later, they reached the Wild Woods, and the dimness of its depths, Melisha took in a long, gasping breath. She sighed in relief as she took in the dank, musty smell of the rotting leaves and debris kicked up by the donkey's hoofs. Elpme looked round at the witch in alarm; it sounded as though she was about to expire.

The dankness of the woods and the strange noises of the woodland inhabitants were much more to Melisha's liking than the open countryside of Elumbria. She relaxed as the donkey carried her further into the dark interior of the woods – the animal plodding wearily along as Elpme hummed another tuneless song and picked unripe nuts, berries and mushrooms so they could eat something when they finally stopped. They had been travelling for hours and had not eaten since breakfast. Melisha began to nod drowsily and was almost dropping off in a doze when a sudden shout brought her abruptly to her senses.

"Stop! Stop! Who goes there? Who goes there?" squealed a high pitched voice.

Standing in front of them, and with a long spear almost touching the end of Elpme's nose, was a wizened little creature dressed in shades of dark green and brown. Its bark-like skin and gnarled features blended in perfectly with the

148

woods in which it obviously resided. It jabbed the spear a few more times in Elpme's direction as the young elf leant further and further back to avoid being poked in the eye.

"Who are you? Who are you? What brings you to my woods? What brings you to my woods?" the creature demanded.

Melisha cocked her head to one side and eyed the little creature disparagingly. How dare this hobgoblin question her? She crossed her arms and stared at it.

"Who dares to ask me who I am and why I travel through these woods?" she threw back at him.

"I asked first. I asked first," the hobgoblin shouted, hopping up and down and stamping his feet and spear on the ground. The action seemed to be a signal, as from behind the trees close by him, four more, identically dressed hobgoblins suddenly appeared; all of them carrying spears or little daggers and shields. Elpme took a big step backwards at the other hobgoblins' sudden appearance and stood close to the donkey's side as if it would afford him some protection, his bright blue eyes wide in fright.

Melisha sighed as though weary with the interruption to her journey. "I'm just a tired old lady travelling through 'ere and we thought we would rest the night in your luvverly woods," she simpered. There was little point in aggravating the tiresome creature further, so she might as well try to butter him up.

"You've got to pay the toll. You've got to pay the toll," the hobgoblin demanded, hopping up and down again.

"Oh for gawd's sake, do you have to say everyfink twice?" she said wearily. "I ain't bliddy deaf."

The hobgoblin stood still and stared at Melisha. His comrades shuffled up close behind him and whispered to each other excitedly. "All right, all right," the first hobgoblin murmured to his mates. It seemed to take him great effort, but he then managed to speak without having to replicate each sentence.

"You've got to pay the toll," he said slowly and deliberately. "You can't pass by unless you do."

"Why?" Melisha challenged.

The hobgoblin was taken aback; he wasn't used to being questioned. Not many visitors passed through this way, and the few that did were usually nervous enough of his threatening behaviour that they would just pay him so they could be on their way. He thought for a moment and then said, "Coz it's the law."

"The law? Whose law?" Melisha quizzed. She could see that the hobgoblins were unused to having to answer questions, as the little group whispered amongst themselves, getting more and more agitated with each passing moment. The head hobgoblin spoke again.

"Our law. We make the law here, for we are the guardians of these woods," he said proudly, standing as tall as his little body would allow.

Melisha was starting to lose patience; he really was a tedious little man. "Right, how much is this bliddy toll?" she asked wearily, thinking that she would rather just zap the creature out of the way but that would blow her idea of travelling incognito out of the water.

"The toll changes and today you must pay with a song," the hobgoblin replied. "A song, a song," his comrades echoed, jumping up and down enthusiastically.

Melisha nearly fell off the donkey. The thought of singing a song to an audience horrified her. She didn't mind singing while she worked or when she very occasionally had a bath, but in front of people, well, that was something else.

"I don't know any songs," she said, trying to get out of paying this particular toll. "Give me something else to pay by."

"It has to be a song or I cannot let you pass," the hobgoblin replied emphatically, crossing his arms as if to demonstrate his determination. The other hobgoblins crossed their arms too and adopted fierce looking expressions. Melisha wasn't impressed.

She thought for a bit, and then looked at Elpme and an idea struck her that maybe he could pay the toll instead. He obviously knew the odd tune and so she suggested as much to the hobgoblin.

The little man looked at the young elf dubiously, tipping his head from side to side as he weighed up the youngster.

"Only the leader of the party can pay the toll. He is obviously not your leader but a servant, so we cannot take the toll from him. You must pay," he stated, pointing his spear at Melisha to drive home the point. She really didn't like this little creature and it would give her great pleasure to send him sprawling with a flattening spell, but she took a deep breath and resigned herself to the fact that she was going to have to sing these obnoxious creatures a song. She took a deep breath and began to sing.

There once was a woman from Elvedom

But no-one could call her handsome

Till one fateful day

She travelled this way

And left a small man on his bum.

The hobgoblins, and Elpme, stared at Melisha in horror. The noise coming out of the witch's mouth was horrible. Her caterwauling jarred their senses and a couple of the hobgoblins waggled their fingers in their ears as if to clean out the terrible noise that assaulted them. Melisha grinned. She liked the song she'd just made up and thought herself very clever; so, oblivious to the pained looks on her audience's faces, she began again.

There once was a wom…

But before she got any further, the hobgoblin held up his hands as if halting traffic.

151

"Stop! Stop! You have paid enough. You may pass and pass quickly," he squealed. His fellow hobgoblins agreed, "Yes, yes! Pass quickly, pass quickly."

Melisha patted her thin hair, as if preening herself, and took on a slightly hurt expression. "Well, if you're sure," she said.

"We're sure, we're sure," the hobgoblins replied in unison. Then, standing aside, they allowed Melisha and her little party to finally continue on their way.

Watching from behind some trees away to the left of the toll paying activities, the two small creatures spying on Melisha's progress were also holding their hands over their sensitive ears. As the witch and her captives moved off, they took it as a sign that it was safe to remove their hands and continue with their surveillance.

The density of trees and undergrowth of the woodland floor became more difficult to navigate as the little group went further into the depths of the woods. The branches of ancient oaks and elms appeared to join arms to prevent their moving forward, so that in some places they had to turn around and find another way through. Old, gnarled yew trees seemed to contain the faces of long dead spirits, as the twists and turns of the trees' boughs and bark formed strange shapes. The birdsong that had got on Melisha's nerves for much of the journey through the woods faded and died, and the silence was only broken by the plodding of the donkey's feet and Elpme's light tread rustling through fallen leaves.

For a while, Melisha rode with her eyes closed and her nose sniffing the air. She could sense that they were close to the Pool of Elsabet, but she would know for sure when she could smell it. She could always smell something magical a mile away. The donkey was becoming increasingly reluctant to move, as it struggled over roots and bracken that scratched at the poor creature's legs and belly. Elpme coaxed and cajoled the animal as Melisha, frustrated at the slowing of their progress, dug her heels into the donkey's sides and called it rude names to try and urge it on.

Finally, they came across an avenue of trees that formed an archway over a track that seemed to lead into a clearing. They stopped at the entrance to the archway and Melisha closed her eyes again and drew in a long breath through her bulbous nose. There it was; the smell of magic. It was difficult to describe but she would consider it closest to a mixture of spices and the pungent scents of exotic blooms. It was totally unmistakeable. A slow smile drifted across Melisha's ecstatic face. They were here and the full moon was still a night away. They would use the interim time setting up camp and resting in the clearing close to the pool, so that she could soak up the magic in the air and prepare herself for the next night.

Melisha urged Elpme and the donkey on, and the three travellers walked through the avenue of trees and out into the clearing; in the centre of which was a pool of still water. The blue of the sky above reflected in the mirror-like surface of the water, and reeds, grasses and irises grew around the pool's edge; the purple of the iris flags the only splash of vivid colour in an otherwise sea of green.

Melisha clambered down from her perch on the donkey's back and the poor beast almost seemed to groan in relief. Released from its burden, it trotted off and, when it felt it was a safe enough distance from its heavy load, tucked into the luscious grass that grew by the side of the pool.

Meanwhile, Elpme busied about making a supper of the foodstuffs he had foraged on the journey through the woods. It would be a measly meal, but it would have to suffice for that evening and he would search for more the following day. He picked up the water pouch that was now almost empty and went to fill it at the pool. He jumped backwards as if scalded when Melisha screamed at him to stop.

"You can't take the water from the pool, you fool!" she yelled. "No-one touches the pool but those with magic themselves. Go and find some elsewhere. I'm sure I heard a stream or running water just before we got 'ere." Elpme ran back towards the archway that led back into the woods, a hand cupped to his ear as he listened out for any sign of running water.

Melisha stood by the pool and gazed at the surface of the water. A sense of calmness swept over her and the creases in her face caused by years of scowling and frowning seemed to smoothen. She inhaled the scent of magic in the air and she knew that she had done the right thing in coming here before she journeyed further north to the realm of Elcaledonia. What she could achieve here would ease her passage into that wild and hostile land.

Elpme was soon back from finding a source of water and, having built a small fire, he set about making supper for himself and Melisha. As the sky darkened overhead, the witch and the young elf ate a strange concoction of the nuts, fruits and other food in silence. When they had finished, they settled down for the night. Melisha's head was full of plans for the ritual she would perform the following day.

From behind a dogwood bush, two little spies settled down to take it in turns to watch the travellers sleep.

The following morning, bright and early, Elpme disappeared off to find something edible for them to eat that day. Melisha, meanwhile, went to the pool side and found an old tree stump that formed a table of sorts. She took numerous small objects and amulets from her pack and laid them on the stump, chanting various incantations as she did so. Then she threw one of the items into the centre of the pool as an offering to the spirit of the Great Sorceress, Elsabet.

As each hour passed, yet another offering was made until all the objects and amulets, except one, were thrown into the waters. Melisha placed the final amulet – a large bloodstone on a leather cord – around her neck. She then removed her boots and, with bare feet and in a trance-like state, began to circle the pool's edge in a slow plodding gait, her eyes staring straight ahead seemingly unseeing.

Elpme, who had returned from his foraging much earlier, sat silently on the trunk of a nearby fallen tree and watched the witch's progress. His confused brain was mesmerised by the sight of the bulky form of Melisha as she trudged around the pool's perimeter.

The day had passed swiftly and the reddening of the sky above them showed that evening was fast approaching. Melisha suddenly stopped walking, faced the pool and threw back her head, looking up into the wide expanse of sky above her. She then opened wide her arms and stepped forward into the waters. As she moved further into the pool's depths, her rough, brown dress floated up around her but still she walked on with her arms raised. The water eventually reached her chest and, as it did so, Melisha took a deep breath and dipped down under the water's surface. At that moment, the moon rose above the treeline and its fullness shone down on the ripples caused by Melisha's submersion. What seemed like several minutes passed before suddenly, she burst forth from the pool's depths.

Elpme, who was still sitting watching the events unfold, almost fell backwards from his seat on the fallen tree. His mouth hung open as the witch stepped out of the Pool of Elsabet. But where had his mistress gone? Who was this stranger walking towards him?

A beautiful, porcelain skinned woman with long, shiny, raven hair and dressed in a baggy sack cloth dress approached him and smiled bewitchingly. She ran her hands down the sides of her voluptuous body and her hips swayed from side to side as she walked. Elpme couldn't help but smile back at her. Then, opening her ruby red lips, she said:

"Where's me bliddy supper boy?"

As Elpme rushed about getting this strange woman something to eat, behind their dogwood bush, two little imps, exhausted from barely any rest over the past two days and bored from watching the repetitive ritual that they had witnessed that day, lay curled up fast asleep.

# CHAPTER 17

## The Citadel of Elavalon

The Companions raced across the plain towards their refuge for the night; the pack mules doing well to keep up with the pace. As they approached, the Citadel walls perched on their rocky tor, loomed high above them. Suddenly, a shout rang out from one of the ramparts.

"Halt! Who goes there?"

Reining the horses to an abrupt stop, the travellers looked up to see an elf leaning over peering down on them, the setting sun's rays glinting off his armour. Prince Finnion spoke on their behalf.

"We are on King's business and wish to take rest here this night," he called in reply.

The elf on the ramparts called back, "If you are on King's business, identify yourselves."

Elenya stood up in her stirrups and called out to the elf. "It is I, Elenya, your Sovereign Princess and these are my companions."

The elf straightened his body to attention and called down once again. "I beg your pardon, Princess. I shall arrange for the gateway to be opened."

With that, he disappeared and, very soon afterwards, there appeared in the stone wall ahead of them the beginnings of an outline of an enormous arch. As the image became stronger it revealed an opening into a great courtyard. The riders rode over the granite surface of the entrance way into a beautiful marble cloister. A number of white haired elves in shining silver breast-plates and light armour ran forward to assist the travellers from their mounts, leading the horses away through a portico over to the left of the yard. Mrs Longton, Lizzie and her friends stared around

156

with open mouthed appreciation of their incredible surroundings.

White marble pillars and carved arches encircled them and a huge, richly ornate fountain played in the middle of the courtyard; its waters creating a peaceful energy about the place. Through the arches, they could see paths and narrow roadways snaking away into other parts of the citadel. Opposite the entrance arch were a number of white marble steps leading up to a massive doorway, which led into the interior of the building. Standing before it was an elf dressed in a long, silver grey robe, pinched in at the waist by a silver rope from which hung a large key. His grey flowing hair and beard matched his garb perfectly and there was a serenity about him that seemed to fill the void between him and his visitors. A soft smile played on the lips of his lined face and his piercing blue eyes fell upon Elenya.

The elf walked slowly down the steps towards her and she strode towards him as the rest of the Companions watched silently. Elenya and the elf stopped in front of each other and then, much to Lizzie's surprise, Elenya curtseyed. The elf bowed his head in return and the two then embraced.

Elenya beckoned Lizzie forward. As she went to them shyly, her grandmother not far behind, a smiling Elenya introduced them to the elf.

"Lizzie, let me introduce you to our uncle, Eladrian, the Guardian of Elavalon and High Priest of Elvedom. Eladrian is my mother's brother."

Lizzie looked at Eladrian in amazement. This was her uncle? She'd never had an uncle before and no-one had told her that she had one in Elvedom. He bowed to her and so Lizzie thought it appropriate to follow Elenya's lead and curtsey to him.

"I am pleased to meet you at last, Elizabeth," Eladrian said; his voice was soft and deep. "I am, of course, a Great Uncle to you as your mother was my niece, but I am here at your service, as I was at hers." Elenya then introduced Mrs

157

Longton and the rest of the Companions in turn. Eladrian welcomed them all.

"Welcome to Elavalon. I have expected your arrival, and accommodation has been arranged for your comfort this night. Please follow me," he said. He turned, and with Elenya and Lizzie to either side of him, led the party through the doorway into the citadel's interior.

The visitors found themselves in a spacious entrance hall with a high vaulted ceiling. White marble glistened everywhere, as it had in the courtyard, and marble statues of mythical creatures looked down upon them. The party walked through the hall in silence, taking in their surroundings, until they reached a stairway leading into the upper reaches of the building. Standing to either side of the stairway were several elven maidens. They looked identical in their long white dresses, with their long white hair falling in a silken sheet down their backs. Eladrian turned to his guests.

"These maidens will escort you to your accommodation for the night where you can refresh yourselves before supper. They will then await your pleasure until you are ready to come to the dining hall." With no further instructions, the maidens turned and began to lead the party up the stairway. The peace of the place stifled any discussion amongst the guests as they trailed mutely behind their guides. Eventually, they were led along a hallway lined by a number of doors. As each maiden stopped in front of a door and opened it, one of them spoke to their guests.

"These are your rooms and we hope you will be very comfortable. We trust that all you will require for the evening is in your rooms but please let us know if you need anything further. We have organised that the children share, as we thought they would prefer having company, and so the two young ladies are in this room here." She indicated a room to her right. "And the young gentlemen are in the room opposite." She pointed to the door of a room on her left. "If the rest of you would like to come this way?" she asked, as the older members of the group entered their respective rooms.

Lizzie and Eloise went into their room and looked around. It was spartan but spotlessly clean and functional and was a million miles away from the more grand rooms that Lizzie and her grandmother had occupied at Elvedom Castle. Two single beds covered in plain white linen dominated the room and the few other pieces of furniture dotted about appeared to be made of light oak wood. On a table to one side of the room was placed a bowl of fruit and a jug of water with two glasses. To the left of the table was a door which Eloise opened and saw that it was a simple bathroom. Everything in Elavalon seemed to be coloured white and the bathroom was no exception.

Lizzie suddenly felt awkward. Last night, sleeping out in the open had been the first experience of sharing a space with others at night. She had, however, never shared a room with anyone in her life before and it felt strange that she would not have the privacy that she had always been used to. Lizzie had never been invited to the sleepovers that she knew other girls in her class had often talked about, and realised that this was probably going to be something like that.

"What if I snore?" she thought to herself and, even worse, "What if Eloise does?"

Eloise seemed more relaxed about the situation and ran to the window and peered out.

"Oh look, Lizzie, our room overlooks the courtyard. Isn't it beautiful?" she trilled, turning around and beaming at Lizzie. Seeing the look of uncertainty on her face, Eloise asked if she was all right.

Lizzie felt silly. What was she worrying for? She would be spending the time with her friend and it would give them a chance to really start to get to know each other. They'd had so little time to talk together and no time on their own, so this would be an opportunity to share some girly stuff. She smiled at Eloise and said she was fine, making the excuse that she was just a little tired after the long day's ride.

"Of course you are," Eloise said understandingly. "Which bed would you like – the one next to the window or the one nearest the door?" Lizzie looked at the beds. She preferred the one nearest the window but instead said that Eloise could choose and was relieved when the girl flopped down on the one nearest the door.

"Well at least the bed's comfortable after sleeping on the floor last night," laughed Eloise.

Deciding to check out the state of the bed for herself, Lizzie flung herself down on it; it was indeed comfy. She lay on her back and stared up at the ceiling. The white plasterwork was peppered with sparkling stones in the shape of stars. She wondered what this place was. It had an air of something mystical about it. The closest feeling that Lizzie could recall having had in a building was when her grandmother had once taken her visit a huge Cathedral. Lizzie turned onto her side and, propping herself up on her elbow, looked at her friend.

"Do you know anything about this place, Eloise?" she asked. Eloise adopted the same pose as she turned to face Lizzie.

"Only through stories and legends," Eloise said. "To be truthful, I didn't think it really existed. It's supposed to be the spiritual home of the elves and it's said that if Elavalon falls, so shall the House of the Kings of Elvedom," she continued, almost in a whisper.

"Wow," breathed Lizzie. Then, flopping onto her back, she stared once more at the ceiling. "And to think my uncle's the guardian of it." As she was pondering the thought, there was a knock at the door. The two girls sat up and stared at it.

"Come in," called Lizzie.

The door opened and in walked Elenya. She was still in her travelling clothes and the whiteness of the room emphasised her dusty and slightly dishevelled appearance.

As she strode into the room, with her confident but graceful style, she grinned at the girls. She went over to the bowl of fruit and picked up a shiny red apple.

"Well," she began, turning round and looking at the two girls sitting on their beds, "What do you think of Elavalon?" She bit into the crisp apple and wiped a dribble of juice that trickled down from the side of her mouth.

"It's beautiful," sighed Eloise, a dreamy smile on her face.

Lizzie looked at her friend and smiled at the pleasure spread across Eloise's features. She then looked at her aunt.

"Eloise told me that this is the spiritual home of the elves. What does that mean?" she asked.

Elenya sat down on a plain wooden chair by the window. "This place is said to be the heart of Elvedom. In ancient times, the Kings of Elvedom held court here. When Eldorth cursed my father's house, evasive action needed to be taken to ensure that he could not attack the citadel and overthrow its inhabitants. So, Elavalon has been placed under a concealment charm and the priests and priestesses that now live here keep it under their protection. It will only be revealed when they allow it to be. One day, when Eldorth is no longer a threat, we hope that Elavalon will return to being the seat of the Kings of Elvedom."

Lizzie looked confused. "But if it's under a concealment charm how could we see it from so far away?"

Elenya laughed, "Good question, Lizzie. Well, our uncle, Eladrian, knew of our journey and that King Elfred wanted his granddaughter to witness the place for herself and so he lifted the charm for a brief designated time. If something had happened to delay our progress, and it very nearly did with that pterotorial visit, then the citadel would have no longer been visible to us."

Lizzie nodded in understanding. "So who is our uncle Eladrian?" she asked.

161

"As I told you when I introduced you, he is my mother's brother and he is the guardian of Elavalon whilst it is under concealment," Elenya explained. "He is also High Priest of Elvedom, although his correct title is Keyper of Elavalon. Did you see the large silver key that hung from his belt?"

The two girls nodded.

"Does he have to lock the place up?" asked an incredulous Eloise, her brown eyes wide in wonder.

Elenya laughed her strong, clear laugh again. "No, Eloise. The key is a symbol of his position. It is a very precious object because of its symbolism, but it is not used in the physical sense."

Elenya stood up and took another bite of her apple as she walked towards the door.

"Anyway, that's enough explanations for now. I just wanted to make sure you two were okay. You'd better get yourselves washed and changed for supper, as should I. There should be some robes hanging in the closet there for you to put on and you should wear them." Then, just before she closed the door, she popped her head round it one last time to say, "And don't take too long about it, supper's in half an hour."

As Lizzie made her way to the bathroom, Eloise ran over to the closet, pulled out two white robes and held them up to show Lizzie. The long, soft fabric touched the floor at the girl's feet and hanging at the robes waists were silver plaited belts.

"Well, at least we don't have to worry about what we're going to wear to dinner," laughed Eloise.

Having washed away the day's grime and dust, and dressed in their identical robes, the two girls left their room to make their way down to supper. As they entered the hallway outside their bedroom door, it seemed that the rest of their party had telepathically communicated, for they all appeared in the hallway at the same time. Lizzie looked across at Max and Elrus and eyed them up and down. The boys' white robes hung down from their shoulders, but the elves in Elavalon had obviously under estimated Max's height, as his stopped short of his silver sandaled feet and finished somewhere just above his ankles. He looked uncomfortable with the image as he pulled at the sides of the robe, as if trying to make it longer.

"Nice dresses guys," giggled Lizzie.

"I thought so," grinned Elrus, doing a quick twirl. The children laughed and even Max seemed to relax a little. They looked along at the other Companions in their white garb and, as usual, Elenya stood out as the most stunning. Then Lizzie looked at her grandmother and thought she looked beautiful too. She went to her and gave her a hug.

"You look lovely, gran," she beamed, looking into her grandmother's face.

"Thank you, darling," smiled Mrs Longton, hugging Lizzie back and placing a gentle kiss on the top of her granddaughter's head. "I feel rather lovely," she laughed.

"Well, I feel a fool," grumbled a voice from somewhere along the hallway. Lizzie looked and saw Digby, a frown etched on his rugged, bearded features. He tugged at the belt, as if it were too tight.

"Well, I think you look very handsome," smiled Elenya at the dwarf. Digby seemed to preen for a moment at the compliment before once more adopting his grumpy expression.

"Mine's too long." The complaint, in a squeaky high-pitched voice, came from Gorin. Everyone looked in his direction. The goblin appeared to be swamped by his robe as it drooped to the floor. Lizzie wanted to giggle and she heard a stifled chortle come from Elrus just behind her.

"Oh dear, would you like me to help you pull it up a bit," offered Mrs Longton, her motherly instincts coming to the fore. She took a step towards the goblin.

"No thank you," replied Gorin quickly, recoiling from her, a horrified look on his face at the thought of being treated like a child. "I can manage," he added, bunching up the material of the robe and trying to tuck it around the belt.

As Gorin struggled with his robe, the maidens who had escorted them earlier reappeared and the one who had spoken earlier addressed them once again.

"If you would like to follow us, we will show you to the dining hall," she said, and, turning, led the white clad procession along the hallway and down the stairs towards the huge entrance hall.

Lizzie, walking beside her aunt, could hear the mumbled complaints of Gorin following along behind and found it hard to keep a straight face as she heard her grandmother and Digby still trying to offer their assistance to the goblin.

"You're going to fall bum over face down the stairs if you don't pick it up," she heard Digby's gruff voice say.

Once down stairs, they were led to a large doorway leading off the main entrance hall and, looking ahead of them, the visitors could see that the room contained a long, plain wooden table. It was laden with silver platters full of food, and crystal jugs and goblets were laid out next to plain white plates and silver cutlery. Standing at the head of the table was Eladrian. Each of the maidens stood behind a chair and these were soon occupied by one of the Companions. It was then that Lizzie noticed that the only one of them not in a white robe was Flaxon. He was, however, wearing a lightweight silver breastplate that covered his usually bare chest.

Eladrian spoke. "Before we sit and feast upon the gifts that Mother Earth has provided for us, may we give thanks to her." The congregation stood as Eladrian then spoke in a language that Lizzie didn't understand.

In a deep and resonant voice that seemed to reverberate around the hall, he chanted, *"Sa en Griane niamhr emaicht er dairther. Sa en Gelacht niamhr emaicht ar seirfur. Sa en brethain deofer carum si methair. Muat*

164

*Methair Domane ca giel miut beile ajas laef ajas ama, sa miut bie fairfer ir huer sierbhis."*

Lizzie watched Eladrian in fascination. She then looked around the table at her Companions. Apart from her grandmother, who was also taking great interest in the proceedings, Lizzie could see that all the elves and other races amongst them, had their heads bowed and their eyes closed. She saw Elwood open one eye and peer at her. He indicated that she should follow their lead. She quickly did as she was told and the magical sound of Eladrian's words seemed to wash over her in a wave. At that moment, it didn't seem to matter that she didn't have a clue what they meant.

When he had finished, Lizzie slowly opened her eyes. Eladrian then sat down and the company took this as the signal that they should follow suit. Once the diners were seated, all ceremony seemed to disappear as the group tucked into the delicious food on offer, and the sounds of lutes and flutes filtered through the air, creating a calming ambience. Lizzie sat opposite her aunt, with Eladrian to her right and Max to her left. Lizzie looked around and saw that the maidens had placed them alternately male and female wherever possible. As she took some steaming creamy potatoes and sliced chicken and munched on them ravenously, she realised how hungry she was.

"So, Elizabeth, how are you finding our world of Elvedom?" The question came from her uncle and she swallowed a mouthful of the potatoes before being able to answer him.

"Oh, it's brilliant!" she beamed at him. "I'm learning new things every day about it and about myself too," she continued enthusiastically.

"That is as it should be. We are all on a journey through life and we will discover new things all the time. When we stop learning, we stop breathing," he said, smiling at her gently.

Lizzie nodded at him shyly. He was so spiritual she felt quite inhibited in his company. She looked across at Elenya who smiled at her encouragingly.

The gesture gave her a boost of courage. "Please sir, can I ask you something?" she asked him.

"Of course, Elizabeth, ask away," he replied.

Without looking at him, Lizzie sensed Max's ears prick up at this. She could see Elrus, sitting opposite Max, in animated conversation with Eloise next to him.

"Could you please tell me what you said before we sat down?"

Eladrian laughed a deep and infectious laugh that sounded as if it was something he did often.

"Oh, my dear; of course I'll explain. It is a prayer to the Mother Earth and I recited it in Old Elvish, the language of our ancestors. It translates thus; 'May the sun never leave his Daughter. May the moon never leave her Sister. May the brethren always tend its Mother. Our Mother Earth who gives us home and life and love, may we be forever in your service.' As you have probably learnt, we elves are the guardians and protectors of our most precious Mother Earth. Without her we are nothing."

Lizzie nodded in understanding. "It's a huge responsibility that elves have," she said, suddenly feeling the weight of it on her shoulders.

It seemed that this mystical place had made her realise the enormity of what the future held for her. One day she would rule this world in place of her grandfather and the impact of this hit her like a physical blow. She would never be able to do this, it was much too big an expectation of little Lizzie Longton. Up until now, she had somehow been swept away by the excitement of living this new fantasy life as if it were just that – fantasy, unreal, imagined. But sitting here next to this man, she knew that it was no fantasy but her real life. She suddenly felt very sick and dizzy and was aware of beads of sweat popping out on her forehead. She felt distinctly unwell and quickly stood up.

"Excuse me, but I need the bathroom," she said, and ran stumbling from the room.

# CHAPTER 18

## Midnight Max

Lizzie ran as hard as she could out into the fresh air of the courtyard. Some elven soldiers sitting on a wooden bench nearby jumped to attention as she passed. Running to the fountain, she placed her hands upon its sides and leant over, looking into the clear waters of the fountain's pool. She sucked in the air in huge gasping breaths and the sense of panic that had risen in her chest seemed to subside a little. The feeling of sickness passed and she shook her head as if trying to dislodge the thoughts swirling around her brain.

Lizzie then felt the light touch of someone placing a hand gently on her shoulder and, turning, she looked into the worried face of Max. Looking beyond him, she could see the figure of Elwood standing on the steps to the citadel, an anxious look on his face as he wrung his hands in agitation.

"Are you all right, Princess?" Max asked gently, his concern for her etched across his handsome young face.

Lizzie began trembling uncontrollably and shook her head.

"I don't think so," she said, her lips quivering and her eyes filling with tears. "What am I going to do Max? I don't think I'm cut out for this. I mean, I haven't had any training. There's so much I don't know or understand."

Max placed a comforting arm around Lizzie's shoulders, their differences in status forgotten as Max's care for his friend over-rode any other rules. Max encouraged her to sit down as her legs were shaking so much and so the pair sat on the low marble wall that edged the fountain's waters.

"You're doing a brilliant job so far," Max said reassuringly. "Look; how many days have you actually spent in this world?" Lizzie shook her head and shrugged her shoulders.

"Not many," she admitted.

"Exactly," Max continued. "And in those few days you have had an enormous amount happen to you and you've coped fantastically. I bet you've surprised yourself at what you've done since you've been here." He looked at her with his big blue eyes showing their admiration of her.

She nodded. "I have actually," she agreed.

"Every one of our companions has been in awe at what you have been able to achieve without any training. You are born to this, Princess. It's in your blood – well, half your blood anyway," he grinned cheekily.

Lizzie smiled. The feeling of total panic was easing and she let out a big sigh. Elwood, still standing on the steps, also sighed with relief. It appeared that the crisis seemed to have been averted, for the time being anyway, and he turned and walked back towards the dining hall, to reassure some of the others who had also wanted to come after Lizzie. It had been Flaxon who had told them to leave the situation to Max.

"You should take more deep breaths," advised Max, as he watched the colour begin to filter back into Lizzie's face. Her pallor had been something akin to a washed out dish rag when he had first come to her aid. "My master has always told me to do the same if I have become over anxious about something."

Lizzie did as advised and after taking several exaggerated breaths, admitted that she felt a lot better. Max asked if she would like to return to the hall but she said she wasn't ready to face everyone yet, so he suggested that they take a walk until she was.

As Lizzie stood up from her perch on the side of the fountain, her legs felt decidedly wobbly and so she placed a steadying hand on Max's arm. As the pair took a few steps, Lizzie began to feel the circulation coming back into her shaky legs and Max supported her as they walked slowly around the courtyard. Through one of the arches, Lizzie spotted what looked like an ornamental garden and she asked Max if they could take a stroll around it.

The full moon above them cast a silvery glow over the flowerbeds and plants of the garden. The aroma of night blooms filled the air with their pungent scents and the peace of the place seeped into Lizzie's frazzled nerves, soothing them and making her feel heaps better. She saw a white wooden bench under an ornate arbour and said that perhaps they could sit there for a while. Now feeling much stronger, she let go of Max's arm. They sat down on the bench and Lizzie fell back against it, peering up through the arbour at the moon high in the night sky. They sat quietly for a while, soaking in the peaceful atmosphere, reluctant to break the garden's spell.

Finally, Lizzie turned to Max and thanked him.

"You're a real friend, Max. I'm so glad that it was you who came to my rescue. I feel a lot less embarrassed about my outburst than if one of the others had come out to me," she said gratefully.

"No problem, Princess," Max said, bowing his head to her.

She looked at him earnestly. "Why do you insist on calling me Princess when I've told you to call me Lizzie?" she asked.

Max looked down at his sandaled feet. "It is because I am servant to His Majesty, King Elfred, and so, as his granddaughter, I must pay you all due respect. I am not comfortable calling you... Lizzie." He said her name quickly, as if he would be struck dumb by doing so.

She placed a comforting hand on his arm and said it was okay. "I actually quite like it, so I give you permission to continue calling me Princess. Actually Elrus calls me it so I guess it's something I've got to get used to," she said, pulling a face of resignation. Max looked relieved as they grinned at each other companionably.

She then looked at him long and hard and he squirmed slightly at her stare. It was as if she had suddenly realised something for the first time, as she said, "Max, all this time we've spent together, it's just occurred to me that you don't have pointed ears like the other elves. Why is that?"

Max smiled shyly. "Because I am not an elf."

Lizzie was stunned. She had always assumed that he was.

"What do you mean, you're not an elf?"

"Just as I say, Princess, I am not an elf. Don't you find my ears unusual. I mean, even fairies have slightly pointed ears," he grinned, turning his head from side to side, showing her each ear in turn.

Lizzie laughed. It was funny to hear him describe his ears as unusual when they looked very like most human ears. "Well, if you're not an elf what are you? I mean you can't be human, can you?" she asked, eager to know what type of being he could possibly be.

"No! I'm definitely not a human. I've heard about them. No, I am told by my master that, like him, I have the blood of magi running through my veins," he continued.

"Magi?" Lizzie wasn't sure she'd ever heard the word.

"Yes, magi. The magi are an ancient race from which all the sorcerers, wizards or witches in the worlds are descended. I, according to my master, am one of those descendants," Max told her.

"Are your parents magi then?" Lizzie suddenly realised that she had never heard Max ever mention his parents at all; he only ever referred to his master, Marvin.

"That I do not know. I was abandoned at birth and left as a baby at the castle of Elvedom to be placed under the care of my master. I guess that at least one of them must be for their blood runs through me too," he acknowledged.

"Why don't you ask them?" Lizzie asked.

"I do not know if my parents are alive or dead as they have not been in my life since they left me." Max said this

171

without a hint of sadness, but pragmatically, as if talking about someone else.

"So you're like me," Lizzie said with understanding. "We're parentless."

Max smiled at her. "I suppose we are," he agreed. "Although you know that you still have your father out there somewhere."

Their conversation was abruptly interrupted by someone calling to them and they turned to see Elrus, closely followed by Eloise, walking through the archway into the garden.

"So there you are," boomed Elrus, shattering the peace completely. He was carrying a big platter of what appeared to be a selection of snacks. Lizzie grinned at her friends. She now knew that with their friendship, she could face whatever the future had in store for her.

Eloise came and sat down next to Lizzie, scooching her along so she could squeeze onto the bench. Eloise looked at Lizzie closely, a worried frown on her pretty face.

"Are you okay now, Lizzie?" she asked, placing her warm hand over Lizzie's own.

"Yes thank you, Eloise," she said, giving her friend a hug. "I had a bit of a wobble I'm afraid."

"Well that was pretty evident," said Elrus, plonking himself down on the grass in front of them. "I brought you some grub as you didn't seem to get to eat much in there," he added, offering her and Max the platter. The pair took a sandwich each and, while Max ate his hungrily, Lizzie took a tentative bite as her stomach still wasn't totally recovered.

"So come on then, what was all that about?" asked Elrus, looking at Lizzie as if she had been behaving daft.

Lizzie explained the reason for her panic attack and said that she now felt much better.

"So, did we miss anything interesting during our absence?" she asked Elrus and Eloise.

172

"Nah," said Elrus, through a mouthful of ham sandwich. Did the boy ever stop eating, Lizzie wondered. "It was all pretty boring really. Well, once the commotion you caused had settled down it was," he continued.

"I couldn't hear much of what was being said because of this one here going on about stupid football," said Eloise, giving Elrus a feigned look of annoyance.

The little group laughed and Elrus reminded Max that they'd agreed to have a game whilst they were there.

"Well, I don't think we're really dressed for a game of football, do you?" Max said, indicating their white robes and silver sandals. Elrus nodded and said that he had a point.

The friends chatted and laughed together, munching their way through the sandwiches and cakes on the platter until all that was left were just a few crumbs.

As Elrus told them about one of his exploits, when a few months earlier he had tried helping to catch one of the villager's pigs that had escaped from its sty and run riot through the village, Elwood entered the garden. He watched the four friends for a short while from a distance, laughing along at Elrus's description of himself hanging onto the pig and being dragged through the mud by the village pond. Eventually and reluctantly, he interrupted them.

"Ma'am, I am sorry to spoil your fun but the hour is now late and we must leave early in the morning. I think that it is time for you and your friends to go to bed," Elwood said.

The four friends got to their feet and followed the little elf back towards the inner part of citadel and to their bedrooms.

They said good night to each other in the hallway outside their bedroom doors before entering their spartan rooms. Slipping out of her robe, Lizzie put on a nightdress that had been laid out on the bed ready for her. She smiled as she heard Eloise cleaning her teeth in the bathroom and humming a tune as she did so. Lizzie felt exhausted. Eloise came into the room and wriggled into the comfort of her bed sighing in contentment.

Having completed her own ablutions, Lizzie too climbed into bed and pulled the sheets up to her chin. Cocooned safely within the bed's linen embrace, she felt secure. Nothing could touch her here and she wished that it would always be so. She turned to say good night to her friend but Eloise's soft steady breath told Lizzie that she had already drifted off into dreamland. At least she doesn't snore, Lizzie thought briefly.

From her bed closest to the window, Lizzie turned her face to gaze out at the silvery disk of the full moon. As it sent its lunar rays across the bed's counterpane, her thoughts were full of what the future could possibly hold in store for her before tiredness finally swept over her and she drifted off to sleep.

Several hundred miles away to the North, a less innocent face was doing likewise.

# CHAPTER 19

## In the Stars

Eldorth stared up at the moon from the window of his bed chamber. Its luminosity cast shadows across his cruelly handsome features, making his high chiselled cheekbones stand out white, whilst his hard grey eyes glinted from their deep set sockets and his thin lipped mouth worked as he ground his teeth together. He turned away from the window and paced across his room, his dark blue silken robe billowing out behind him as he walked. He was unable to sleep.

Once again, he churned over in his mind the fact that he should never have let Melisha out of his sight. What was the witch up to? He should have had a report of her whereabouts by now. What were those two spy imps playing at?

He ran his hand through his thick black hair, pushing it away from his forehead as he sat down in a large chair facing the window. An old myth said that the full moon led men to lunacy; he wasn't sure about that but he was pretty mad at himself for not keeping a tighter rein on Melisha. She could be up to anything out there alone and unrestrained by his controlling hand. He needed to be in control and at the moment, he wasn't sure that he was.

Earlier in the day, Eldorth had gone down to the witch's rooms. He wanted to search for any clues as to what Melisha might have planned on the trip she was making. He didn't trust that she had told him the whole truth when she had said that she was just travelling to Elcaledonia to the Great Library of Eldinburgh for spell books. He was sure she was up to something else but what, and to what purpose, he didn't know.

When he had tried to enter her rooms, he found that she had placed a repelling charm on the door. He called upon spells that he had learnt from her to break the charm but the door held fast. Finally, frustrated at being thwarted in his attempts to gain entry, he had called upon the services of his henchman, the ogre, Orfwit. The great lumbering idiot had tried to barge the door down but the spell had, as its name suggested, resisted his efforts as, time and again, Orfwit bounced off the door and was propelled across the hallway and sent crashing into the wall opposite. Dazed and confused, the stupid ogre had been worse than useless and Eldorth stopped him before he damaged the castle wall. The strength of the spell cast by Melisha to secure her rooms gave Eldorth even more reason to believe that she was hiding something, and he was determined to discover what it was.

Eldorth closed his eyes. He was tired and needed rest but sleep eluded him as it did most nights; too much was on his mind and sleeplessness was his punishment. His thoughts drifted back to the time he had met and begun his collusion with Melisha.

*

*The land beyond the grounds of Elvedom Castle stretched away down into a deep hollow where a stone hut stood, built into the side of a hill. Its peat and grass covered roof blended in perfect camouflage with its surrounding environs and only the tell-tale plume of smoke gave away its location.*

*The young elf sat at the top of the knoll and, from his hiding place behind a large boulder, peered upon a slovenly looking woman. She was digging at a patch of earth that was planted with rows of vegetables and herbs. He had heard rumours at court that the witch, Melisha, had returned from her travels and was now living somewhere nearby, but that the King's men had not yet located her. Eldorth was pleased with himself as he had done what the King's men had not. This was the third day he had come here to watch the witch and had decided that she was pretty boring, as all she seemed to do was potter around her little plot of land and not much else. How threatening could she be? Why, she hadn't even spotted him spying on her!*

*"Ere again, boy?" the witch's coarse tones assaulted Eldorth's ears. He fell behind the boulder in his attempt to remain hidden. He'd obviously misjudged her.*

*"What? D'ya fink I didn't know you were there?" Melisha called. "I ain't stupid; I knows when someone's watchin' me."*

*Eldorth remained hidden, now sitting behind the rock with his back leaning against its cold surface. He could hear the witch shuffling around down in her garden, when suddenly a shadow fell across his legs that were stretched out in front of him. He looked up and into the face of Melisha.*

*Her bloated, ugly face with its slobbery mouth and bulbous nose repelled him and he nearly fell over sideways in surprise. Her thinning hair was plastered to her head, no doubt caused by the exertion of digging her plot of ground. Eldorth took in her dishevelled clothes and was struck by the thought that they, and, judging by the unpleasant stench emanating from her, she herself, could do with a good wash.*

*"What ya doin' spying on me?" she spat at him.*

*Eldorth's arrogance rose up in him and he said haughtily, "I wasn't spying, I was observing." He got gracefully to his feet and, even at his mere 16 years, he towered over the witch; it gave him an immediate sense of power.*

*Melisha was struck by the handsome youth standing in front of her. With his shock of black hair, his piercing grey eyes and his gangling but already athletic frame, she could sense something special about him. She beamed a brown, chipped toothed grin at him.*

*"And what did you observe?" she asked, placing particular emphasis on the last word of the question.*

*Eldorth raised his chin so that he seemed to peer down his aquiline nose at her, "That you live a very boring existence."*

*Melisha let out a loud cackling laugh. "Well, youngster, one of the first fings you should learn is never judge a book by its cover," she said, giving him an exaggerated wink. Eldorth recoiled at the overly familiar gesture; Melisha appeared not to notice as she turned and beckoned the boy to follow her.*

*"Come on, you might as well 'ave a drop o' drink while you're 'ere. I suppose you'll need refreshment before ya make ya way back to the castle," she said, as she shuffled down the side of the knoll towards her hut.*

*"How do you know I'm from the castle?" Eldorth called to her in surprise.*

*"There's not much goes on that I don't know about," Melisha replied, not bothering to turn to look at him.*

*Eldorth watched her shambolic progress for a short while before following on behind. He saw her disappear into the recesses of her hut and, with just a slight hesitation, he entered through the low doorway. The outward appearance of the hut was deceptive, as the interior of the witch's abode was more extensive than expected. As Eldorth's eyes adjusted to the change in light levels, he could see that the hut was cavernous. It appeared to stretch away under the hill into which it was built.*

*A brazier burned brightly in the middle of the hut, above which was a gap in the roof through which the smoke from the brazier's fire escaped. Above the heat hung a cauldron, and a sickly yellow vapour lingered around its brim. There was a putrid smell in the hut and Eldorth deduced that the cauldron's contents were probably something to do with it. He wrinkled his nose in disgust.*

*Melisha was standing over to one side of the hut, rifling through the contents of an old wooden cupboard; she turned to face Eldorth, holding two chipped mugs and a bottle containing a pale green liquid. Eldorth eyed the bottle suspiciously. Melisha, noticing the look on the boy's face, held up the bottle and smiled her slobbery grin.*

*"It's just a bottle of me own homemade pea-pod cordial. You'll love it," she said, reassuringly.*

*Eldorth doubted that very much, but his curiosity about the witch was too great to pass up an opportunity of finding out more about her, so he joined her at the table on which she had just placed the mugs and bottle of cordial.*

*As he sat down, he asked, "How come I could find you but the King's men, who've been searching for weeks, haven't?"*

*"Coz I don't want 'em to," she said simply. Eldorth looked quizzically at her. "I've got a concealment charm on the place so that only those I wants to find me can do so," she explained.*

*Eldorth sat on the wooden bench at the side of the table and watched as Melisha poured the pea-pod juice into the mugs. She passed one to the boy.*

*"So, let's drink to a productive partnership, shall we?" she announced, raising her mug in salute. Eldorth looked at her bemused.*

*"Partnership?" he queried.*

*"But of course," Melisha said. "I've been expecting you."*

*Eldorth could not disguise his surprise at this pronouncement. "Expecting me?"*

*"Oh yes," she said. "Our futures are very much entwined. It's in the stars, see?"*

*No, Eldorth did not see. "In the stars?" he asked.*

*Melisha looked at the boy as if he was suddenly a bit on the simple side. She put down her mug, got up from the table and walked towards the back of the hut where there was a trestle table, littered with scrolls of parchment and other detritus. Deciding upon one of the scrolls, she picked it up*

179

*and unrolled it as she made her way back to Eldorth. Laying the document on the table before him, she placed her mug on one corner and the bottle of cordial on another to stop the scroll from springing back into a roll.*

*As Eldorth looked at the parchment before him, it made no sense to him as it just appeared to be a series of stars and planets, under which were scribbles of some hieroglyphs that he didn't recognise.*

*Melisha eyed the boy with pleasure. This was going to be so much fun. She had wanted an apprentice for years, but the right one just hadn't come along. So, okay he was obviously an elf and not a descendant of the magical Magi tribe, but no matter; he had the desire and traits that she could mould to her ways. The house of Elderen was going to suffer for the years of torment and misery that she had endured, and the great Marvin would get his comeuppance too.*

*Eldorth looked up from the scroll and into Melisha's face as she said, "Come back again tomorra' boy and your lessons in the arts of magic will commence."*

*Getting up from the table and walking to the door, he turned and looked at the witch as she shuffled to the back of her hut to replace the scroll, which was once again rolled and safely secured. He had found his true destiny in this hut and he could tell the witch thought she had the upper hand but she was in for a surprise, he smirked. He turned and strode off, back towards Elvedom Castle.*

\*

Eldorth opened his eyes slowly. The moon had moved across the sky and he could no longer see her silvery disk from his place in his chair. He raised himself from his seat as something from his memory pricked away at his conscience. There was something in that recollection that he knew was relevant to what Melisha was up to now, but what was it?

Eldorth found that he always thought more clearly when he paced, and so he decided that he would think better if walking through the passageways of his castle. He pulled his robe tighter and walked out of his chamber. The silence of the castle was just what he needed as he made his way down into the depths of his domain. Still, the memory eluded him until eventually he found himself in a corridor that led to the dungeons.

Eldorth didn't come to this place usually – he left the dirty work of torture and incarceration to his minions – but something had drawn him here and so he walked slowly past each of the cells, occasionally glancing into their emptiness.

Finally, he glanced into the last dungeon on his left where the moon was once again sending her eerie light into the recesses of the cell. Lying on a thin mattress on the floor of the cell, he could see the body of a small, white haired girl. Her hair had fallen across her face but he could see her thin arms encircling her body as if she was hugging herself for comfort. He could see the dark bruises that marred the perfect whiteness of her skin and he felt a strange sensation that was unfamiliar to him. Was that a feeling of compassion? He suppressed it quickly – compassion led to weakness and he was not weak. He saw the girl stir and her hair fell back to reveal a swollen eye and grazes on her cheek. He recognised her as the elf who had been caught outside the castle walls.

He knew that Melisha had been working on the girl to get her to reveal what she had been doing outside the castle when she had known it was forbidden to go beyond the castle walls. The witch had not been successful; this either meant that the girl had been telling the truth – that she had been collecting herbs – or that she was indeed a Secret Keeper.

Eldorth remembered an old saying, "Keep your friends close and your enemies closer". Eldorth didn't have friends but if this girl was an enemy, then he needed to find out more about her. He decided that he would instruct the Dungeon Keeper to bring her to him in the morning.

As Eldorth turned to make his way back to his chambers, the thing that he'd been trying to recall from his memory suddenly struck him.

"Don't judge a book by its cover." That was what Melisha had said when they had met all those years ago. Whatever Melisha was up to had something to do with that saying. All he needed to do now was to find out what that something was.

# CHAPTER 20

## Into Elcambria

Lizzie must have eventually dropped off to sleep, as she was woken with a start by someone knocking on the door to her and Eloise's room. Upon Lizzie's mumble of, "Come in", a maiden, who had escorted them to their rooms the previous day, entered.

"Good morning, Your Highness, and to you also, Miss Eloise. I have come to tell you that it is seven of the hour and breakfast is at eight." The girls thanked her sleepily as the maiden, dipping in a brief curtsey, backed out of the room.

Lizzie threw back the covers and, swinging her legs out of the bed so that she was sitting facing Eloise still snuggled under the sheets, stretched and yawned.

"Good morning, Eloise," she said, to the mop of black curls spread across the brilliant white pillow of the bed opposite.

"Morning," came the muffled response.

"I'll use the bathroom first then, shall I?" Lizzie grinned, as the curls made a nodding motion.

Lizzie made her way to the bathroom but, before she reached it, she stopped at the bedroom window and looked out. The sun beat down on the courtyard below and she could see soldiers and servants already going about their business. She would be sad to leave this place, as she knew that by staying here she would be safe and secure. She then thought, "But for how long?" Lizzie knew that her destiny lay elsewhere for the time being but she hoped that one day she might return to Elavalon for longer.

When the two girls had finished dressing, they made their way down to the dining hall where Lizzie had briefly spent some time the previous evening. Most of the rest of their party were already there and the girls could see Elrus and Max tucking into the simple breakfast of cooked ham, eggs, delicious fresh baked breads and preserves.

Mrs Longton was in animated discussion with Elwood, but they stopped upon spotting Lizzie and Eloise and Elwood jumped to his feet; something he did whenever Lizzie first entered a room, should he be caught sitting down at the time.

"Good morning, darling," Mrs Longton said brightly, as Lizzie ran over to her grandmother and hugged her tightly. The older woman kissed her granddaughter lightly on the cheek as she hugged her back.

"Did you sleep well?" Mrs Longton aimed the question at both girls.

"Yes thank you," answered Eloise, eyeing the breakfast fare hungrily; then remembering her manners, returned the question.

"Like a baby," smiled Mrs Longton, although the dark bags under her eyes told a different story.

She had had a restless night worrying about what she and Lizzie had got themselves into and had seriously considered demanding that they be returned to Longton Hall and pretend that the past few months had never happened. She had talked to Elwood and Elenya at length the previous night about Lizzie's future and the argument against taking such action was strongly put by the two elves.

Elenya had calmly but forcefully stressed that it wasn't only the world of Elvedom and its peoples that were at risk, if Eldorth was not defeated in his attempt to overthrow the House of Elderen; all the worlds surrounding Earth would be in peril.

"Like it or not, Mrs Longton, as heir to the throne of Elvedom, Elizabeth is key in this battle of good over evil," Elenya had said.

"But what can a child, who isn't even a full elf, do against such a person as this Eldorth?" pleaded Mrs Longton.

"That I do not know for sure," Elenya said, resignedly, "But if my father and Marvin say that her involvement is imperative, then that is good enough for me. Of one thing I can be sure; my father would not put his grandchild at risk if it were not so. He lost his beloved daughter and he would not want to lose her child."

Mrs Longton watched Lizzie as she joined her three friends further along the table, and smiled at seeing her laughing happily at something Elrus had just said. It was a sight that she had thought she would never witness back in Chislewick, but was it too high a price to pay to see it here? She sighed deeply at the thought and took a sip of her green tea.

Lizzie, meanwhile, was biting into a soft bread roll spread liberally with strawberry jam and nodding at Elrus, who was saying that he'd heard Prince Finnion telling Filip and Fidora that it was going to be a long ride that day.

"From what I heard, I think they're hoping to reach the Mountains of Snow by nightfall," Elrus said.

"I've never seen snow. Are the mountains really covered in it?" asked Eloise, her eyes showing her excitement at the thought.

Max shook his head. "They are in winter, but not at this time of year. Although," he said thoughtfully, "the tops might be."

"Oh," Eloise said disappointedly.

Finally finishing their breakfast, the children left the dining hall and joined the other Companions, who had gathered in the courtyard to say goodbye to their Elavalon hosts.

Eladrian was talking to Elenya, who was standing by her stallion holding the magnificent beast's harness and stroking its pure white neck.

"Thank you, uncle, for your hospitality this past night," Elenya said.

"You and your companions are most welcome, niece. It is a shame that the circumstances do not permit you to stay a while longer," Eladrian replied.

Elenya then spotted Lizzie and her friends and called them to come and join her. Eladrian, resplendent in his white robe and silver belt with its symbolic key, turned at their approach. The other companions followed the children until they had joined Elenya.

Eladrian then spoke to Lizzie. "I am sorry I was unable to join you for breakfast this morning, Elizabeth, but I had pressing business to attend to," he said, bowing his head to her.

"Oh, that's okay, uncle," she said, the term of address was still strange to her ears. She realised as she said the words that she had not seen either Eladrian or Elenya at the breakfast table, and thinking about it further, Prince Finnion had been missing too.

"I trust you had enough rest to enable you cope with the long day's ride ahead," Eladrian said. "This is a trying journey for ones so young."

"Oh, we're fine, sir. We've loads of energy to keep us going," chipped in Elrus.

Eladrian smiled at the young elf. "I'm sure you have, Master Elrus," he nodded sagely.

Mrs Longton, who was standing behind her granddaughter, with a hand resting gently on Lizzie's shoulder, relayed her own thanks for the hospitality shown to them.

"I hope we may meet again, when all this business of relics and the like are done and dusted," she said to Eladrian.

He looked at her as if a little uncertain of her exact meaning but he had certainly gathered the gist of her words.

"I look forward to it Mrs Longton," he smiled.

There was a commotion as a phalanx of soldiers came marching into the courtyard. Their white and silver uniforms gleamed in the bright morning sunlight. The soldiers then formed themselves into two rows. Each row faced the other, creating a pathway that led towards the great arch through which the travellers would pass back into the world beyond the citadel's sacred walls.

The Companions, together with enough supplies for the remainder of their journey, prepared to leave. After the final goodbyes and the embraces of Elenya, Lizzie and Eladrian, the riders mounted their horses.

As if as one, the soldiers drew their swords. Then, holding the weapons with the blades flattened against their faces by way of salute, they formed a guard of honour. The little group, led by Elenya and Prince Finnion, passed by the soldiers silently and then, with a final wave of farewell, rode out onto the plain that stretched away towards Elcambria.

The heat of the morning sun beat down on the group as they rode across the open plain. There was no shelter from its relentless rays to be seen in any direction. Mrs Longton peered out from under her wide brimmed hat and looked up into the blue expanse of sky; if any of those horrid flying creatures appeared now there'd be nowhere to hide, she thought.

For most of the journey, the riders had ridden either in single file or two abreast, but in the vast plain surrounding them, they rode side by side. Some travelled in silence, lost in their own thoughts; others, such as the twins Elwood and Elwind, chatted away cheerily. The four young friends, however, played guessing games to while away the time. Lizzie tried to teach the others I-Spy, but given that there wasn't much to spy upon, other than grass, sky and the occasional cloud, they soon ran out of ideas. They then turned to teaching each other songs and Lizzie went through her repertoire of nursery rhymes but got fed up with Elrus insisting on analysing the meaning of each one.

The final straw came when he asked, "But why wouldn't Jack Sprat eat fat?"

The morning passed quickly into afternoon and the landscape gradually changed from the wide open plain to more rugged and hilly terrain. The way became increasingly difficult to navigate and the conversation and singing faded as they guided their horses over the more challenging ground. Filip and Fidora had resumed their roles as scouts and had ridden ahead to see what the land held in store.

After they had travelled some miles, they could hear the pummel of hooves as Filip came riding back into view. Elenya held up a hand for the group to stop and wait for Filip to relay his findings. Reining his mount to a stop, the fairy told Elenya and Prince Finnion that the great river, Elsevern, that divided the lands and barred their way into Elcambria, lay about a mile ahead of them.

"Is the way clear for us to cross?" asked Prince Finnion.

"Fidora is riding along to the Bridge of Elsevern to ensure our passage is not hindered, Sire," Filip replied. "Its great structure can be seen off to the west of here."

Prince Finnion thanked the fairy and said that he should return to Fidora and wait for them by the bridge. Filip bowed his head in reply, turned his horse and sped off once more. Elenya then turned towards the little party waiting patiently for instructions.

"We are to travel a few miles west of here to reach the Bridge of Elsevern. Filip and Fidora will wait for us there. I must warn you that the Bridge may be guarded by the Elcambrians and that they may challenge our crossing. You must be prepared. Just follow my lead and do as I say and all should be well," Elenya announced.

"Challenged? In what way?" asked Mrs Longton nervously. "Will we be in danger?"

"I hope not," Elenya replied. "We come as a travelling party and not a warring one. The Elcambrians have been allies of ours for years, but there are some who do not like what they perceive to be the undue influence of the elves of Elvedom upon their country."

"Well, that's reassuring – not," Elrus said sardonically to Max, sitting on his horse next to him. Max looked at his friend with worried eyes and nodded.

Elenya swung her horse about and began trotting off in the direction that Filip had just taken, and the party followed suit. The ground beneath them soon began the descent down towards the valley of the river and, above the noise of the horses' hooves on the stony surface, they could hear the sound of the river's rushing waters.

When they reached the valley floor, the breadth of the great river stretched away ahead of them. The water bubbled and churned as it made its way over the rocks and boulders that littered the river's bed, and it was clear to see that it would be impossible to cross it by any other means than a bridge. Looking along the river bank towards the west, the group could see the large structure of the Bridge of Elsevern spanning the river's width. They then began making their way towards it.

As they reached the bridge, Filip and Fidora re-joined them.

"Well, what have you discovered? Is the Bridge guarded?" asked Elenya.

"As you can see, Princess, this side of the river is clear. We cannot discover any resistance anywhere but that is not to say that we will not meet any once we cross," replied Fidora.

Flaxon then stepped forward.

"May I recommend that we stay together as a group for now, Princess," he said, directing his suggestion to Elenya. "If we do meet with hostility, Filip and Fidora will be exposed to it without support. I think it would be better if you led the way across the bridge. The Elcambrians will not feel threatened if they think that a Princess of Elvedom is prepared to ride into their midst."

Elenya nodded her agreement.

"Flaxon is right. I will lead the party from here," she said. Then, turning to the faun, requested that he walk alongside her. "Finnion; you, Filip and Fidora should ride behind me. Lizzie; you and your friends must stay behind the fairies." She then turned to the rest of the group. "Mrs Longton, Elwood and Elwind protect the children from the rear and Willo, Gorin and Digby must ride behind the pack horses to calm them should they be spooked by anything that should occur." Finally, she directed the elven archers, Elbie and Elgin, to bring up the rear of the party. Duly organised, the little group set off across the bridge.

The wooden span of the bridge spread out ahead of them as they took their first steps on its vast framework. Lizzie's nerves jangled with every clop of Whisper's hooves beneath her. The anticipation of imminent attack was almost too much to bear. She looked at Max riding to her right and saw the fear etched on the young apprentice's face, as he stared straight ahead into the back of Fidora's multi-coloured wings. Lizzie then turned to her left and saw that Eloise was looking down into the mane of her horse as if afraid to look up. Beyond Eloise, she could see Elrus with his head held high as if daring any potential foe to mess with him; it made Lizzie smile. He was such a great friend to have around. Lizzie chose not to look behind her as she didn't want to see the worry that was sure to be fixed on her dear grandmother's face.

The sound of the river rushing past under them thundered in their ears as they crossed the bridge. They had just passed the half way point of the bridge when Lizzie heard a sharp intake of breath from behind her. She turned and saw her grandmother staring wide eyed ahead of her and pointing her finger towards the far end of the bridge. Lizzie followed her gaze and could see that the way was now hindered by a body of men gathered there. They were armed with what looked like an array of weapons, including spears and swords.

Lizzie's first impulse was to rein in Whisper and stop, but the steady trot of Elenya and the others ahead of her did not falter and so she continued in their wake. Every pair of eyes of the Companions was fixed on the troop at the end of the bridge. When the travellers were several yards away, Elenya held up her hand as a signal for them to stop. She then jumped down from her horse and she and Flaxon stepped forward. As they did so, two members of the band confronting them broke ranks and strode towards them; shields protected their bodies and they held spears in their hands.

"Cau!" shouted one of the men.

The word was strange to the ears of the travellers but the meaning was clear and Elenya and Flaxon stopped in their tracks.

Elenya spoke. "We mean no harm. We are just a group of travellers on our way to meet our kin in the Mountains of Snow."

Lizzie, peering from behind Prince Finnion, could now see, from the pointed ears that stuck out from their long wild hair, that the two men blocking their progress were elves. They were short and stocky of stature and their unkempt hair and scruffy beards added to their threatening image.

"Who are you? And what makes you think that you may travel our lands?" called one of the elves in a lilting accent.

"They're Welsh!" Lizzie heard her grandmother exclaim from behind her, as if speaking to herself. "Well, they sound Welsh," her grandmother added.

Elenya planted her legs in a stance of defiance and, raising her head, so that her regal countenance was unmistakable, declared that she would only discuss that with their leader.

191

The Elcambrian elves spoke in hushed tones to each other and glanced from Elenya and Flaxon, to the group of riders behind them. Then the spokesman announced, "That is what you will do then. You will follow me and my men and there will be no funny business. Your archers and those carrying other weapons will be disarmed before we will allow you through."

"I can only allow that if you guarantee us safe passage to your leader," Elenya stated emphatically.

"You have my word, on the life of our great prince, Elowen ap Elowen, that you will come to no harm whilst you are within our company," the elf said, his melodic tones ringing out loud and clear. He then turned to the band of elves behind him and shouted instructions for them to gather the weapons of those on the bridge.

Elenya, meanwhile, returned to her horse and told the group to hand over their weapons without any fuss.

"Are you sure this is wise, Your Highness?" asked Prince Finnion, removing his sword from its scabbard.

"We need these elves on our side, Finnion, and this is a sure way of demonstrating that we are not their enemies," Elenya said simply.

Lizzie watched as the members of the Companions relinquished their weapons and almost giggled nervously at the reluctant Digby giving up his axe, as he glared at the elf taking it from him. If looks could kill, thought Lizzie, that elf would be floating off down the river by now.

With the Elcambrian elves now surrounding them, the party made their way across the remainder of the bridge and into Elcambria.

As they stepped onto Elcambrian soil, more elves appeared from under the bridge, bringing sturdy brown ponies with them. The Companions' captors quickly mounted their ponies and the whole group headed off into the hills beyond the river's edge.

After several miles, the party entered a valley, through which ran a tributary of the great river they had crossed earlier. On a motte by the side of the water, they could see a grey stone castle dominating the surrounding countryside. Its rugged walls looked heavily fortified and a flag was fluttering on a mast towering above one of its turrets. As they drew closer, Lizzie could see that the flag held an image of a red dragon upon a white and green background.

The bustling activity of a busy garrison confronted them as they rode into the castle's main stronghold. There seemed to be market stalls around the central yard's edges and the business of the day seemed in full swing as the group passed by. Some of the castle's inhabitants stopped what they were doing to watch the visitors' arrival. Upon reaching the castle's Keep, the Companions were instructed to dismount. Then, surrounded by their captors, the travellers were marched into a great hall.

At the far end of the hall was a dais, upon which was a huge wooden throne. Seated on the throne and leaning back, with one leg thrown casually over one of the throne's arms, was a tousle haired person. A crimson cloud of curls topped by a gold circlet encrusted with emerald, surrounded a pretty but sharp featured face that was in the process of knocking back the contents of a large pewter goblet.

Two of the elves leading the small party into the hall suddenly stopped and used their spears as a barrier to signal that the visitors stop. Then, the elf who had challenged Lizzie and her party at the bridge strode towards the dais. He stopped, bowed, and then said a few brief words to the throne's occupant who must have made some response, unheard by the waiting visitors, as he beckoned them to come forward.

The woman occupying the throne turned towards the visitors and languidly looked them up and down as, with the back of her hand, she wiped the residue of the liquid she had been drinking from her moist lips.

"And to what do we owe this honour?" she said indolently, putting down the goblet and rising slowly to her feet. She placed her hands on her slim hips. It was obvious from her regal bearing and the gold circlet she wore that she was an elf of some importance. Then, as if suddenly amused by something a broad smile, displaying perfect white teeth, spread across her striking features. Her bright green eyes sparkled as she said, "Why, if it isn't the great Princess Elenya herself!"

# CHAPTER 21

## There be Unicorns?

"Elgawen?" Elenya peered at the elf standing before her as if she wasn't seeing her clearly. Then, to the shock of almost everyone in the hall, she screamed, "Elgawen!"

The two elves ran towards each other and hugged one another tightly, dancing around in circles and laughing and screeching like a pair of teenagers. The rest of the hall's occupants stood and stared at the two in bemusement; their behaviour was not what was expected of two high ranking elves. The Elcambrian elves looked at each other with raised eyebrows and shrugged in confusion.

"Oh my giddy gods; what are you doing here?" squealed Elgawen.

"It's a long story," said Elenya, her face suddenly serious. "Oh, Elgawen, it's wonderful to see you." She hugged Elgawen again.

Lizzie grinned with pleasure at her aunt's excitement at meeting this very obvious good friend; it seemed that they hadn't seen each other for some considerable time, given their exuberant exchange.

Then, as if she had suddenly remembered that there were others in the hall with them, Elgawen looked over to where Elenya's travelling companions stood watching them.

"So, who do we have here?" Elgawen asked, as she took in the various members of the little group.

Elenya proceeded to introduce each of them in turn, leaving Lizzie until last.

"Lizzie, this is my very good friend and partner in crime, Princess Elgawen of Elcambria." Then, holding her niece by the shoulders in front of her, she said proudly, "And this is my niece, Elizabeth, or as she likes to be known to her friends, Lizzie."

Elgawen stared hard at Lizzie and Lizzie felt as if Elgawen's bright green eyes were boring into her very soul, so intense was her gaze. Then, to Lizzie's surprise, the woman's eyes seemed to mist over as if she were remembering something really sad, but as she blinked the mist away, a friendly smile spread across her face.

"Eletheria's daughter," she stated, as if coming to some kind of conclusion. Then, sticking out a hand in greeting, said, "Welcome, Lizzie, it is good to meet you." As Lizzie took Elgawen's hand with the intention of shaking it, she was suddenly drawn into a tight hug that nearly squeezed the breath out of her. With her face almost buried in the elf's torso, Lizzie was fascinated to see the intricate detail of a tattoo that encircled Elgawen's upper arm. It was similar to Celtic designs Lizzie recalled having seen before in the human world.

Releasing Lizzie as abruptly as she had embraced her, Elgawen welcomed the group to Elcambria and invited them to break bread with her and her people. She then yelled at some servants to bring food and ale for her guests as she invited the group through to her inner chamber where they could rest and refresh themselves.

"We can talk more openly in my chambers than we can here. Loose talk costs lives," she whispered to Elenya. Then, turning to her followers who had brought the Companions into her presence, she beckoned the two leaders of the group and waved the rest away with a dismissive hand.

In Elgawen's inner chamber, there was a long, rough wooden table with enough chairs around it for all the Companions to sit upon. As they seated themselves, the servants reappeared, carrying jugs of ale and wine for them to drink, and bread, cheeses and cooked meats to eat.

As the group tucked into the fare on offer, Elenya expressed their thanks. "We are grateful for your kind offer of rest and refreshment, Elgawen, but sadly we cannot stay long," Elenya apologised. "We must reach the Mountains of Snow by nightfall."

Elgawen peered suspiciously at her friend. "And why would you be venturing into the Mountains?" she asked. "There are hidden dangers that lurk in the deepest recesses of them. You must travel with the greatest care, Elenya." Elgawen leant forwards as if to emphasise the point.

Lizzie, sitting close by listening to the exchange, shuddered as a frisson of fear passed through her. As if sensing the shudder, Elgawen turned her green gaze upon her. Then, speaking to Elenya but not taking her eyes from Lizzie, she said, "So the stories that Elethria had a child were true then? There is certainly no mistaking her; she is her mother's image."

Elenya smiled lovingly at Lizzie. "Yes, the stories were true."

"But where's she been until now? The whereabouts of Elethria was never made clear; all we were told was that she had died," Elgawen pursued her intense scrutiny of Lizzie; it made the girl squirm.

"She has been kept safe a world away from here but she is here now and King Elfred wants her to see as much of Elvedom as will allow," Elenya said. The tone of her voice made it clear that the subject was closed, and so Elgawen turned her gaze towards her friend instead.

The topic of conversation then changed to catching up with what had been happening over the period of time since they had last met. Lizzie soon discovered that she had been right about the intervening time having been quite considerable.

Lizzie enjoyed listening to their reminiscences but wanted to know more about the times they had spent together that might shed light on her own mother's part in their history. Finally, she could bear it no longer and plucked up the courage to interrupt their conversation.

As Elgawen finally seemed to draw breath, Lizzie asked, "Did you know my mother well?"

Elgawen seemed surprised by the question but her face softened as she nodded and said, "Indeed I did. As children, the three of us – your mother, your aunt and me – spent a number of summers together. Your mother was a calming influence on your aunt and me when we got ourselves into a number of scrapes."

Elenya laughed. "Oh my, do you remember that time when we crept up on the Unicorn mother with her foal and I wanted to capture the foal to train it for riding. What a shock we got when the father Unicorn came charging at us from out of those woods. If it hadn't been for Elethria putting herself between us and calming the creature, the father would have flattened us." Elgawen joined in the laughter and said that the look on Elenya's face at the time had been classic.

Lizzie listened in open mouthed awe. She wasn't sure if she was more shocked at hearing of the daring thing her mother had done or the fact that there were unicorns.

"Unicorns? There are unicorns?" she almost whispered the words.

The two princesses turned and looked at her; a puzzled frown crossed Elgawen's face. "You sound surprised, Lizzie." Elgawen flicked a questioning glance at Elenya as if to ask why the girl was questioning the existence of unicorns.

"There aren't many unicorns where Lizzie's been living; are there Lizzie?" Elenya said quickly, shooting Lizzie a look to be careful. The secret of where Lizzie had been kept for the first eleven years of her life was only known by very few people. Although Elgawen was a good and old friend, she had not been amongst those who were privy to the secret of where Elethria had gone and what had happened to her child.

"Um, no there aren't," Lizzie replied, trying to look casual about it whilst her brain whirred with the excitement of knowing that the magical creatures really did exist in this world. It was something that she hadn't thought about but, thinking about it now, she decided that she was absolutely going to ask her aunt about seeking out the creatures.

The meal over, Elenya said that they really should be on their way.

Elgawen stood up and accompanied her friend as she and her party prepared to leave.

"Well, your horses should be well rested by now, so they will be ready for your onward journey," she said.

As they left the inner Keep and went out into the bustling courtyard, it could be seen that the horses were ready and waiting for the Companions' departure. As Lizzie looked for her own little horse, Whisper, she could see there was a large raven coloured mount that she hadn't seen before. There were also two of the sturdy brown ponies that had been ridden by the Elcambrian elves who had accompanied them earlier that day, tethered alongside Whisper and the other horses.

Elrus, standing behind Lizzie, whispered in her ear, "I think we may be having some company on the next leg of the trip." She whispered back that she thought he might be right.

Spotting the additional horses herself, Elenya turned a questioning face to her friend. Elgawen shrugged. "Well, you didn't think I'd let you travel through our lands unprotected did you?" she said.

"That's not necessary, Elgawen. We have protection enough. This does not need to involve you and your people," Elenya insisted.

"As soon as you crossed the Bridge of Elsevern, it involved my people," Elgawen said. She placed a hand on Elenya's arm. "Look, I know you can't tell me what you're up to but nobody knows these lands better than my men and me. I have a strong suspicion that I know who you may be planning to meet with in the mountains, and I'm sure that my people and I can get you there quicker than if you were left to your own devices."

Before Elenya could refuse the offer of help, Elgawen held up a hand to stop her. "You can say what you want but it won't change anything. My men and I will guide you to the Mountains of Snow at least. What happens from there will be in the lap of the gods."

Elenya grinned and shook her head. "Is there any point in arguing with you?" she asked.

Elgawen shook her head. "What do you think?" she laughed.

Elenya accepted that to argue with her friend would achieve nothing and so announced to the Companions that they would be joined on their journey by Elgawen and two of her followers. Elenya turned once again to Elgawen.

"Well, if you insist that you and your men are to travel with us, I think it would be helpful if you perhaps introduced them," she suggested.

Elgawen grinned and called to the two elves who had led the group that guarded the Bridge of Elsevern. She introduced the leader as Eleuen and his second in command as Elaled. The elves bowed low to Elenya and then to Lizzie and the rest of the Companions. Eleuen said it would be an honour to guide them on their journey.

"Well, we'd best be on our way if we are to make the mountains before dark," announced Elgawen. "There is an encampment at the base we can spend the night in, as it would be unwise to try to navigate the mountain paths in the dark."

Elgawen then turned and spoke to Flaxon. "We will need to pick up the pace as there are still many miles to go before we reach the mountains. I understand that you have travelled by foot up until now but, as it will be tiring for you to keep up with us, I have taken the liberty of arranging a mount for you."

Flaxon began to protest and said he did not wish to ride and would prefer to continue on foot, but Elgawen was determined and waved away his protest and said she must insist. Before Flaxon could say anything more, a short, brown, shaggy haired pony was led over to him. Peering from under the fringe of hair almost hiding its soft brown eyes, the pony eyed the faun warily. Flaxon introduced himself to the animal and the pony whinnied in response. Much to Lizzie's surprise, Flaxon responded by saying, "Nice to meet you, Patience. I hope that your nature lives up to your name as you are going to need to be very patient with me; this is my first experience of riding." The pony whinnied again, nodding its head up and down as it did so, while the group watching the pair laughed at the exchange.

Without further ceremony, the travellers quickly mounted their horses and, with an awkward looking Flaxon bumping along in his saddle, made their way out of the confines of Elgawen's castle.

The two Elcambrian elves, along with Fidora and Filip, scouted ahead of the party, as the remainder of the group were led by the two princesses, Elenya and Elgawen, and Prince Finnion. The pace of the journey did indeed speed up as the riders cantered onwards. Lizzie was pleased to see that Flaxon gradually appeared to adapt to the rhythm of his pony's gait and began to seem more at one with the animal.

They travelled through some of the most stunning landscapes that Lizzie had yet witnessed during her time in Elvedom. The Elcambrian countryside was green and lush in the valleys and ruggedly beautiful as they made their way through rock strewn gullies.

The journey passed peacefully enough until finally, in the distance, they saw the imposing outline of the Mountains of Snow. The sun was now lower in the sky as it cast its golden rays on the snow capped tips of the great massifs. It was a wonderful view and Lizzie smiled at the thought that they would soon be at their destination, and finally discover the reason why they were travelling there.

Suddenly, a cloud of dust indicated that riders were approaching and they could see the four scouts who had gone ahead, riding towards them at full tilt. Bringing their mounts to a clattering halt in front of the group, Filip spoke on the scouting party's behalf.

"We bring bad news. We will not be able to rest the night at the encampment. It has been vandalised. Some of the cabins have been burned to the ground and others smashed and broken," Filip recounted.

"Some of the burnt embers of the huts are still smouldering, and so we are not sure whether or not the perpetrators of this attack are still in the vicinity, Highness," Eleuen added, directing his report to Elgawen.

Elenya and Prince Finnion looked at each other and an unspoken agreement seemed to pass between them. Finnion then said, "We will proceed with caution to the encampment. From what you have said, Elgawen, it is sited at the approach to the mountains and so this is the direction we must take." Then, standing up in his stirrups, he spoke to the rest of the party.

"You must all stay vigilant and keep close together. We do not know if these renegade creatures, whatever they are, are still about but there is strength in unity and so we must remember that."

There was a rumble of agreement amongst the little group and Lizzie heard her grandmother's voice as she said, "Oh dear, what are we going into now?"

Lizzie made her way back to her side; the older woman had been riding towards the back of the group in the company of Elwood towing one of the pack horses. She tried to reassure her grandmother.

"I'm sure we'll be okay, gran," she said softly, reaching across to place a comforting hand on her grandmother's arm.

Mrs Longton patted Lizzie's hand gently and said she certainly hoped so.

The group quickly formed themselves into a tight knit unit and they made their way slowly towards the site of the encampment, watching out for any sign of potential attack as they went. As they approached the site, the pungent smell of burning and burnt wood was very evident. It was now dusk and the light was fading fast. As the riders entered the encampment, Elenya's stallion suddenly reared up, taking her by surprise, but she was an experienced horse-woman and quickly settled the horse with strong handling and soothing words. The incident seemed to unsettle the rest of the horses and, as the riders did their best to keep them in check, a shout from Elenya brought everyone's attention to her.

"This is not a good sign. Prepare yourselves for –" but before Elenya could say more, a howl came from up above them. From behind a rocky escarpment that overlooked the camp, a number of bodies, wielding various weapons, came charging down at the group of travellers. Lizzie felt herself being dragged from her horse, and looked around to see that Elrus had got hold of her arm and was pulling her down behind Whisper and his own horse so that the horses were shielding them. Mrs Longton, Max and Eloise quickly joined Lizzie and Elrus as their horses too formed a ring around them, protecting them all from the skirmish that was taking place outside of their living barrier.

Lizzie looked up and saw a volley of arrows flying past overhead. With the horses' reins tightly held in each of their riders' hands, Lizzie and her companions crouched down by the animals' sides. Lizzie was surprised at how calm the creatures were, given their earlier skittishness, until she was sure she could hear the sound of pan-pipes; Flaxon, she thought.

"We should be helping," Lizzie hissed to the others.

"No!" cried Mrs Longton, terrified at the thought.

"Your grandmother's right. Leave the fighting to the experts," yelled Elrus, above the yells and cries of the ensuing fight. He then turned to Max. "Quick, mate, cast the protection spell," he yelled. Max looked confused for a moment and then, as if suddenly coming to his senses, drew his wand from his pocket and, stooping over the group huddled together, waved the wand in a circular motion above all of their heads, including his own. As he did so, he muttered strange words and Lizzie felt a sensation that resembled someone pulling a blanket over them. Even the sound of the fighting seemed as if it was coming from further away.

Outside of Lizzie and her protective cocoon, the fight was being fiercely fought. The attackers turned out to be a small band of renegade hobgoblins and they were proving tricky opponents. They were small and wily and, due to their size, were able to get under and between the legs of the larger horses. The peaceable Flaxon and Willo had removed themselves to a safe distance, as they had been travelling at the back of the party, close to Elbie and Elgin. Flaxon had jumped down from Patience and quickly clambered up the side of a cliff face opposite to the direction of the raiders' attack; his goat-like feet made short work of his climb. Overlooking the scene unfolding below, he began to play his pipes, preventing the frightened horses from taking flight.

Elenya and the others had quickly jumped down from their respective mounts to even up the height disadvantage. The small bandits realised too late that they had underestimated their target and were getting a sound beating. The Elcambrian elves were particularly ferocious combatants and the skirmish was over in a matter of minutes as several of the hobgoblins lay dead or wounded. A number of them managed to high-tail it away up into the mountains, carrying or dragging some of the wounded with them, and were followed by Elaled wailing like a banshee in their wake.

Eleuen was bending over one of the wounded creatures lying on the ground; a patch of dark red blood was seeping across the front of its leather jerkin. Elgawen strode over and looked down at the hobgoblin, disdain etched on her face.

"Where have you come from? And why did you destroy this camp?" she asked pitilessly. She was joined at her side by Elenya. The hobgoblin looked up at the two princesses and the look of hatred in his fading eyes shocked Elenya.

Then, with his last breath, the creature spat, "Down with the House of Elfred."

Elgawen turned away just as Elaled trudged back into the camp, grumbling that the little vermin were too quick for him and had disappeared up into the mountains. Elgawen said that they were unlikely to return that night and that they should start making camp. She instructed her two followers to get rid of the bodies of the fallen attackers and make prisoners of the wounded.

Elenya was still standing over the body of the hobgoblin who had shown his hatred of her and her father's house. As she shook her head sadly, she felt a hand on her shoulder and turned and looked into the face of Prince Finnion.

"Why, Finn?" she asked, using the familiar mode of address that she only used when they were alone. "What happened to make these hobgoblins feel such hatred of us? Hobgoblins used to be a peaceful race."

Prince Finnion looked at her sadly, "Propaganda, Elenya. Eldorth is no doubt using divisive messages to call the less intelligent beings to his cause. Hobgoblins have never been known for their quick wit."

Elenya turned away from the little body in front of her and walked back toward her horse, when a thought suddenly struck her. "Lizzie!"

The little ring of horses was still in place and Elenya ran towards them; as she did so, she was joined by Flaxon who had clambered down from his perch above them. Elwood and Elwind had already reached the group and Elwood was pulling at the reins of Whisper. As the little horse was gently eased away from the side of his mistress, Elenya, Flaxon and the twin elves could see the little group huddled together in the midst of the horse barricade. Max turned his head slowly towards the onlookers and smiled in relief. Then, with a wave of his wand, the protection spell dissipated and Lizzie, Elrus, Eloise and Mrs Longton seemed to come out of some kind of trance.

Elenya reached down, took Lizzie's hand and pulled her to her feet. Flaxon assisted Mrs Longton to her feet as she let out a huge sigh.

"Oh my giddy aunt; I'm getting too old for all of this," she said, looking around at the carnage and placing a hand over her mouth at the horror of it.

Elgawen and her men walked over and joined the little group and, as they did so, Elgawen said, "Well, it looks like we'll be sleeping under the stars tonight. It's just a good job it's not raining!"

Elwood quickly piped up, and said cheerily that he would use some of the glowing embers from the huts to get a fire going and make some drop scones and hot chocolate for supper. There was a general nodding of agreement that this was a good idea.

As Lizzie and her three friends led their horses over to an area on one side of the encampment, where a number of the other horses were already tethered, Lizzie turned to Elrus and asked, "Does it ever rain in Elvedom as it never has since I've been here? I mean, it's been so hot lately."

"Oh, it rains all right," he said, nodding knowingly. "And if it'll rain anywhere it's likely to be here, as the mountains seem to create their own weather."

"And looking up at those dark clouds forming above the peaks up there, Elgawen may have spoken too soon," added Max, as the rising moon disappeared behind a drifting cloud bank.

# CHAPTER 22

## Take the High Road

Melisha sat at the edge of the still pool, peering down at the reflection looking back at her. Yesterday's spell had worked even more effectively than she had believed it would. The magical waters of the pool had exceeded all expectations and she was delighted with the results. No one but no one would recognise her now. She had been sitting there gazing at her reflection for some considerable time, enjoying the new version of herself. Inside nothing had changed and the only give away of her true identity was when she spoke. This was all too evident when she finally tore herself away from the pool's side and turned towards Elpme, who was sitting next to his donkey staring at the beautiful stranger before him.

"You ready boy?" Melisha yelled; the coarseness of her speech was at odds with her image. Elpme jumped to his feet in a flash and looked around him in confusion, as if the voice had come from elsewhere.

Behind a bush at the edge of the glade, the two imps were hopping up and down in panic. They had woken earlier and after a brief squabble, with one blaming the other for not staying on watch when they had realised that Melisha had disappeared. What were they to do? Who was this beautiful woman and where had she come from? Eldorth would have them flayed alive if he knew that they had lost the witch. The only thing they didn't understand was why the elf, Elpme, and his donkey were still there. They were in the midst of arguing in low hissed insults when they heard Melisha's voice. They peered quickly around the side of the bush but Melisha was still nowhere to be seen. Perhaps the witch had gone on ahead through the woods on the other side of the clearing, they thought. They decided to follow the beautiful stranger and see if she led them back to the trail of Melisha.

In the meantime, they needed to collar a crow in order to get a missive to their master, telling him the route they were taking but making sure they omitted the bit about the missing Melisha.

On the other side of the clearing, Melisha was clambering up on the donkey to continue her journey to Eldinburgh. The bemused Elpme kept looking around to see if he could spot his mistress. He had definitely heard her shout at him, but he could only see this beautiful stranger sitting upon his donkey and so, with the Servitude Spell he was under still binding him to the witch, he was compelled follow this woman's orders.

The little group set off once more through the woods, with Elpme leading the donkey along a narrow winding pathway that cut through the woodland undergrowth. After a few miles, the density of the trees began to thin and they came out to a more open and rugged terrain. Eventually, they came to a small stone bridge with a sign marking the border of Elcaledonia.

A tremor of excitement passed through Melisha as the donkey carried her across the bridge and into the land of Elcaledonia. Not long now until they reached Eldinburgh, she thought. She told Elpme to stay off the main routes to the city and keep to the byways so that they would avoid meeting anyone.

The weather on the Elcaledonian side of the border was noticeably cooler as they continued their journey north. In Elvedom it had been hot for so long that Melisha had forgotten what it was like to be in a more temperate climate. She began to quite enjoy the journey now that she was no longer dripping with sweat. This new body without its folds of fat had its advantages in more ways than one. The motion of the donkey plodding onwards allowed Melisha to doze.

Behind her the two imps kept their distance, running between rocks and gorse bushes to stay hidden should the woman on the donkey turn around. Melisha, however, was too focused on her destination and so the idea of being trailed by Eldorth's spies never occurred to her.

Staying on the higher paths and roadways became increasingly more hazardous, and the normally sure footed donkey stumbled and struggled over the uneven ground. Melisha was almost jolted off her perch on the donkey's back numerous times until, finally, it became so uncomfortable that she decided to walk for a while. Elpme and the donkey walked a little ahead as Melisha strolled along behind, enjoying the feeling of freedom that her new, trimmer body allowed her.

Gorse and heather covered the hillsides of the land they were now travelling through, and everywhere seemed to be under an enormous purple and white blanket. Melisha knew the old superstition about heather supposedly being lucky and thought that a little luck wouldn't go amiss. She bent and picked a bunch of tiny purple flowers and, as she lifted the posy to her nose and took in its earthy scent, she spotted the fleeting movement of something darting behind a gorse bush several metres back along the track from whence she'd come.

Melisha stopped mid sniff. She peered over the posy, watching the bush out the corner of her eye, but nothing moved. She stood up slowly; every fibre of her body told her that it was no rabbit or other small animal that she had seen, but some other creature that ran on two legs. She turned her head so that she appeared to be turning away from the bush, but kept her eyes locked in its direction, and as she did so, the bush rustled as if something was moving behind it.

Melisha kept the posy close to her nose, whilst with the other hand she reached down to a deep pocket in her dress. Before whatever was hiding behind the bush could move, Melisha had whipped out her wand and cast a freezing spell. There was a dull thud as the spell had the desired effect on its targets and they fell to the ground, unable to move. Melisha sauntered over to the bush and, peering behind its prickly fronds, saw the prone bodies of two blue skinned imps. Their little scrawny limbs were splayed out as if they had been mid star-jump, and their large black eyes were sprung wide in surprise.

Melisha put away her wand and stood over the pair with her hands planted firmly on her waist and a sneering scowl on her face.

"You dirty little sneaks," she snarled. "I bet you've been following me all along, 'aven't ya?" She prodded the imp closest to her with a battered boot covered foot. The imp's eyes stared up blankly. Melisha crouched down beside the little creatures, looming over them threateningly.

"He sent ya, didn't he? Eldorth!" she hissed, more to herself than to the horizontal imps. "That boy's got a lot to learn if he really thinks he can get the better of me. I'll show 'im." She stood up quickly, something she'd never have been able to do with her previously cumbersome body. She then called to Elpme who was some distance away, oblivious of the drama that had just unfolded. He turned obediently in her direction, pulling the donkey to a halt.

"Come 'ere and pick up these pieces of Eldorf's poop," she ordered the poor hapless Elpme, indicating the prone imps with her foot. "And sling 'em on the donkey's back. I might have use of them later." Elpme quickly did as he was told and the group carried on their way.

The long summer's day was drawing to a close as Melisha and her little entourage finally approached the outskirts of the great city of Eldinburgh. So as not to draw unwanted attention to the stricken imps, still lying across the back of the donkey, Melisha pulled her old cloak from out of her bag and threw it over their little bodies. She had planned to avoid the main road to the city but its heavily fortified walls meant that she had no choice but to enter through the huge gateway that led to its myriad of cobbled lanes and streets. A bored guard sat in a sentry box next to the gate and cast a cursory glance in the little party's direction before returning to his perusal of the newspaper in his hands. A lone woman with her servant and donkey were of no interest to him.

Lamps lit the main thoroughfare through the city and, ahead of her, sitting high upon its rocky plinth overlooking its citizens' homes and businesses, loomed the ramparts of the castle. Next to its craggy neighbour, Melisha's eyes fell upon her true destination, The Great Library of Eldinburgh.

Eldinburgh was the biggest city in Elcaledonia and its residents came from many different races and creeds. Melisha took in the smells and sounds of the streets around her, relishing the effects on her senses; being in a city was quite different from being in the countryside. An evil smile spread across Melisha's face as a shiver of anticipation rippled through her at the thought of what might lie in wait within the city's darkest recesses. Many years previously, Melisha had travelled to Eldinburgh and had stayed at an inn where no questions were asked of its visitors. She decided that The Goblin's Goblet was as good a place to spend the night as anywhere else. Now leading Elpme and the donkey, they entered one of the dark twisting lanes that led away from the bright main street of the city.

As they approached the inn, the noise of raucous laughter and merrymaking could be heard wafting through the still air. A young servant girl sat outside on an upturned wooden barrel, and looked them up and down as they came towards her; her grubby, beer stained apron and straggly hair was evidence that her master cared little for her.

"D'ya know if there's a room free this night, girl?" Melisha asked. The girl shook her head.

"None of our rooms is free, missus. They all costs money," the girl responded.

Melisha looked at her disdainfully. "I didn't mean if they were free, as in they didn't cost anything, ya stupid fool. I meant have you any that don't have guests in 'em," she explained.

"None of them's got guests in at the moment. The guests is all in the bar," the girl said helpfully. Melisha shook her head in disgust at the idiocy of the child.

"Oh, never mind, I'll go and see ya master. Is he in the bar?" she asked, speaking slowly and clearly so that the girl understood her meaning. The girl nodded. "Good. You fink you can help my servant to stable the donkey and find 'im a bed for the night?" The girl looked amazed.

"Your donkey sleeps in a bed?" she asked incredulously.

"No! Of course it don't.... Oh, for gawd's sake, just take me servant and the donkey to the stables; they'll sort 'emselves out," Melisha huffed, exasperatedly. As the girl hopped down from the barrel and beckoned Elpme and the donkey to follow her, Melisha suddenly remembered the imps. She called Elpme to her and whispered that he should hide the little creatures until she was ready to deal with them in the morning.

"In the meantime, make sure they get some water in 'em," she instructed. Elpme nodded emphatically. "And don't drown 'em," she called after his retreating back.

As Melisha put her hand on the ring handle of the door to the inn, she stopped a moment. Removing her hand, she ran both of them down her dress to smooth out the wrinkles as best she could, and then patted her hair into tidiness. Then, placing her hand on the door handle once more, she turned it, opened the door and entered the inn.

The laughter, singing and loud discussions taking place in the inn's bar was almost deafening. A thick smog of tobacco smoke mixed with the pungent smell of beer, wine and strong spirits assaulted her senses and she closed her eyes as she breathed it in with delight.

"This is more like it," she thought to herself. "Much better than that namby-pamby country fresh air – yuck," she quivered at the horrible memory of it.

As she stood taking in the aromas, she felt an arm slide around her shoulders. She opened one eye slowly and, turning her head, looked into the rough, scarred face of a feral-elf. His dark leathery skin and black beady eyes bore into her lecherously.

"Allo darlin'," he leered.

This was a new experience for Melisha. In her usual form, no-one would dare to call her darling, let alone put an arm anywhere near her. She squirmed.

"Take your arm off me," she said; her voice low, slow and threatening.

"Ouch, don't be so unfriendly to Elmac, bonny lass," the elf said.

The term of address threw Melisha for a moment – Bonny lass? Bonny? She'd never been called that before! Who did this creep think he was, talking to her like that?

She looked deep into Elmac's eyes and the contempt in hers caused his smile to flicker and falter for a brief moment.

"If you don't get your arm off me, I'll break it in three places so that you'll never wield a sword again and all you'll be fit for is shellin' peas," Melisha snarled.

"Well, we are a feisty one, aren't we?" Elmac grinned. "Aye, lads," he called to his companions propping up the bar. "I have a young lass here who says she's going to break my arm. Now isn't that nice?"

The gang of six other feral-elves, supping copious amounts of beer and spirits at the bar, guffawed loudly.

"Well ya like them fiery, Elmac," called a young ginger topped accomplice. His accent was that of the race of elves that came from across the Elirish Sea.

"I do that, Elcon" laughed Elmac, his face cracking with mirth. Suddenly an excruciating pain shot through his arm and he collapsed onto the floor, gripping it tightly. "Owww…," he howled, sweat breaking out on his weathered brow.

Melisha stood over him, glowering down at his pain-wracked face, a wooden stick gripped in her white-knuckled

213

hand. The laughter from the elves at the bar froze and silence spread around the room as though a blanket had been thrown over it to stifle the noise. All eyes were turned on Elmac by the door and the woman who was obviously the cause of his discomfort.

"I warned you," Melisha growled. Elmac, still gripping his throbbing arm, peered up through watery eyes at the beautiful but cruel face staring down at him.

She bent down and whispered quietly and velvety in Elmac's ear. "Now, if you're a good elf, I'll fix that poorly arm for you, but there's going to be conditions attached. You're gonna 'ave to do something for me."

# CHAPTER 23

## The Secrets of the Mountains

The dark clouds that had hung over the Mountains of Snow the night before still clung to the high peaks like a heavy, grey blanket, leaving the party of travellers thanking their lucky stars that the night had remained dry.

After Eleuen, Elaled, Elbie and Elgin, ably and expertly assisted by Digby the Dwarf, had buried the small bodies of their dead attackers, the travellers had settled down to a supper of hot broth and crusty bread, the latter having been brought with them from Elgawen's castle earlier that day. The evening passed without further incident and Lizzie and her companions listened with pleasure as Elgawen and her two liege elves, Eleuen and Elaled, sang songs in the beautiful haunting language of Elcambria.

Finally, exhausted from the events of the day, Lizzie had slept dreamlessly, snuggled in her sleeping blanket between the warm bodies her grandmother and Eloise. Her grandmother's gentle snoring had been reassuringly comforting, after the fright of the hobgoblin attack, and so Lizzie was soon lulled to sleep.

She was woken, as dawn broke over the mountains, by the smell of bacon frying and coffee brewing. She opened a lazy eye and, lifting her head slightly, spied Elwood and Elwind busying around two small fires, one with a billy can dangling above it and the other with a skillet supporting a large pan full of the sizzling bacon. Lizzie felt her stomach grumble as it informed her that it would welcome a plate of bacon and eggs. She raised herself onto her elbows and watched as other members of the party began stirring from their sleeping blankets and getting ready for the day ahead. The two Elcambrian elves were walking into the camp, their hair and beards damp from having just carried out their ablutions in a stream a short distance away. They were speaking in their strange lilting language and laughing loudly at something that Elaled had just said.

Following the Elcambrian elves' lead, Lizzie scrambled out of bed, waking her grandmother and Eloise as she did so, and quickly made her way down to the stream. She bent down beside the crystal water and plunged her hands into its depths. Her breath caught in her throat, as the water was icy cold from its journey down from the mountains. Lizzie splashed the refreshing liquid onto her face, making her skin tingle and erasing any lingering sleepiness that may have been loitering there. She really could have done with a shower but this would have to do for now, she thought. As she dabbed her face dry with a small rough towel that she had brought from her travel pack, she heard someone approaching. Turning, she saw that Elrus was about to join her. She was relieved that she'd only been washing her hands and face or it could have been embarrassing.

"Good morning, Princess," he greeted her, chirpily.

"Good morning, Elrus," she smiled. He was always so upbeat that she wondered if anything ever made him sad. As the young elf reached the water, he quickly stripped to the waist and Lizzie shyly averted her eyes. Suddenly there was a loud splash and a yelp, and she turned to see Elrus waist deep in the stream, splashing water over his upper body and rubbing his head and arms vigorously.

"Brrr...., it's freezing!" he jabbered, shaking the water from his red hair.

Lizzie couldn't help but laugh, but then blushed a vivid shade of pink as she noticed that Elrus's trousers had also been discarded at the side of the stream along with his shirt. She quickly turned away again and called that she'd see him back in camp, as she made a hasty retreat in its direction.

As Lizzie scurried back into camp, she could see several of the party tucking into their steaming breakfasts, including Digby and Gorin who seemed to have become firm friends over the past few days. Others were busy packing up their belongings and preparing for the ride ahead of them. As her eyes travelled around the campsite, they fell upon the four small mounds of freshly dug earth, beneath which lay the small bodies of their attackers. A shiver of sadness mixed with fear rippled through her as she wondered what other possible dangers lay ahead as they made their way up through the mountains.

Elenya and Prince Finnion had still not told the group what awaited them at the end of this journey into the Mountains of Snow but Lizzie knew that whatever it was, it must be important. She had gathered that this trip wasn't just a progress for her to see more of the world she would one day rule over.

A loud rumble from Lizzie's stomach reminded her how hungry she was, and so she made her way over to Elwood who was loading bacon onto a plate being held out eagerly by Max. The young apprentice smiled at her as she approached.

"Good morning, Princess," he grinned. She repaid the greeting as she too took a plate full of bacon, eggs and toasted bread from Elwood's outstretched hand. The two friends sat in amiable silence as they munched on the delicious fare. Mopping up the last traces of egg yolk from his plate with another piece of bread, Max turned to Lizzie and grinned.

"Why does breakfast always taste better when you eat it outside?" he mused. Lizzie nodded her agreement and mumbled, through a mouthful of toast, that it must be all that fresh air.

As the pair washed up their breakfast things, Lizzie spotted her grandmother and Eloise coming into camp from a different direction to that which she had taken down to stream. They were both carrying their wash bags and so Lizzie wondered where they had been.

"We've been down to the ladies bathroom," Mrs Longton said cheerily. "I thought you'd already been there," she added, looking at Lizzie quizzically.

Lizzie shook her head and said that she'd been down to another part of the stream, pointing in the direction of the place where she had washed earlier. Just as she was explaining, Elrus sauntered back into camp, swinging his towel and whistling happily.

"But that's the boys' area!" exclaimed Eloise, looking slightly shocked. "There's a part screened off for us girls to use."

Elrus had now joined them and, giving Lizzie a cheeky smirk, said how refreshing his dip in the stream had been. Lizzie flushed red again at the thought of their earlier encounter and glared at him as if daring him to embarrass her further.

Breakfast over, the group quickly packed up camp and, mounting their horses once more, began picking their way up through the rocky passes that took them further into the mountain range.

As they navigated their way through a particularly narrow gully, Elgawen's elves led the way on their stout, sure footed ponies. The heat of the early morning sun began to diminish as they travelled higher into the mountains, and the first wisps of low cloud touched the heads of the taller riders amongst them.

"This will ruin my hair," grumbled Mrs Longton, in mock annoyance.

Suddenly from above there could be heard a raucous cawing sound, and a flash of black and white feathers, with traces of vivid blue, swooped down and flapped around the head of Max.

Startled by this unexpected presence, Max's horse seemed to stagger a little in fright. Max had become quite the horseman over the previous few days, and so he quickly pulled his mount back under control before exclaiming, "Mag!"

The magpie landed lightly on his shoulder and nuzzled her shiny head into Max's neck, making the young sorcerer chuckle as the bird's feathers tickled him. Riding just behind Max, Lizzie was astounded by the bird's sudden appearance.

"How did she find you?" she called ahead to him.

"I told you, don't you remember," he replied over his shoulder. "Magpies are great at finding things."

Elrus, who was riding in front of Max, turned around and asked why Mag would suddenly turn up now.

Max shrugged. "I don't know, maybe my master sent her. Or maybe she was just missing me," he said, taking a hand from his reins and stroking Mag's sleek feathered back. Max secretly knew, however, that the magpie suddenly turning up was likely to mean that there was danger ahead. Mag would act as another pair of eyes to warn him of that danger. What he didn't know though, was why she had left it until now to arrive.

They were now high into the mountains and were riding through the clouds that clung there. A thick fog surrounded them, making it difficult to see where they were going, and their only view was the rider in front. The moisture in the air caused the travellers' hair to cling lankly to their faces and necks, and their clothing hung damp and uncomfortable against their skin. Lizzie kept her eyes firmly fixed on Max's back as she encouraged Whisper to continue plodding onwards and upwards into the ever thickening cloud.

At the point where even Max's back was becoming indistinct, Lizzie began to feel a quiver of fear shudder through her. Where were they going to end up? Elenya called out to the group occasionally, making sure that the party was still intact, and as she called out once more, Lizzie felt reassured as she heard each member, and in particular her grandmother, call back that they were there.

The journey through the clouds seemed to go on endlessly and Lizzie felt a sudden empathy for people whose sight impairment meant they lived their lives in a permanent misty world. Her acute hearing listened out for any sounds that might imply imminent danger, but the cloud cover seemed to dampen even noise so that all she could make out was the muted clip clopping of horses' hooves on the rock and shingle beneath them.

Gradually, when Lizzie thought they would never see clearly again, the back of Max's blond head began to become increasingly visible. The warmth of the sun's rays penetrated the cloud's thinning tendrils and Lizzie closed her eyes and lifted up her face in welcome.

As more of the front riders became visible once again, Lizzie turned to see the pretty face of Eloise, just behind her. The girls smiled at each other in evident relief at finally being rid of their uncomfortable blanket. Then Lizzie's beloved grandmother appeared and, one by one, other members of the party came out of the mists. Lizzie turned to face the front again and found that they had finally escaped from their cloud cocoon. The party of Companions reined in their horses as they discovered themselves on top of a plateau, overlooking a stunning scene that lay before them.

The bright blue sky, with its sun high above, stretched out before them and Lizzie could see the tops of the mountains poking their glistening snow covered tips through the clouds now below them. The staggering beauty of the scene almost took her breath away. In the distance, one of the mountains stood high above the others and Lizzie could just make out what looked like a fortress carved into the mountain top. Below the fortress walls were a series of caves or openings hewn into the mountainside. Lizzie heard her grandmother gasp as she took in the view.

"Oh, how beautiful," Mrs Longton sighed.

Lizzie looked across at Elenya and saw that her aunt had a faraway look on her face as she stared across the mountains to what was obviously their destination that day.

The look betrayed other thoughts of something more than just the distance to be travelled between them and the fortress. As if sensing that she was being watched, Elenya turned and smiled gently at Lizzie. Then becoming leader once more, Elenya spurred the party onwards.

The Elcambrian outriders went on ahead, leading the way over the distance left between them and their destination, until finally they came to an immense stone bridge that spanned the gap between themselves and the mountain fortress. Two huge granite statues of winged creatures guarded either side of the bridge's vast expanse.

As the party took their first steps onto the bridge, Lizzie expected a repeat of their experience at the Bridge of Elsevern, when the Elcambrian elves had challenged their presence. But, other than the two enormous stone guards, eyeing them with their boulder sized eyeballs, no one appeared to mind the group of riders being there.

Clouds swirled in the abyss below the bridge and Lizzie pushed away the terrible thought of what would happen should the structure give way, concentrating instead on getting to the other side as quickly as possible. A strong acrid smell assaulted Lizzie's sensitive nose and she blinked rapidly as her eyes stung from the powerful aroma. She felt sure she had smelt something similar in the past but couldn't recall when or from what. Mrs Longton put her finger on it by asking why there was such a strong smell of sulphur in the air. Elwood and Elwind glanced at each other knowingly but refrained from replying.

Upon reaching the end of the bridge, they were confronted by two massive, studded iron-work doors barring their way. Elenya held up her hand and the little group stopped in their tracks. The Princess, with Prince Finnion and Princess Elgawen on either side of her, rode up to the doors that dwarfed them. Elenya then held her arms outstretched above her and called out in her clear, strong voice:

"We come to seek the help of the great and powerful Y Draig Goch and the Draig Goch Flyers."

At her words, the huge doors began to swing silently open into an enormous cavern that seemed to stretch away into the depths of the mountain.

Elenya turned to the group and beckoned them to follow her. Lizzie looked around at her companions and saw the trepidation etched on the faces of her grandmother, Max and Eloise. Elrus's eyes, however, were bright with excitement at what lay ahead. The rest of the group's faces betrayed nothing other than their complete trust in their leader's command.

As they entered the cavern, Lizzie could see, with the aid of an unknown light source, that the walls glistened with what appeared to be fool's gold. To the side of the cavern, there was a row of troughs and Elenya led the party over to them. Dismounting, she took her horse to one of the troughs which was filled with water, whilst others proved to be full of food for the horses and mules. Prince Finnion and Elgawen followed suit and so did the rest of the group.

Elenya announced that the horses would remain there for their safety and that the rest of their journey would now be on foot. Lizzie was surprised at this as there was no one around to look after the mounts, but before she could express her concern for her little Whisper, her grandmother must have read her mind because she asked the very same question.

"Please don't worry, Mrs Longton, arrangements will be made to ensure the horses come to no harm and that they are cared for," Elenya assured her.

"But why is it safer for them to stay here rather than coming with us?" Lizzie asked, not satisfied by the answer given.

Elenya smiled. "All will become clear very soon, Lizzie. I don't wish to spoil the surprise."

Intrigued, Lizzie let the subject drop. The group tethered their horses and ponies to a number of iron rings embedded in the cavern wall next to the troughs. They then slung their bags over their shoulders and made their way towards the back of the enormous chamber. There Lizzie could see steps carved into the rock that led up higher into the mountain. No natural light lit their way, only the strange glow of the indeterminate light source. The smell of sulphur became increasingly more powerful and Lizzie and the others placed their hands over their noses to try to prevent its stinging effects.

At the top of the steps, another enormous cavern opened out before them and suddenly they were confronted by a scene that Lizzie couldn't have imagined in her wildest dreams. A loud roar filled the air, causing Mag to flap her wings frantically and the rest of the party to almost jump out of their skins. The roar was then followed by several others and Lizzie and her companions clamped their hands over their ears to protect them from the onslaught.

Lizzie stared in disbelief as – her voice lost in the cacophony of noise coming from their direction – she mouthed, "Dragons!"

# CHAPTER 24

## In the Dragons' Den

The smell and noise of the place was overpowering and Lizzie's senses were reeling from the magnitude of what she was experiencing. She felt someone grip her arm and turned to see her grandmother staring in open mouthed shock, her other hand was placed firmly on her chest, as if trying to stop her pounding heart escaping from her rib cage.

"Oh my, oh my, oh my," Mrs Longton repeated.

Elenya came over and stood behind the pair, placing a comforting hand on each of their shoulders.

"Surprised?" she asked, her face flushed with excitement.

"You could say that," Lizzie breathed, as she stared at the enormous creatures. Each one was contained within a separate pen made from a strong metal framework. Elves dressed in black leather jerkins and leggings attended to the great beasts.

Elrus sidled up to Lizzie, not taking his eyes from the dragons. "Wow!" he exclaimed.

Lizzie looked past Elrus to where Max was standing, his face frozen in fear, and Mag, sitting stock still on his shoulder, seemed to sense that flapping her wings or making a noise might not be a good idea in the circumstances. Eloise looked equally terrified so Lizzie was glad to see Elgawen place an arm around the young girl's shoulder and say something into her ear, making Eloise smile in the process.

Elrus also noticed that his friend was struggling with the situation, and so went over to Max and punched him playfully on the arm. The young apprentice's fixed attention was brought abruptly from the dragons to Elrus and he blinked at his friend as if seeing him for the first time.

"Got a spell big enough for that lot, mate?" Elrus grinned. Max couldn't help but grin back at him and shook his head.

"Not sure my wand's big enough," he chuckled uneasily. He was grateful that Elrus always seemed to make light of even the tensest of situations.

"It's quality not size that matters," said a voice from just behind them and, turning, the boys found a grinning Flaxon looking down on them, a twinkle in his soft brown eyes. The boys nudged each other and laughed at the innuendo. Max staggered from the knock he took from Elrus, making Mag dig her sharp feet into his shoulder and causing him to yelp in pain. The magpie cast Elrus a steely glare with her black beady eyes, in admonishment at almost being dislodged from her perch.

One of the Dragon Elves finally appeared to notice the new arrivals and, wiping his hands on a rag, came walking over to them. He suddenly noticed Elenya amongst the party and fell to one knee, bringing his arm, with a clenched fist, across his chest in salute.

"Welcome, Your Highness. You were expected. May I escort you to the Dragon Master?" he said, rising to his feet. Elenya thanked the elf and said that she would be glad if he would lead the way. So, with the little group following in his wake, the elf led them past the dragon pens.

The visitors glanced nervously at the huge creatures as they passed. Mrs Longton expressed her concern that, should one of the dragons decide to breathe fire at that precise moment, they would all be burnt to a frazzle.

The Dragon Elf cast a look over his shoulder and told them not to worry. "They are fed a special diet to create the fire within them, and are only fed that when needed. Their fire ability is currently dormant," he assured the visitors. A sigh of relief rippled around the little group.

The heat in the dragons' vast cavern was stifling, and the faces and bare, muscled arms of the Dragon Elves glistened with sweat as they tended the massive creatures. As the visitors passed by, they could see that, close up, the dragons were stunningly beautiful. Each one varied in colour; some were different shades of green or blue and others' red through to orange. Fascinatingly, their scaly skin gleamed as if lit from within. Lizzie was interested to see that some of the creatures were smooth headed, like huge lizards she remembered having seen in a zoo once called Komodo Dragons (and thought that perhaps they were really related after all). Other dragons had sharp horn-like bulges on top of their heads that gave them an even more fearsome appearance. Most of the dragons kept their great wings folded neatly along the sides of their bodies, but a couple of the creatures rustled them slightly, like huge birds of prey, as they watched the visitors suspiciously with great amber coloured eyes.

As she passed each one, Lizzie counted thirty dragons in all. She felt strangely drawn to them in a way that she couldn't explain, and although she knew that she should probably be terrified of the breath-taking creatures, she wasn't. She just felt elated.

At the rear of the dragons' cavern, there were a number of tunnels which led away in different directions through the mountain. Amongst them was another flight of steps, and the party quickly made their way up the steep treads. When they reached the top, they found themselves in a large open space, along the sides of which were high stone balustrades opening out onto the stunning views of the mountains surrounding them. Stone benches and statues of dragons and elven warriors were strategically placed below and alongside the balustrades.

At one end of the space was the entrance to what was quite clearly the central keep of the mountain fortress and, striding down the steps from it, with an entourage of similarly clad elves, came an elf dressed completely in black leather; his shoulder length black hair flew out behind him as he walked purposefully towards them.

Lizzie heard a sharp intake of breath and looked up at her aunt, from whose direction it had come. The look on Elenya's face surprised Lizzie, as it seemed sad and tears glistened on the rims of her beautiful brown eyes. The look was fleeting, however, as Elenya quickly blinked away the threat of tears and adopted a more serious and regal expression. Lizzie looked from her aunt to the approaching elf and could see that he was strikingly handsome. His black hair was complemented by a neatly trimmed black beard and moustache, above which was a straight masculine nose. His high cheek-bones and strong brow gave him a proud air and he was obviously an elf of some significance.

As he reached the group, he stopped directly in front of Elenya. With piercingly blue eyes, he looked deep into the Princess's own before falling to one knee and taking her proffered hand and kissing it. The rest of his followers each fell to a knee with the same clench fisted salute as the first Dragon Elf they had met. The elves stood up and their leader spoke.

"Welcome to Eldragonia, Your Highness, we are glad that you and your party have arrived safely." The Dragon Master had a low, slow voice and Lizzie thought she saw a flush of pink seep into Elenya's pretty cheeks. The elf then turned to Lizzie and bowed his head in welcome before nodding to each of the visitors in turn.

"Thank you, General Eldron. We are glad to be here," Elenya said, as she dipped her own blond head in respect. Lizzie then remembered that she had seen this elf before; he had been at the Great Council meeting with her grandfather earlier that year.

With the greetings concluded, the Dragon Master suggested that the visitors would no doubt be in need of rest and refreshment.

"Quarters have been prepared for you," General Eldron said. "My elf-servant has arranged for your rooms to be made as comfortable as possible, given that we are a garrison of soldiers who are used to more simple accommodation."

"Please don't put anyone to any trouble, General. We are quite capable of coping with simple lodgings," Elenya said haughtily. Lizzie looked at her aunt in surprise. She was unused to hearing her speak in such a high-handed manner as she was now with General Eldron. She looked at the General, who seemed to wince at the words before inclining his head and saying, "As you wish."

He then turned and called to some servants who were hanging back from the welcoming party. They hurried over and, after bowing to the visitors, were instructed to show the guests to their rooms.

As Lizzie and her companions followed the servants, she glanced back at the Dragon Elves and saw General Eldron watching the back of Elenya, with an unreadable look on his face. Lizzie turned back just in time to see Elgawen link arms with Elenya.

"Not got over him yet then?" Lizzie heard Elgawen say; to which Elenya, with her nose firmly in the air, replied, "I most certainly have."

The grand entrance hall of the fort was in stark contrast to previous castles and fortresses that Lizzie had been to in Elvedom. Even Elgawen's castle, though more functional than the Castle of Elvedom or the Citadel of Elavalon, had a bustling, homely feel to it. This place however, had the distinct feel of an army garrison. There were no fripperies or furnishing to soften its appearance, unless you considered some large tapestries that hung on the walls, depicting fire-breathing dragons flying over burning buildings or elves in armour wielding bloody swords, as soft furnishings. Rows of neatly stored weapons stood in racks along one side of the hall, and on the opposite side and flanking one of the large tapestries, hung shields and more weaponry.

As the fortress's guests made their way through the hall, they could see a courtyard out to one side where rows of elves were going through a vigorous exercise routine. Elrus's eyes lit up at the sight.

"Hey Max, that looks like a good place to play a game of football," he called to his friend, brightly. Max looked through to where Elrus was pointing and nodded sagely.

"Perhaps we could challenge those guys to a game," Max said with his tongue firmly in his cheek.

"Yeah, good idea," agreed Elrus enthusiastically.

"I was joking," laughed Max. "Look at the size of them! They'll slaughter us."

"Well, just remember what Flaxon said, it's not the size that counts – it's the quality," Elrus grinned, winking exaggeratedly at Max. The pair laughed loudly causing the others in the group to wonder what was so hilarious.

As the visitors reached their rooms, Lizzie could see what the General had meant by the accommodation being simple; they weren't so much rooms as cells. Each one was small with barely a slit of a window, and contained an iron bedstead with a mattress and a single pillow, white sheets and a rough grey blanket. There was a small bedside table, a wooden chair and some hooks on the wall.

"There are showers and toilets along the hallway," said the elf-servant, pointing in the direction of the facilities. "We've separated them for males and females," he added, with the tone of someone who had been inconvenienced by having had to go to so much trouble.

Elenya, obviously sensing the elf's disgruntlement, turned on the charm.

"Thank you so much. You really needn't have gone to such lengths for us. We really do appreciate that you've considered our privacy, don't we ladies?" she said beguilingly, almost fluttering her eyelashes as she touched the elf's arm gently for good measure. The females of the group agreed vigorously, eager to press home the point. The elf-servant's face flushed briefly as he accepted their thanks. Bowing his head, he told them that dinner would be at seven of the hour and then trundled off down the hallway, back to his more pressing chores.

As each cell was identical to the others, the visitors entered their chosen accommodation. There was a slight scuffle as Gorin and Digby tried to pick the same room, but Digby won out due to his superior strength as he barged the little goblin out of his way.

Once in her room, Lizzie flopped down onto the bed and closed her eyes. The rough blanket scratched at the skin on her arms and the mattress beneath it felt hard and a little lumpy. Still, at least it was a bed, she thought, and turning her face into the pillow, smelt the freshness of the clean linen that encased it. She breathed a sigh of relief, at having reached the relative safety of this place. Her brain buzzed at what she had just witnessed down in the cavern below her. It seemed inconceivable that dragons would be sleeping where she would sleep this night. She still had no idea why they had travelled to Eldragonia. Why had she been brought here? She felt sure that it wasn't purely a sight-seeing trip. No, there was more to it than that; she just knew it in her bones. Keeping her eyes shut tight, in her mind she conjured up the images of the magnificent beasts below and could feel their heat and even smell their distinctive odour – something akin to sulphur and burnt matches. The long journey up into the mountains began to take its toll on her and she felt herself drifting off to sleep.

\*

*Wind tore through her hair and whipped against her face as she soared ever higher and higher. The powerful sinewy body beneath her felt at one with her own as its huge wings beat slowly and deliberately, taking them both up into the clear blue atmosphere.*

*"Onwards and upwards, Dronan," she yelled, ecstatically.*

*"Your wish is my command," growled the deep thundering voice of her companion, as his wings beat faster.*

\*

Lizzie woke with a start. She had been flying; flying on the back of one of the enormous dragons. It had felt wonderful and yet natural to her. Her nerve endings were jangling and she knew that somewhere within the fortress, she must find the dragon in her dream – she must find Dronan.

# CHAPTER 25

## A Secret Shared

There was a knock on Lizzie's door and Mrs Longton's damp haired head poked itself around it.

"Hello darling! Aren't you washed and changed yet?" she asked, as her body followed her head into the room. She looked suitably washed and refreshed herself.

"I can see *you* are," laughed Lizzie, as her grandmother sat down on the bed next to her. Mrs Longton shook her wet hair over Lizzie, making her granddaughter squeal. She then began tickling her.

The door to the room burst open and Max, Elrus and Eloise almost fell into the room. The shock on their faces quickly turned to grins of amusement as they saw what had caused their friend's screams of, "Stop! Stop!"

"We thought you were being murdered," laughed Elrus.

Mrs Longton looked at the three friends standing in the doorway and could see that at least the two boys were dressed and ready for the dinner ahead of them. Eloise, however, was still in her travelling clothes but was holding a towel as though she had been on her way to the showers. Lizzie noticed Eloise's towel too and decided to join her friend, so quickly grabbing up her things, the two girls made their way to the showers.

As they reached the shower-room they could see that a roughly scrawled drawing of a female had been carved on the door. Upon pushing it open they found themselves in a functional room, devoid of any frills that might have made it appear in any way feminine. All along one side of the room they could see shower heads sticking out of the stone wall, below each one was a large tap and next to that a glass receptacle that contained some opaque liquid, which Lizzie assumed must be some form of soap or shampoo. In between each of the showers there were what appeared to be hastily erected wooden partitions, at the front of which hung curtains, creating flimsy doors to protect the privacy of the person inside. Lizzie assumed these alterations were what the Dragon Master had meant by making things more comfortable for the ladies in the group.

Along the wall opposite the showers was a row of cubicles and upon inspection Lizzie and Eloise discovered that they were basic toilets. They were more akin to latrines but with wooden seats above. The girls looked at each other and wrinkled their noses in disgust. Taking a sniff of the air around them, Lizzie breathed a sigh of relief, as the fragrance at least proved that the facilities were spotlessly clean.

The inspection finally over, the girls each entered one of the shower cubicles. Lizzie quickly stripped off and stood beneath the shower. As she fumbled with the tap, she heard the shower next door suddenly spurt into life and there was a loud yelp from Eloise as the water hit her.

"Owww…," Eloise yelled.

"Are you okay?" Lizzie called, in concern.

"Fi.., fine… it's just it's a bit powerful that's all," Eloise called back.

Lizzie gently turned the tap of her own shower in the hope of having more control over it than Eloise seemed to have over hers. However, a jet of hot water pummelled straight into Lizzie's chest almost knocking her back through the shower curtain. She gave an involuntary gasp at the power of the shower then, regaining her feet, she turned her back to it. The stream of water felt like dozens of tiny needles pricking her skin. As she tipped her head back the hot shower pounded into her hair and she had the sudden horrible thought that it might be washed away by the force of the water. It was difficult to stand the shower's strength for too long, so she quickly extracted some of the soapy liquid from the bottle next to the tap and rubbed it through her hair

233

and over her skin. Every part of her tingled from the water massaging her body and, whatever was in the soap, was certainly invigorating. Having rinsed off every trace of foam, Lizzie grabbed up her towel and rubbed herself briskly. Slipping on the bath robe that she'd brought along too, she popped her head out of the shower cubicle at precisely the same moment as Eloise.

The two girls looked at each other and giggled. Eloise's perfect brown skin shone like a polished button and her black curly hair glistened with droplets of water. Lizzie's normally pale complexion was bright pink from its pummelling.

"Well, that was quite some shower," laughed Eloise breathlessly. Lizzie nodded in agreement.

"It certainly was," she chuckled.

Back in her room, Lizzie quickly donned a fresh set of clothes and met her grandmother and her friends in the hallway just outside her door. The boys said that they had been having a look around whilst the girls were, in Elrus's words, "Titivating themselves."

"We've found the Great Hall where dinner's going to be held," explained Max. "Come on, we'll show you the way. The others went down a few minutes ago," he continued over his shoulder, as he began walking along the corridor.

They soon arrived in the Great Hall and Lizzie was staggered by the beauty of what she saw. The Hall itself was not particularly stunning, as it was just a large expanse with a high vaulted ceiling and the long trestle tables laid out beneath it. There was one table set at right angles from the others and this, judging by the place settings upon it, was obviously where the higher echelon of the company would sit.

What stunned Lizzie most though, was what she could see through the huge mullioned windows that ran down either side of the Hall and, in particular, through an enormous window behind the top table. Through the clear glass that filled the window frames were views of the mountains surrounding the fortress, the snow tipped caps of which glistened in the early evening sun. The orange glow of the sun's rays shone through the biggest window, lighting up the room, and the window's glass panes sent the sun's glittering golden beams bouncing off the walls and statues that adorned the vast space.

Lizzie spotted her aunt standing to one side of the room, in discussion with Prince Finnion, Flaxon, Elgawen and the twins Elwood and Elwind. Elenya, as always, looked amazing. Lizzie's first thought was that she too must have had a shower because Elenya's skin and golden hair seemed to shine in the glow of the sun's rays. Elenya looked across at Lizzie and smiled a dazzling smile.

The other members of their party were also present and Lizzie almost giggled at the sight of Gorin and Digby short bodies having to stand on a long stone bench by one of the windows to look out at the mountains beyond. The archer and Elcambrian elves, together with Willo and the two fairies, Filip and Fidora, were with them.

Suddenly Lizzie heard the sound of many marching feet and into the Hall, led by the Dragon Master himself, strode the Dragon Elves. Their leathery uniforms shone as if regularly polished to a high sheen. General Eldron held up his right hand and the elves came to an abrupt halt, standing to attention as they did so. The General then marched up to Elenya and, inclining his head in a brisk bow, apologized for not being there to welcome her.

His face seemed to soften, as he said, "I am proving to be a poor host, Your Highness. I never seem to be in place to greet you."

Elenya swallowed hard, as if a little taken aback by the comment, and then tipping up her chin as she regained her composure and smiling gently said, a little less tersely than she had spoken upon their first meeting, "Not at all, General."

At that point the General offered his arm to her and Elenya, with a slight hesitation, placed her hand upon it as he then led her and her entourage to their seats at the top table. Lizzie found the whole procedure fascinating. There was definitely a history between those two, she thought to herself, as she watched Elenya take her seat beside General Eldron. "I'm going to find out what it is," she decided.

When all the guests were seated the General gave the signal for the Dragon Elves to continue to proceed into the Hall and take their places at the tables. As soon as they were seated the whole place seemed to relax and, as servants appeared with platters of food and flagons of beer, wine and other non-alcoholic beverages. The atmosphere in the hall was that of the boisterous camaraderie of any army garrison.

Lizzie, because of her royal position, had been placed to the left of General Eldron and next to her grandmother. Elenya on the other side of the General was seated next to Prince Finnion and he was next to Elgawen. Lizzie kept trying to peek around Eldron to see the interaction between him and her aunt but it was proving tricky. He seemed to spend most of the time staring straight ahead, a distant look on his face as he picked at his food, whilst Elenya seemed determined to keep Prince Finnion entertained as she laughed, somewhat falsely from what Lizzie could hear, at things the Prince was saying. Even Prince Finnion looked a little perplexed at Elenya's over friendly touching of his arm at regular intervals.

Lizzie suddenly felt saddened by her aunt's behaviour towards the General, as it seemed to be making him uncomfortable. The fixed look on his face showed traces of hurt and so, unable to bear it any longer, Lizzie reached out a hand and placed it on his forearm. From wherever his mind was, as he stared off into the middle distance, it was brought back to the present by the light touch of Lizzie's hand. He turned slowly and looked down at her small slim fingers, as they gently squeezed his strong muscular arm.

His eyes rose from looking down at her hand to gaze with the full intensity of their blueness into Lizzie's own.

"Princess?" he quizzed, simply.

"Excuse me, General," Lizzie said, removing her hand from his arm, as she now had his attention. "I was wondering how you became the Dragon Master."

The General looked surprised by the question.

He thought for a moment and then said, "That is easy to answer but perhaps more difficult to understand."

"Try me," Lizzie said, smiling brightly to compensate for her aunt's off-hand behaviour towards their host.

The General laughed and his whole demeanor changed as he did so. His handsome features, with his sparkling blue eyes and straight white teeth would be the envy of any of the human world's movie stars, Lizzie thought as she looked at him. His laughter caught the attention of Elenya and Lizzie felt a sense of satisfaction at the look of puzzlement on her aunt's face as she watched him. It was the look of someone who hadn't seen or heard that person laugh in a long time. Seeing Lizzie watching her she quickly turned her attention back to Prince Finnion.

General Eldron smiled down at Lizzie. "The simple answer is that I was born to be a Dragon Master," he said quietly.

Lizzie looked at him as if to say that the answer wasn't quite good enough. The General grinned.

"Okay," he said. "I was born to it because I inherited the gift from my mother's family. Her father and the generations before him were Dragon Masters. It usually falls to the first born son in the family but for some reason the gift was not passed to my older brother but to me, thank the gods."

Lizzie was surprised by the last thing he said, which was almost whispered. "Why thank the gods?" she asked.

The General looked at her slowly as if surprised that she need ask such a question. "Because only they know what he would have done with the power of the Dragons," he said mysteriously. Continuing with his story, he said, "I knew from an early age that the gift was mine. I would dream of dragons; dream of flying with them, talking with them, training them. I would play at being Dragon Master. My mother knew and she sent me to stay with my grandfather and he trained me to control the power within me. Then I became a Dragon Elf and well, the rest is history as they say."

Lizzie smiled. "Can you speak Dragonian then?" she queried.

The General looked surprised but smiled. "But of course."

"But can you speak it without knowing you are?" she asked eagerly.

The General looked genuinely confused. "Um... I have never thought about it. I have just always been able to do so," he said hesitantly, as if the thought had never occurred to him. "Why do you ask?"

Lizzie sighed and looked at the General intently, then leaning in closer, as if sharing a great secret, she said, "Because I can too."

It was the first time she had voiced the fact of her amazing ability since Flaxon had explained it to her in the Forest of Neuwe. It was another thing that made her different from others and so she found it hard to tell anyone for fear of their reaction. The General could speak Dragonian too, so surely he would be sympathetic.

The General looked at Lizzie in disbelief. Then, as if he hadn't heard her correctly, said, "I'm sorry? You can what too?"

Lizzie leant in towards the General and with a beckoning hand, brought him close. As he bent his head to listen to what she was about to say, she whispered, "I can speak to dragons too."

General Eldron leant back in his chair and stared at her. The look of shock on his face was startling, it was as if he hadn't heard her correctly. Lizzie nodded as if to say he had heard her right.

"But..., but how long have you known this?" he stammered.

"I only found out the other day," she said, matter-of-factly.

The General was now completely flummoxed and it showed on his handsome face.

"The other day?" he asked disbelievingly. "How would you have only discovered this the other day? When would you have come into contact with dragons? They are strictly controlled creatures, due to the nature of their powers."

Lizzie looked at him reassuringly. "Oh, I never spoke to a dragon before. It was a pterotorial that I spoke to," she said.

The look on the General's face was now truly comical and she would have laughed at it, if it hadn't been rude to do so. He stared at her wide eyed and his mouth opened and closed like a fish gasping for oxygen. Lizzie thought she should explain and so recounted the story of the injured pterotorial and how she had reassured the creature and sent it on its way. The General just continued to stare at her, shaking his head slowly from side to side in total amazement.

"I know," Lizzie said, giving him a wry look. "I would never have believed it myself but it was Flaxon there," she nodded towards the Faun sitting along the table next to Max and Elrus, "who told me that I had just spoken Dragonian. Flaxon knows lots of things you know."

The General followed Lizzie's gaze towards the Faun and nodded mutely. Fauns were creatures of great knowledge and wisdom, Eldron knew that for sure.

"So, do you think I was born being able to speak Dragonian then?" Lizzie asked. "I mean, I would never have

239

known before as there aren't any dragons where I come from. At least I don't think there are," she added.

General Eldron looked at Lizzie as though she were from a different planet. "No dragons?" he said quietly. He had known that Elethria's child had been hidden and kept safe during her formative years but where in this world did they have no dragons? She was an odd little thing he thought to himself but a child that could talk to dragons? Now that was truly special.

"What does your aunt Elenya say to this special gift of yours?" the General asked.

Elenya, who must have had a lull in her own conversation, suddenly picked up on the exchange between Lizzie and Eldron upon hearing her name and so turned her attention fully upon the pair beside her.

"What gift?" she asked, looking at them both suspiciously.

Lizzie leant back out of Elenya's line of vision and put a finger to her lips, to indicate that the General should say nothing; Eldron gave a slight nod in mute understanding. Mrs Longton, sitting alongside Lizzie, was also now showing an interest in the discussion taking place beside her.

Lizzie's face told the General that she wasn't yet ready to share her secret with anyone else and so he gave her a look that showed that it was safe with him. Winking conspiratorially at Lizzie he said, "Oh, well it looks like the secret is out, Princess." Then turning to Elenya continued, "I have a special gift for the Princess in honour of her visit to Eldragonia. I thought that we would name the first young dragon to hatch during your visit after her."

Elenya didn't look convinced. "Isn't Elizabeth an unusual name for a dragonlet?" she asked, eyeing him quizzically.

General Eldron agreed that it was but said that these were exceptional circumstances. "It's not every day that we have a visit from the heir apparent," he added proudly.

240

Although she still looked sceptical, Elenya seemed to accept the explanation and Mrs Longton clapped her hands together in delight.

"Oh how wonderful, Lizzie," she beamed. "A baby dragon named after you. What do you think of that?"

Lizzie grinned at her grandmother and said, feeling pretty guilty as she did so, "It's great, gran. Great!"

Her grandmother reached across and put an arm around Lizzie's shoulder and squeezed her tight. "Oh, if those Bray brats could see you now, they'd be green with envy." Lizzie laughed at the thought of the Bray twins turning green – like two miniature versions of the Incredible Hulk and the "not so" Jolly Green Giant.

"I will send instructions for the Hatchery Master to take you down to the hatchery tomorrow," General Eldron continued. Elrus, sitting next to Mrs Longton, poked his red head around her and grinned broadly; showing that he too would be a willing visitor to the hatchery. And so it was agreed that the guests would visit the dragon hatchery the next day.

Lizzie leant back in her chair and grinned to herself as she looked out at the revelry taking place in the hall. Popping a piece of ripe cheese into her mouth and wincing slightly at its powerful flavour, she thought to herself, "This is all too exciting." Here she was, little Lizzie Longton, sitting next to a Dragon Master, amongst Dragon Elves and her nearest and dearest. Tomorrow she would find if she truly could talk to dragons and to top it all, she was going to have one named after her. Amazing!

# CHAPTER 26

## Moonlight Madness

The meal over, there followed some entertainment which included singing and lute playing by Elgawen and the Elcambrian elves and a couple of fire eaters from the Dragon Elf contingent. The Dragon Elves obviously enjoyed a good time and so, when after quite a few jugs of beer had been consumed the songs became a little bawdier, much to the pleasure of the cheeky Elrus. Mrs Longton suggested that perhaps the time had come for the younger members of the group to go to bed. It had been a very exciting day after all, she added. Elwood offered to accompany the children to their rooms but Lizzie said it wasn't necessary, as they were old enough to put themselves to bed.

After kissing her grandmother goodnight and wishing everyone else the same, Lizzie and her three friends made their way to their rooms.

"I'm not a bit tired. I can't see why we couldn't have stayed and enjoyed the songs," grumbled Elrus, as he trudged along behind the others.

"Actually, I'm not sure my father would have liked me listening to some of those songs," exclaimed an indignant Eloise.

Max laughed. "Well I wouldn't have told him if you didn't," he said, giving her a gentle nudge.

Lizzie walked along silently, lost in her own thoughts about her conversation with General Eldron. She was also intrigued by what was going on between him and her aunt. Eloise looked at her friend with concern etched on her face.

"You're very quiet Lizzie," she said.

Lizzie turned and smiled at Eloise. "Sorry, I was just thinking, that's all."

Elrus pushed forward and walked alongside her. "So what were you and the DM talking about then?" he asked. Lizzie shrugged.

"Oh, nothing much," she said, not giving anything away.

Elrus grabbed her arm and linking it with his own, as they continued up the stairs towards their accommodation for the night said, "Oh, come on now Princess! We saw you chatting away with him for ages. What would hold a Dragon Master's attention for so long? I'm pretty sure it wouldn't have been *nothing much*," he teased.

"Well, if you must know, I was asking him what it was like being a DM, as you called him," she said haughtily, her eyes sparkling with enjoyment at the banter between them.

It was Max's turn to be interested now and so linking Lizzie's other arm, he asked, "And what did he say?" Eloise, not to be left out, joined arms with Max and the four of them marched along together.

Lizzie felt as though her heart would burst with happiness. Her three friends were there with her and they were interested in what she had to say. How would they react if she really told them what she had been talking about with the General? Something told her that they would still be there for her but something else held her back – a long history of being different and ostracized for it. She would tell them but when *she* was ready to.

"He just explained that he was born with the knowledge that he would be a Dragon Master," she explained. "Apparently, his mother's side of the family has a long history of being Dragon Masters. Although, he did say that it was usual for the eldest son to inherit the ability but that it had fallen to him instead. He seemed pretty relieved that it had been him and not his older brother," she added thoughtfully.

"Well of course he'd be relieved," said Elrus, as though he was amazed that she should be surprised. Lizzie looked at him quizzically. "Well, come on! It's pretty cool being *The*

243

*Dragon Master.* I mean it must go down well with the ladies."

"Oh Elrus!" Lizzie and Eloise cried in unison, as Elrus fell forward from the playful shove Lizzie gave him in feigned outrage. Laughing uproariously, Elrus ran a little ahead, then turning, called to Max.

"Hey Max! D'ya fancy trying out for Dragon Master? You'll be a big hit with the ladies," he drawled. The friends laughed as Max and the girls chased the squealing Elrus up the remaining stairs that led to their rooms.

Breathless and still falling about in fits of laughter, the friends finally found themselves outside their rooms.

"I am *so* not tired," wheezed Elrus, his face as red as his hair from the chase.

"Me neither," agreed a puffing Eloise.

"How about we go and explore?" Lizzie suggested, eagerly.

Max looked appalled. "No! Absolutely not! No!" he said, shaking his head emphatically. "This place is…" His face worked as his mind sought the words. "… is, full of dragons!"

Lizzie looked disappointed. "But you said that you and Elrus went exploring earlier," she pouted.

"We only went to find the Great Hall so that we knew where to go for dinner," he stressed. Then giving her a knowing look, continued, "You must be careful, Princess. You know how daring you can be and your grandfather will be most displeased if you put yourself in danger."

Elrus put a friendly arm around Max's shoulder. "Come on, mate; live a little."

Max looked at Elrus as though dealing with a naughty child. "You shouldn't be encouraging her, Elrus," he admonished. "We're meant to be protecting her."

Elrus looked at Max earnestly. "But we will be looking after her," he said. "Look; if we don't go with her she'll just

244

go on her own. Remember what she was like when you met her?" he continued, indicating Lizzie, who was staring at the ceiling, doing her best to whistle, unsuccessfully, and trying to appear nonchalant.

Max looked at Lizzie thoughtfully. Elrus was right, of course, but Max thought it would be madness to go exploring somewhere with such evident dangers. Elvedom Castle after all was a safe place – that's if you didn't go falling through Thresholds into the domains of your worst enemy.

Eloise stood and watched her three companions. She felt a strong bond between them but felt she was still on the edge of it all. The fact that she was there with them, she knew meant that she had a role to play but what that role was to be, she didn't yet understand. Eloise could see that Max was worried, he was a bit of a worry-wart, and so she placed a gentle hand on his arm.

"I'm sure that there will be signs warning of any particularly dangerous places, Max. So, if we stick to the corridors and passages and don't go into those marked dangerous (at this point she gave Lizzie and Elrus a warning glance as if to say don't you dare enter them), we'll be fine, " she reassured him. Max seemed to relax a little at her words but his face showed his uncertainty. Then, as if resigning himself that it was going to happen whether he liked it or not, he agreed to join the little exploration party.

They decided that they would wait until the older members of their travelling group had gone to bed and then meet up in Lizzie's room; they didn't want to risk Mrs Longton coming in to check on Lizzie and find her room empty and so raise the alarm.

Alone in her room, Lizzie went to the slit of a window and peered through at the sliver of a view. The darkness outside obliterated the mountains she knew to be there, instead all she could see was a multitude of stars in the clear black sky and the silvery beams of the moon up high. She walked over to her bed and lay down, staring blankly up at the ceiling above her. She was wide awake and her brain buzzed, as, once again, it churned over the events of the day.

It felt as though hours had passed, when she finally heard the tread of footsteps coming along the corridor outside her room. Whispered voices, obviously believing the young people to be asleep, said their goodnights and Lizzie quickly turned on her side, facing away from the door and closed her eyes. Seconds later she heard the handle of the door to her room turn and someone come in.

"Ah, bless!" she heard her grandmother's voice say quietly. Her soft footsteps came closer to the bed and Mrs Longton, who must have been talking to herself, said, "She must have been exhausted, falling asleep fully dressed."

As Mrs Longton reached the bed, she bent and pulled the blanket that was draped over the edge, across Lizzie's apparently sleeping body. Lizzie smiled inwardly at her grandmother's gentle touch, as she smoothed Lizzie's hair away from her face and she found it hard not to reach out and hug Mrs Longton. Turning from the bed Mrs Longton tip-toed out of the room and closed the door quietly behind her, leaving Lizzie feeling more than a little guilty; she had now deceived her beloved grandmother twice in one evening. Flopping onto her back, she stared up at the ceiling and decided that tomorrow she would tell her grandmother everything but that tonight she was going on an adventure.

After waiting several minutes she went to her bedroom door and placing her ear on the cold hard surface listened. The corridor outside was silent. Opening the door slowly, she prayed that it wouldn't creak; it didn't. Glancing left and right along the length of the passageway, she breathed a sigh of relief that there was no-one to be seen. As if they had sensed her presence, the doors to Elrus, Eloise and Max's rooms also opened slowly and three young heads popped out.

At Lizzie's signal, the four friends left their rooms and made their way quickly and silently back to the main stairway. Elrus began creeping down the stairs, holding up a hand as a sign for the others to wait until he knew that they wouldn't bump into anyone making their way up them.

"I hope he's not going to do that weird, creeping thing he did when we were in the woods that time," Max hissed in Lizzie's ear, causing her to chuckle.

Beckoning the others to follow him, Elrus did the weird creeping thing – on his tip-toes, bent at the knees with his back to the wall - as he made his way further down the stairs. At the bottom and out into the open courtyard with its balustrades to either side, the four friends made their way over to their left where more stairs led down towards the dragon caverns. As they reached them and Elrus took a step onto the first rung, Max's hand shot out and grabbed him, pulling him back from the brink.

Elrus looked surprised as Max shook his head vigorously. "No way are we going down there," Max almost spat at him. Lizzie, placed a soothing hand on Max's arm.

"It's okay, Max. The dragons are penned in, they're not going to get at us," she said, trying to calm the now shaking Max; although she wasn't sure if the trembling was caused by fear or anger, as his face looked very fierce.

"I mean it Princess, we are not going down there without someone trained to deal with dragons. It would be madness! We haven't got Flaxon here with his magical calming pipes should something go wrong," Max insisted, his blue eyes flashing in warning.

"Okay, okay," agreed Elrus, wrenching his arm from Max's tight grip and rubbing it.

Eloise looked at Lizzie and her dark eyes showed that she too was having second thoughts about this moonlight adventure.

"Maybe we should wait until tomorrow when we go to visit the hatchery," she said quietly. "Hey, we could then do a recce of the place as we pass through," she suggested, more enthusiastically.

Lizzie sighed and was about to reluctantly agree when suddenly Elrus began pushing her and the others in the direction of a large statue of a dragon over by the balustrade closest to them.

"Quick, someone's coming," he urged. His sharp hearing had picked up the voices of people coming into courtyard. The four friends crouched down behind the statue and out of sight of whoever had just entered the space.

"Why? Why do you insist on tormenting me so?" said a male voice; the hurt in it was almost palpable. There was no reply. Maybe he's talking to himself Lizzie thought until she then heard a sharp intake of breath and a woman say:

"Let go of me!"

Lizzie had to stop herself from jumping out from behind the statue as she recognized the voice of Elenya. The four friends looked at each other with wide eyes and pricked ears. With the utmost stealth, Lizzie peered around the statue's plinth and saw her aunt standing several metres away, the moon's luminous rays cast their light over her aunt's perfect features and her long blond hair shone like spun gold. Standing close to her, his head down and with his back slightly turned towards Lizzie, she could make out the black clad figure of General Eldron holding onto her aunt's arm. Lizzie was captivated by the scene.

"I'm sorry," Eldron was saying, releasing his grip. Then raising his head and staring into Elenya's face, he said with his voice almost breaking, "I should not have touched you, Your Highness. It was inappropriate." He bowed his head briefly once more before bringing it up to look at her directly again and saying so softly that, even with her acute hearing, Lizzie had to strain in order to pick up his words, "You know I would never hurt you."

"But you did," Elenya cried scornfully. "You left me without a word of explanation and hid yourself away here in this isolated eyrie."

"I did not want to leave you but I had no choice," Eldron said resignedly. "Your father would never accept a union between us, you know that. Until Eldorth is defeated …." His voice trailed away as he hung his head into his hands.

Elenya looked at Eldron sadly and reached out to touch his hands but stopped before making contact with him. Her hand dropped to her side.

"If you had loved me, you would have fought for me," she said, so sadly that Lizzie felt a terrible lump form in her own throat as she sensed the sharp pain of her aunt's lost love. Eldron's hands dropped from his face and he reached towards Elenya. She took a step back from him.

"I will love you always, you must know that Elenya," Eldron said earnestly. "One day we will be together. We must. Until then can you not at least be civil to me?"

Elenya tossed her hair and raised her chin defiantly. "I may not be prepared to wait that long but I will do my best to be civil, as you put it." Then brushing past him she strode across the courtyard towards the stairs that would take her to the sanctuary of her bed chamber. As she got half way across she began to run and Lizzie watched with a heavy heart as her aunt ran past her with her hand over her mouth and tears streaming down her face. Elenya was always so strong and in control of things that it made it even more difficult to witness her distress.

As Elenya disappeared up the stairs, Lizzie turned to see Eldorth almost stagger towards a balustrade and, with his hand placed on it for support, stare up at the crescent moon with pain etched on his handsome face.

Lizzie fell back and sat down next to her friends and they stared at each other. "Well, now we know why the General was getting the cold shoulder treatment," Elrus said quietly.

"Yes," Lizzie nodded. "But why would grandfather never allow them to be together?" she asked. The others just shook their heads and shrugged. There was definitely more to this than they had just witnessed, Lizzie thought, and decided that she was going to find out what was keeping the lovers apart.

# CHAPTER 27

## Dragon Dilemma

"Ma'am! Ma'am! If you don't get up soon there will be no breakfast left in the place. Those Dragon Elves eat like, like – well, dragons!" Elwood exclaimed impatiently. He was standing at the end of Lizzie's bed and pulling at the blanket whilst Lizzie gripped the other end tightly, holding it up under her chin.

She finally let go, almost causing Elwood to fall over backwards, and dragged herself out of bed. Lizzie had spent a restless night, tossing and turning as she replayed in her mind everything that had happened over the past twenty four hours. She had finally fallen into an exhausted sleep only to have been woken, a seemingly short time afterwards, by the increasingly irritated Elwood.

"Okay, okay," she grumbled, yawning loudly just to emphasise how tired she was.

Elwood picked up the blanket, which had fallen to the floor, and the pile of clothes that Lizzie had discarded the previous night; muttering under his breath about having to pick up after her as he did so. He quickly tidied the room while Lizzie went off to get showered.

"Breakfast's in the refectory," he called after her, as she disappeared out of the door.

After a very brief shower, the power of which blasted away any remnants of sleep that may have lingered, Lizzie dressed hastily and made her way downstairs. She knocked on each of her friends' bedroom doors to see if they would accompany her but when she got no answer, she assumed that they were either still sleeping or they were already having breakfast.

In the courtyard she was greeted by the rasping caw of Mag, on apparent lookout on the head of the dragon statue that Lizzie and her friends had hidden behind the night before. The image of Elenya running past in tears, flashed through Lizzie's mind and she felt again the pang of sadness that she had experienced at the time. Turning to the magpie she asked where Max was. Mag flapped her wings and Lizzie almost believed she understood Mag's rasping reply of, "He's through there!" as she turned towards the entrance to the mountain top fortress's inner Keep.

Entering the large entrance hall, she could hear the hubbub of voices coming from somewhere off to her right. Following the noise she found herself in a large chamber full of tables and chairs, most of which were occupied by elves chatting amongst themselves whilst they tucked into plates piled high with food. She looked around for familiar faces and finally, across the room at one of the tables, she could see her friends and her grandmother engrossed in something a Dragon Elf was saying. Eloise suddenly noticed Lizzie and waved frantically for her to join them.

As Lizzie reached the table, much to her surprise, the Dragon Elf jumped up and saluted her. She blinked and almost took a step back at the elf's sudden unexpected act, and wondered if she would ever get used to this sort of treatment but she smiled politely and inclined her head in acknowledgement. The elf was tall and muscular, like the other Dragon Elves she had seen, but he appeared much older. His black hair was flecked with grey, as was his neatly trimmed beard and moustache, and his grey eyes under a broad brow were defined by crows feet lines at the corners or, as Lizzie's grandmother liked to call them, his laughter lines.

Elrus, noticing Lizzie's reaction to the Dragon Elf's salute, grinned and introduced him.

"Princess, this is Eldrid, he is the Hatchery Master."

Eldrid saluted. "I am honoured to meet you, Your Highness," he said, bowing his head.

"Likewise," Lizzie smiled. Eldrid waited until she had sat down and then followed suit.

Before Lizzie had a chance to ask where she got her food from a plate of what her grandmother would call a "Full English", was placed in front of her by a young serving elf. Thanking him she tucked hungrily into her breakfast, it was delicious.

Watching her in fascination from the corner of his eye, as he didn't wish to appear rude, Eldrid went on to explain that they would go down to the hatchery after breakfast.

"There are a couple of eggs that are almost fully incubated," he said. "They should hatch any day now."

"How exciting," breathed Eloise. "Oh, I do hope we get to see them hatch." Her pretty face beamed with the thought of seeing a baby dragon enter the world.

"I'm sure that can be arranged," Eldrid said, smiling at her.

"When you say incubated, how do you incubate them?" Mrs Longton asked. "I mean are they like chicken eggs, in that the mother has to sit on them?" Her face showed that she was worried by the idea as she had hoped not to come into close contact with the creatures again, after the shock of seeing them the previous day.

Eldrid threw back his head and let out a loud laugh. Then, eyes twinkling, he turned to face her.

"Oh, very funny, Mrs Longton. A dragon sitting on its eggs! Ha, ha!"

Mrs Longton looked a little affronted by the reaction and as Eldrid realized that she was being quite serious, he cleared his throat and put on a straight face.

"Umm, no. Dragons don't sit on their eggs. The weight of their bodies would crush them. No, the eggs are normally incubated by heat. If the eggs were left for the mothers to incubate they would use their fire. For safety reasons, we do not allow the dragons to use fire unless we choose to do so.

Therefore, we remove the eggs and they are heated in the hatchery until they are ready to hatch," he explained.

With their breakfast over, Lizzie and her companions accompanied Eldrid and made their way out of the refectory and towards the dragon hatchery. As they were leaving, Lizzie noticed Elenya across the room in animated conversation with Elgawen. She was shaking her head at something that Elgawen was saying and looking very serious. Lizzie paused to watch and, as she did so, Elenya noticed her. She smiled and waved and blew Lizzie a kiss. Lizzie waved back before following Eldrid and the others out of the room.

Crossing the courtyard they made their way to the stairs that led to the caverns below. Mag flew down and landed on Max's shoulder but, as he ran his hand along her sleek, feathery back, he told her to wait there.

"I don't think the dragon caverns are the best place for you Mag. You'll be much better off up here," he said, sending the bird back to her perch.

The warmth of the caverns below became increasingly evident as the group made their way down the stairs. As they passed the tunnel to take them into the main cavern, where they had seen the dragons the day before, Eldrid explained that the hatchery was on a lower level. Following him carefully down the steep steps, Mrs Longton began to puff.

"My, it's very warm down here," she huffed, waving her hand in front of her face in an attempt to fan it cool. She watched the back of Eldrid as he led the way and thought that the leather garb he was dressed in must be unbearably hot and decided that she would ask him about it at some point.

Finally, they reached a level that went in three different directions. Eldrid stopped.

"The hatchery is down this tunnel here," he explained, pointing the way to the left. "This one straight ahead contains the facility for the juvenile dragons that are in the early stages of training." He then turned towards the tunnel leading to the hatchery.

"Excuse me!" called Lizzie. "But what's down that tunnel there?" she asked, pointing down the one to the right.

"Restricted access, Your Highness," he said and without further explanation strode off down left hand tunnel. Lizzie and Elrus looked at each other quizzically. Max noticed the look and his heart sank. He could read those two like a book and that look meant trouble. If they weren't meant to go there, then that was exactly where they would try to go.

"Don't even think about it," Max hissed in warning, into Lizzie's and Elrus's ears as he guided them towards the tunnel that led to the hatchery.

"What?" asked an innocent faced Elrus. Max just shook his head.

In the hatchery the heat was stifling, it was like walking into a hot oven. Around the sides of the room were a series of bowls hewn out of rock with a recess beneath each that contained a burning fire. Several of the bowls held a single dragon's egg, each one resembling a large rugby ball in shape. The eggshells differed in colour, some were blue, some green, others red or orange but each one glowed with an iridescent gleam. They were beautiful.

Eldrid removed a large leather apron from a hook by the entrance to the room and donning a pair of thick padded gauntlets he picked up a large pair of iron tongs.

"The eggs have to be turned regularly to ensure they are properly incubated," he explained, walking to the nearest one and using the tongs to rotate the blue egg.

"Do the colours have a particular significance? I mean does it indicate the incubation stage?" asked Mrs Longton, mopping her forehead with a handkerchief she had taken from a pocket in her trousers. She was sweating profusely and it was running down her forehead into her eyes and dripping from the end of her nose; like the children around her, her face was a brilliant shade of red. Eldrid on the other hand seemed to be quite cool, and although there was a sheen to his skin there was no sign of a drop of sweat.

"It's usually an indication of the colour of the young dragon but it has been known for a blue egg to produce a purple dragon," he told them. Mrs Longton nodded in understanding, her hair was now plastered to her head and she was obviously feeling very uncomfortable. Lizzie looked at her grandmother in concern.

"Are you okay gran? You look awfully hot," she asked.

"I think I may have to wait outside for a bit," Mrs Longton said, wafting the handkerchief in front of her face in the vain hope of it cooling her down. "Do you have any water here?" she asked, trying to appear calm but feeling that she was getting to the point where she might faint if she didn't get a drink soon.

Eldrid, busy with his egg turning, didn't seem to notice her increasing distress but when asked, he indicated, with a jerk of his head, that there was a water fountain back along the tunnel where the three tunnels joined. Lizzie took her grandmother's arm and said she would go with her.

Upon reaching the water fountain, which looked very like the dragon egg bowls but with a continuous stream of water flowing from a spout above it, Mrs Longton almost stuck her whole head under the flow. The water was ice cold and she sighed in relief as it splashed over her face. Opening her mouth beneath the spout she swallowed the cold sweet liquid.

"Ahh…," she sighed, standing back and letting the water drip from her face. Lizzie laughed at the sight of her and Mrs Longton grinned. "I needed that!"

Lizzie then did the same and guzzled down the water, letting it flow over her flushed cheeks and cooling them. As she stood up, she suddenly heard a roaring sound as though an animal was in terrible pain; it made her blood run cold.

"What was that?" she exclaimed, looking around her with eyes wide.

"What was what?" asked Mrs Longton, who was in the process of wetting her handkerchief under the spout.

"That roar; something's in trouble," she said. The roar came again, followed by a pitiful whining. "There it is again!"

Mrs Longton looked confused. "I didn't hear anything, darling. I must be going deaf in my old age," she smiled.

"No gran. It sounds terrible. Something's in trouble, I can sense it," she said, her ears pricked and listening out for the troubled creature. Her acute hearing could hear the whimper of a distressed creature and following the noise she discovered it was coming from the tunnel that Eldrid had said had restricted access.

Lizzie turned to her grandmother. "It's down there," she explained. "It needs my help gran."

Mrs Longton shook her head emphatically. "No Lizzie. Let's go and get Eldrid he'll know what to do."

Lizzie shook her head slowly. "No, I don't think he will." The whimpering had stopped and now Lizzie could hear the sound of someone or something pleading to her.

"Save me. Save me."

Mrs Longton, was in a dilemma. She knew that the right thing to do would be to go and seek Eldrid's help, but she also knew that Lizzie was discovering new things about herself all the time. So maybe Lizzie was right and she was the one who must deal with this. Mrs Longton wrung her hands together.

"Oh Lizzie, I don't know. You could be placing yourself in real danger. There's got to be good reason why it's a restricted access tunnel," she said, pacing up and down.

Lizzie put out a hand and held her grandmother's arm to stop her.

"But I do know, gran. It's like when I helped the pterotorial – it's something I have to do," she said gently. "Just wait here." Then, before Mrs Longton could stop her,

257

Lizzie left her grandmother standing and watching as she disappeared into the restricted tunnel.

The tunnel seemed to go on for an age and sloped gradually downwards as she walked along it, listening out for the sound of the injured or troubled creature as she went. The whimpering came intermittently as if the source of it had resigned itself to its situation, before it whimpered once again.

The light in the tunnel was very dim with only an occasional burning torch to break up the darkness. Lizzie surprised herself at how unafraid she felt, considering she really had no idea of what possible danger she was walking towards. She kept her ears pricked to listen out for the sound of the distressed creature but it had gone very quiet.

"Maybe it's heard me coming and is frightened," she thought to herself. So, she decided to call out to it.

"Hello, hello! Are you okay?" she called, trying to sound as friendly as she could.

"I am here!" a voice replied.

The sound came from a little way ahead of her and so moving forward, she could see to her left a large wooden door with wide bands of reinforced metal across its width to strengthen it. She could see no place for a key but a large metal ring served as a handle and so placing her hand on it, she turned it slowly.

The door was thick and extremely heavy and it took great effort to push it open enough to enable her to squeeze through the gap. A torch was burning close to the doorway but apart from that, there was no other source of light. She found herself in a large cave that seemed to stretch away into a dark recess. Taking the torch from its sconce, she began to walk towards the recess and as she did so something moved and she heard the sound of what appeared to be a heavy chain clank against the stone floor.

She lifted the torch higher and suddenly could see a pair of large amber eyes staring back at her. It took her so by

258

surprise she almost dropped the torch. The eyes blinked and Lizzie got the intense feeling that the creature behind them was racked with pain and sadness.

"Hi. My name's Lizzie. I heard you calling out," she said gently. The sound of chains rattling could be heard again as the creature shifted its body once again.

"I can feel that you're in need of help in some way," Lizzie continued.

"How can *you* help me?" the creature replied dismissively. "You're such a small thing."

Lizzie relaxed a little. She felt that there was a connection between her and the creature and that it wouldn't hurt her so she moved a little closer. As she did so the light of the torch fell upon the scaly skin of a silvery white shape. The bright amber coloured eyes never left her face. Lizzie's own eyes were now beginning to adjust to the dim light level and as they did so she found that she was looking at a young dragon. Its beautiful silvery skin glimmered in the torch light and its huge horned head turned to face her full on. The sight of the dragon almost took her breath away with its magnificence but then she could see that it was tethered by shackles around its legs and neck and chained to the wall. Sadness welled up inside her at its plight. The poor creature could barely move.

Lizzie spotted another sconce on the wall and placed the torch in it before once more walking slowly towards the dragon.

"I won't hurt you," she said gently as she approached.

"But how do you know that I won't hurt you?" the dragon replied.

"Because I don't think you will. I trust you not to," Lizzie said. "Why are you chained in this way? And why are you on your own in here?" she asked.

"Why do *you* want to know?" the dragon asked, almost petulantly.

"Because I'm interested," Lizzie replied.

The dragon looked away from her for the first time since she had entered the cave and shifted his body as if trying to make himself comfortable.

"Well?" Lizzie asked encouragingly. I think this needs firm handling, she thought to herself.

"Because I'm dangerous!" he roared. The dragon's breath as it roared was like being blasted by a very large hairdryer and Lizzie closed her eyes against it. Silently she thanked the Dragon Elves for not allowing the dragons their fire or she'd have seriously singed eye-brows. She stood her ground and, once the roar had petered out, sat down on the floor and crossed her legs. The dragon looked taken aback at her lack of reaction; she hadn't even faltered.

"Well that's silly," she scoffed. "How can you be any more dangerous than any of the other dragons here? Surely all dragons are potentially dangerous," she continued.

The dragon was confused by the small girl sitting crossed legged in front of him. Why was she unafraid of him? The Dragon Elves kept him chained here because they were afraid of the powers they knew he possessed. He cocked his head to one side as he eyed Lizzie carefully. Perhaps, this was the special one that he had been waiting for.

"Well, maybe I'm more dangerous than you seem to think I look," he said, raising his head proudly despite the restriction of the huge metal collar and chain around his neck.

Lizzie noticed his lack of movement and said sadly, "You must be very uncomfortable."

The dragon sneered and turned away from her. "I cope."

"You know it's okay to tell me how you feel," she said soothingly. "I won't tell if you don't want me to but maybe I can get them to make things better for you."

The dragon swung his head around and looked at her, his eyes sparkled with pent up anger. "The only thing that's going to make things better for me is to get out of this place and see the sunlight." His head suddenly dropped and he looked defeated.

"I've never seen sunlight."

Tears welled up in Lizzie's eyes and a shooting pain of sadness whipped across her chest. She felt this creature's misery as if it were her own and knew for certain that she must help him.

"That's terrible and I'm going to make sure you get out of here," she said, her voice full of determination. "By the way, you haven't told me your name."

"I cannot," the dragon replied.

"Why not? I told you mine, so it'd be rude if you don't tell me yours," she said.

"I do not have a name to tell you," was the reply.

"But everyone has a name, so why haven't you got one?" Lizzie responded in surprise.

The dragon's eyes flared as they showed his irritation at Lizzie's questioning.

"I have never been given a name. Dragons are named by the Dragon Elf that they are assigned to and I have no Dragon Elf to name me."

"Then you should choose your own name," said Lizzie happily.

"I do not think you understand what you are saying," the dragon replied, suspiciously.

Lizzie was confused. "Well, I think it's pretty straight forward, just pick a name that you like," she replied.

It was the first time that Lizzie sensed that the dragon was smiling at her in his own way.

"When I say I do not think you understand, I feel that there is something I should explain to you before you give me the right to name myself. By allowing me to do so you are giving me my independence. I cannot be owned by any

Dragon Elf and will not be under anyone's control but my own," he said.

"But that's a good thing, isn't it?" Lizzie replied. "I mean, who wants to be someone else's slave. Go on! Choose a name," she encouraged.

The dragon looked deep into Lizzie's eyes and she returned the stare.

"You know my name," he said slowly.

Lizzie blinked hard and then, staring into his eyes once again, the connection between them was complete.

"I do," she said, remembering her dream of the night before. "You are Dronan!"

As the dragon's name left her lips the door to the cave crashed open and Eldrid and General Eldron strode in.

As Lizzie scrambled to her feet and faced them, she could see her grandmother and three friends hovering in the background by the door.

"Move away, Princess," General Eldron said softly, beckoning her towards him. "Just back away slowly."

Lizzie stood still. "It's okay," she said confidently. "Dronan and I are fine, aren't we Dronan?" she said turning back to the dragon now behind her. Dronan made a low rumbling noise, not unlike an enormous purring cat, as he eyed the new arrivals warily.

"You've named him?" In his shock, the General almost whispered the words.

"Not really," Lizzie replied. "I just knew it was his name, didn't I Dronan?" Dronan rumbled in agreement. She looked at the dragon in confusion. "Why won't you speak for yourself? Go on tell them," she urged. Dronan remained silent.

"The dragon will not speak. We don't even know that he can," Eldrid said, disparagingly. "The creature is untrainable and should have been destroyed at birth."

262

Dronan let out a deafening roar. "It's okay, Dronan!" Lizzie soothed, trying to calm him. Then, glowering at the Hatchery Master, she said, "He didn't mean it, did you Eldrid?"

Eldrid looked down at his feet and mumbled, "No Your Highness."

"I think we should leave now, Princess," General Eldron said, with more authority this time.

"I'm not leaving until those shackles are taken off Dronan," Lizzie sat down on the floor once again and this time crossed her arms as well as her legs.

"Elizabeth Longton, come out of there at once," came the stern tones of Mrs Longton, as she peered around General Eldron and Eldrid, who were now staring at Lizzie disbelievingly.

Lizzie defiantly stayed put. The General hunkered down and spoke gently to her.

"Your Highness, you would be safer coming with us now," he cajoled.

"I am perfectly safe where I am," Lizzie reiterated. "General, last night when we spoke about – you know what – I didn't ask you whether or not you work with a particular dragon. So, do you?"

The General nodded.

"So how did you know which dragon you would work with?" she asked.

The General seemed to think for a moment before saying, "There was a connection between us."

Lizzie's face broke into a broad grin. "Exactly!" she exclaimed. "It's the same with Dronan here. We have connected. He called out to me somehow and sought my help. I'm meant to be with him," she explained.

The General looked at her sadly and shook his head. "This is not possible, Your Highness," he asserted.

263

Lizzie raised her chin boldly and asked why. Dronan and the others present watched with interest as the General eased himself down and sat on the floor facing Lizzie.

"It is not possible because he is a male dragon," the General explained. Lizzie looked perplexed. "Dragon Elves only work and fly with female dragons. Females are more manageable as male dragons are difficult to train due to their strong independent nature. They cannot be trusted to do as they are bid."

A loud snort and the sound of rustling wings came from Dronan and Lizzie looked around at him as she sensed the contempt with which he held the General's words. General Eldron looked over Lizzie's shoulder at him and uncertainty flickered across his handsome face. Dronan settled down and laid his great head across his folded front legs, his huge amber eyes still fixed on the pair sitting just a few metres away.

The General returned his gaze to Lizzie. "This dragon is a Silver male and they are the most fearsome of all dragons," he said quietly. "We control the births of dragons and will not incubate male dragon eggs but this one was not discovered until he hatched. We thought that he may die if neglected but, like all elves, we could not allow this cruelty to happen, so we have kept him here. Attempts were made some time ago to train him but he would not obey our instruction as he did not connect with any of the Dragon Elves. Now he stays here until he is old enough to use for breeding to produce eggs with our female dragons."

Lizzie gave the General a puzzled look. "You say that you could not allow him to die because it would have been cruel but look at him," she turned and looked at Dronan and he lifted his head in response. "This is cruel. It would have been kinder to have had him killed than locked away in this cave for years. He's magnificent and he should be allowed to fly and train with the other dragons. It's not his fault he's a male. Let me train with him?"

The General sat back in amazement. "Let, let you train with him?" He laughed in disbelief. "I think not, Your Highness."

"Please," Lizzie implored. "I promise you that he will work with me. Won't you Dronan?" The dragon grunted. She turned around and faced Dronan fully. "You will won't you Dronan? Just think you will see the sunlight, have the wind beneath your wings, won't that be wonderful? You just have to promise to work with me and you will lose the shackles."

"They will never free me," Dronan moaned sadly.

Eldrid almost fell backwards into the others standing behind him in shock as he heard Dronan speak for the first time, whilst General Eldron leant back on his hands and shook his head.

"Just tell them that you'll work with me, please Dronan," Lizzie pleaded.

Dronan looked past her at the Dragon Master still sitting on the floor and with his huge amber eyes boring into General Eldron's said, "I will only work with you Princess."

"Lizzie!" interjected Lizzie.

"With Lizzie," Dronan added. "I will do all that she, and only she, bids me to do. I will not use my fire unless she bids it or it is absolutely what must be done."

Lizzie laughed, "Oh Dronan. They won't let you do that anyway."

General Eldron had got slowly to his feet by this time and helped Lizzie to hers. "That is not strictly true, Your Highness. Male dragon fire is not the same as that of the females. Dronan here still has his fire within him and although as a young dragon it doesn't yet have the full power of an adult, it is still strong. It is why you could have put yourself in real danger."

Lizzie's eyes flew wide as she stared at Dronan. "So you could have fried me!" she exclaimed.

Dronan's eyes twinkled brightly as he acknowledged that he could. "You've not enough flesh on you to appease my appetite," he said jokingly.

General Eldron eyed Dronan warily. He still wasn't convinced he was doing the right thing but his princess was determined. "Well Princess, it would seem you have yourself a dragon," he declared.

Eldrid, who had remained by the door, came forward at the General's request. He was instructed to make arrangements for Dronan to be moved down to the training stables where other young dragons were housed. Lizzie moved closer to the young dragon.

"This is going to be so great," she smiled at him. Dronan dipped his head to her then looking up into her eyes said, "I will do my best to make it so."

As she left the cave with her grandmother and three friends she glanced back to see Eldron and Eldrid removing the shackles that bound Dronan's legs and sighed in relief. She had saved him and, in doing so, there was now a bond between them that she knew would last her life-time.

# CHAPTER 28

## Enemies Enmity

The atmosphere in the Great Hall of Maladorth Castle was as icy as the temperature. Although the sun beat down on the lands surrounding it, none of its heat filtered through the castle's impenetrable walls.

Eldorth hadn't slept well in weeks and the lack of it showed in his face, which looked drawn and lined. His haunted eyes had dark shadows beneath them but their piercing intensity was undiminished and showed the bitterness that was gnawing away at him. The spies that he had sent to follow Melisha had failed to report back to him for too long and he was furious that he had no idea of what the witch was up to.

The apparition floating just off the ground in front of Eldorth radiated a malevolence that even he found a little disturbing. The air around the wraith smelt of rotting flesh, even though it was not of solid matter. A dark, tattered flowing robe floated about its wasted frame and Eldorth grimaced at the sight of its skull, which was just visible through the dripping flesh of its translucent form. Everything surrounding the wraith was dark and menacing; in life, hundreds of years before, it must have committed unthinkably wicked acts to have been condemned to its current existence. The silence of the wraith was eerily threatening, but as Eldorth had summoned up the being and its fellows it owed him its loyalty.

"So there has been no sighting of her?" Eldorth asked, the exasperation in his voice clearly evident.

The wraith shook its head slowly from side to side.

"Damnation!" yelled Eldorth, hitting the arm of his chair with the side of his fist in frustration. "Where has the woman gone?" The question was rhetorical and so required no answer but the ghostly presence appeared to shrug its shoulders all the same.

"Well, just keep some of your troops on the lookout for her whereabouts," Eldorth instructed. "I want her brought back here as soon as possible." The wraith dipped its head in acknowledgement.

Although Eldorth found Melisha repugnant and despised her slovenly ways, he knew that he needed her, because not only did she hold the magic that he so desperately craved for himself, but she was also his only real confidant. She must be found and quickly as he did not trust her completely.

"I take it the Chalice is still safely guarded?" Eldorth queried. The wraith dipped its head again to indicate that it was.

"Well, make sure your guards ensure it remains so. They must be extra vigilant as I have reason to believe there may be attempts to steal it."

Following Lizzie's healing of the wounded pterotorial that had attacked her and her party, its accomplice had returned with its wraith rider to report that a group of travellers had been seen in the south. The description of one of the individuals in the group sounded very like the daughter of Eldorth's most hated enemy and he knew that if Princess Elenya was on the move then it would only mean trouble for him. The last piece of intelligence that he had received was from a hobgoblin messenger, who had said that there had been a skirmish in the foothills of the Mountains of Snow between some of his people and a group who sounded very similar to those previously spotted by the wraith rider. If this report was accurate, then Eldorth had a good idea of where the party was heading and, if he was right, then it was a worrying turn of events.

Eldorth had considered having the Chalice moved to a different location but that in itself presented problems, as it could draw unwanted attention from prying eyes. He decided that it was better to leave it where it was but with enhanced protection. However, if Elfred had resorted to enlisting the help of those who Eldorth suspected, then it would not be an easy task to keep the relic safe.

Eldorth slumped back into his chair wearily and briefly closed his eyes. With Melisha gone he had no one to make the draughts that would aid his sleep at night or give him the energy with which to cope during his waking hours. His mind never rested and so sleep eluded him, leaving him feeling listless and drained. So, in her absence he had had to turn to another who had said she was adept at herbal remedies.

He turned his attention back to the wraith still hovering in front of him and with a dismissive wave of his hand indicated that it should go.

"Oh, and tell that half-wit, Orfwit, to send in the girl with my herbal draught. I need to replenish my energy," Eldorth instructed the departing apparition.

Moments later the door to the Hall opened and a young blond she-elf came in carrying a tray containing a pewter jug and goblet. She stood in front of the dais, where Eldorth sat with his eyes closed.

"Your energy draught, Lord," Ella said, looking at him in feigned adoration, as Eldorth opened his eyes.

"You know the routine," Eldorth said lazily.

Ella did know the routine and began to pour some of the liquid from the jug into a small glass beside the goblet. Lifting the glass to her lips, she swallowed its contents. After a few moments to ensure that the liquid was safe to drink, Eldorth indicated that she could pour him a goblet of the draught. He still did not trust the girl fully but he would use her until the errant Melisha showed up once more.

After spending several days in the dungeons of the castle, Ella had finally managed to persuade Eldorth that she had been doing nothing more than foraging for herbs when she had been caught outside the castle walls. She had been lax in ensuring that she was not seen and had suffered the consequences when she had been discovered. However, with Eldorth's accomplice Melisha out of the way, her lie about collecting herbs must have resonated with him and he had called for her. Like many of her kind, Ella did have knowledge of the types and uses of herbs and plants. She was in no way a healer but she could make simple concoctions to aid common ailments and so she used her understanding of herbal properties to make the draughts that Eldorth demanded. She knew they had limited benefits but she hoped they would suffice to keep Eldorth satisfied as to her usefulness.

Eldorth kept Ella under strict surveillance, which was inconvenient, but she was now able to follow the instructions she had received from King Elfred during her incarceration in the dungeons below and wheedle her way back into Eldorth's inner sanctum. Here she hoped she would, once again, elicit pieces of useful intelligence that she could pass to her true master back at Elvedom Castle. She hoped the last piece of information she had sent King Elfred, which had been the cause of her capture, was proving to be invaluable - the location of the sacred relic, the Chalice of Elaria.

*

Several hundred miles away to the north, Melisha approached the Great Library of Eldinburgh. She was surprised to see that it was guarded on all sides by elven soldiers; the silver breastplates of their uniforms sparkled in the morning sunlight. The soldiers had travelled from lands in the south of Elvedom to a sea port several miles distant to the Elcaledonian capital and had marched across land until they had reached Eldinburgh. Their task was to ensure that the security of the Great Library was not breached and they had orders to keep close watch for any approach by the slovenly witch, Melisha.

Two soldiers guarding the vast doors to the Library stood statue-like. Only their eyes, which swivelled in their sockets to watch the approaching woman, gave away the fact that they were not hewn from the same stone as the building they protected. As Melisha drew near the doors, the soldiers turned as one and the spears in their hands barred the witch's way.

"Halt! Why do you seek entrance to the Great Library of Eldinburgh?" barked one of the soldiers.

Melisha peered up into the face of the soldier and batted her eyelashes furiously in a flirtatious way. Then using all the womanly charm she could muster, and putting on a girlish voice, said, "Oh, excuse me sir but I am a healer. I have walked a long way from my village south of here to seek out the recipe for a medicine to heal a very sick child." She cast her eyes down subserviently.

"Do you have proof of what you say?" the soldier asked sharply, not in the slightest bit moved by the flirty Melisha.

Melisha's temper flared in her, "How dare you ask me for proof?" she almost spat at him but swallowing down her anger just simpered and said, "Sorry sir, I did not know I would need proof. I had to travel light and quickly and so had no time to think of bringing any." She raised doe eyes to him again.

The soldier softened and looking to his comrade for reassurance, which the other gave with a curt nod of the head, he agreed that Melisha could pass. Thanking him profusely, Melisha bowed her head and, unseen by her challengers an evil smirk spoiled her now beautiful features. Having talked her way past the soldiers the Librarian sitting at the huge wooden desk situated in the magnificent entrance hall to the building posed no threat and Melisha entered the building's vast interior.

Many years previously, Melisha had been banished from ever entering the Library's hallowed halls again by the guardians who cared for and catalogued its precious contents. The reason for her banishment was due to her attempt to steal one of its most valuable volumes. The enchantments protecting all the books had worked their magic and she had been discovered. Melisha had been furious with herself for thinking that she could have got away with the theft so easily and it had taken her years of searching to discover a way of fooling the guardians into allowing her access once more. The magic of the Pool of Elsabet had been the solution as, not only did the magic alter her body and features, it also cast a concealment charm over her inner personality. She was satisfied that she had enough vials of the magical waters to keep her in her present form for as long as she needed, this meant other magical means could not reveal the true Melisha, only she, herself, could do that.

She had learnt her lesson though and had no intention of attempting to steal another such book. Instead she had hidden a pen and parchment in her clothing to record the spells that she needed. Keeping vigilant, she secretly wrote down each of the most important of the spells. The process was tricky as the guardians periodically walked along the aisles and passages between the huge book cases and tables and was made doubly difficult by the fact that Melisha appeared to be the only person present.

She had arrived at the library three days previously and had visited daily since then. Her current disguise had made it possible for her to pass easily through the library with only an occasional appreciative glance from the library's few occupants. Melisha was now engrossed in the contents of the large book she was reading. Its ancient pages crackled as she turned them. Her now smooth skinned finger, with its perfect nail, trailed the hieroglyphs that covered the aged parchment. The beautiful and intricate writing was not easy to read for an ordinary person but Melisha was well versed in deciphering many of the ancient symbols.

Apart from the periods she spent in the Library, Melisha had used the rest of her time in Eldinburgh in the recruitment of more of the feral-elves and their ilk. She was in her element, the dregs of society were her kind of people and she relished the power she felt in rallying them to her service.

The feral-elf, Elmac, had begged her to fix the arm she had damaged, when he had tried to molest her on the night of her arrival in the city. Melisha had only done so when he had pledged himself to her service and so the following morning he had been dispatched, with some of his gang, to discover the whereabouts of the ancient tribe of Elpicts, an isolated group of elves that lived somewhere in the highlands of Elcaledonia. The Elpicts had the reputation of being ferocious warriors and Melifcent knew that if she was successful in gaining their help, she would have the bargaining power that would put her on more even terms with Eldorth. They also had amongst their tribe, elders called the wise ones, who were versed in ancient magic and it was their knowledge that she desired most. They would help her to translate some of the ancient text that she had discovered and the spell that was contained within it.

Melisha raised her eyes from the book, and rubbed them. She had been reading for hours and was now tired. Slipping the last of the scraps of parchment that she had been scribbling on into her cloak, she closed the heavy tome and replaced it on the shelf. Gathering the folds of her cloak around her, she pulled the hood over her head and walked past the librarian at the desk and out into the night. The elven soldiers still stood on their silent sentinel as she swept past.

Melisha scurried through the cobbled streets heading to the Goblin's Goblet inn where she was staying. As she reached the back street where the inn was located, she could hear the sound of raised voices coming from inside. Suddenly the doors crashed open and two bodies came tumbling out onto the paving stones outside. Standing in the doorway and rubbing his hands together, was the burly form of the inn's landlord.

"And stay out you vermin! No one gets away without paying for their ale," he bellowed. The two individuals scrambled to their feet and scarpered off down the street past Melisha and disappeared into the labyrinth of alleyways that spread throughout the city, like a huge spider's web.

"Good evening, Mistress," greeted the landlord upon spotting Melisha's approach. "I trust you've had a pleasant day."

"That's my business," snarled Melisha, as she brushed past the landlord's rotund belly and into the noisy, smoky bar behind him. The landlord eyed her warily; for such a beautiful woman she was nasty piece of work, he thought. He had some very dodgy customers enter his premises but she was something else. He couldn't quite put his finger on it, but he could sense there was an evil about her that caused even him to be uneasy. He turned and followed her into the bar, as he heard her shout for wine.

Standing at the bar, looking typically dishevelled and grubby and supping from a tankard of ale, Melisha could see that the feral elf Elmac was back. She strode up and stood beside him as he chatted to his gang member, a battle scarred individual with a shaven head and half his ear missing. Elmac didn't notice her at first and continued talking until she interrupted him with, "Oi! Don't ignore me!" she spat as she took the goblet of wine from the landlord who had quickly returned to his post of serving his dubious clientele.

Elmac almost choked on his ale in surprise and as the liquid dripped from his stubbled chin, turned to face Melisha.

"Apologies mistress," he said. Elmac was not easily scared but this woman made him nervous. His arm still ached from his first encounter with her.

"Well? What news do you bring me?" Melisha demanded.

Elmac wiped his chin and cleared his throat before telling her that he believed he had discovered the likely whereabouts of the Elpicts. "They're a nomadic tribe but I've got two of my scouts still out there trailing their tracks. I suggest that if you wish to meet with them we make for the Uplands as soon as possible," he said.

"Then you'd better go and make sure arrangements are made for us to leave at daybreak," she ordered. Then downing the wine, she swept her cloak around her and made for the stairs leading to her room above.

Sitting high up on the roof of the building opposite, unnoticed by Melisha and the landlord, sat a magpie; his jet like eyes watching the scene below. He had been following the witch since she had left Maladorth and his keen eyes and ears had taken in her every move. His master had sent him on this mission after he had received the news of Melisha's intended journey and he knew that whilst she remained in Eldinburgh, then he would too. Only when her plans changed would he fly south to his master with that information. Pi could fly like the wind when the need was on him but for now, he would keep his post.

He swooped across the street and landed on the inn's sign of a wrinkled skinned Goblin drinking from a goblet, which hung from its grey stone façade. He peered through an open window just above it. Inside the room beyond he watched as Melisha came through the door and took off her cloak. She threw it at Elpme and demanded he fetch her food and ale for her supper. The little elf scuttled off on his errand as Melisha extracted the scraps of parchment containing ancient spells from inside her dress and placed them on the table. She leant back in her chair and sighed loudly, stretching her arms above her head lazily. Then, with an evil smile spoiling her beauty, she said aloud, "Soon I'll have all I need. I just hope those Elpicts can translate these ancient spells.

# CHAPTER 29

## Dragon Days

The following days in Eldragonia passed in a haze of activity, as Lizzie and her companions filled them with working alongside the Dragon Elves.

After discovering Lizzie in the Dronan's cave, her three friends had questioned her excitedly about how she had been able to communicate with the young dragon. She had explained that she hadn't been sure how they would feel if she told them that Flaxon had told her that she appeared to speak dragonian after the episode with the pterotorial. Instead of thinking she was odd but that her newly discovered ability was wonderful.

"How amazing!" Eloise had breathed. It had made Lizzie feel even more special having the support and understanding of her friends.

After his move from his solitary cave to reside with the other young dragons undergoing training, Dronan seemed to grow in size and stature. Lizzie took great pleasure in seeing the change in the young dragon, who had been so crushed by his isolated existence. She spent time with him each day, tending to his needs and learning how to train him in the art of flying, let alone fly with a rider on his back. Lizzie had been told that it would be quite some time before Dronan would allow her to climb upon him.

In the early stages she was shown how to strap on the equipment that would be needed to carry a rider but Dronan behaved like a young stallion. The first time a harness and saddle was placed upon him, his reaction had been to rebel against it. Lizzie had to summon up all the strength and authority she could muster to rein the young dragon in, as he bucked and flapped about trying to dislodge the saddle. She was rescued when one of the Dragon Elves held on to the training leash with her until she had managed to calm Dronan. All the while Elrus, Eloise and Max looked on in awe and amazement at her courage in taking on the task.

"You wouldn't catch me getting that close to that creature," commented Max, shrinking back from the scene of Lizzie being dragged hither and thither by the bucking Dronan. Elrus looked at Max with a wry grin.

"Now why doesn't that surprise me mate?" he chuckled.

"I think she's awfully brave," added the wide eyed Eloise.

At the end of each day a tired, bruised and battered Lizzie would fall into the showers and be thankful for the powerful jets of water, as they blasted away the dirt and grime and massaged her aching back and limbs. Now she understood why the elves liked their fierce power showers.

After the first week of training, Dronan seemed to have concluded that it was easier to just accept the strange feeling of the equipment upon him and became much more compliant to the training regime. The next couple of days saw him plodding around the training cavern behind Lizzie, as she led him around on the long training leash, like an extremely large pet dog, much to the amusement of the Dragon Elves looking on.

On the evening of the second day of Dronan's compliance, a tired but happy Lizzie was having supper in the refectory with her friends and some of the other companions, including her grandmother and Elenya.

"So how's Dronan's training coming along, Lizzie?" asked Elenya.

"It's going better now that he's got used to the saddle and stuff," Lizzie smiled. "It was exhausting trying to hang on when he was leaping about all over the place," she laughed

Her companions laughed along with her.

"So when will he be ready to fly?" Prince Finnion asked.

"General Eldron said, that because he hasn't been out in the sunlight before, he will have to start learning to fly after sunset and that he must get used to daylight gradually or it may damage his eyes," Lizzie explained. Elenya's slight wince at the mention of Eldron's name had not gone unnoticed by her.

"Well, he should know," Elenya said, looking down at her food and stabbing at it with her fork.

"We haven't seen much of you over the past week, Elenya," observed Mrs Longton.

"No, I am sorry for that Mrs Longton, but I have been busy with the Dragon Elves and other members of our party making plans for our next course of action," Elenya explained. "I hope you have not been bored," she continued looking at Mrs Longton and the four young people sitting with her.

"Oh no, I've been having a lovely relaxing time after that long ride here," Mrs Longton smiled.

"I certainly haven't," Lizzie said, through a mouthful of mashed potato, causing her grandmother to give her a stern look for speaking with her mouth full as the rest of them laughed.

"Me neither," said Elrus. "Just watching Lizzie fighting with that dragon has been entertainment enough." He grinned.

"We've also been helping the Dragon Elves with mucking out and stuff," added Max, wrinkling his nose at the memory of having to remove great heaps of manure from the dragon pens whilst they were out on exercise.

"It was smelly," grimaced Eloise, causing them all to laugh again.

At that moment General Eldron came striding across the refectory towards them. Upon reaching the group he grabbed a spare chair from a neighbouring table and pulled it up between Lizzie and Elrus, who had been sitting next to her.

278

"Good evening everyone," he said cheerfully.

"Good evening," they responded. Elenya just stared across the table at him. The General's eyes flicked uncertainly from her down to Lizzie sitting next to him.

"I have some good news, Your Highness, well two pieces actually," he announced. "A dragon has just hatched and, as promised, she is to be called Elizabeth."

A ripple of pleasure spread through the occupants of the table at the news, with Mrs Longton crying "How wonderful!" and Eloise's squeal of, "That's brilliant!"

"There can't be many Princesses that have *two* dragons," grinned Max, at the beaming Lizzie.

"Can I see it?" asked Lizzie. "What colour is it?"

"Trust a woman to ask the colour of her dragon," Elrus chimed in, making the males amongst them nod their heads in agreement and the females to protest at his cheek. They then laughed when he added, "It's a good job it was a girl too otherwise a male dragon would have never have lived down being called Elizabeth!"

The General said that the dragon was pale green but added that she might darken as she got older. "Maybe you can go down with your friends tomorrow to see her," he suggested.

"Oh, how lovely," Mrs Longton sighed. Her granddaughter had a green dragon named after her, she so wished that she could tell Bob and Mary back in Chislewick. They would be thrilled too, that was if they didn't think she had lost her mind.

"So, what's the second piece of news?" asked Elenya, her tone icy.

"Well, we are undertaking a flying exercise tomorrow and I thought it would be the right time for you and your companions to join my men," he explained.

"Oh wow!" blurted Elrus. "We get to ride on dragons?"

The General nodded. "In tandem, of course," he said.

279

"What's 'in tandem'?" asked Eloise.

"It means that you will sit with one of my men. You do not possess the skills of flying for one thing but, more importantly, each dragon only answers to their Dragon Elf."

"Is this just for the children or for all of us?" queried Elenya.

"For you all, Princess," the General smiled. "And due to your position within the party, I think it best that you accompany me."

Elenya's beautiful face flushed in annoyance. "Is that absolutely necessary?" she asked indignantly.

"I believe so, yes," General Eldron said smoothly, a flicker of amusement playing on his lips.

"Is it compulsory?" A small voice came from the direction of Max. His face looked even paler than usual, under his shock of blond hair, and his worried eyes showed the fear lurking behind them. He was sitting next to Eloise and she reached across and placed a comforting hand upon his arm.

"It's okay, Max, you'll be with a Dragon Elf. I'm sure they'll look after you," she smiled at him.

Max nodded but it was evident to all that he was not happy at the idea of climbing up on one of the enormous creatures, let alone fly through the air on it.

"Well, I shall leave you to your supper," the General said, standing up and replacing his chair. "I bid you goodnight and I shall see you all after breakfast tomorrow." They bade him goodnight and he strode out of the refectory, watched, out of the corner of her eye, by Elenya.


Lizzie and the rest of her companions were up early the next morning. Some time the previous evening, outfits similar to those of the Dragon Elves had been placed in each of their rooms. As Lizzie arrived for breakfast, she found it amusing to see that most of her companions were dressed in the same soft leathery jerkins and trousers as their hosts. The only exceptions were her grandmother and Willo. Even Flaxon had a black jerkin over his usually bare top half. When Lizzie asked Willo why he wasn't joining them, he explained that Wood Sprites were not meant to leave the ground, like the trees they were close kin to, and so he could not fly upon dragons.

"What about you, gran? Aren't you coming?" Lizzie asked.

Mrs Longton placed an arm around her granddaughter's shoulder. "No darling, I don't think so. I think I'll leave all that excitement to you youngsters. Besides, I'm not terribly good with heights."

After breakfast the party gathered in the courtyard where General Eldron was waiting for them; he was accompanied by a thin faced Dragon Elf, who the General introduced as his Flying Captain – Elgor. The captain gave the clenched fist salute that Lizzie had become so familiar with.

"I am honoured that you have joined us this morning, Your Highnesses," Captain Elgor said, directing his statement to Elenya and Lizzie. He then turned to the rest of the group and gave each of them a sharp bow of his head.

"He'll give himself a headache if he does that too much," Elrus whispered in Lizzie's ear, from where he was standing behind her. Lizzie suppressed a grin.

Lizzie thanked the captain for the outfits that they were all wearing.

"You are all welcome, Highness, but they are necessary to protect you whilst flying. It gets very cold at altitude and dragon skin has excellent thermal properties," he explained.

"Dragon skin!" exclaimed Lizzie. "You kill dragons for their skin?" She was horrified at the idea.

"Indeed no, Your Highness. Dragon's are far too precious to kill purely for their skin and we should never be so cruel. Also, adult dragon skin would be far too hard to manipulate

281

into wearable clothing," he assured her. "Our flying suits are made from the shed skins of young dragons. As each young dragon grows into their next stage of development, they shed their skin. The skin is then collected and tanned and made into our protective clothing. The tanning process darkens the colours slightly but you will see hints of the original colour if you look closely enough."

Lizzie and the others did as he suggested and did indeed see an almost two toned effect to the amazing material.

The General then invited the group to follow them and so they made their way down into the depths of the mountain to the dragon cavern. As they entered, Lizzie was surprised to see that the dragons were not there. The General and Captain Elgor marched past the pens and through a large arch carved into the rock that led into another massive cave. At the far end of it were a number of apertures through which could be seen the snow capped peaks of the surrounding mountains. Eloise sighed in contentment at seeing the white glistening stuff that she had never experienced in her home of Elcarib.

The cave was buzzing with activity as the Dragon Elves went about the business of preparing several massive dragons for departure. As Lizzie drew closer the enormity of what she was about to do hit her and she felt the electric shock of fear, mixed with excitement, flood through her small frame. She looked around at her friends and they had similar looks on their faces, although Max's was just a little more acute in the fear factor. Lizzie smiled at him reassuringly and mouthed that he'd be fine.

The General introduced them to the Dragon Elves who would be riding with them.

"May I introduce you to the Dragon Flyers," he announced. The elves turned and saluted. Then the General and his Captain assigned each member of the party to a Dragon Flyer.

"Your Highness, you will fly with Captain Elgor," the General said, turning to Lizzie. The Captain made his usual abrupt bow of the head.

"A privilege, Your Highness," Captain Elgor said. "Please come this way." Lizzie began to follow him and as she did so she glanced back and saw each of her friends being introduced to the Dragon Flyer that they would be accompanying.

"Excuse me, Captain?" she called, catching up with Captain Elgor who was striding towards a magnificent blue beast, whose reins were being held by a young Dragon Elf.

The Captain stopped and looked at her quizzically. "Your Highness?"

"The General just introduced us to the Dragon Flyers but I thought you were all Dragon Elves. What's the difference?" she asked.

"We are all Dragon Elves, Your Highness. Dragon Elves are the soldiers who work and care for dragons. Dragon Flyers are the elite flying corp of the garrison. All young Dragon Elves aspire to be a Dragon Flyer because, as the name denotes, you get to fly upon dragons. Only after years of training and hard work may a Dragon Elf achieve this position and only then if he is able to bond with a dragon of his own," the Captain explained.

"You said *his* own dragon; aren't there any girl Dragon Elves?" Lizzie asked. She had been in Eldragonia a number of days now but it had only just dawned on her that she hadn't actually seen any female elves there.

The Captain looked amused. "No, Highness. There are *no* girl Dragon Elves. It takes great strength to handle dragons," he said dismissively, then turning towards his own dragon, he began to walk towards it once more. Lizzie followed on with pursed lips.

No, girl Dragon Elves! You wait, I'll show you what girls can do, she thought, irritated by the arrogant way in which the Captain had dismissed the idea of females being able to handle a dragon. After all, wasn't she handling Dronan!

As Lizzie stood next to the fully grown dragon beside her, she could truly appreciate the size of the beast. Its stunningly beautiful scaled skin shone with the inner glow she found so fascinating and the magnificence of the creature left her almost breathless. She watched as the Captain ran his hand slowly down the length of the dragon's neck and spoke softly to it; the action reminded her of watching her grandmother do something similar to the horse she had ridden here from Elvedom Castle.

The Captain asked Lizzie if she would allow him to assist her into the saddle. When she agreed, she found herself lifted, as though she weighed nothing more than a feather. The soft padding of the sumptuous leather tandem saddle, strapped to the dragon's back, was surprisingly comfortable. Sitting between the dragon's neck and its vast wings, the floor seemed a long way down.

The dragon's skin felt warm against Lizzie's own as she placed a hand on the creature's back just behind her seat. The softness of the scales surprised her, as she had expected them to feel hard and rough. It feels like a big old stuffed leather sofa, she thought. Lizzie could feel the rise and fall of the dragon's massive rib cage as it breathed slowly in and out and sensed the pulsing throb of its heartbeat. She felt as though she was in some kind of fantastic dream that she really didn't want to wake up from. Perched upon the dragon's back she looked over at the others as they too mounted their dragons, it was a surreal experience. Lizzie smiled when she saw Elenya being lifted up into her saddle by General Eldron, whose hand seemed to linger just a little longer than was necessary on her aunt's back. When all the visitors were mounted, the Dragon Elves climbed up behind them, the agility with which they did so demonstrated clearly that this was something they were used to.

The huge bodies of the dragons seemed cumbersome as they made their way the short distance to the exits. The rolling gait of the dragon beneath her made Lizzie feel as though she would fall from its back. She gripped tightly to the strap attached to the front of the saddle, even though the Captain had strapped a safety harness around her slender waist, and dug her feet firmly into the stirrups to steady herself. As the dragon stepped out onto a wide ledge, just beyond the apertures, Lizzie's heart began to race. The ledge jutted out over a deep valley below and she dared a peek over the edge only to quickly look away to the distant peaks of the mountains straight ahead of her, when her stomach lurched at the sight.

Suddenly there was a shout off to her right as she heard General Eldron's call of, "Dragon Flyers, Ho!"

The Dragon Flyers responded with a cry of Ho! and then, with the sound of dragons roaring in their eagerness to be away, the flying party launched themselves from the precipice.

A silent scream welled up inside Lizzie, as it felt as though she was falling through the air; it was like that horrible feeling you sometimes get just before falling asleep, when your body suddenly jerks awake again. For what seemed an eternity, the dragon continued to plummet down to the rocky floor of the canyon below and she closed her eyes to avoid seeing the ground hastening towards her. The wind rushed against her face, almost taking her breath away but then the steady beat of huge wings slowed the descent and she felt a lightness in her body, as they began to rise up into the air.

Lizzie opened one eye and peered around her. It was a wonderful sight and so, opening her other eye, she took in the vista surrounding her. The mountains spread out before them, their icy tips glinting in the bright sunshine. In the valley below she could see a huge lake, its still surface reflecting the blue of the sky above. Her body began to relax as the tension of fear subsided within her and a feeling of utter joy filled the space that the fear had left.

She looked around for the others and could see Elenya behind General Eldron on his dark blue dragon, the look of elation on her face was evident for all to see. Lizzie sought out her friends and spotted Elrus. She laughed to see that the daring young elf still had his eyes closed and the tension in his jaw showed that he might not be so brave about dragons as his casual attitude might have indicated. Eloise's face was bright with the excitement that filled it and she looked across at Lizzie and waved happily at her. Waving back, Lizzie then looked around for Max, concerned that he wasn't coping with the experience. Then she saw him and a huge smile spread across her face.

Max was chatting animatedly to the Dragon Flyer in front of him and pointing down at the ground below. He was obviously enjoying himself and, as his eye caught Lizzie watching him from her place on Captain Elgor's dragon, he smiled at her and punched the air. Lizzie laughed; of course he would be in his element, after all hadn't he once said that he'd hoped to one day be able to fly a broom, or besom as he'd called it. Flying on a dragon was heaps cooler than flying a dusty old broom.

The dragons began to draw together in a formation led by General Eldron's beast. They flew further up into the atmosphere like a massive skein of geese, before suddenly swooping down towards the lake below. It was exhilarating and Lizzie couldn't help herself from screaming, "Weeee….." as the wind whistled through her ears, pushing them flat against her head.

The tips of the dragons' wings almost skimmed the surface of the lake before they wheeled around in tight formation and began to ascend once more. Lizzie could see flocks of sheep grazing on the lower slopes of the mountains as they flew over them and watched with amusement as the animals scarpered across the grassy terrain to hide from the huge beasts overhead.

After several circuits of the valley, the General led the others back in the direction of Eldragonia and, all too soon, they were landing on the wide ledge that they had launched from earlier.

As Captain Elgor lifted her down from the back of his dragon, Lizzie thanked him excitedly.

"Oh thank you so much, Captain; that was just amazing!" she enthused.

The captain smiled and said she was most welcome as he bowed his head. Lizzie looked across at the others as they clambered or were lifted down from their mounts. She could see Gorin and Digby being helped down and grinned as she watched the little goblin and dwarf high five each other.

Elenya was elegantly dismounting, gently assisted by the hand of General Eldron. Elgawen close by could be seen flirting with the Dragon Flyer who had accompanied her and the handsome elf took her hand and kissed it gallantly.

Other party members could be seen thanking their respective Flyers and Lizzie was happy to see the beaming faces of Eloise and Max as they shook the hands of their flying partners. Elrus however, did not look too well. His usually robust colour was decidedly pale and he seemed to wobble slightly as he was helped down to the ground. Lizzie grinned wryly at the sight and began to walk over to him. Spotting her, he straightened his back and put on a jaunty expression but as he walked towards her his gait was more of a stagger than a swagger.

"So, that was cool," he said, trying to look unfazed by the experience.

"Really? I thought you looked a little tense from where I was sitting," quipped Lizzie. Elrus feigned surprise.

"Me? Tense? Nah!" he denied, stumbling forward from a heavy thump on his back.

Turning to see who had inflicted it, Elrus stared into the beaming face of Max. "Well wasn't that brilliant!" he exclaimed, flinging an arm around his friend's shoulder.

"It was wonderful," grinned an obviously happy Eloise, who had also joined them. "Do you think that they'll take us out again?"

"I really hope so," crowed Max. "If I wasn't going to follow in my Master's footsteps and be a Sorcerer one day I think I'd love to be a Dragon Flyer."

Elrus looked at his friend in amazement. "Personally, I prefer to be a bit closer to the ground," he admitted. "Not that I was scared or anything," he quickly added, trying to convince them that he was just as cool about it as his companions so evidently were.

Lizzie just shook her head slowly. She wouldn't give the game away and spoil her dear friend's reputation, it would be their little secret she thought as Elrus looked at her with a "don't you say anything" expression on his cheeky flushed face.

Later that afternoon, after a long, leisurely lunch, which was very welcome as the dragon flight had left them ravenous, Lizzie and her grandmother together with Elenya, Elrus, Eloise and Max went to meet her new namesake.

The baby dragon was a funny looking little creature, not unlike a strange lizard but with stubby, little wings.

"Ahh, looks just like you," crooned Elrus, for which he received a sharp punch on the arm from Lizzie. "Ow! Well, I mean – it is a bit odd looking."

"Oi! Who are you calling odd looking?" Lizzie said indignantly, much to the enjoyment of the others present.

"Well, I think she's beautiful," Max said, peering at the little creature. "Er, the dragon I mean," he continued, blushing bright red at the thought that he'd just told Lizzie she was beautiful.

Lizzie giggled but then, adopting a more serious expression, teased, "Am I not beautiful then, Max?"

"Of course, Princess," Max mumbled, looking down and shuffling his feet in embarrassment.

The baby dragon seemed to spend a lot of time sleeping and so, with the inspection over, they made their way back up the stairs to the courtyard above.

"Well thank goodness the nursery wasn't as hot as the hatchery," breathed a relieved Mrs Longton.

When they reached the open air they could hear the sound of chanting coming from the exercise yard that they had spotted the day they had arrived. Mrs Longton said she was going to have a nap before dinner and disappeared off to her room, whilst Elenya said that she had a meeting with Prince Finnion and some of the others of their group.

"Can we come?" asked Lizzie.

Elenya placed her arm around her and said it would be really boring for them. "It's just strategic stuff," she explained.

"But I need to learn that sort of stuff," Lizzie pleaded.

"In time Lizzie, but for now you should be having fun and enjoying yourself," Elenya said, ruffling Lizzie's hair affectionately and chucking her under her chin. "Come on smile," she encouraged, taking in her niece's disappointed face. Then looking earnestly into Lizzie's eyes she said, "One day, Elizabeth, you will have to do all this *stuff* as the weight of responsibility will be put firmly on those little shoulders of yours but until then make the most of your freedom."

"Okay," Lizzie conceded. So with a final squeeze of Lizzie's shoulders, Elenya strode off towards her meeting.

"Hey, I've got an idea," announced Elrus. "Why don't we go and join the Dragon Elves at their exercises?"

"I've a better one," declared Max. "Why don't you go and get your football and we'll give them a game?"

"Brilliant idea!" whooped Elrus and without a second thought rushed off to get his ball.

In what seemed like no time at all the young elf was back, carrying his most precious possession. Lizzie and Eloise looked at each other in the way girls do when they think, "Boys!" and followed Elrus and Max into the exercise yard.

The four friends watched as the Dragon Elves concluded their exercise routine and as they began to leave the yard, Elrus approached some of them and asked if they'd like to play football. The elves looked at the ball in Elrus's hand in bemusement.

"Look we'll show you," Elrus said enthusiastically. "Come on Max!" The pair then ran onto the exercise square and began kicking the ball to each other. After watching for a bit and talking amongst themselves, the Dragon Elves joined the two boys and began passing the ball to one another. There was much hilarity as the ball was often miskicked or missed altogether but the elves soon began to get the hang of it.

"Why don't you try heading it to each other?" called Lizzie from the sidelines, to where she and Eloise had been relegated.

"What do you mean?" replied Elrus. "Come and show us."

With that Lizzie, followed closely by Eloise, joined the group on the square and bounced the ball on her head a couple of times before bouncing it towards Elrus.

"I'm not very good at it," she admitted, "but you get the idea."

By the end of the afternoon the session had turned into an almost recognizable game of football, with Elrus explaining the rules and Lizzie chipping in when he was unsure of certain aspects of the game. Two teams were formed with Elrus and Max as captains and one of the girls on each team. The shouting and yelling from disputed decisions and goals scored attracted more of Eldragonia's residents until they had quite a crowd. Elrus and Max found themselves flattened more than once by the more muscular and powerful Dragon Elves but would be quickly dragged to their feet to carry on with the game. When Lizzie or Eloise got the ball, however, they wouldn't be tackled but were allowed to continue on their way much to the chagrin of Elrus and Max.

Finally, after what seemed like hours, Lizzie fell exhausted onto the floor and lay back looking up into the darkening sky. Eloise took this as a signal that she too could rest and so lay down next to Lizzie. The rest of the players stopped playing and looked at the two girls. Elrus marched over and leant over them, his red face glistening from the sweat he'd worked up during the game.

"What are you doing?" he asked, irritably.

"We've been playing for hours and we're tired," sighed Lizzie.

"Well, can't you lie down somewhere else?" he glowered. Lizzie sat up and leant back on her elbows.

"Elrus! A game of football is meant to last for ninety minutes," she declared.

Elrus looked taken aback. "Really?" he asked.

"Really!" Lizzie confirmed.

"Oh," he said, standing up straight. Then looking back down at her said, "How long's ninety minutes?"

Lizzie flopped back down onto the ground; she'd forgotten elves didn't have the same concept of time as humans. They didn't have watches or clocks but measured the passing of time by the movement of the sun, moon and stars in the sky – much like men had hundreds of years ago.

She gazed up into Elrus's face and said that it was a lot less than what they had played.

"Okay folks," he called to the other football players. "It would seem that the game's over for today."

Grumbles and moans rumbled through those gathered around them, as they reluctantly agreed to finish the game. The ball was passed back to Elrus and hands were shaken as it was agreed that they would play again the following day. Lizzie and Eloise got wearily to their feet and, together with

291

Elrus and Max, happily made their way to the refectory for supper.

That night as the four friends made their way to their beds they all agreed it had been the best day ever.

"How long do you think we'll be staying here?" Eloise asked.

Max shrugged his shoulders and said, "I guess until Princess Elenya tells us it's time to leave."

Just as the words left his lips they heard footsteps coming up the stairs behind them and looking around they saw Elwood and Elwind.

"Ma'am, you and your friends are to come with us. Princess Elenya has requested your presence," Elwind said.

"What *now*?" exclaimed Lizzie, surprised at the request coming at such a late hour.

"Yes ma'am," Elwood confirmed.

Lizzie looked at her friends and excitement flushed her face and every trace of tiredness seemed to fly out of the window.

"It must be something important for the Princess to call for us now," Elrus said eagerly, voicing Lizzie's own thoughts.

So, turning to Elwood and Elwind, she said, "Well, lead the way guys."

# CHAPTER 30

## Night Flight

In a chamber, down in the depths of Eldragonia, Elenya was poring over a large map. As Lizzie and her friends entered the room she, together with the Companions, General Eldron and Captain Elgor who were discussing the map's contents, looked up and greeted them.

"Come in kids," Elenya said, beckoning them over to her side. "You're probably wondering why I've called for you at this late hour." The friends nodded.

"Well, we are to leave tonight on our mission to retrieve the Chalice of Elaria – we are calling the mission, Challenge Cup," Elenya announced. Lizzie and her friends looked at her in shock.

"Tonight?" asked Lizzie incredulously, her voice barely above a whisper.

"Yes, tonight," reiterated Elenya. "We want to ensure that we have the element of surprise on our side. The Dragon Elves are preparing for our departure as I speak."

"But how long have you known that it would be tonight and why haven't I been included? Don't you trust me?" asked Lizzie, her face showing her disappointment at not being party to the plans.

Elenya turned to her niece and placed her hands lightly on Lizzie's shoulders.

"How can you possibly think that I don't trust you, Lizzie?" she asked earnestly. "Of course I trust you but only three people, including myself, knew of the plan to go this night. We could not jeopardize the mission by the possibility of details leaking out."

Lizzie looked at the faces of the others in the room and knew from their expressions and the occasional nod that

Elenya was not lying. Lizzie spotted her grandmother across the room and could see she was worried. She then heard someone clear their throat and turned towards Elrus from where the sound had come.

"Ahem! Excuse me Your Highness but did you just say that the Dragon Elves are preparing for our departure?" Elrus's usually ruddy complexion looked a tad pale and was going paler by the minute.

"That's right, Elrus. We fly with them tonight," Elenya confirmed. "That is why we came to Eldragonia, to train with the Dragon Elves so that they can help us in our mission. There is no other way to get to Elcaledonia without going through Eldorth's lands, which we can't do for obvious reasons, or going by ship which would take too long. By flying at night we can pass over Maladorth unseen."

There was a buzz around the room as its occupants all seemed to begin speaking at once. Lizzie looked at Elrus and saw him swallow hard and it upset her to see her usually brave and carefree friend look so scared. She placed a comforting hand on his arm.

"But you never said that we would be flying with dragons," Elgawen said. "I mean, it's fantastic and all that but, are we ready? We've only flown with them today; we're not exactly experienced flyers."

"We didn't come here for fun," Elenya said, her striking features were set in serious expression. "It was always planned that the Dragon Flyers would assist us. Dragons are our main defence against the pterotorials and the wraiths that fly them. We have dallied here too long and so tonight we must fly."

Mrs Longton now stepped forward.

"When you say we, Princess, you surely don't mean the children too," she said.

Elenya said that she did also mean the children.

"But this is madness," exclaimed Mrs Longton. "They are too young to be going on such a perilous assignment. I mean, flying with dragons into heaven knows what! The children aren't prepared for something like this; they haven't even had any sleep. How can you expect them to stay awake, let alone be of any possible use?" Mrs Longton continued to rant, as she shook with anger.

Elenya took a deep breath and seemed to brace herself ready to deal with the fury that was flooding into Mrs Longton's face.

Suddenly the sound of pan-pipes began drifting through the air and the soothing music seemed to cast a calming effect over the troubled Mrs Longton and she ceased her tirade. Lizzie looked across at Flaxon as he played his pipes and saw him wink at her. Elenya walked over to Mrs Longton and spoke softly to her.

"If I could avoid the children coming, Mrs Longton, I would; please believe me. But I cannot. I have instructions that I must ensure that they come on this mission as they have a vital role to play. As you recall when we successfully retrieved the Harp of Elvyth, it was Lizzie's presence as the true heir to the Kingdom of Elvedom that made all the difference. The other children must come with Lizzie because of their relationship to her, they are her friends. The circle of friendship is a magical thing, our friends surrounding and supporting us can help us to achieve what, on the face of it, seems impossible. It is why I surround myself with friends." Her arm swept through the air, indicating the rest of those present in the room. "We may come from all races and creeds but when we join together, we can make the world a better place."

Mrs Longton stood and stared at the beautiful woman before her and her eyes filled with tears. The terror was still deep inside her, despite Flaxon's musical intervention, but she nodded her acceptance at the situation. She now understood the true reason behind King Elfred's insistence that Lizzie's friends accompany her on this journey. In the human world people talked about their circle of friends, it would seem that in Elvedom this "circle" truly had magical properties.

"But how can they form a circle when there are only four of them?" Mrs Longton asked.

Flaxon now spoke. "You can form a circle with only three people if they join hands, Mrs Longton. However, four make the circle stronger but if you have too many friends then the circle will become weaker and may break as the bonds are not as strong."

Lizzie and her friends looked at one another and smiled, each one linking hands with the person standing next to them. Lizzie with Elrus and Max to either side of her felt a surge of strength rush through her and she knew that everything she had just heard was true. It filled her with the confidence she needed to see her through the coming night.

Elenya turned to the group gathered around her and went back to the business at hand.

"Willo has used his skills and knowledge of plants and trees to prepare an energy drink that will keep us all awake and alert so there will be no need for sleep tonight," she announced.

As Lizzie listened and watched her aunt and the others talking about the plans for the foray into the night, she suddenly felt a slight detachment from the proceedings as a voice seemed to filter into her brain.

"Take me with you. Don't leave me behind."

Lizzie looked at the people gathered around her but they were all listening in rapt attention to something General Eldron was saying.

The voice spoke again to Lizzie. "I must go with you. Come and get me." She knew in her heart who was speaking to her. She let go of Max's hand and raised it into the air, to attract Elenya's attention, in the same way she would have done with her teacher, Miss Finley, at school. Elenya looked at her in bemusement.

"Is something wrong Lizzie?" Elenya asked.

"I have to go and get Dronan," Lizzie announced. The group turned as one and stared at her in surprise.

"I don't think that is wise, Your Highness," General Eldron said.

"Sorry General but I'm afraid it is. I have to go and get Dronan. He needs to come with us. I know he does," Lizzie assured him.

"Sorry, Your Highness but that is not possible. The dragon is a juvenile and he has not had the discipline instilled in him to go on such a mission as this," Captain Elgor said stiffly. "Besides, he has barely flown let alone had a rider on his back. No, Your Highness, the dragon must stay here."

The old Lizzie would have just accepted what her elders said and would never have challenged them but this Lizzie, the one who was now the heir of Elvedom, knew that she must have her way and was prepared to stand up for herself.

She looked directly at the Dragon Master and his captain and said, "I must insist." Then, turning to Elenya, she added, "You said you trust me, Elenya." Her aunt nodded. "Then you must trust me when I tell you that I know that Dronan must come too."

Elenya ran the fingers of both hands through her beautiful blond hair, pushing a loose tendril away from her forehead as she did so. She took a deep breath. "Lizzie, I do trust you," she said, as her hands dropped to her sides, "But as Captain Elgor said, Dronan is young and inexperienced. You could be putting yourself and the dragon at unnecessary risk. Are you absolutely sure about this?"

The feelings buzzing through Lizzie's body and brain convinced her that this was something that must happen. She nodded slowly. "Yes Elenya. I'm absolutely sure."

Elenya's back straightened in determination as she then turned to General Eldron and said, "Then so be it. Please arrange for the young dragon to be made ready for the journey." The General went to protest but, seeing the determined set of Elenya's jaw, nodded and instructed his captain to do as the Princess had bid. As the Captain left the room, Lizzie sighed in relief and in her mind she sent the message to Dronan that he too would come with her on the mission to retrieve the Chalice.

With final instructions delivered, the group left the confines of the chamber and made their way down to the dragon caverns where they changed into the leathery clothing of the Dragon Flyers. The soft supple material of the clothes clung to them like second skins and would keep them warm against the cold that the night ahead would hold.

In the departure cavern the dragons were saddled and ready to leave. As they walked towards the huge creatures, Lizzie could see the smaller bulk of Dronan; his silvery white scales shimmering with the strange inner glow that all the dragons had. His large amber eyes turned towards her and Lizzie felt, rather than saw, him smile with excitement and pleasure at the adventure that lay ahead of them.

Captain Elgor was speaking to Dronan brusquely, "You had better do as you're told or it'll be back to the isolation cavern for you, young dragon."

Lizzie felt her face flush angrily at the Captain's words. "Don't worry Captain, he will. Won't you Dronan?" The young dragon just stared insolently at the Captain.

"I just want it known, Your Highness, that I think this is a foolhardy plan," Captain Elgor said firmly, as he gave the straps of Dronan's saddle one last jerk to ensure they were tightened. Lizzie just smiled at the captain although in her head she was saying, "You're entitled to your opinion but it doesn't mean I have to agree with it."

As the Captain walked off to join his own mount, Dronan cast Lizzie a sidelong glance and she knew that he had telepathically picked up her thoughts.

General Eldron joined Lizzie. "I must insist that you ride with me for the main part of the journey north, Your Highness. I say this is because Dronan has very little flying experience and may tire if he has to carry a rider any great distance. It is for both your sakes that I say this," he stated. Lizzie saw that this made sense.

"How can we make sure that Dronan keeps up and is not too far from me?" she asked.

"I have thought about that and decided that he will be tethered to my own dragon so that he will fly just behind us. I hope that is agreeable to you both," the General said, bowing his head to them.

Lizzie said it was.

As the General tied a long piece of leather rope to Dronan's halter, the noise and bustle of the departure buzzed around them. Lizzie placed a gentle hand on the neck of Dronan and the warmth of his scaly skin was comforting beneath her palm. She took the risk of stroking him slowly along the length of his neck, unsure of how he might react to her touch but he seemed to relax and the low rumbling purr that he had made the day she had found him vibrated through her hand. In the days since she had been training with him, there had been little in the way of physical contact but now it felt right that she should make the move and his reaction had proved that she had been correct to do so.

Suddenly a shout went up. "Dragon Flyers mount!"

The General quickly mounted his dragon and taking Lizzie's hand, pulled her up to sit behind him. Anticipation flooded through her as she looked around to see her friends and companions sitting behind their Dragon Flyers. The fear and excitement was evident on each of their faces and it made her smile. She then turned around and looked at Dronan. He was ruffling his wings as if eager to be off.

Looking around for her friends and the other companions she could see them all climbing onto their dragons and saw that Elenya would now fly with Captain Elgor. She then looked across at her grandmother who was standing with Willo and was anxiously wringing her hands. Lizzie waved and blew her a kiss. Mrs Longton stopped twisting her hands together and made as if to catch the kiss, then bringing both hands to her mouth she returned it in an exaggerated gesture and mouthed, "I love you."

Before Lizzie had time to reply in kind, the General shouted, "Dragon Flyers, Ho!" and as the Dragon Elves responded "Ho!" the huge beasts launched off from the ledge overlooking the Mountains of Snow.

Once again the exhilaration of the initial plummet from the ledge left Lizzie breathless and she felt the leather tether between Dronan and the General's dragon tighten and pull at the saddle beneath her. Then the steady beat of the dragons wings began to lift them up into the air and she glanced back to see Dronan beating his smaller wings just a little faster than the enormous beast he was tied to.

The cool night air whipped across Lizzie's face as she peered around the General in order to see the direction in which they were flying but the new moon that was just appearing in the sky cast little light. The darkness that now enveloped them kept them hidden from prying eyes and Lizzie, looking around at the others flying close by, could only just make out the shapes of the other dragons and their riders.

The flyers made their way steadily northwards flying high above the Mountains of Snow until they passed the coastline of Elcambria then over the Elirish Sea beyond. Lizzie looked down at the pale moonlight glinting off the sea's surface. It seemed an awfully long way down. She felt the taut leather rope at her side tethering them to Dronan behind her and wondered how the young dragon was faring. She turned back to look at him and her heart seemed to miss several beats when she could no longer see him flying behind them. An involuntary squeal escaped her. The General swung around in shock.

"What's wrong, Highness?" he exclaimed.

"It's Dronan! I can't see Dronan!"

As the words left her lips, she felt rather than heard the young dragon say, "I am here." Lizzie spun round to see two amber eyes peering back at her but couldn't see what they were attached to. She stared back at the eyes and only then could she start to make out Dronan's shape. She gasped in surprise.

"But, but, he's invisible!" Lizzie stammered.

General Eldron let out a roar of laughter.

"You knew he could do this?" Lizzie called back at the General.

The General shook his head. "Not exactly, but we had the suspicion that he had the ability to become so. Although technically, Dronan is camouflaged, he is not invisible. His silvery white skin is able to take on the colours and shades of his surroundings making him appear invisible. It is what makes him a very special dragon, and in the wrong hands a very dangerous one."

Lizzie looked back again into the eyes of the young dragon following in their wake and smiled. "Well, thank goodness you fell into my hands," she called to Dronan in their telepathic way of talking. A low rumbling purr greeted her words as the group continued their journey towards the rescue of the Chalice of Elaria.

# CHAPTER 31

## The Art of Persuasion

Away to the East the rising sun began to cast its orange rays across a pink and lilac sky. The Dragon Flyers were now over the lowlands of the Elcaledonian mountains and Lizzie could see that in the distance the peaks rose even higher than the Mountains of Snow they had left behind the night before.

Conversation between the Dragon Flyers had been impossible during the night flight. They usually communicated with a series of signals but that wasn't feasible under the cover of darkness. Now, in the gradual dawning of the day, they greeted one another with salutes and waves. Lizzie could see her three friends and the other Companions sitting behind their Flyers and it reassured her that they all seemed safe and secure in their pillion positions.

Lizzie had tried to speak to General Eldron a few times through the night but had given up, as attempting to shout above the rush of the wind and the beating of the dragon's wings had proved too tiring. She was glad that her ability to communicate with Dronan in their silent way had meant that she could ensure that the young dragon was coping with the journey north. He had always replied that he was good and she now took the opportunity of looking back to see for herself.

Dronan's amazing skin had taken on the hues of the early morning sky and he was startlingly beautiful to behold. Lizzie had half expected to see that he appeared to be fading in energy, due to the great distance they had already travelled, but instead he seemed to have gained in strength. His wing beats were slow and strong and it was as if each passing mile was helping him to develop his flying ability further. She smiled and sent him a telepathic "Good Morning."

302

Dronan's brief response of "It is" made Lizzie giggle. I suppose that a greeting that was so familiar in the human world would not be known to a dragon in this one, she thought. It seemed strange that considering their ability to talk to one another with their thoughts, they didn't appear to read each other's minds. It was as though a section of her brain just tuned into that of Dronan's when she wanted to talk to him and vice versa. It was intriguing and when the opportunity came she would have to ask the General if he understood why this was.

The rising sun was now casting its beams across the ground below them and onto the mountains that they were rapidly approaching. Mother Earth could be seen in all her morning glory and she was beautiful. The scenery reminded Lizzie of the stunning landscapes of Scotland that she had seen in a book her grandmother had in the library at Longton Hall. The thought of her home hadn't crossed her mind much lately, what with all the distractions of her adventures in Elvedom, and she felt a sadness and guilt that she hadn't considered how her absence may have affected Basil and Rathbone. Lizzie loved her dogs with all her heart and a lump formed in her throat as she thought of how pleased they would be to see her when she got back. Suddenly a shiver of fear passed through her at the thought that, should this mission go badly wrong, she might never see them again.

Her mind was brought sharply back to the present as the sound of a horn split the air and she looked across to see Captain Elgor blowing a hunting horn for a second time. In response, the General swept his arm above his head and in doing so attracted the attention of the Flyers and their pillion riders. He pointed down below away into the distance and, when Lizzie leaned over the side of the dragon to see where he was indicating, she saw a long loch carved into the mountain range. As the party of Flyers began their descent Lizzie spotted a string of islands stretching across the width of the loch like a necklace of precious emeralds. The largest of the islands was rimmed by what appeared to be ancient trees and it was clear from the gestures of the General, that this was their intended landing place. The huge wings of the dragons almost skimmed across the loch's surface before they swooped above the tree tops and landed with the utmost ease, given their huge bulk, and settled upon the grassy centre of the isle. The Dragon Flyers and their passengers disembarked from the backs of their mounts to allow the beasts to take some rest after the long flight.

Lizzie's first thought as she clambered down from behind General Eldron was to check upon Dronan. The young dragon was now clearly visible as his silvery white skin no longer appeared to be adapting to its surroundings. This surprised Lizzie. "Maybe he's only in camouflage when he's flying," she thought. Dronan stretched and ruffled his wings as if loosening up after the flight. He blinked his huge amber eyes at her and Lizzie thought she could detect a hint of a smile on his face, if that was at all possible.

Lizzie was quickly joined by her three friends and it made her smile to see Max with his arm slung around the shoulder of Elrus as the pair laughed together. Eloise's face was flushed bright with excitement and where the wind had whipped through her black curly hair, it seemed to have grown by several inches as it framed her pretty features.

"Well, how brilliant was that?" beamed Eloise, as she reached Lizzie's side. "Even Elrus seems to have enjoyed the ride," she added, looking across at the boys.

"Hey, I might have been scared on that first flight but I've now got used to flying," Elrus said indignantly. "Although I have to admit I'm definitely an Earth Elf at heart," he grinned as an aside.

"Ahem!"

Lizzie heard someone make a noise as if clearing their throat from just behind her and she turned to see Elwood standing there.

"Excuse me ma'am but your aunt has asked me to request that you and your friends join her and the others," he said, dipping his head in a brief bow. Lizzie thanked him and, together with her friends, followed Elwood towards the rest of the group who were gathered on the other side of the clearing.

Elenya, who was in conversation with Prince Finnion, turned and smiled at Lizzie and her friends as they approached.

"Lizzie!" she beamed, holding out her arms and taking Lizzie into a tight embrace. "How did you find the flight?" she asked, releasing her niece but keeping an arm draped around her shoulders.

"It was a bit chilly up there but wonderful all the same," Lizzie grinned. "Why did we have to stop?"

Elenya looked serious. "We need to discuss the next stage of the mission. Come, we'll join the others." Then beckoning Lizzie's three friends to follow, they made their way to a small mound which Elenya proceeded to use as a platform to call everyone to attention.

"Friends and allies!" she began. "We are about to embark on the final stage of this mission. You know that we are to retrieve something of national importance to Elvedom. Our intelligence is that it is now secreted somewhere in the depths of the highest mountain to the north of us; Mount Elben. We understand that it is protected by forces in the service of Duke Eldorth."

Lizzie, who was standing between Elenya and General Eldron, heard a shuddering intake of breath and looking to her right was surprised that it had come from the General, whose eyes seemed to be drawn resolutely to the ground at his feet. His cheeks were flushed with a high colour and his lips were drawn into a thin bleak line. Looking down from his face she saw that his hands had clenched into tight fists. She was unsurprised at such a reaction at the mention of Eldorth's name, as it had a similar effect on others when it was uttered. But Lizzie sensed there was something much deeper within the General regarding Eldorth; she felt that something really terrible had happened to him at Eldorth's hands and she had a sudden urge to reach across and place a comforting hand on his arm. The urge was suppressed however, when he raised his head and stared defiantly across the heads of the gathered group.

Prince Finnion standing to Elenya's left took up the briefing.

"We must maintain the element of surprise and once the dragons are rested we leave for Mount Elben forthwith. We have learnt that the Mount is the eyrie of a group of pterotorials and it is they that protect what we seek."

There was general murmuring amongst the gathering.

Lizzie jumped at the sudden shout of "Silence!" that came from General Eldorth. As the murmuring stopped, the General continued:

"The pterotorials are no match for the dragons but they will be driven on by their riders, the wraiths and will prove tricky to out-maneouver. You must be careful to ensure that you are not dislodged from your mounts by any that may attack us. Wraiths, as we know, can only be destroyed by dragon fire and that is why the dragons have been made ready for this."

Lizzie heard Elrus, who was standing close by with Max, Eloise and Elwood, say with just a hint of horror, "Do you mean to say those things are now fire breathing?"

General Eldron's lips twitched in amusement as he replied, "Indeed it does." He then gave the order for the Dragon Flyers to prepare the dragons to leave within the half hour and so the gathering dispersed to get ready for departure.

Lizzie and her three friends made their way back to Dronan. As they approached the young dragon he had his eyes closed as though napping but Lizzie sensed a deepening calm in him as though it were more like he was meditating. As she came near he slowly opened his eyes and looked at each of the friends one by one before finally turning to Lizzie.

"He's so beautiful," exclaimed Eloise, in a hushed voice, as she took in his silvery shimmering scales.

"Thank your friend for her kind words," Dronan said silently to Lizzie.

"He says thank you," Lizzie smiled at Eloise, who flushed shyly at the fact that Dronan had heard her.

"You know, it's pretty cool that you can talk with him without having to actually speak," Elrus said. "But can you speak out loud? You know like, in words?"

"Of course we can!" said Dronan, quite clearly to Lizzie's ears but that sounded like a series of loud grunts and snarls to the others. Elrus winced.

"What was that?" he grimaced.

"He said, of course we can," Lizzie translated.

"I think you should stick to the silent conversations in future. What a racket!" Elrus moaned.

Lizzie and the others laughed and she went on to explain to Dronan in their silent way, what Elrus had meant. She then told the young dragon of the plan to leave soon for Mount Elben and that maybe it would be best for him to stay safely on the island.

"No. That is not how it is meant to be. You do know that you must fly me into the enemy's lair don't you?," Dronan announced.

Lizzie stared at him in disbelief and shook her head.

"What's wrong Princess?" Max asked; concern etched on his face. She turned to him with worried eyes.

"Dronan says I should fly him on the mission but of course I can't. He's too young and inexperienced," she explained.

"Oh, and you are old and experienced?" Max asked, looking at her wryly.

"No but..." Lizzie was unsure how to respond, now aware of the very obvious irony of what she had just said.

Dronan's voice entered Lizzie's thoughts. "You know in your heart that I am right. My special ability to camouflage myself within my surroundings will protect you. I am smaller than the other dragons and they can keep the enemy busy and draw them away from our target."

For a young dragon, Dronan was very wise and Lizzie knew that he was right. She nodded her agreement as Max watched her.

"What's going on?" asked Elrus, with Eloise looking on with interest.

Lizzie explained what Dronan had said and then taking a deep breath said, "He's right, of course. We've only one chance at this mission and so it's got to work. Come on, I need to speak to Elenya." Then turning she ran towards her aunt with her three friends in hot pursuit.


"This is madness!" exclaimed Elenya, as Lizzie finished telling her of the plan.

General Eldron and Prince Finnion, who were also party to the conversation, didn't give the impression that they thought it was madness.

"I think the Princess may have come up with the best plan to retrieve the relic. As she says, we can draw the pterotorials out and keep them preoccupied whilst she enters the lair. She and the dragon are small and could easily be overlooked in the general fracas," General Eldron said.

"But the dragon can only carry her. I cannot allow her to go unaccompanied. No! Absolutely not," Elenya stressed, shaking her head vigorously.

"I won't be alone, Elenya," Lizzie said reassuringly. "I'll be with Dronan."

"And I'll go too. I'm sure he could cope with two of us. After all I'm quite light."

All eyes swung round in the direction from where the offer came and alighted on Eloise. Lizzie shook her head.

"No, Eloise. It's too dangerous. I'll be fine with Dronan," she insisted.

"Why would it be any more dangerous for me than it would be for you? There's strength in numbers and anyway, aren't friends supposed to stick together," Eloise added keenly.

Elenya was shaking her head emphatically.

"Is this some kind of mad dream that I'm in the middle of," she spluttered. "You are categorically not going to go into that lair alone or, two of you, or whatever. Now let's get back onto Mother Earth and not away on some mad parallel world where young girls think they can take on wraiths."

A quiet, soothing voice then spoke. "You should listen to your niece, Your Highness." It was Flaxon, his sensible, calm nature ever the sound of reason. Elenya turned and stared at him.

"Your niece has abilities that she is still discovering and I believe that those special traits will enable her to succeed where others may not. I also think that friendship has its own magical power that can help us achieve our aims in moments of doubt. The young dragon was sent to the Princess for a purpose. I believe that this mission is one such purpose. Dronan will be able to fly almost unseen if the rest of the party makes sure they keep the eyes of the enemy drawn in their direction."

Elenya's eyes flitted from face to face as if seeking out an ally who would also see the madness of the idea and agree that it should not happen. Finally, admitting defeat she clasped her hands to her cheeks and nodded her head.

"My father is going to kill me," she groaned. "And Elroy will pick over my bones. And what your grandmother will do to me, doesn't bear thinking about."

Lizzie flung herself at her aunt and hugged her around the waist.

"Don't worry, Elenya. I won't let any of them lay a finger on you," she vowed. Then looking across at Eloise, she smiled nervously as her friend smiled nervously back.

"Excuse me General but the dragons are ready to leave," Captain Elgor saluted the General as he made the announcement.

Elenya turned worried eyes to her niece.

"Now don't do anything stupid or too risky. Oh my, what am I saying… this whole thing is stupid and risky. What I mean is, please, please be careful – both of you," Elenya pleaded, placing an arm around each of the girls and squeezing them tight.

"You need to get in and out of there as quickly as possible," Elenya continued. "If you are in any real peril you must promise me to abandon the mission and get out."

The girls nodded mutely as the reality of what they were about to do began to sink in.

The General then spoke. "Use the dragon as your protection. Make use of his ability to change his skin to hide you from the enemy. When in flight lay low against his body, it will shield you from prying eyes."

Holding hands to strengthen their feeling of resolve, the girls nodded in unison.

Prince Finnion took up the instruction. "You will need to give us a signal when you are out of the lair and have the relic in your possession. This will then enable us to make a quick retreat." He then added, "Can either of you blow a horn?" He called over to Fidora and asked if she still carried her hunting horn. She withdrew a hollowed out goat's horn with a silver mouth-piece from a pouch that hung from her belt and passed it to him.

Eloise held out her hand and taking the horn from Prince Finnion blew into it. A loud blast made it clear that she could indeed blow a horn.

"My father taught me how to blow a conch shell back home in Elcarib. It's not much different," she grinned shyly.

"Well then, let's get going. There's no point in drawing out the agony any longer." Elenya blew out a sigh of resignation as they made their way to their mounts.

Dronan, who once again appeared to be in deep meditation, opened his eyes as they approached and peered at Lizzie and Eloise. Lizzie explained the plan to him and he nodded his head slowly in understanding.

"Do not worry. I shall protect you both with my life," he said. Lizzie relayed this to Eloise, who thanked him, it gave them both some comfort to know the depth of the young dragon's commitment to them. Then without further ado the two girls climbed up on Dronan's back. He seemed to puff up with pride as they felt him draw in a deep breath and then stretch out his wings. With Eloise sitting close behind Lizzie and holding tight to her waist, Dronan took several steps forward to accustom himself to the extra weight that he would be carrying.

From where they were sitting Lizzie looked across and could see Elrus and Max watching them. Max was such a worry-wart, Lizzie thought as she looked at the anxious frown pasted on his pale face. He mouthed the words, "Be careful" and she smiled at him reassuringly, even though her stomach was churning like the contents of one of his master's cauldrons. Elrus grinned at them encouragingly, and called out "Good luck!" just as Captain Elgor's hunting horn blew the signal to get ready. General Eldron's shout of "Dragon Flyers Ho!" told them it was time for the dragons to be off.

Without the ledge from Eldragonia to launch from, the dragon's almost vertical take off took Lizzie by surprise. There was no stomach lurching decent, like the plummet

311

from the ledge, but a gradual rising into the air with a great flapping of enormous wings. She was worried that Dronan would struggle with both her and Eloise as an extra burden but he seemed to be coping with admirable ease.

Lizzie was pleased to see that her place behind General Eldron had been taken by Elenya and smiled to see her aunt holding tightly to the General's waist. The other Companions each accompanied a Dragon Flyer and the party quickly formed into a flying V shape. Dronan and his precious cargo fell in behind the General's dragon that formed the head of the V. The young dragon was no longer tethered to the larger creature that he tailed, so that he would be able to quickly split away from the group when the time came for him to do so.

Lizzie felt the reassuring presence of her friend clinging onto her but she also felt a huge responsibility; Eloise wouldn't be in this situation but for her friendship with Lizzie. She would once again have to trust her instincts and these told her that Dronan would be true to his word and protect them with his life.

# CHAPTER 32

## Challenge for the Chalice

Mount Elben loomed large and forbidding ahead of the raiding party. As Lizzie looked up towards its peak a mist hung around the summit shielding it from prying eyes. The vapour reminded Lizzie of the enchantment that had once protected the Harp of Elvyth, when they had retrieved it from Eldorth's castle all those months before.

As the dragons ascended higher Lizzie's sensitive ears suddenly heard a piercing screech and from out of the mist there appeared several dark shapes. With black leathery wings folded back and their sharp beaked faces like lethal darts pointing straight at them, several pterotorials were heading towards them. The manoeuvre had taken the Flyers unawares such was the speed of the creatures' approach.

Just as unexpected as the pterotorials' attack, was a deafening roar. It sounded like dozens of hot air balloon burners all firing up at once, as the dragons' fire burst from the huge beasts' gaping mouths. Lizzie was thankful that she and Eloise were sheltered to the rear of the action.

Their attackers wheeled about, turning steeply away from the heat and flames of their opponents. Like a squadron of fighter jets the pterotorials then came from the rear but were once again thwarted in their attack when, belying their great bulk, the dragons turned quickly and, almost as one, reformed in a counter attack. As quick as lightening, Dronan took advantage of the distraction and flew upwards and away from the foray and headed towards the top of the mountain. So steep was his ascent that Lizzie and Eloise had to hold on for their lives. Lizzie looked back down at the aerial battle below and couldn't help but smile wryly at the sight of Digby the Dwarf swinging his axe at an approaching pterotorial causing the creature to whirl away to avoid injury.

313

Lizzie's heart was in her mouth as she watched another pterotorial, the wraith on its back clearly visible in the rays of the heightening sun, heading straight at Max and his Dragon Flyer. A shuddering sigh of relief escaped her as she saw General Eldron and Elenya intercept the attack on her friend, the fire from the General's dragon catching the wing of the attacker causing it to spin away out of control down towards the ground below, the wraith on its back evaporating into thin air.

As Dronan flew upwards the trio appeared to have gone unnoticed and the nerves jangling through Lizzie's body seemed to relax a little when they found themselves entering the concealing mist near the top of the mountain. The thickness of the mist made vision almost impossible except for a few feet in front of their noses and so Lizzie's other keen senses took over. She listened out for the sound of anyone or anything approaching and even her sense of smell seemed to become more acute as the sulphuric smell of Dronan's breath wafting in her direction became almost overwhelming. Taking a deep breath in through her mouth to avoid the young dragon's aroma, Lizzie could taste the mist and it reminded her of how once, as a small child, she had tried eating a snowball. Her clothing now clung to her damply as the moist air soaked her and she felt Eloise shiver as she too suffered the coldness of the mist surrounding them. Lizzie began to feel uneasy as they seemed to have escaped the fray too easily.

As though the thought had tempted fate, she suddenly heard the flapping of leathery wings close by and from out of the mist the sharp black features of a pterotorial was headed straight at them. Dronan instinctively dived to avoid the attack and Lizzie and Eloise squealed in terror at the speed of his descent. Lizzie felt Dronan seeming to swell in size beneath them, as if his lungs were taking in air like huge a pair of bellows. Then just as quickly, he turned and headed straight back towards his attacker. The move seemed to take the pterotorial unawares as it didn't have time to avoid Dronan's fire when it burst from him like a blast furnace.

314

The fire caught the creature's tail and it spun uncontrollably, screaming in pain as it plummeted downwards. Some of the heat of the young dragon's fire blew back towards his two riders and Lizzie was thankful for the protective clothing and the gauntlets that they were both wearing.

Turning once again towards his destination, Dronan flew with increasing power and speed as Lizzie and Eloise clung on even tighter for fear of being thrown off. With every wing beat the mist around them became thinner and through it Lizzie could make out the rocks that formed the side of the huge mountain. It was bereft of vegetation and its grey granite sides were peppered with ledges, crags and boulders. As they flew along the mountainside searching for any gaps or crevices in its surface it suddenly occurred to Lizzie that they had no idea of where within the mountain's depths the Chalice was concealed.

"Dronan!" she called silently to the young dragon.

"What is it you want?" he replied. His tone indicating that he was obviously more concerned with his search for a way into Mount Elben than anything she had to ask.

"How are we ever going to find the Chalice in this monstrous mountain? It'll be like trying to find a needle in a haystack."

"Why would you want to find a needle in a haystack?" Dronan asked irritably.

"I don't want to find a needle, it's just a saying," she replied. She really should remember that dragons seemed to take the things you said quite literally.

"Elves are such odd creatures," Dronan huffed.

"I mean it's a saying that emphasises the point that it's going to be difficult to find something really small in the middle of something so big," she continued quickly, trying to explain herself and not be offended by his remark about elves.

"Well why didn't you just say that?" Dronan said irritably. "It will be fine. I will help you find it."

Lizzie was sceptical. How could this young dragon possibly know where to look?

Dronan finally seemed to spot what he was looking for. Turning, he flew towards a narrow ledge on the mountain's side. At the rear of the ledge Lizzie could see a fissure in the rock and Dronan clambered onto the ledge. It was evident that the opening was large enough for him to enter with ease but that his two passengers would have to dismount. The girls quickly unharnessed themselves from his back and climbed down onto the rocky outcrop. They peered into the inky black depths with trepidation.

As they were about to step into the gap Dronan swivelled his head towards the two girls and stared at them; his huge amber eyes glinting at them in the morning sunlight. He then spoke aloud as he told Lizzie that she and Eloise must do exactly as he told them at all times.

"I shall act as a shield between you both and any adversary we may come upon. No matter what happens you must keep close to me," he said. Lizzie translated for Eloise and her friend nodded slowly in understanding, her dark eyes betraying the fear she was feeling. Lizzie placed a comforting hand on Eloise's arm even though she too was more than just a little scared about what might lie ahead of them.

Taking Eloise's hand into her own she said, "We're here now, so there's no going back until we retrieve the Chalice." Her voice cracked slightly as her throat seemed to constrict with the fear that was bubbling away in her rib cage. Her heart was racing and she felt the weight of responsibility fall heavily on her shoulders at having got her dear friend into this perilous situation.

"We must place our trust in Dronan. He'll keep us safe, won't you Dronan?" she said, turning to the dragon and looking at him in a way that said, come on reassure us both.

"I have said I will and I will," Dronan said, as though she was somehow labouring the point. "Come now, we must not delay any longer," he continued impatiently.

Lizzie placed her free hand against Dronan's neck as if ready to be guided into the mountain's interior but just before they entered the cavern she spoke to the dragon again.

"Can I just ask you once more, how do you think you are going to find the Chalice?"

Dronan turned to look at her again. "Do you know nothing of dragons? We can sense gold from miles away. The Chalice is made of gold I suppose."

Lizzie suddenly realised she had no idea what it was made of and so looked at Dronan uncertainly. Swallowing hard she admitted that she didn't know whether it was made of gold or not.

"Well, if it isn't, then we're in big trouble," Dronan said, shaking his head sadly. Then looking back up at her, a twinkle very evident in his beautiful amber eyes, he said, "I think that it may very likely be here as I have a distinct sense that there is something gold and magical somewhere in the vicinity. So trusting my senses, I shall follow my nose in its direction and let us hope that whatever it is, it's what we seek." And with that the three accomplices stepped into the mountain.

The cold air of the mountain's interior smelt dank and unwelcoming as they entered a narrow passageway just wide enough for Dronan with the two girls tucked in close by his side to pass through. Lizzie's exceptional eyesight quickly adjusted to the low light levels and she was surprised at how much she could actually see given the lack of a light source. As they walked along Eloise suddenly stumbled over the uneven ground and fell against Lizzie almost knocking her over. Lizzie let out an involuntary yelp and the noise echoed off the solid granite walls. A rush of beating wings was heard and Eloise gasped.

"What's that?" she hissed.

317

"It is just bats nesting up in the roof of the cave. Your voices disturbed them but they will not harm you," Dronan assured them. Lizzie passed his message on to Eloise who breathed a sigh of relief.

"I can't say I'm terribly keen on the thought of bats but they're preferable to those horrible pterotorials, unless they're the blood sucking type of course. They aren't are they?" Eloise whispered urgently into Lizzie's ear, looking up nervously into the reaches of the cave above them.

"What! You mean like vampire bats?" replied Lizzie, also raising alarmed eyes to the ceiling.

Dronan gurgled in his throat as if chuckling to himself.

"Are there vampire bats in Elvedom?" Lizzie asked.

"Well we have them in parts of Elcarib," Eloise said.

"Would you like me to send my fire up at them if they bother you so much?" Dronan asked wryly.

"NO!" Lizzie and Eloise almost yelled in unison, causing the bats to flutter and flit about just above their heads once more and causing the girls to duck.

After a while the narrow passageway began to widen, although the little party still had to keep their heads quite low to avoid hitting them on some of the longer stalactites that hung down. Dronan suddenly stopped. In front of them a huge cavern stretched out to both left and right. The hard surface of the floor beneath them had disappeared and they were confronted by a large expanse of water. An eerie light, the source of which they were unable to determine, cast its glow across the still surface of the pitch-black water.

"What now?" asked Eloise, whilst Lizzie peered around as though looking for some magical solution to their dilemma.

"Perhaps it's just a big puddle and we can wade across," suggested Lizzie. Dronan shook his head slowly from side to side.

"I don't think that we can take a chance on that," he said doubtfully.

"Ok. If we can't wade across, maybe we should try and skirt around the edge," Lizzie replied, peering around to see if there were any sign of solid floor at the water's edge.

Dronan once again shook his head from side to side as Eloise pointed out that the water appeared to go right up to the cavern walls.

"I will carry you across," Dronan announced.

"But you can't fly across there with us on your backs," insisted Lizzie. "The ceiling is too low."

"What's he saying?" Eloise asked her friend.

"He says he'll carry us across but that's impossible," Lizzie explained.

"I didn't say I would fly you across, did I?" was Dronan's response. "I shall carry you on my back and if the water becomes deep, I shall swim across."

"I didn't know that dragons could swim," Lizzie gaped at him in surprise. Was there no end to his talents, she thought.

"I don't know if they can either but we can find out together," Dronan said nonchalantly. Lizzie explained what he had just said to Eloise and the two girls stared at each other, their faces riddled with doubt.

"Come on! No time to waste," Dronan urged them impatiently. Lizzie shrugged her shoulders in resignation and clambered up onto the young dragon's back, whilst taking Eloise's hand and pulling her up behind her. They really didn't have any other choice as Dronan's scales would no doubt dry off quicker than their leathery clothing they were wearing would.

In order to keep their feet dry, the two girls knelt on Dronan's back clinging onto his harness to stabilise themselves as he began to plod through the shallows of the mountain lake. The shallow water suddenly gave way and when Dronan felt the floor beneath his feet disappear, he spread out his wings so that they acted as floats as he began to paddle frantically with his legs, using his long tail as a rudder. The girls were joggled about on his back and they clung to him desperately so as not to be dislodged from their precarious perch. As Dronan found his balance he gained confidence in his newly found skill and they were soon leaving the shore of the lake behind them.

Things were going swimmingly when suddenly just ahead of them the surface of the lake began to churn.

"What's that!" squealed Lizzie, spotting the disturbance first from her place just behind Dronan's head.

"Oh my!" breathed a frightened Eloise as from out of the water a huge serpent-like head emerged. The creature's fiery red eyes glared down at them as its long slithery body swayed above them, the dark waters it had come from dripping from its smooth skin. A long yellow tongue flicked out in their direction as the creature lunged at its prey.

The girls' screams echoed around the cavern, multiplying the sound so that it seemed as though an army of screaming teenagers had invaded the serpent's lair. It reared up in confusion at the sound, flailing its long body around as though in some sort of pain, making the girls scream even louder as they clung onto Dronan who was being buffeted about like a cork on the lake's surface. Dronan took advantage of the creature's obvious confusion. He raised his head as high out of the water as he could and shot a blast of his fire straight at the serpent's middle.

The creature cried out in agony and fell back, disappearing under the water which continued to bubble and churn as it slithered and writhed under the surface. Stretching out with his strong legs Dronan powered across the remainder of the lake and soon his feet found solid ground beneath them. In front of them was another narrow passageway and as the young dragon's body left the water he urged the girls to quickly dismount and run ahead and away from the lake's shoreline in case the water serpent should follow them. Giving one last blast of his fire as though

320

daring the creature to come after them, Dronan quickly followed the girls.

Lizzie had needed no second bidding and dragging Eloise with her, did as she was told; the pair running as hard as they could. Given the wobbly nature of Lizzie's and Eloise's legs, after such a terrifying experience, it was amazing that they had been able to run at all but with Dronan pushing them on from the rear, they soon put what they considered a safe distance between themselves and the odious creature from the lake. They stopped and looked at each other.

"Well, I think that it might be wise to avoid coming back *this* way," Eloise said, her eyes wide with relief at their lucky escape.

"Let's just hope that there's another way out if we ever find the Chalice," agreed Lizzie. She looked at Dronan and could see that he was sniffing the air, his eyes narrowing in concentration. He took a deep breath in and then turning to Lizzie said, "I smell gold."

The girls looked at each other and grinned, then taking their places close to Dronan's side once more, the three of them began following in the direction that Dronan's nose was leading them. It wasn't too long before the narrow passageway they were negotiating gave way to yet another enormous cavern. This time, however, there was no lake to bar their way but instead the ground dropped away into the bowels of the mountain. In the middle of the void, rising out of its depths, was a huge mound with a level platform at its summit. High up in the sides of the cavern walls were a series of openings allowing shafts of light to filter down on the scene below. Large dark shapes could be seen flying around the vast space as each one passed through a channel of light. Pterotorials!

The smell emanating from the mound in front them was nauseating and the girls quickly clamped their hands over their noses and mouths to block its effects. Dronan, seemingly oblivious to the smell, turned to Lizzie.

"I can smell the thing that you seek is upon the summit of the mound before us," he said.

"How can you smell anything other than that horrible stench?" mumbled Lizzie from behind her hand. "Eew... What is is?"

"Pterotorial droppings, I should imagine," came the muffled response from Eloise.

"You will become accustomed to it," Dronan said blithely. The girls looked at him doubtfully. "But in answer to your question, the smell of gold is stronger to me than that of which you complain. Now, you and your friend must climb once again onto my back. Keep as low as possible against me so that I may shield your presence with my wings," he instructed them, as Lizzie translated for Eloise. "My camouflage will keep us hidden from the sight of those creatures, plus they seem more concerned about an attack coming from the direction of those openings up there" He flicked his head in the direction of the pterotorials flying around the gaps in the walls above their heads.

"I will try to avoid using my fire for as long as possible but it may be necessary if we are to get to the treasure. We must all now trust our instincts to do what is needed," he continued. The two girls nodded mutely in understanding. Then without further ado they climbed up on Dronan's back. Eloise flung her arms around Lizzie's waist in a tight hug.

"Good luck," she whispered, her voice hoarse with the fear that had welled up inside her. Lizzie squeezed her friend's arms tight and glancing back briefly wished Eloise the same. Then with the two girls laying low against his scaly skin, the young dragon launched himself off into the void.

With slow wing beats Dronan began to rise up towards the platform. Warm thermals drifted up from beneath him and aided his ascent, enabling him to make quick progress with the minimum of effort. His amazing skin quickly took on the colours of his surroundings so that he became

322

virtually invisible to those around him. As Dronan had observed, the pterotorials guarding the mound's summit seemed more preoccupied with any possible attack from the openings above them. Lizzie was grateful for the distraction that her aunt and the other companions were creating in their aerial assault on the outside of the mountain and hoped that they were all safe. But then she put those thoughts aside knowing that she needed to concentrate on the action that she was now about to undertake.

As the three raiders reached the platform, Lizzie could see that in its middle was a huge nest and sitting upon that was what seemed to be the biggest pterotorial of all. Its sharp beaked face was turned up towards its fellows flying above it and it let out a screech that reminded Lizzie of the injured pterotorial she had tended what seemed like an eternity ago.

Still unseen, Dronan landed softly on the platform's edge and, with the girls still low on his back, he began to creep towards the immense nest.

"It's in there," he said silently to Lizzie. "I know it. Now just stay where you are, we must use the element of surprise." Lizzie sent back the message that she understood but just as the thought left her mind to find its way to Dronan's, the huge pterotorial sitting on the nest swung its head around and stared directly at them.

Lizzie almost fell off Dronan's back in shock, as she realised that her silent means of communicating with the young dragon had somehow been picked up by the creature before them. The pterotorial looked at them as though uncertain of what or who they were. It cocked its great head to one side, like some huge black curious bird. Its eyes blinked rapidly as its brain seemed to start registering the fact that there were interlopers in its mountain eyrie.

Dronan had stopped dead in his tracks and Lizzie and Eloise felt his body beneath them begin to swell and they knew that he was preparing the fire within him. The pterotorial seemed to suddenly decide that these visitors should not be there but as it opened its mouth to call to its mates still flying above, Dronan let rip his fire.

Screeching in pain as the fire burned its flesh, the huge black creature flapped its massive wings and raised itself out of range of the fire breathing creature below it.

Lizzie was off Dronan's back in a flash, pulling Eloise with her, and avoiding the next blast of Dronan's fire they ran towards the now vacated nest. The suddenness of Dronan's attack had thrown the pterotorials into complete chaos, their ear splitting screams reverberating around the vast cavern. Lizzie and Eloise crouched down beside the twisted pieces of wood and vegetation that formed the nest, as Dronan bravely blasted his fire at the now panicking pterotorials. As Lizzie watched she could see shadowy figures on the backs of their flying foes. "Wraiths," she thought with a shudder.

The huge pterotorial that had been guarding the nest was now flapping around above Dronan and, in between dodging the fire being aimed at it, attempted to stab the young dragon with its terrifying beak. Lizzie knew that there was no time to waste and that she needed to take full advantage of the commotion that Dronan was causing so, dragging Eloise with her, the pair climbed up the side of the nest. Clambering over the jagged branches and stems, Lizzie was thankful once again for the leathery clothing that they had had to wear for their flight to Mount Elben.

As the two girls reached the top of the nest and looked down into its centre there, glittering in a beam of light, was a hint of gold. Eloise had spotted it too and pointed at it excitedly. As Lizzie began to edge her way down into the nest the two girls suddenly heard a sound that made them want to yell out loud with relief. A hunting horn blared out over the sound of the screaming pterotorials. Looking up Lizzie could see three huge dragons had entered the cavern through the openings above them and were heading straight at the pterotorials, blasting them with fire as they came.

Lizzie spotted her wonderful aunt sitting astride the back of one of the magnificent beasts. Elenya's golden hair was flying out behind her as the shafts of light beamed down like great spotlights over some enormous stage. With one arm around the waist of General Eldron, Elenya wielded her sword more in a token of power than in actual attack. Lizzie then glanced quickly at the accompanying two dragons and a grin split her face when she spotted the blond head of Max and the red hair of Elrus sitting behind their Dragon Flyers. The two boys were whooping and howling like banshees, although Lizzie thought that the dragons' fire was probably having more effect than all the noise two small boys were making. The dragons were circling above the pterotorials, raining their fire down upon the now scattering creatures.

Lizzie quickly reached the glittering object that was tucked into the nest's interior and pulling aside some of the vegetation pulled out a golden goblet. She had it in her grasp: The Chalice of Elaria!

As Lizzie clambered back up toward the top of the nest, Eloise reached down and grabbed her hand. Eloise's strength surprised Lizzie as the young elf pulled her quickly up next to her with ease. The pair quickly jumped down and began running back toward Dronan who was still doing his best to fend off his huge attacker. Lizzie could see that he was beginning to tire and she heard his silent call for her to hurry.

Suddenly the pterotorial turned away from Dronan and instead its black beady eyes spun in Lizzie's and Eloise's direction. It flapped its great wings and flew towards them. Lizzie looked around swiftly but there was nowhere for them to hide. She looked across at Dronan but the young dragon seemed almost spent and she could see that he was gasping in great breaths of air in an attempt to raise enough fire to attack the pterotorial once again. Holding Eloise's hand tightly she looked up for some help from the three dragons that had appeared moments earlier but they were busy chasing away a final few pterotorials. Lizzie flung herself to the ground, pulling Eloise down with her as she went, cradling the Chalice in the crook of her other arm. Maybe if we make ourselves as small as possible, she thought hopefully, we won't be such an easy target.

As she braced herself for the onslaught, Lizzie heard the creature suddenly scream out and daring to look up she saw that her attacker was now under attack itself but not from one of her allies. For there, flying around the huge beast's head and pecking at its face, was a smaller one of its own kind. It was giving Lizzie time to get away and so scampering to her feet, she pulled Eloise with her towards Dronan. The young dragon seemed to have regained some of his strength and was staring at the sight of the two pterotorials, the smaller of which seemed to be at the advantage. Dark spots of blood from the larger creature were now splattering across the platform's surface and it was waving its huge head about in an attempt to avoid the onslaught from its kin.

"Come on let's go!" yelled Lizzie, as she and Eloise quickly climbed up onto Dronan's back. With no further encouragement needed Dronan took off, his wings beating hard to get up and away as quickly as possible. Lizzie looked down at the two pterotorials and she knew why the smaller creature had turned upon its own kind; it was the one she had helped to heal previously.

She called out to it. "Come, come with us. You must come or you won't survive here."

The smaller pterotorial ceased its attack and flew upwards after Lizzie and her companions, leaving its battered and bleeding kin flapping about and whimpering in pain on its platform. Despite its pain and obvious injuries, it seemed to realise that its attackers were getting away. It began to rise up off the platform in order to follow them, its great wings making its ascent more rapid than those of its smaller assailants. It was just within touching distance of them when out of nowhere a round black and white ball hit it squarely between the eyes. The impact seemed to stun the creature and, much to the relief of those watching from above, it wheeled away to search for the thing that had hit it. Lizzie, who had heard the sound of its approach, had been looking back and watching it getting ever nearer when the ball hit. She realised immediately from whence it had come and turned her eyes towards Elrus. Her dear friend had sacrificed his treasured possession to save them.

As they rose up towards the three dragons that had seen off the remaining pterotorials, Eloise let out a blast on Fidora's hunting horn. The circling Dragon Flyers turned at the sound to watch their approach. As Lizzie, Eloise and Dronan reached them, Lizzie waved the Chalice of Elaria above her head in triumph and the raiders crowed with delight at the sight of the golden chalice glinting in her hand.

"What just happened there?" called out General Eldron, as they headed for the openings above them. "Why did that pterotorial turn against its own?"

"I saved his life and now he's saved mine," Lizzie yelled back. "We're even now but he has to come with us or else his life won't have been worth saving. Now let's get outta here!"

So without further delay the raiding party, with their newest member, flew out of the mountain and, with the concealing mist having evaporated, into the fresh, clear Elcaledonian air.

# CHAPTER 33

## Return of the Raiders

As the four dragons sped away from Mount Elben, trailing in the wake of Dronan was the dark forbidding shape of the pterotorial. Lizzie had been determined that it should not be left behind to some fate worse than death.

Having successfully seen off the enemy attack, the other Dragon Flyers had headed back to the safety of the isle in the middle of the loch. As Lizzie and her accomplices approached the isle there were yells of delight from the Companions and Dragon Flyers. Suddenly the group below spotted the pterotorial following the mountain raiders and their yells turned to shouts of alarm as they began frantically pointing at the black winged creature at Dronan's rear. The archers amongst them drew their bows and pointed up at the group but, unable to get a clear shot at the creature for fear of hitting one of their own party, they waited. General Eldron's dragon was the first to land and he quickly reassured those gathered on the isle that there was no danger. As Dronan landed the pterotorial settled silently beside him and looked around warily at those standing before it.

Lizzie dismounted from Dronan and walked over to her new ally; placing one hand on the creature's neck, she looked deep into its eyes.

"Thank you for protecting me," she said. The pterotorial stared back at her, tilting its head to one side like an enormous black dog would do when listening to its mistress. Something extraordinary passed between the pair, an undefinable bond that they would always share and at that moment Lizzie realised that the creature was a female. She didn't know why but it made the link even more special. Lizzie's attention was brought sharply back to the celebrations going on around her when Eloise blasted a long note on Fidora's hunting horn before shyly handing it back to her. Fidora thanked Eloise and putting an arm around her shoulders placed the horn to her own lips and blew it loudly.

As the celebrations continued, Elenya made her way over to Lizzie's side. "I think that, as the Chalice's champion, it would be good if you could say a few words, Lizzie," Elenya suggested. Lizzie looked at her aunt in panic.

"Me?" she squeaked nervously. Elenya nodded.

"I think that talking to this lot," she began, indicating the ecstatic crowd whooping, hugging and leaping around in front of them, "will be nothing compared to what you have just done." And with that, Elenya held up her arms to draw the attention of the company.

Lizzie swallowed hard to remove the lump of fear that had formed in her throat, speaking formally to the group felt almost scarier than fighting off a huge beast with a pointy beak. Then summoning up her boldest voice she thanked them and said that their success was only possible because of all their efforts. Then pointing to each of them in turn, she continued, "But in particular I must praise the determination and love of my dear friend Eloise, the resolution of the brave and bold Dronan and the courage and strength of this wonderful creature here." She looked into the face of the pterotorial beside her and saw the flint like eyes soften as they looked back at her.

Elenya came forward and took Lizzie in her arms and hugged her tight.

"I'm so very proud of you, my darling," she said, tears teetering on her lashes. "You are not only brave but modest too and you acknowledge and value the contribution of those who serve along side you. These qualities are signs of the great ruler you will one day become." She then turned and addressed the gathering, "But enough talk! We should be off. We must return pass over Maladorth before the night is out. Also we cannot risk Eldorth having back up for those that we have defeated here today." And with that she went to organise their departure.

Max and Elrus, not wishing to interrupt the exchange between Lizzie and her aunt, were watching nearby. At Elenya's exit they came over to Lizzie and, joined by Eloise, grinned at their friends before falling together in one big huddle of relief.

Pulling away and staring into Lizzie's eyes Elrus said, "You did well, Lizzie." He yelped as Max punched him playfully on the arm, grabbing his limb as though he'd suffered a terrible injury.

"Did well? Did well?" exclaimed Max, giving Elrus a withering glare. Then looking at Lizzie like some proud father, said, "Princess; you did brilliantly!" "And you!" he said, looking at Eloise as if seeing her for the first time, "You were amazing."

Eloise blushed prettily and spluttered that it was nothing; the biggest understatement that Lizzie thought her friend could possibly make.

Lizzie then took Elrus to one side. "Thank you Elrus," she said simply. The young elf looked at her as if confused that she had singled him out.

"Princess?" he asked.

"You gave up your football to save us," she replied.

Elrus's face flushed and then he smiled. "Princess, I'd give up a lot more than a football to save you; and Eloise of course," he said. "I told Elwood it would come in useful. Anyway, you can buy me a new one next time I visit you," he winked.

Lizzie looked around at the rest of the group getting ready to leave and saw Elwood standing by his dragon watching her. His face looked sad and it made her heart ache a little. She ran over to him and almost knocked him over as she flung her arms around him.

"We did it Elwood! So, why the sad face?" she cried, pulling back and looking earnestly into her dear little guardian's face.

"I failed you, ma'am. I should have been there with you to ensure your safety. I failed in my duty to do that," he blushed and he stared down at his feet as though ashamed.

Lizzie grasped the little elf's arms and gave him a shake. He looked at her, startled by the action.

"Don't you ever think you've failed me," Lizzie said, crossly. "It is because of you that I was able to do this. All these months you have been teaching and guiding me to be able to take on the things I need to. I would never have had the courage to do what I have done today and go through the adventures we've had on this journey without you. Just knowing you are there for me is all the help I need."

A broad smile spread across Elwood's face. "You are too kind, ma'am. I am and always will be your most loyal servant." As he bowed his head, Lizzie had the urge to kiss him on the top of it but wasn't sure how Elwood would react. He took his role as her servant and guardian so seriously that certain protocols had to be adhered to and she could tell that the hug she'd just given him had shocked him enough for one day.

After a discussion with her aunt and General Eldron, they had finally conceded that Lizzie could return to Eldragonia on the back of Dronan. The General insisted however, that Eloise should fly back with the Dragon Flyer she had left with and Lizzie would fly with him once more.

"Dronan will be very tired after your adventure in the mountain," the General said. "The flight back will be too arduous for the young dragon to cope with carrying you girls."

The Dragon Flyers were soon mounted and ready for departure and before long they were heading south-west and back towards the safety of the Mountains of Snow and Eldragonia.

With a tail wind behind the dragons pushing them on, the return flight was much quicker than the journey north and they were soon flying out over the sea where, in the distance, the Mountains of Snow could be seen in all their glory. The sight of them spurred the dragons on to even greater speed as the magnificent creatures sensed that they would soon be home.

Eldragonia's ramparts could be seen clearly as the dragons flew over the peaks of the lower ranges of the Mountains of Snow. Some of the dragons let out roars of pleasure at returning to their home and the Dragon Flyers accompanied their mounts with shouts and yelps of gladness at their triumphant return. Captain Elgor's hunting horn blasted out as the dragons swooped in for their final approach to the ledges that led to the inner refuge of the fortress.

Dragon Elves were waiting, ready to aid the Dragon Flyers and the Companions to dismount and lead the dragons back to their pens for much needed rest and nourishment. Lizzie quickly dismounted from General Eldron's dragon and went to untether Dronan and passed the reins his harness to a young Dragon Elf. He assured her that he would take good care of the young dragon. Lizzie thanked the elf and then looking at Dronan said her silent thanks to him.

"You were a real hero, Dronan," she smiled, patting his neck gently. "I could never have done what I did without you. Thank you."

"You are most welcome, Princess," Dronan replied. "I think it is clear that our destinies are now joined and that we will forever be united."

Lizzie swallowed hard as tears pricked at her eyes. "That's good to know," she said finally. She watched as her Dronan, as she would now always think of him, was led away for his much deserved rest. Her attention was then brought round to a commotion that seemed to be happening on the other side of the dragons' cavern.

"Well, how do we communicate with the thing?" she could hear someone saying amongst the Dragon Elves gathered there. "Well, they're supposed to be related to dragons aren't they? I suppose we'll just have to see if there's anyone here that can get through to it," said another. Lizzie could see that the subject of their discussion was the pterotorial. The poor creature looked very confused and backed away from any attempt to approach it.

"Well Princess, any suggestions?" came a voice from just behind her. Looking around she discovered Elbie standing there. His lilting voice sounded amused at the scene they were both witnessing. "We saved the creature and now we have the responsibility of it but these Dragon Elves, they're just what they say on the label – "*Dragon*" elves. These creatures now, well they're a whole different matter."

Lizzie looked at Elbie and again at the frightened creature which was now snapping its long beaklike mouth at the hastily retreating Dragon Elves.

"Well if I can talk to it then surely there must be someone else here that can," Lizzie said. The other Companions were now beginning to gather beside Lizzie and Elbie. Elenya draped an arm over Lizzie's shoulder.

"It seems that you have a special gift for communicating with different creatures, my darling," Elenya said. "Your mother did, so it looks like she's passed on the ability to you."

Lizzie felt pride swell in her chest. She had inherited something else from her mother; proving once again that loved ones always leave a little of themselves with those whose lives they touch.

As Lizzie walked over to the pterotorial, it stopped pecking at the elves that were trying to get close to it and looked at Lizzie as if seeking reassurance. She was quick to give it and slowly explained that the elves were only trying to help. "You'll be an honorary dragon," Lizzie said. It seemed to understand and relaxed a little. Then turning to the Dragon Elves she told them to just be patient with the creature.

"She saved my life and so she's very precious to me. Please make sure she is well cared for." The elves bowed and assured Lizzie that the creature would be given every possible attention. "Once we can get near the thing," she heard one of them grumble. Smiling to herself, Lizzie thanked them and re-joined her friends as they made their way out of the cavern and into the upper levels of the fortress.

Climbing up the stone stairway towards the open courtyard above, the returning party chatted animatedly amongst themselves. Patting each other on the back and praising one another on the part they had played in the retrieval of the Chalice of Elaria, the tensions of the mission began to ebb away.

"Some adventure, aye Lizzie?" grinned Elrus, as he trudged up the steps beside her.

"It certainly was," she laughed. "I bet you're glad to be back on solid ground though. No more dragons to fly?"

"Oh, I don't know," Elrus shrugged. "I was getting used to it at the end. I might even consider training as a Dragon Flyer myself one day."

"Yeah but you have to keep your eyes open instead of squeezing them shut every time the dragon takes a dive," laughed Max, slinging his arm over Elrus's shoulder.

"And you need to be able to talk to dragons," chipped in Eloise. "That's the really tricky part."

"Hey, Lizzie; what did you do with the Chalice?" asked Elrus suddenly as if he'd just realised that she no longer had it in her possession.

"Oh, Elenya has it," Lizzie explained. "She put in a pouch that she apparently brought along especially for it."

"Good job you got it back then," smirked Elrus. The four friends were still laughing together as they stepped into the bright sunlight of the courtyard.

"Lizzie! Oh, Lizzie!"

Looking in the direction from where her name was being called Lizzie saw her grandmother rushing towards her, her face flushed with a mixture of excitement and relief at seeing her beloved granddaughter. Lizzie found herself crushed against her grandmother's bosom and her hair being showered with kisses. Freeing herself enough to speak she managed a, "Hi gran!" before finding herself engulfed once more. Finally releasing Lizzie, Mrs Longton called the other children to her and gave them much the same treatment.

"Oh my darlings, you're back and all in one piece. I've been so worried. There was no news of what was happening. I haven't slept a wink and I've nearly worn a trough in the courtyard here where I've paced up and down so much," she blabbered, tears of relief now streaming down her cheeks.

A calm voice interrupted Mrs Longton's flow.

"Elizabeth!"

Looking in its direction Lizzie saw her grandfather walking towards her with her aunt Elenya, her arm linked to that of her father's. Close behind them strode General Eldron and the large and imposing figure of Max's master and mentor, Marvin.

"Grandfather!" exclaimed Lizzie in surprise. "You're here. How? When?" she spluttered.

King Elfred smiled warmly. "Marvin arranged for a Threshold so that we could be here for your return," he explained, as he took her in his arms and hugged her.

"I, I don't understand. If…?" Lizzie stammered.

"I know!" The indignant sound of Mrs Longton's voice cut across the courtyard. With her arm still around the waist of Eloise she continued, "You can imagine how I felt when the pair of them strolled into the dining hall this morning. Bold as brass, not a saddle sore between them. Well, I was cross, I can tell you. Why? I asked. Why did you make us travel half way across the country on the backs of those poor horses when you could have just got us here as quick as a wink by a Threshold?"

King Elfred chuckled. "I did explain, Mrs Longton, that the journey here was part of Elizabeth's education. She needs to learn about the world she will one day rule and she won't see much of it or understand it by hopping about between Thresholds. Each part of your travels these past weeks will have enhanced her abilities and skills as well as teaching her more about this world," he expounded.

"Humpff..." scoffed Mrs Longton. "Well I could certainly have done without the saddle sores, I can tell you."

Lizzie giggled. "Oh gran, you enjoyed every minute of it really. Didn't you? Come on admit it?" she encouraged.

Her grandmother smiled. "Well, maybe not every minute. Anyway, that aside, I'm extremely relieved that you're all back safe and sound, I can tell you," she said, giving Eloise an affectionate squeeze to emphasise her point.

Lizzie looked around at the rest of the Companions who had travelled with her and smiled as she watched them all chatting amongst themselves. Elwood and Elwind were deep in discussion and she could see Max and Elrus telling Marvin about their adventures, their arms waving about animatedly as they demonstrated the part about the dragon flying.

Lizzie breathed a sigh of relief and pleasure as she watched her friends' flushed and excited faces and began to feel the tension that had gripped her body begin to relax. She felt a warm glow of contentment in the reassuring presence of her grandfather and grandmother. Lizzie once again had the sense of belonging in this world but knew deep inside that she must soon return to her home at Longton Hall. She torn between leaving her beloved home and her dear friends Bob and Mary Crowther and now there was Granny Fimble. She then thought of her two faithful dogs, Basil and Rathbone and suddenly realised that she missed them all terribly. The events of the past few weeks had pushed all thoughts of her life in Chislewick to the back of her mind and she felt the sting of guilt at not having considered how those who cared about her had felt during her and her grandmother's long absence. Her torment must have shown in her face as Elenya looked down into it with concern etched on her own beautiful features.

"Are you okay, Lizzie?" she asked.

"I'm fine. I'm just a bit tired," lied Lizzie, although she did feel quite weary.

"Well I think it might be a good idea for us all to go and have a nice hot shower and some rest because tonight we celebrate!" exclaimed Elenya as, turning to the crowd gathered in the courtyard, she pulled the Chalice from the pouch hanging over her shoulder and shook it above her head. Everyone cheered and applauded and Lizzie felt the adrenaline course through her veins once again as she too got caught up in the excitement of the moment. She suddenly found herself being dragged by the hands by Max, Eloise and Elrus as the four of them spun around in a mad version of a game Lizzie had played when she was very young called Ring a Roses. Falling down exhausted, the four friends roared with laughter as they watched King Elfred prise the Chalice from his daughter's grip and place it in the pouch slung from her shoulder. He then passed it to Marvin and Lizzie saw it disappear into the voluminous folds of Marvin's cloak. She knew that he would take care of its future safe keeping.

After a stingingly hot, fierce shower, a sparklingly clean Lizzie, and her equally refreshed friends, took well deserved naps. Waking some hours later they met up in the dining hall and were surprised to see that the stark surroundings had been transformed with celebratory banners and trappings. In the absence of anything fancy to wear they had all dressed as smartly as their travelling clothes (which had been cleaned and pressed by the dragon elves servants) allowed. The cooks had prepared a sumptuous feast of roasted meats and steaming plates of vegetables, accompanied by pies, breads and cheeses and was followed by wonderful cakes and puddings.

After the feast the company were entertained by the two Elcambrian elves, Elaled and Eleuen who, together with Elgawen, sang ancient folk songs of love and legend much to the enjoyment of all present. Lizzie looked around at her friends and family and smiled. For now, at least, she had a sense of well being. Looking along the table at those dearest to her she spotted Elenya listening in rapt attention to the words of a love song that Elgawen was singing so enchantingly. A gentle smile played on Elenya's beautiful face as though she was living the words of the song. Lizzie then looked across to see General Eldron gazing at Elenya and his longing for her aunt was clear for all to see. It saddened Lizzie to see it and she decided that she would speak to Elenya about why the two of them could not be together.

"Surely it can't be because he isn't royal," thought Lizzie, hotly. "Royalty in the human world can marry people who aren't princes or princesses. If that's what's keeping them apart, maybe if I tell them about human royals then they can persuade grandfather to let them be together."

With the celebrations finally over, the tired and happy gathering began making their way to their beds for the night. King Elfred had told Lizzie that Marvin would prepare a Threshold that would take her, her grandmother and Elwood back to the barn at Hogs Trough Farm the following morning.

"Won't we be coming back to Elvedom Castle with you?" she asked. "I'd love to see it one more time before I go home. We haven't spent any time there this trip," she added sadly.

The King expressed his sorrow that it wasn't possible this time but that he hoped she could soon return and, Eldorth's behaviour allowing, spend a good long spell at the castle.

"Tomorrow you must return to your human home, Elizabeth. Soon you will be starting the next stage of your human education, I believe," he said gently.

In all the excitement she had been through over the past few weeks, the thought of starting her new school at Markham High hadn't even entered her head. Her heart skipped a beat at the thought of it.

Knowing that she may not have time to make her farewells the next day, Lizzie said goodbye to most of her dear Companions at the end of the feast. She had decided, however, that she would make a final visit to Dronan in the cavern below them the next morning before her departure for home.

As the four young friends reached the hallway that led to their bedrooms, they said goodnight and arranged to meet for breakfast. Lizzie took a last look at the stairway for any sign of her aunt but was disappointed to find none but, upon entering her bedroom, she was surprised and delighted to find that Elenya was sitting on the edge of her bed.

"Hi!" she said brightly but the smile she had given her aunt faded when she saw the sadness that blighted Elenya's beautiful brown eyes. She went and sat next to her aunt and looked into her face.

"What's the matter, Elenya?" she asked softly.

"We haven't really had any time to ourselves, have we Lizzie?" Elenya said sadly. "We seem to spend what little time we have together running around finding things or caught up in events not always in our control. I hope that some day we shall have some time to do the sorts of things aunts and nieces should be doing."

"What sorts of things do aunts and nieces do?" asked Lizzie uncertainly.

Elenya laughed. "I've no idea but I'm pretty sure that they don't usually fight pterotorials and retrieve sacred relics." Lizzie giggled and agreed that they were pretty unusual in that sense.

"Well, maybe one day we can just do some fun stuff like, like… Actually, I can't think of anything more fun than fighting pterotorials and retrieving sacred relics," Elenya said, making them both fall against each other laughing until tears ran down their faces. As the laughter faded Lizzie turned to face her aunt and looked at her earnestly.

"Elenya, can I ask you something?"

"Of course, Lizzie, you can ask me anything," Elenya replied.

Lizzie took a deep breath. Well, here goes she thought.

"Why can't you and General Eldron be together?"

The question seemed to rock Elenya as she took a sharp intake of breath at the unexpectedness of it. She blinked rapidly as if trying to gather her wits about her.

Lizzie realised that she had put her aunt on the spot and began blathering on about human royals and how they could marry non-royals. Then seeing Elenya's discomfort at the situation, Lizzie began apologising for asking and said that it was none of her business.

Elenya placed a comforting hand onto Lizzie's arm and said it was all right and that she had just been surprised at the question.

"What made you ask it, Lizzie?"

"Well, it's pretty obvious that you're mad about each other. Anyone can see that," Lizzie replied, matter-of-factly.

"Really?" asked Elenya. Her face showed her surprise.

"Er, duh! Yes!" Lizzie exclaimed, as if her aunt was slightly stupid.

Elenya smiled softly.

"Eldron and I have loved each other since we were children. Our fathers were great friends and we were brought up together. We had similar interests and as we played together our friendship and childish love blossomed into something deeper. But then Eldron's father died suddenly and everything changed. Our vows of undying love were broken when Eldron said that he could no longer be with me. I've now discovered that my father had told him that he

340

could not, or rather would not, agree to any union between us," she said sadly.

"But why? Eldron's brave and loyal isn't he?" Lizzie cried.

"Yes. Yes he is, totally," Elenya agreed.

"But if you love him, why do you give him such a hard time?" Lizzie asked.

Elenya let out a wry laugh. "Because he didn't fight hard enough for me, I guess," she admitted. I know it isn't really Eldorth's fault and I am 'hard on him' as you describe it, in order to protect my own feelings."

Lizzie thought that being an adult sounded awfully complicated and seeing the puzzled look on her face Elenya continued.

"The truth is Lizzie, there are reasons or rather, there is one very important reason why we cannot be together."

Lizzie looked at her aunt expectantly, waiting for the reason to be revealed. A shuddering sigh escaped Elenya lips and she shook her head as though the words were too hard to voice. Then looking deep into Lizzie's face she said, "Eldron is Eldorth's younger brother."

The announcement of this fact shook Lizzie to her socks. "But, but…!" she blurted.

"I know. Father cannot look at Eldron without being reminded that his brother was the cause of Elethria's death. It doesn't help matters that he also looks very like his older brother," Elenya explained. "It's impossible for us to be with one another whilst Eldorth is alive and the curse on our family still stands."

"But it isn't his fault that his brother's bad," argued Lizzie. "Why should he be punished?"

Elenya looked at her sadly. "Blood ties are strong in Elvedom and there are bonds between family that are hard to sever. Eldron is tied to Eldorth whether he wishes to be or not. Until Eldorth is either defeated or changes for the good,

341

which is most unlikely, then we must be apart. It is something we both have to bear, even though our hearts ache from the knowledge of it."

Lizzie placed her arms around her aunt and hugged her tightly. "Then we had better beat him good and proper," she said earnestly, as Elenya planted a kiss on the top of her niece's blond head.

When Elenya had left the room, Lizzie climbed wearily into bed. She soon fell into an exhausted sleep and dreamt of dragons, chalices, harps and other assorted things and places from her time in Elvedom. Over it all, however, was a deep feeling of foreboding that there was someone or something that would yet cause her and her loved ones more pain and anguish before they could all be at peace.

# CHAPTER 34

## Demons Divided

To the north and west of the Mountains of Snow Duke Eldorth sat on his ornate chair in the great hall of his castle. A dark clad apparition floated eerily just above the flagstones in front of him, bowing its ghostly head in deference to him.

The news it had just delivered caused its recipient's head to fall back as his fisted hands pounded the arms of his chair. The noise that left Eldorth's throat made those who heard it shudder in dread. As the howl he had released subsided, his breath came in short shallow gasps and his eyes glared madly in their sockets.

"NO! NO! NO!" he bellowed. "How was this possible? How did they know where the Chalice was hidden?" His eyes flicked around the room as if searching for something unseen as his hands flew up to his hair and began almost pulling it out by the roots. He looked like a man possessed as he gradually got to his feet and stepped forward. The wraith before him drifted back slightly.

Its voice, like its appearance, was wispy. "We could not withstand the dragons' onslaught, Sire," it breathed. It was barely audible but it still held a hint of the accent it had born during its living years.

"Dragons?" Eldorth stopped tugging at his hair and stared at the wraith with a puzzled expression on his face.

"Aye Sire, dragons," the wraith repeated. "They were too powerful for us but we fought as best we could."

Eldorth slumped back down onto his chair. A look of pure hatred spoiled his darkly handsome features. So, his suspicions had been correct when he'd heard the reports of the travellers heading to the west. His mouth worked and his teeth ground together as he tried to control the anger that was welling up inside him. He knew that he must contain the anger and hatred and channel it towards the retribution he would mete out to his enemies.

"Go!" he spat. "Get out. I will tell you when you and your troops are next needed. Go tend the pterotorials and make them ready for when next needed."

As the wraith drifted towards the Great Hall's intricately carved oak doors that were silently swinging open, Eldorth called after it. "Wait! You can make yourself useful and appease my wrath by doing a task for me." The wraith turned and looked once more at the imposing elf now slouched in his chair. "Find the witch Melisha. Find her and report back to me of her whereabouts and activities." As the wraith turned away Eldorth shouted after it. "And be quick about it!"

The wraith bowed its head in obedience and exited the hall.

Eldorth laid his head against the cushioned rear of his chair and ran his fingers through his black hair, smoothing it as he did so.

Things were slipping away from him and he needed his accomplice back to get things back on track. Where was the witch? He got up from his chair and began pacing. He needed to think. These minions he'd surrounded himself with were no use when it came to planning strategies; they were only good for carrying out his orders. Then again, they didn't seem to be carrying those out particularly well. How had his enemies discovered the Chalice? He had been assured that the stronghold it was held in was impenetrable. What secret weapon did they have that could have penetrated his defences? His thoughts then turned to the news that the wraith had brought.

"Of course, dragons!" he hissed, a sneer crossing his lips. "So, they have the Dragon Flyers at their disposal now." Then, as if looking into the face of an absent foe, he snarled,

"So, you want to take on your big brother do you? Well Eldron, we'll see about that!"

*

Away to the north in Eldiburgh, a small band of travellers had gathered in the early morning light outside an inn in a back lane of that great city.

Cloaked and booted Melisha climbed up on the back of the donkey that had brought her there. Her hapless servant, Elpme put the finishing packages into the panniers to her rear and then stood ready to lead the donkey on their journey further north. Melisha had been assured that the Elpicts whereabouts was now fairly certain and with the feral elves help she was sure that they would find them to glean their help. They had better find them, she had threatened, or there would be trouble to pay.

"They travel by foot mistress, so we should be able to catch up with them easily enough," Elmac, the feral elf gang leader assured her. "It would be best if we travel as light at possible. Is it necessary that you bring those with you?" He indicated the two still spell-bound imps that had been plonked in one of the panniers.

"Who gave you the right to question what I do or don't bring?" Melisha spat at him. "If they're there, then I'm bringing 'em. You just concentrate on your job of finding those Elpicts."

Melisha had decided to keep the two imps and work on a spell to convert them to her service. She couldn't risk that they escape and report back to Eldorth and they were too valuable an asset to destroy them. Spy imps were not a common commodity and she had been impressed that Eldorth had come across a pair of them. Given time she would get them on her side.

With the party finally ready to depart, they set off along the cobbled lane and away from the Goblin's Goblet Inn without so much as wave to their hosts. The burly landlord, with his urchin of a servant girl, stood watching them go.

"Good riddance to bad blood, Elmin," he said, wiping his hands on his beer-stained apron as though wiping his hands of the departing company. The little servant elf nodded eagerly.

"She's a mean one, boss," she agreed.

"She is that, girl. She is that," he concurred. With that, the two of them went back into the inn to prepare for the day ahead.

Up on the roof of the building opposite, Pi sat watching the events below unfold. The clever magpie hadn't been fooled for a moment by the witch's elaborate disguise. No, he knew exactly who was riding off on that poor pack animal's back. It was now time for him to return to his master and report the latest turn of events.

As the witch and her gang began their journey north, a black and white bird, with a tail wind behind him urging him on his way, flew quickly south.

# CHAPTER 35

## Pastures New

Lizzie looked at herself in the mirror. The girl staring back at her appeared like a stranger. Her battle scarred insides showed no evidence of their existence on the outside of her still small, lithe body. Her blond hair was neatly brushed and swung silkily against her shoulders, as she turned her head from side to side to once again inspect her long strangely shaped ears. Her "dear, dear ears" as she now thought of them. She touched them proudly and winced when she thought of the years that she had wished them away. They were now her constant reminder of her wonderful friends and family in Elvedom.

Her startlingly pale blue eyes peered down at the new uniform she was wearing. Its royal blue blazer looked stiff and uncomfortable and she wriggled her slight shoulders at its unfamiliar feel. Her grey pleated skirt hung to her knees and she took a deep breath as her hand slid to the secret pocket that her grandmother had sewn into its waistband. The reassuring presence of her mother's locket eased the sense of terror she was feeling at the thought of her first day at Markham High School. If I can survive an aerial battle on the back of a dragon, then the first day at High School should be a doddle, she thought to herself with a wry smile.

The memory of her last morning in Elvedom came flooding back.

*

Lizzie peered into the depths of the dragon pen but there was no sign of Dronan being there. She knew that his amazing skin could take on the colours and shades of his surroundings and that he was able become almost invisible to the naked eye, so continued to stare. She turned to Captain Elgor beside her.

"Are you sure he's here?" she asked.

Before the captain could reply a large amber eye suddenly materialised at the rear of the pen, closely followed by its mate.

A broad grin spread across Lizzie's face.

"Dronan," she said simply.

"Princess," the young dragon replied.

"I've come to say goodbye. I have to return home for a while. You will be good won't you?" she spoke to him as though she was talking to one of her dogs.

"Good?" was Dronan's indignant response.

"Well, okay perhaps good wasn't the right choice of word. You won't be difficult for the Dragon Elves who will be training you, will you?" she continued.

Dronan blinked slowly and said that he would do what he felt was right. "I will be true to myself as all beings must be," he finally announced.

Lizzie nodded. What he said made sense. Something inside her told her that their time together was far from over and when she at last said goodbye, she told him so. "I'll be back!"

"I know," were Dronan's parting words.

Before heading back to her grandparents and the rest of her friends, Lizzie paid a quick visit to the pterotorial. The creature looked comfortable and more relaxed than it had the previous day when it had first arrived at Eldragonia. It was housed in one of the dragon pens slightly apart from the others, "to allow it to settle in" she was told.

"We had no idea what these things ate," explained the Dragon Elf that had been given the task of caring for the creature. "I've tried giving it what the dragons eat, you know – sheep, calves, pigs and stuff but it just wasn't interested. I've now found that it seems to like bird flesh so we're going to have to increase the breeding of our poultry stocks." Lizzie nodded in understanding and wished the elf luck. She

348

didn't want to stay talking for too long in case he went into the gory details of how dragons and pterotorials actually devoured the poor creatures that were fed to them.

Accompanied by Captain Elgor, who reassured her that both Dronan and the pterotorial would be well cared for, Lizzie made her way to the huge entrance hall of the mountain fortress. There she found her grandparents, Elenya, Elwood and Elwind, her three dear friends, Marvin and General Eldron all waiting for her. The other Companions, she was informed, had now left and were on their way back to their own peoples.

"The Threshold is ready, Your Majesty," Marvin announced. King Elfred thanked the sorcerer and turning to Lizzie held out his arms. She fell into his tight embrace.

"It is time to leave, Elizabeth. You have learnt much and grown immensely during your brief time here, I think," he said softly.

"Yes grandfather," she agreed. Then looking up into his face said, "I can come again soon though, can't I?"

He smiled his gentle smile as he looked into her face. "You will come again when the time is right for you to do so. You need some normality back in your life."

"But I don't like normality. Normality is not always very nice in Chislewick," she said, looking down sulkily.

She felt another arm slide across her shoulder and looked up to see her grandmother looking down lovingly at her. "But think of Basil and Rathbone and how much they're missing you," Mrs Longton said.

"I know and I miss them too," Lizzie said sadly. "I've been thinking about them a lot lately." Then turning back to her grandfather asked him when he thought the time for her to return to Elvedom would be right.

He shook his head slowly. "We cannot know for sure. We are hoping that we may be in for some peaceful times for a while as the retrieval of the Chalice of Elaria is quite a set back for Duke Eldorth. Until all the relics are reunited the full power of the Chalice cannot be used to heal the land and stop the poison from spreading. However, having it back in our possession will slow down the destruction Eldorth is wreaking."

The mention of Lizzie's arch enemy's name caused her to look straight at General Eldron. She saw his face tighten at the sound of his brother's name and it suddenly occurred to Lizzie that she could be looking at the face of Eldorth himself; after all Elenya had said he looked quite like him. The previously faceless being, that was making her life so difficult in Elvedom, looked like that. The thought startled her. General Eldron looked back at her sadly as though he had read her mind and a gentle smile gradually touched his lips, as if to reassure her that although he may look like his older brother, he was otherwise nothing like him. Lizzie returned the smile and then turned her attention to her aunt.

She hugged Elenya tightly and said that she was looking forward to that "aunt and niece time" that she had been promised. Elenya laughed and said that she would start planning it as soon as she got home to Elvedom Castle.

Finally, Lizzie turned to her three friends. She embraced them all in turn, much to the embarrassment of Max whose face flushed so hotly that Lizzie felt she could have cooked an egg on it.

"I shall miss you all so much. I just wish you could all come home with me," she said, her voice catching in her throat.

"We'll miss you more," cried Eloise, clinging on to Lizzie as if she would never let her go.

"Not possible," Lizzie wept as the tears now flowed freely down her cheeks.

"Hey girls, stop it will you or you'll have me at it next," said Elrus, his voice trembling with emotion.

Finally, letting go of each other Lizzie turned to Max once again. The young sorcerer's apprentice was staring down at his feet as though afraid that if he looked at Lizzie his resolve might also crumble. Lizzie touched his arm softly and, unable to ignore the gesture, he raised his sad blue eyes to hers.

"Keep up those magic lessons, right?" she ordered.

"Of course, Princess," he replied.

"And while you're about it, ask that Master of yours if there isn't some way that he can arrange for the four of us to keep in touch while I'm back in my other world," she suggested.

Max grinned at her. "Will do, Princess," he said, more brightly than he felt.

After the last farewells had been said Lizzie, Mrs Longton and Elwood followed Marvin down into the bowels of Eldragonia to where they found a number of what appeared to be prison cells. One of the doorways had a blurred look about its edges and Lizzie knew that this was the Threshold that would take them home. Thanking Marvin and wishing him goodbye Lizzie, Mrs Longton and Elwood stepped through the door.

*

"Lizzie! Lizzie! Are you ready darling? The school bus will be along soon. You don't want to miss it on your first day." Mrs Longton's voice carried up the stairs and along the wood panelled hall to Lizzie still standing in front of the mirror. She took a deep breath and turned towards the door.

"Coming gran," she called back.

As she walked towards her bedroom door Basil and Rathbone got up from their places by the foot of the bed and followed her. They had barely left her side in the week since she had returned home from Elvedom and had even taken to sleeping next to her bed rather than their usual place down by the Aga in the kitchen.

As Lizzie entered the kitchen, Mary Crowther was at the table holding a brand new lunch box in her hand. Giving it to

351

Lizzie with a, "Here we are me chick" and a "Well, don't you look smart", she once again expressed surprise at the lovely tans that Lizzie and Mrs Longton had caught whilst on holiday.

Upon their return to Longton Hall, where Mary and Bob had been looking after the place, they were met with excited questions about what they had done on their holidays.

"You must have had wonderful weather," Mary had crowed. "Look at the tans you both have. I didn't know that Greenland got such hot sunshine," she'd exclaimed.

"Neither did I," agreed Bob, eyeing the pair suspiciously.

"Oh, it's something to do with the ozone layer being a bit thinner up there," Mrs Longton had lied, looking at Elwood for back up. Bob's eyebrows rose even higher at this remark; there was something amiss about this Greenland visit, he thought, but he'd wait until Mrs Longton or Lizzie felt they wanted to divulge where they had really been.

Elwood had appeared momentarily flustered at having to lie on the spur of the moment but had quickly concurred.

"Oh, yes indeed. The ozone layer is very thin in Greenland."

Mrs Longton had looked at him and shaken her head, her face distinctly showing that he could have done better. He'd shrugged his small shoulders and pulled a face to show that he hadn't been able think of anything better at the time. Both gestures had not gone unnoticed by the eagle-eyed Bob but were completely missed by his wife who had been more preoccupied with putting on the kettle for "a nice cup of tea".

Mrs Longton looked at Lizzie and smiled. Her heart swelled in her chest at the love she felt for her only grandchild.

"You look so grown up, darling," she said. "Here, let me take a photo of you," she continued, picking up her camera and pointing it at Lizzie.

Mary, now standing at the sink, turned and watched them as Mrs Longton snapped away at Lizzie who was pulling a series of poses as though modelling for some fashion shoot.

"It was such a shame you forgot to take your camera on holiday with you," said Mary disappointedly. "I'd have loved to have seen some holiday snaps of Greenland. They don't sell disposable cameras there either did you say?" she added, shaking her head sadly.

"No!" replied Lizzie and Mrs Longton in unison.

Just at that moment Elwood managed to divert any further questions from Mary by saying that the school bus was expected at any moment.

Giving Mary a quick hug, Lizzie picked up her new school bag and swung it over her shoulder. Waving to Mary and Bob standing at the front door with Mary fluttering a tea towel in her hand, Lizzie walked along the drive with her grandmother and Elwood.

"It's going to be okay, darling," Mrs Longton reassured her, looking at the apprehension etched onto Lizzie's face. "New school; new start," she added, breezily.

"But same old people," Lizzie mumbled. Her grandmother placed a comforting hand on her shoulder.

"But the Brays will be small fish in a rather large lake at Markham High, whereas they were big fish in a little pond here in Chislewick," Mrs Longton replied.

"Especially Regina!" chipped in Elwood, making Lizzie giggle. Elwood was pleased that his quip had made his mistress smile.

"Don't forget what you have been through this summer, ma'am," he continued. "You have fought on the back of dragons. Nothing surely can be more frightening than that!"

Lizzie grinned at him and then her face became more serious as she said, "But I had my friends there with me. Nothing seems impossible when you have your friends there to help you."

353

A lump formed in Mrs Longton's throat. Lizzie was right of course; people could cope with any adversity in life if they had the love and support of those they held dear. She pulled Lizzie into her arms.

"As I've said my darling, Markham High is a big school, there are bound to be other children that will need to make new friends. I'm sure that you will find them." Then as she kissed her granddaughter on the top of her head one last time, she spotted the school bus coming along the lane.

"Here it is! Here it is!" squeaked Elwood, hopping up and down excitedly. "And don't forget, ma'am. I shall be making sure that all is well but keeping well out of sight." Lizzie thanked him and knew that he would be true to his word. She would look out for the flashes of green from time to time.

The school bus stopped just outside the gates to the Hall and Lizzie said a last goodbye to her grandmother and Elwood. Giving them a final wave, she climbed onto the bus. Looking down the aisle for a spare seat she was relieved to find one just behind the driver. As she slid across to sit next to the window she heard a sound that once again turned her blood cold.

"Oh look, it's Lizzie Long Ears." "Yeah! What a freak!"

A quick glimpse over her shoulder confirmed that the comments had, as expected, come from her human nemeses, Regina and Veronica Bray.

"Oh well," thought Lizzie, placing a discrete hand on the pocket with her locket. "Here we go again!"

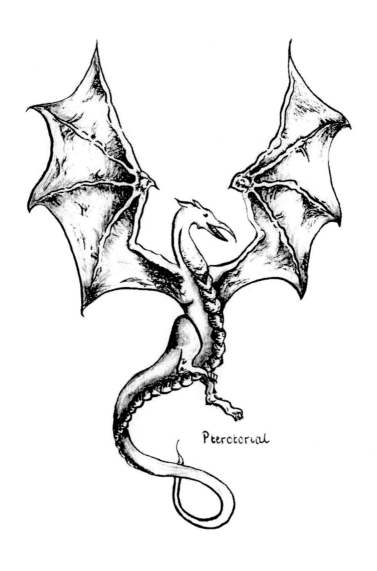

Pterotorial

J2B/13/P

9 781784 079307